LONG BLACK CURL

LONG BLACK CURL

ALEX BLEDSOE

A TOM DOHERTY ASSOCIATES BOOK

NEW YORK

This is a work of fiction. All of the characters, organizations, and events portrayed in this novel are either products of the author's imagination or are used fictitiously.

LONG BLACK CURL

Copyright © 2015 by Alex Bledsoe

A Tor Book
Published by Tom Doherty Associates, LLC
175 Fifth Avenue
New York, NY 10010

www.tor-forge.com

Tor® is a registered trademark of Tom Doherty Associates, LLC.

The Library of Congress Cataloging-in-Publication Data is available upon request.

ISBN 978-0-7653-7654-1 (hardcover)
ISBN 978-1-4668-5141-2 (e-book)

Tor books may be purchased for educational, business, or promotional use. For information on bulk purchases, please contact the Macmillan Corporate and Premium Sales Department at 1-800-221-7945, extension 5442, or write to specialmarkets@macmillan.com.

First Edition: May 2015

Printed in the United States of America

0 9 8 7 6 5 4 3 2 1

To Tuatha Dea:
Danny, Rebecca, Tesea, Brandon, Kathy, Chris,
Nikki, and Adam—
as close to the Tufa as you're likely to get on this earth

ACKNOWLEDGMENTS

Special thanks to the two newest honorary Tufas,

Alice Peacock
Lou Buckingham

and to

Kezzie Baker
Jon Mayhall of the Spook House Saints
Henry Harrison and the Rockabilly Hall of Fame
Kevin MacNeil
Melissa Roelli
Marlene Stringer
Paul Stevens
and, as always, Valette, Jake, Charlie, and Amelia.

When they lay my body in the green, green grass
I will whisper quiet secrets to the animals that pass
about the times I swore I was never coming back,
but I lied.

—JOSIAH LEMING, "Appalachia"

LONG BLACK CURL

1

The small airplane, a Piper Comanche, soared above the Cumberland Plateau and approached the Appalachian Mountains. The moon was full and cast its glow on the clouds and snowy landscape below, but the three passengers did not notice. They were cold and cramped in the small passenger cabin but elated from adrenaline and anticipation.

The youngest of them was Guy Berry, in one of the two bucket seats. He was only seventeen, a lanky, bespectacled kid from Texas, so he was totally unused to this sort of weather. He drew his knees up to his chin and wrapped his coat around them.

The oldest was P. J. "Large Sarge" Sargent. In his forties, he was one of those irrepressible types who smiled no matter what. He looked on the other two as little brothers, offering advice and surreptitious sips from his flask when no one else was looking. They in turn adored him like a favorite uncle.

The biggest by far was Byron Harley. Billed as the "Hillbilly Hercules," he had to fold his six-foot-four frame into the plane almost like a contortionist. He wasn't tall and skinny, but thickly muscled from a childhood of hard manual labor. He sat on the bench seat along the back cabin wall, with his long legs stretched out straight before him. His heels reached the far end, and he had to keep his head bent forward because of the contour of the wall behind him. This accommodated both his height and the brace that supported his left leg. It was a miserable position for five minutes, let alone for an hour, but it was still better than the alternative.

He'd been hurt in a motorcycle accident while working as a courier during his stint in the army, and his choices were to wear the brace or lose the slowly withering leg entirely. It gave him almost constant pain and discomfort, but most of the time didn't dampen his friendly personality. And for those times it did . . . well, he had his own hidden flask. And while the alcohol helped his leg, it did the opposite for his temperament.

But he was sober now, and delighted to be on the plane, which would accomplish in an hour what their old, broken-down tour bus would need almost a day to achieve. They would be in Knoxville soon, checked into a warm motel, where they could sleep in beds, eat freshly cooked food, and wash their sweaty stage clothes.

These were, in fact, at that moment, the three most popular musicians in the country. Their songs were known by everyone sixteen and under, and by many older than that. They had appeared on national television, and in the movies, lip-synching their hits to the screams of studio audiences. And now their joint winter tour, in this new genre called "rock and roll," played to sellout houses across the Southeast.

"Did you guys meet that old banjo player that opened the show?" Guy said. The boy had had two small regional hits in Texas before his third single, "Bonnie Jo," skyrocketed him to stardom.

"What about him?" Byron asked.

"He had six fingers on each hand. And they worked! I ain't never seen nothing like it!"

Large Sarge nodded. He coasted on a single novelty record, "That's What I Think," but understood exactly how lucky he was, and how to maximize his time in the spotlight. He knew that by this time next year, he'd be back at his old radio station spinning platters, and that was okay. He appreciated the ride while it lasted. "His name was Rockhouse Hicks," Sarge said. "Used to play with Bill Monroe, I think."

"Hell, everybody in these parts used to play with Monroe," Byron said. Byron had the most substantial career of the three, with a half-dozen hits for himself, and three songs he'd written for others on the charts as well. In his last movie, *Riot in P.S. 105,* he'd even been given a few lines of dialogue, and there was talk he might be up for bigger parts in the near future. "He finds 'em, trains 'em up, and then off they go. I hear he's a mean SOB."

"Well, if he trained this fella, he did a great job," Guy said. He shook his head and repeated, "I've never heard anything like it."

"Well, that's 'cause he's a Tufa," Large Sarge said.

"What's that?" Guy asked.

"Nobody knows for sure. They got black hair like Indians, but you saw him—he don't really look like one. A lot of 'em look like they could be part Negro, too, but they swear they're not." He gestured toward the window. "They live up in these mountains somewhere, and don't come out very often, but when they do, it seems like every last one of 'em is a great musician."

"They all play banjo?"

"Naw, they play all sorts of things. And they know damn near every song you can think of. But you can't get much out of 'em otherwise." He took a drink from his own flask and offered it to Guy, who politely shook his head. He continued, "Some folks say they were here when the first white folks came over from Europe. Hell, some stories say they were here when the first Indians arrived."

"What do they say?" Byron asked.

Sarge laughed. "They don't say shit."

"So they ain't Indians," Guy said.

"Nope. Nobody knows what they are. But if you're around one, watch yourself. They're sneaky, like Gypsies."

"Somebody's pulling your leg," Byron said. He slapped his injured leg. "And believe me, I know about leg-pulling."

"Maybe. But you didn't hear that ol' boy play tonight, did you?"

"Naw, I was restin' my leg in the dressing room," Byron said. It sounded like an excuse for partying, or meeting a girl, but it was the literal truth—his leg needed all the rest he could get before a show, because he performed like his injury didn't matter at all. Oftentimes it meant flinging his leg about like a dancer might, except that the extra weight of the brace was even harder on its already weak muscles. But the crowd loved it, and he couldn't imagine not doing it; the screams of the girls alone made the pain worthwhile. Right now it throbbed with a dull regular beat, 4/4 time, which was the rhythm he'd used for most of his hit songs.

"Man, the sound in that place tonight was awful," Guy said. "I hate playing in gymnasiums."

"One time I had to go into this gym, and they didn't have a stage or nothing," Sarge said. "They just had bleachers on both sides, and they sold all the seats. Then they made the whites sit on one side, and the coloreds on the other. So I had to set up in the middle and try to play to both of 'em. Everybody was too nervous to be the first one to start dancing. It wasn't until right before the end that a few people came down from each side, but they stayed in little clots, making sure they got nowhere near each other. Man, I tell you what, we need to stop screwing up our kids with our problems, you know that?"

"I had something worse happen," Guy said with a grin. "It was my first band in high school, the Furious Ones. We had this guitar player named Pete who thought he was hot shit on toast.

He liked to sneak Dexedrine from his cousin who was narco-leptic, and toss one down before the show. Usually it didn't do much—he was pretty wild anyway, and this actually kind of calmed him down—but I think he took more'n usual on this night. So he was bouncing off the damn ceiling.

"Anyway, he had this super-long cord for his electric guitar, and he liked to dance all around. So on this night, he got his feet all tangled up, but he was too into his music to realize it. He jumped way up in the air, like he always did, and usually he came down with his feet spread apart. But this time he couldn't, and he landed flat on his back. His guitar flew headfirst into his amplifier, and it made this god-awful shriek that I swear probably messed up my hearing to this day. The drummer jumped over and unplugged his guitar, and we looked up to see everybody starin' at us. Then the announcer's voice came over the PA: 'Let's give a big thank-you to Guy and the Furies.'"

They all laughed. Byron took a swig from Sarge's flask; then Sarge said, "What about you, Byron? You got to have a story, too."

"Hey!" Guy cried. "Did you see that?"

"What?" Large Sarge asked.

"Outside the window. Something flew past."

Sarge leaned over and looked. He saw the plane's wing, the moonlight on the clouds, and the stars in the cold air. "I don't see anything."

"Maybe it was a bird," Byron said.

"At night?" Guy protested. "And it was *big*!"

"Owls are pretty big," Byron suggested.

"Do they fly this high?" Guy asked.

Before anyone could respond, the plane suddenly lurched and threw them first against the right cabin wall, then the ceiling. Guy screamed, his voice high pitched and panicked. Large Sarge, who'd been in the marines in World War II, reacted calmly and tried to find a handhold. Byron, who'd been in the army but never saw combat, was blinded by pain as his limp leg wrenched in its socket.

Then there was noise, and fire, and the sensation of being inside a blender, followed by stillness and cold.

Byron Harley took a deep breath and pressed his palms flat against the metal covering him. It was hot to the touch.

His head ached like his first hangover, and he felt tight and hot all along his left side. He'd lost consciousness at some point, because he remembered seeing treetops scrape the cabin windows as they shot past, and then he was here, trapped under some big sheet of steel.

He pushed with all his considerable strength, and felt the weight mostly in his back where it pressed against the ground. They didn't call him the Hillbilly Hercules for nothing, after all. The plane's wing rose enough for him to get his pinned leg out from under it.

He slid his bad leg to one side. Ironically, the brace had taken the wing's weight, protecting his damaged limb. Then again, that leg was numb in so many places, he couldn't be sure it wasn't snapped in half.

"Okay, okay," he said aloud. "One more time."

He lowered the wing slightly, gathered his strength again, then pushed hard and fast, flinging it up into the air. He rolled, and the wing crashed back down onto the spot where he'd been pinned. A cloud of sparks from the smoldering leaves rose around it.

Byron lay on his back gasping, staring up at the bare branches silhouetted against the orange-tinted haze high above. The air smelled of burning gasoline and heated tree sap. Smoke rose from the wrecked plane, mixing with the fog and blocking all view of the stars. The ground beneath him was cold and wet, now that the heat had melted the frozen leaves.

He coughed and rolled onto his stomach. With supreme effort he got his hands and knees under him, then shoved himself to his feet. His leg brace, bent by the impact of the crash, pinched his thigh. He wiped his watering eyes and took his first look around.

The little plane had crashed into the mountain slope at full throttle. There had been no warning: one minute he and the other two passengers were chatting about their upcoming show, and the next their world was filled with screeching metal and screams.

No, wait, there *had* been something. Guy thought he saw something flying around the plane, something big. Could an owl have really caused this, tangling in the propeller and sending them earthward?

His brain gradually sorted out the debris so he understood what he saw. The engine was on fire, the bent propeller blades visible like huge fingers reaching up through the flames. The crash had sheared off both wings, and the fuselage was crumpled like an accordion. The fog and smoke hung close, and the fire turned the whole vista softly orange. *Like a glimpse of Hell,* he thought.

How had he gotten out in one piece? He'd been in the backseat, pinned by his height, and should've been crushed on impact. But somehow he'd been thrown clear. That meant that the others might have . . .

"Guy?" he called. "Sarge?" He didn't recall the pilot's name, so he couldn't shout for him. He kept calling their names as he stumbled to the plane and peered in through the shattered cockpit window.

The pilot was still strapped in his seat. Byron could tell by the limp way the man sprawled forward that he would stay there until someone took him out, and there was no hurry on that. He threw handfuls of wet leaves onto the flames, hoping to smother them, but all it did was generate fresh surges of smoke that blew right into his face. He coughed, wiped his eyes, and gave up. He realized he had no idea where the gas tank was on a plane like this, so he had no idea if the wreck was about to explode.

As he stepped back, he saw something else. Near the front of the plane, a body lay wrapped around a tree trunk, as if thrown there like a child's doll. It wasn't Guy or Sarge: he could tell by the clothes, and the small size.

He knelt beside the body and turned it over. It was a boy of about twelve or thirteen, with jet-black tangled hair. He was bare-foot and wore overalls. His face was stuck in a look of surprise, and there was a huge bloody gash in his side that allowed his insides to fall out.

Byron fought not to throw up. How much dumb luck was that? Some kid wandering through the woods in the middle of the night gets hit by a crashing plane.

"Too bad, kid," he said as he closed the boy's eyes. His skin was still warm. "Too damn bad."

He got to his feet, coughed again, then called out, "Guy? Sarge? Where are you? We gotta get outta here, man!"

Nothing answered, except the crackle of flames and a distant owl. Then he spotted a hand protruding from beneath a seat torn free in the crash.

He hobbled over to it and pushed the cushion aside. Guy Berry lay on his back, his eyes open behind his trademark thick-rimmed glasses. His hair, and the skin from which it grew, was sliced away from the left side of his head, exposing the bone. Like the boy, he looked startled, not afraid. And of course, he was dead.

Byron swallowed hard. He flashed back to the first time he'd heard one of Guy's records. It was on a jukebox in a Utah diner, when Byron had been traveling from Northern California to St. Louis. He remembered thinking that it was the first time he could actually hear the singer's smile, and he just knew Guy had been grinning the whole time he recorded it. And when they finally met a year later, he realized it was true. Guy was infectiously happy when he was performing.

And now that smile, that music, was silenced.

He found Large Sarge still in the plane, crushed between a section of roof and the fuselage floor, his body almost bent in half. His fallen toupee covered his face. He was dead as well.

Byron stumbled back and sagged against the nearest tree trunk. Hot tears burned his eyes, but wasn't sure if they came from the smoke or his own feelings. "Goddamn it," he muttered. Then he screamed at the sky. *"Goddamn it!"*

He thought of his daughter, little Harmony Harley, barely two years old. Perhaps God had saved only him from the crash because he knew there was a baby out there who needed her daddy. Guy had no kids, Sarge's were all grown up, and the pilot had mentioned he was getting married in the spring; only Byron had a young child. Had that made the difference?

If so, then why had God arbitrarily killed the boy hit by the plane?

He was exhausted and sore, but he had to keep moving. He attempted to bend his leg brace back into alignment, but he'd need to take it off and get a hammer to do it right. For the time being, he'd just have to be careful flexing his knee.

Now that he had a moment to catch his literal and metaphorical breath, he felt a rush of total panic. Where the hell was he? Which way led back to civilization? Should he try to move his friends away from the crash site in case it did explode?

Then something at the edge of the illumination caught his eye. "You gotta be kidding me," he whispered.

His guitar case lay flat and undisturbed in the middle of an open space, as if gently placed there by a kind and unseen hand. He stared in disbelief as the firelight reflected off its shiny surface. From this angle, it looked almost as if the case itself were burning but not being consumed, like the bush that spoke to

Moses. He limped over and carefully knelt, wincing at the pinch as his brace bit into his skin.

The case was warm but not hot. He said a little prayer before he reached for the catches. He held his breath as he opened the lid

His Gibson J-45 acoustic, with his first name in pearl inlay along the neck, didn't have a scratch.

"Fuck me," he sighed in wonder.

He looked around at the crash site anew. Byron was not a religious man, despite having been raised in the Pentecostal church, but it was hard not to see the hand of God in his deliverance. "Lord, looks like I owe you one," he said. The Lord did not respond.

Then he remembered that the plane might explode at any moment. He had to get away from the crash, find a road or a house with a phone, and let the authorities know. He had to call Donna, so she wouldn't panic if she heard the news on the radio first. Ever since Harmony had come along, Donna's emotions had been on a hair trigger anyway; if she thought he was dead, it would send her shrieking down the street.

He knew that there would be no help up the slope, toward the mountaintop. All the houses or roads would be down lower, in the valley. He stumbled down the hill through the fog, bumping into tree trunks and low-hanging limbs, wrenching the guitar case free when it wedged into something. Once away from the fire, the ground grew icy and slippery, with patches of snow where the treetops gapped. In no time the glow from the wreck faded, and he was lost in cold, black darkness. He was glad he wore his leather jacket, but the chill would get him soon if he didn't find shelter.

Twice the frozen leaves flew out from under his feet, and once he slid for a frighteningly long way before he slammed into a fallen tree. He had no idea how long he'd been moving when, ahead of him, he saw another orange glow.

At first he feared he'd traveled in a circle and inadvertently returned to the plane. But no, he'd been moving downhill the whole time. As he got closer, he saw that it wasn't the plane burning ahead of him; it was a campfire.

He approached it as carefully as he could, but his footsteps sounded to him like the passage of an elephant, and his exhausted breath rasped loud in his head. Up here in the mountains they could be moonshiners tending a still, working late and not in the mood for visitors. Through the mist the light grew gradually brighter and sharper, until he could make out the camp's details.

Two men sat on logs on either side of the fire. One looked small and shrunken in clothes made of old rags stitched and tied together. He had an immense, bushy beard and wore an old top hat. The other man wore a more modern winter coat and held a large jug.

A big dog lay between them. When he caught Byron's scent he jumped up and barked once, a big *barumph* sound that seemed impossibly loud in the silence.

"Hesh up, Acrasia," the bearded one snapped, and the dog obeyed.

Byron stepped into the open. His size often intimidated people, and sometimes that was useful, but not now. He smiled as much as he could, gave a little wave with his free hand, and said, "Howdy, gentlemen."

The two men turned to look at him. The bearded one's eyes glittered with reflected firelight. The other, clean-shaven and dressed more normally, looked familiar, but Byron's crash-fuzzed head couldn't place him. He did note the absurdity of running into someone he might know in the middle of the Appalachian woods after surviving a plane crash.

"You look plumb lost," the clean-shaven one said. His voice was neither friendly nor suspicious, just neutral.

"My airplane crashed," Byron said, startled at the statement's absurdity.

"That's what that noise was," the clean-shaven man said to the other. "Told you it weren't thunder. Anybody hurt?"

"Everybody but me is dead."

For a long moment, all three were silent.

"Ain't that a hell of a thing," the clean-shaven man said at last. "How many we talking about?"

"Guy Berry . . . Large Sarge Sargent . . . the pilot." Even saying it aloud couldn't make it seem real. They had played before hundreds of people just hours before. There was no way both of them, *all* of them, could be dead. "And some fella the plane hit when it crashed."

"It hit somebody on the ground?" the clean-shaven man said.

"It did unless he was up in the air flying around the plane." This made him flash back to whatever Guy had seen just before the accident, but of course there was no way it could have been a person.

The man in the top hat said thoughtfully, "I might need to go up there and take a look. You got any biscuits or hardtack on you, John?"

The other man felt around and pulled out something wrapped in a napkin. "This is all I got."

"That'll do."

"I need to get ahold of somebody," Byron interrupted. "Let 'em know what's happened. Where you reckon I could find the nearest phone?"

"Well, ain't no way to get down off the mountain in this fog," the bearded man said. "That's why we're sittin' here. Have to wait till daylight or we're likely to walk off a cliff." He raised the jug and offered it. "But that don't mean we can't be sociable. Reckon you need a drink, son."

Byron squatted on the log, his bad leg out straight and his other knee nearly up to his chin, and gratefully took the jug. He winced as the moonshine burned his gullet and exploded in his belly. It took him a moment to get his breath back, but the two men didn't laugh at him. "Thanks," he croaked.

"Whoo-ee, you sure is a big ol' feller," the man called John said. "How tall is you?"

"Six foot four," Byron said as he wiped his mouth with the back of his hand. He was used to questions about his size. "Weigh about two-twenty."

"Your mama must've had a hell of a time feeding you."

Byron laughed. "Well, she did say we needed to have our own truck patch just to make my school lunch." He passed the bottle back to one of the others. "I can pay you if you'll take me down the mountain right now."

"Ain't got nothin' to do with money, son," the bearded man said.

"You don't know the way?" Byron asked.

He grinned, his missing teeth clear in the firelight. "I know the way just fine. But 'tween the fog and this moonshine, I wouldn't trust myself to find my pecker with my left hand." He laughed at his own joke.

Byron said nothing. Now that he was reasonably safe, he felt numb, the evening's experiences too extreme for his mind to absorb.

"My name's John," the better-dressed man said. "Yonder sits Eli. And that's his ol' hound dog, Acrasia."

"Will he bite me?" Byron asked.

"Might slobber you to death," the bearded man said.

Byron scratched the dog between his ears. He'd owned a similar dog as a boy, and after recent events, it was comforting just to touch the short, bristly fur. The animal let out a satisfied whine. "My name's Byron."

"Where you from?" John asked.

"California. Born in Albert Lea, Minnesota."

"Where's that?"

"Down close to the state line with Iowa."

"They done give towns two names like a person now?"

"Not sure how it got that name. Didn't live there long. Moved to Virginia, then out West."

"Either way, you're a long way from home," Eli observed.

"That's the truth," Byron agreed. The liquor's warmth spread through him, muting the panic and urgency he'd felt since the crash. When the jug came his way again, he took another swig.

John reached down behind the log he sat on and produced a fiddle and bow. With no preliminaries, he began to play "Be Kind to a Man When He's Down," its long, mournful notes filling the quiet forest. Byron had heard that song all his life, from a scratchy old record his dad treasured. He and the bearded man sat in silence, listening, the fiddle giving voice to emotions too strong to be expressed any other way.

When he finished, John nodded at Byron's guitar case. "You play that twang plank?"

"I've been known to pick at it," Byron said.

"You know 'The Brown Girl'?"

"About that girl that gets her head cut off and kicked against the door?"

"That's the one."

Byron had an unfailing memory for tunes, and could recall almost anything he'd ever heard, and certainly anything he'd ever played. "I reckon I can find my way around it."

"Why don't you two pick a little," Eli said as he stood, "while I go attend to some business. Be back before you know it."

He wandered off into the dark. Byron assumed he was going to pee, but if he'd been more aware, he'd have noticed that Eli headed off uphill, toward the plane crash.

Byron took out his guitar. When he looked up, John let out a long, plaintive wail from his fiddle, and Byron strummed along.

"Who's gonna sing?" John asked.

"I'll give it a shot," Byron said, and when they began the next verse, he did:

Come riddle me, riddle me, Mother, he says,
Come riddle me all in one,
Whether I'll go to court fair Helen,
Or fetch you the brown girl home.

If it registered on Byron that neither of these men seemed overly concerned with the plane crash or its victims, that neither had inquired about whether Byron was injured, and that the moonshine jug never seemed to get any emptier, Byron pushed it aside. Right now the most important thing was that he was jamming with a great fellow player. And if that seemed impossibly odd as well, out in the middle of the Tennessee woods, he'd just deal with that later, when they'd finished playing.

Unfortunately, he had no idea how long that would truly be.

2

Winter 2015

The first real snow fell quietly that January, without the slicing wind that sometimes accompanied it, and left three inches of powder on the ground, and on every tree branch on the mountainside. Now the sun blazed on it, reflecting in blinding white across the eastern slopes. Luckily, the trail led the woman around to the western side, where it was colder but the light was more bearable.

After hiking for two hours, she stopped to rest and drink from the water bottle in her bag. The trail seemed to take the most difficult path instead of the easiest, going up steep inclines and then sharply down into gullies. Fallen trees blocked it in places. She knew, though, that this all meant she was going the right way. She appreciated that confirmation, since she hadn't been in this area in a frighteningly long time.

She took off her sunglasses. She appeared to be a woman of about thirty, with the dusky skin and jet-black hair typical of the Tufa. Unlike the generally straight or slightly wavy hair of most, though, hers poked long ebony ringlets out from under her ski cap. She had high cheekbones, big green eyes, and full lips. She was attractive, but would never be beautiful. And the determination in her eyes had frightened away many a weak-souled man.

As she rested, she watched a squirrel run down the length of a fallen log, leaving little puffs of snow in its wake. It scampered up a tree trunk and disappeared into the bare branches. She smiled, stretched, and sighed with contentment. She'd been away too long.

She sang:

The snow it melts the soonest when the wind begins to sing;
And the swallow skims without a thought as long as it is spring;
But when spring goes, and winter blows, my lad, and ye'll be glad,
For all your pride, to follow me, be ye either joy or sad.

When she finished, she laughed to herself. Such a simple thing, singing, and she'd been separated from it for so long.

She looked up at the slope. It appeared particularly difficult, which meant she didn't have far to go.

Just then her cell phone rang. She took it out and stared at it, surprised that she got any reception here. Indeed, it was only the faintest single bar. She pushed the TALK button and said, "What?"

A distinctly British voice said, "Hello, my dove. Do you know what I've seen in the last half hour?"

"What?"

"Nothing. Not a bloody thing. I keep waiting for the wonders of nature to appear, but it seems they've taken the day off. Unless you count sticks."

"Bored, huh?"

"One could say that."

"Can't you read your book?"

"I finished it. The butler did it, by the way."

"What was it called again?"

"The Butler Did It."

"Well, play games on your phone, then."

"I don't dare. I'm afraid to use up the battery, in case I have to wander through the forest in search of rescue."

"You go wandering through this forest, my friend, you won't need rescue."

"See? That is not reassuring. You're actually quite terrible at reassuring people."

"You're a grown man, you shouldn't need—"

"Bloody hell!"

"What?"

"Some sort of animal! Just outside the truck!"

"What does it look like?"

"A bloody big bird! Like an ostrich, only it's green!"

"Sounds like an emu. Probably got out of somebody's yard."

"It's gigantic!"

"It's just a bird, you big baby."

"I think it can hear you. It's looking this way."

"It just sees its reflection in the windows."

"Can it break the glass?"

"I don't think so. Just ignore it, it'll go away."

"How much longer will you be?"

She looked back up the trail. "Not long. If I can get a signal, I'll call you when I start back down."

"Well, if a bird answers, hang up."

She put away the phone and resumed her climb.

The old man opened the door set into the side of the hill and squinted out into the light. The trees were bare, and the winter sun filtered through them onto the fresh snow. The air bit at him, cold and damp.

A woman stood on the old railroad ties that made up his front porch. She wore a stylish fur-edged leather coat, expensive boots, and sunglasses.

He put the electrolarynx against his scarred throat and said, "Yeah? This ain't no camp shelter. Get your ass off my property." The voice came out flat and unaccented, an automated shadow of its former, powerful self.

The woman frowned. "Damn, Rockhouse, you sound like one of them video games kids play. You got a remote control that walks you around the room, too?"

Rockhouse Hicks looked more closely at the woman, then recognized her. He hid his surprise and said slowly, "Bo-Kate Wisby."

She smiled and took off the sunglasses. "Was beginning to think you'd forgotten me. How long's it been?"

He rocked back on his heels but didn't quite retreat. "Been a while."

"That's a fact."

She looked around at the stones that formed the doorframe and the inside walls. She nodded at the electrolarynx, and the puckered scar tissue on his neck beneath it. "Your daughter Curnen did that, didn't she? Tore your damn voice out with her teeth, from what I hear. That must've stung."

"What do you want, Bo-Kate?" he said again.

"Can I come in?" She made a complex gesture with her hand, then bowed her head in apparent supplication.

He wasn't fooled. "Not till you tell me why you're here. Last I heard, you was working over in Nashville."

She chuckled. "Rockhouse, a lesser woman would think you didn't trust her."

"I don't. I remember what you did. And I know what your song is, Bo-Kate: 'Young Hunting.' And I ain't gonna be another Lord Henry."

She laughed, a snort of utter contempt, and reached into her bag. "Old man, you ain't never been my Lord Henry. And we ain't close enough related for you to see me that way. You think I don't know why Curnen did what she did? Hell, *everybody* knows. You're a cliché, you know that? An inbred, inbreeding old mountain man who doesn't even have indoor plumbing." Her voice turned hard. "Now let me the fuck inside."

He fumbled and dropped his electrolarynx as he tried to slam the door in her face.

She pressed her lipstick-sized stun gun against his belly. He stumbled back, convulsing. She followed him inside, holding the device against him, careful not to shock herself. When she pulled it away, he fell twitching to the floor. A wet stain spread across his crotch.

She closed the door and looked around the room, waiting for her eyes to adjust. His boots scraped the floor as his legs spasmed.

A tepid fire burned in the hearth, putting out very little heat. A table with two straight-backed chairs, a rocking chair, and a bed were the only furniture. The walls were damp, moldy stone. No windows admitted light; a trapdoor peeked out beneath a tattered rug.

"Great gosh a'mighty, Rockhouse, you really *do* have a rock house," Bo-Kate said as she looked around. "You really *live* like this? With all the power you used to have, you decide to live in a damn *burrow*? You must be part gopher."

Five banjos on stands lined the wall. There were no pictures, no feminine touches, and the place smelled unwashed and sealed off.

"Well, no sense putting off what I'm here for. I'd tell you I was sorry, but that just flat ain't the case. I'm not the least bit sorry for what I'm about to do."

She knelt beside him. Foam collected at the corners of his mouth, and he wheezed. She checked his pulse and, satisfied that he wasn't actually dying, bent close to speak in his ear. "I know you can hear me, so pay attention. When I heard about what happened at the Pair-A-Dice, well, I just knew it was my time to come back. You lost your power that day, and that makes you useless. And it leaves an empty chair."

She opened her purse and pulled out a heavy pair of industrial clippers, the kind used to cut tire rubber or metal sheets. She squeezed them a couple of times; the big spring between the handles squeaked.

"Besides, it's time for somebody new to take over, somebody who won't coddle those damn First Daughters. They're led by a *twelve-year-old,* for God's sake, and you never put 'em in their place. You're too soft, Rockhouse, and I don't mean that little withered pecker of yours."

She pulled his right hand away from his body. The six fingers on it twitched from the shock's aftereffects.

"That's all about to change. I'm going to clean house around here. We've had these two groups tiptoeing around each other long enough. It's time for one person to be in charge of all the Tufa, one person with some damn ideas to move this place into the modern world. And that one person is *me.*"

She nestled his extra pinky finger into the crotch between the clippers' blades.

"Everything special about you is gone," she said. "You can't sing no more. And now—"

His eyes cleared enough for him to focus on what she was doing. He tried to pull back his hand.

She squeezed the handles and snipped off his finger.

He tried to scream, but the only sound was a loud, pitiful exhalation.

She did the same with his other hand. Then she wiped the clipper blades on his shirt, put them back in her purse, and gathered up the two severed fingers into a sandwich bag.

"I need these to prove you're out of the picture," she said, still crouched over him. "But I'd be lying if I said I didn't enjoy doing that. Remember when I was fourteen, and you slid your hand inside the back of my bathing suit bottom up at Sinks Creek? Six fingers, just like some damn bug crawling on my ass, and you old enough to be . . . goddamn, old enough to be fucking *God*. I swore right then I'd get you back for it one day."

He held his trembling, mutilated hands up so he could see them. He still made no sound, but tears filled his eyes.

Bo-Kate stood, brushed off her knees, and looked around. She spotted what she wanted in a dark corner on a warped, ragged shelf.

It looked like a toy axe, no more than three inches long, but she knew the edge was razor sharp and would cut through anything. She held it up to the light. "You won't be needing *this* anymore, either."

She opened the door and looked down at him trembling on the floor. It had begun to snow again, and flakes blew in past her. His injured hands lay on his chest, blood soaking into his shirt.

"You can stay here in your hole. I won't be needing this dump. I'm going to be living in a real house. Maybe the old Overbay mansion. I need something they've got there, too. I always liked the looks of that place, and it can't be too hard to chase that stupid Bliss out of it."

He rose to a seated position, his hands still cradled against his chest. The hatred blazing from his eyes would once have terrified her.

"I'll give you one warning," she said, and pushed him flat again with one boot. "You move against me, old man, and it's the last move you'll make. I'm paying you the respect of letting you live. Don't make me regret it."

Rockhouse raised one bloodied hand and tried to make a symbol with it, but it shook too much. Blood dribbled from the stump of his finger onto the floor.

Bo-Kate laughed. Then she slammed the door behind her.

Rockhouse got to his knees. He could hardly breathe, and it took all his energy to crawl up into one of the chairs and rest his mutilated hands on the table. He sat over them, mutely sobbing. A gust of wind came down the chimney and caused his fire to blaze, as if expressing the rage he could not.

The flurry ended almost at once, and the faded winter sun reemerged from the clouds. As she started the long walk down the mountain, Bo-Kate Wisby sang "Silent All These Years." She had Tori Amos's range, so the words echoed back to her with a purity that almost made her cry.

She loved the woods in the winter. There were no ticks, no deer or snakes, nothing but the dead world glossed over with the cleanness of ice and snow. Most importantly, everything *sounded* different in the winter: music, like her own voice, tinkled like a shattering icicle.

The last time she prowled the winter woods in Cloud County, she'd been nineteen. And *he* had been twenty. They walked hand in gloved hand, harmonizing from the ridges that looked down over the valley, fully aware that they could be heard by anyone with true Tufa blood, no matter how far away. They didn't care. At least, *she* didn't. She still didn't know for sure about him.

She was so wrapped up in her happiness, in her ability to sing after all those years of enforced quiet, that she didn't notice the man hiding behind the trunk of a maple tree. She passed within ten feet of him, and although the tree was too narrow to fully block him, he was dressed in winter browns that didn't draw her eye. He held perfectly still until she passed out of sight.

When she was gone, Junior Damo stepped out and gazed down the trail after her. He recognized her, all right: there was hardly a Tufa who wouldn't have. Bo-Kate Wisby was one of only two Tufa who had been totally, irrevocably cast out of their society, banished from Needsville, Cloud County, and the night wind. Which made her presence here, now, that much more perplexing.

Not that Junior had any doubt where she'd just been. There was only one destination for a Tufa on this mountain, and it was his as well. He resumed climbing.

Junior was thirty, with the standard black hair and perfect teeth of the Tufa, but he had a slightly dazed look most of the time, as if day-to-day events confused him. Along with the forelock that fell across his eyes no matter how much he combed it back, he sported an eternally boyish appearance that helped immensely with the ladies.

As a long-haul trucker for Diversified Transport, he had been out of town in Iowa when Rockhouse was mauled at the Pair-A-Dice, but he knew the story. It would make a great song someday: the daughter-molesting old man hated by everyone, who finally got his comeuppance at the hands of the very child he'd both raped and tried to destroy. The fact that Curnen Overbay had torn his throat out with her very teeth would be tricky to couch in lyrical poetry, but someone would manage it. And the story's end, with Curnen leaving Cloud County along with her non-Tufa lover, would be perfect.

He knew the injury had destroyed the old man's voice, although his musical talent with the banjo would be undimmed. No one, in fact, played anything like old Rockhouse, with his six working fingers on each hand. No one else could.

He reached Rockhouse's dwelling and knocked on the door. "Rockhouse? It's Junior Damo. I need to talk to you, sir." There was no reply.

He glanced up at the chimney, where a solid column of smoke emerged into the cold air. He put his ear to the door, and heard something move inside. He knocked again. "Rockhouse? My feets are getting cold out here." He pushed on the door, and it opened inward.

A bright shaft of clean winter sun cut across the dim interior and fell onto the old man seated at the table. It took a long moment for Junior to understand what he was seeing: the tears, the blood, the mutilated hands. "Great googa-mooga," he said, and made a protective hand gesture.

Rockhouse, whose glare could once reduce even the biggest, bravest man to quivering jelly, waved at the floor with his left hand. Junior saw the cylindrical device and for an instant wondered why the old man had a light saber. Then he realized what it was, picked it up, and put it on the table. The door closed behind him.

Rockhouse put the electrolarynx to his throat. "Bo-Kate Wisby did this," he said, the flat tones a contrast with his distorted expression. "She cut off my fingers."

"I seen her coming down the mountain," Junior said numbly.

"How did she get back here?" the old man asked. "How did that murdering bitch get back here?"

"Beats me," Junior said. He looked around the little room, which had been Rockhouse's home for longer than most Tufa, let alone most humans, could believe. This was where the Fairy Feller landed, and where he lorded over his exiled people until they split into two groups, leaving him in charge of one, and his archrival Radella ruling the other. Radella's wisdom passed down through generations of women, but Rockhouse stubbornly refused to move on.

"But I got a better question," Junior continued. "What does she *want* here?"

"I don't know," Rockhouse said. He was no longer breathing so heavily, and Junior wondered if the pain was sending him into shock.

The handle of his knife, in its belt sheath under his coat, dug into his side, and Junior remembered why *he* had come here. He'd heard of Rockhouse's fall, and figured the easiest way to step into the old man's place was to kill him outright. As usual with his plans, he'd impulsively begun to implement it without entirely thinking it through. But now, faced with this pathetic shell of the towering presence he'd expected, he found he couldn't do it. It would be like killing that cougar who'd mauled his cousin after the animal's teeth, claws, and eyesight had all gone bad.

"Well," he said at last, drawing the word out, "you just take care of yourself, Rockhouse. Might want to pack them hands in snow for a while." He backed to the door, never taking his eyes off the old man.

Rockhouse's face was a mask of self-pity. "You ain't gonna just leave me like this, are you?"

Junior opened the door. When he did, a crow zoomed into the room. In the confined place it seemed gigantic, and its *caw-caw* was so loud, it made Junior want to cover his ears. But before he could, the crow flew back out and disappeared into the forest.

Junior stared after it. A bird flying into your house was an omen of death; everyone knew that.

He looked back at the old man sitting pitifully at his bare table. "Rockhouse, you remember when I was a senior in high school, my ol' truck broke down on the way to Rosalia Mullins's house? You drove right by me in that old station wagon of yours and didn't stop. In fact, you laughed out the window at me. Yelled back that you'd go tell her I just wasn't that interested. She ended up going out with Larry Heard that very night. I might've married that girl, Rockhouse, instead of that porcupine I'm stuck with now, you know that?"

Rockhouse said nothing.

"So I'll tell you now what I shoulda told you then: Fuck you, old man." Then he slammed the door behind him.

Far down the mountain, Bo-Kate paused to listen. Had she just heard a distant hunter's gunshot, the echo of a car backfiring, or, as she really thought, the sound of a door slamming high above her on the mountain, where there was only one door to slam?

It took a fraction of the time to descend that it had for the climb. She stepped around the root ball of an immense toppled tree and reached the head of the logging road, where Nigel and the SUV waited. She heard the engine and smelled the exhaust before she saw the vehicle, its black finish gleaming. She spotted the tracks of the emu that had terrified him; it made her smile to imagine Nigel, so British and urbane, face-to-face with actual wildlife. The man had probably never seen anything bigger than a lapdog anywhere except the zoo.

She crept up on the vehicle, deliberately staying in the blind spot. When she was close, she slapped the side panel and heard him yelp. She stepped back so he could see her laughing, then waited for him to unlock the passenger door.

Nigel Hawtrey stared daggers at her. He was British, of African descent, and his position as her executive assistant—and more—did not keep him from expressing his true opinions, a quality she treasured. He said very properly, "Yes, you gave me a start. Proud of yourself? Shall I alert the media?"

"I only wish I could've seen your face."

"Yes, well, how did your hunting expedition go?"

"I got what I needed." She held up the plastic baggy with the severed fingers.

Nigel's eyes opened wide. Softly he said, "My God, are those—?"

"They are. Don't worry, he still has a full set left, that's the beauty of it."

"I thought you were just going after some bauble."

She held up the tiny axe. "Got that, too." Then she sucked in her breath as the blade nicked her skin. A lone drop of blood appeared on her fingertip. "Anyway, let's get going. I want to stop somewhere in town on the way to my folks."

"The town we drove through?" he said as he put the vehicle in gear. "We could stop *everywhere* and not lose an hour."

"Oh, don't be so snide. Besides, there's more going on there than you think. Needsville's got a lot of secrets."

"Like the ones you told me about your people?"

His arch, superior tone usually amused her, but not this time. "Nigel, I know you think you're funny, but this is no joke. Everything I told you about the Tufa is true. The fact that you don't believe it doesn't change that."

"Oh, my cocklebur, but I do. I grew up hearing stories of the Good Folk. I just never supposed they would also be good ol' boys."

She looked out at the trees as he backed the SUV around and pointed it the way they'd come. Fresh snow fell as clouds slid over the sun. "We ain't that good, my friend," she said almost to herself. "Not at all."

3

Mandalay Harris sat in the back of the school bus, watching the snow come down. School had let out at noon, when it became clear that the snow was going to continue at least sporadically throughout the day.

She was the last student on the route, and her home was located just down the road from the bus driver's. So every afternoon, even on an early release day like this, she and Mr. Dalton rode home together, usually in silence except for the AM radio that played the right-wing talk station from Knoxville. He always turned it up loud when it was just the two of them.

"We live in a fascist state," the radio voice ranted. "Our government at the highest levels is infested with radical, revolutionary, and in some cases Marxist people that no one elected!"

"Damn right," Mr. Dalton said to himself.

Mandalay wondered what all of this meant to the outside world. Her head was so filled with the history of the Tufa, from Radella on down, that it took all her concentration just to make it through the day. Most of the kids in her sixth-grade class were at least partly Tufa, and they understood that she just wasn't like them. They didn't hold it against her, but neither did they go out of their way to cross the boundaries that separated them. She couldn't, and didn't, blame them; it was hard to look and feel like a child but think like a woman with vast swaths of ancient knowledge.

All across the county, parents explained to their children, often in vague and unsatisfying ways, why Mandalay was special and had to be treated with deference. Yet she was also just what she appeared to be: a twelve-year-old girl growing up in the twenty-first century. And if that seemed contradictory to the rest of the Tufa, she thought, just imagine how it felt to her.

When Mandalay was born, her mother had died. That was not unexpected: often, the heads of the clans died passing on their wisdom, experience, and everything else. Her mother had not been the prior leader: that was the semi-legendary Ruby Montana, who had lived high in the mountains and held court on Saturday nights at the barn dance. On rare occasions she would visit the Pair-A-Dice roadhouse, neutral ground where both sides of the Tufa could come together and play. It was said her voice had been so pure, it could melt icicles and summon fish from the bottom of lakes; she also played the autoharp so well, she could produce notes no one, human or Tufa, had ever heard before.

Ruby Montana had been dead for ten years prior to Mandalay's birth, although given the Tufa's rather malleable relationship with time, she'd managed to make sure there was no gap in leadership. Before her death, she'd told the First Daughters who would give birth to her successor, when and where it would happen, and even what to name the girl. But she hadn't warned them that Mandalay's mother would die. There had been no omens, no signs, so no one was prepared for it, least of all her father. Raising a newborn daughter alone was bad enough, but he had no idea how to help her sort through the generations of knowledge lurking in her mind. His extended family had pitched in, as had the entire Tufa community, but none of them had the slightest clue what she was going through when her eyes glazed over, or when the words that others heard as mere whispers on the night wind spoke to her with total clarity.

She was halfway down the aisle when Mr. Dalton stopped the bus in front of her house and opened the door. He said, "Careful on the ice, there, darlin'."

"Thanks," she said. As she walked away, the radio voice said, "A revolution is coming, people, and it won't be pretty. People won't take this forever!" The door closed, cutting off the anger and resentment.

Mandalay lived in a single-wide house trailer with her father and stepmother, Leshell. Her swing set, now half-buried in snow and crusted with ice, sat beside the driveway. No one was yet home, so she got the key from the mailbox and let herself in.

She hung up her coat, put down her books, and went to the stove. Aluminum foil covered a plate of brownies, along with a note from Leshell that said, *Hope you had a good day. Stay warm. Love you.*

Mandalay took one and chewed on it absently as she went to her room. She took down the tiple Bliss Overbay gave her from its place on her wall. She was big enough now for a full-size guitar, but when she needed to find a little peace, she always returned to this.

She sat on the edge of the bed and began to play a song she'd found on YouTube, called "Paranoid." It wasn't the old Ozzy Osborne song; this one, by a Nashville singer-songwriter named Alice Peacock, instead captured in its words and music something that Mandalay thought no one else in the world could understand:

You're making me nervous
You're making me sweat
Confessing to crimes

I didn't commit
I'm looking behind me
And under the bed
You know where to find me
Get out of my head

The song may have been written for a lover, but for an avatar like her, who carried millennia of history and was constantly being whispered to by the night wind, it applied just as fittingly.

As she sang, she closed her eyes. A slowly building noise in her head drowned out first the tiple, then her voice, and finally her very thoughts. The night winds blew over her, into her, through her. At once she was in the air, *of* the air.

Time travel—there was no other word for it, really—was such a basic part of Tufa existence that few even commented on it anymore. It often took place in dreams, or waking visions, moments that gave glimpses through the eyes of someone who lived through the events. Occasionally the night wind took people as they were and let them observe. But for Mandalay, it was a literal experience of being uprooted and dropped into another era, one as vivid as the reality she'd left.

Which is exactly what happened to her now.

She opened her eyes. She knew immediately that she was a different person: her perspective was higher, farther from the ground, and her physical form felt heavier. She knew she was an adult. She stood outside, beneath a heavy sky of surging gray clouds, but it wasn't cold. It was the opposite: heavy, humid, and with the tension of thunder in the air. And she was not alone.

She stood on a flat mountain top: Emania Knob, a place she recognized. No one outside Cloud County knew why trees failed to grow here, leaving only uneven grass; the Tufa knew it was the very spot where, back when the mountain itself was jagged and new, they had arrived to begin their exile, thanks to their leader's hubris and failure. He'd been thrown across the sea by the Queen, and his impact flattened the mountain.

If she looked hard enough into the clouds, Mandalay could see the transitory images of faces, vaguely human but with just enough distortion to make her wish she hadn't seen them at all. Wind moved through the tops of the trees visible below the bare mountaintop, although the air on the peak itself was utterly still.

Mandalay wondered which ancestor's body she now shared. It could have been Radella, who'd come over with the original Tufa and helped them settle this new world. It might have been Scathac Scaith, a warrior woman who essentially divided the Tufa for all time following the Third Battle of Mag Tuired and drove the dark Tufa into the cave they still used as their meeting place. Or maybe it was even Layla Mae Hemlock, the Singing Siren, whose voice could bring angry men to tears and who sang away the threats during the Civil War.

It didn't matter. Whoever she was, Mandalay saw through her eyes now, and *what* she saw was far more important than whoever was seeing it.

All the Tufa, hundreds of them, from both groups, were there on that mountaintop. They formed a ring around two people at the center. Their clothes were of another era, but Mandalay couldn't say whether it was twenty years earlier, or two hundred; her sense of the passage of time, when she was in this vision state, was nonexistent. Everything happened in the present, and she felt it all as if it were life and death. In this case, that didn't seem to be an exaggeration.

The two in the middle, a young man and woman, clutched at each other as if they expected to be attacked. The man was tall and handsome, clad in jeans and a leather bomber jacket that zipped diagonally across his chest. The woman wore a tight blouse and capri pants. They had the Tufa coloring of dark hair, dusky skin, and white, perfect teeth. But the woman's hair was made up of long, wavy curls that fell around her face and danced in the wind. They behaved like two animals herded into a corral, and now being slowly cornered to be harnessed, bridled, and broken.

Or slaughtered.

Rockhouse Hicks stepped into the open. His hair was gray, not the white of his current incarnation nor the black of his youth. And he looked truly worried and afraid, emotions that seldom crossed his typically arrogant, sarcastic countenance.

"Bo-Kate Wisby and Jefferson Powell," he said loud enough for all to hear. "This is where it stops, you two. Enough people have died. Enough property's been destroyed. Enough shit has been spread around." He turned to look straight at Mandalay. "Right?"

Mandalay heard the voice of the head she was inhabiting. "We agree. This all has to end. We don't begrudge you your love, but your actions have left us no choice."

Bo-Kate said, "You go to hell! All of you! You all tried to keep us apart, but we fucking showed you, didn't we? And now you want to destroy us!"

"We want to keep you from destroyin' *us*, you malignant little harpy," Rockhouse said.

"If you really think we can destroy you, old man," Jefferson said, chest puffed defiantly out, "then you're not nearly so powerful as we've always thought. And if that's true, maybe you *should* be destroyed."

"And us?" Mandalay's other voice said. "Your own people? Your family, who raised you and loves you? Should we be destroyed, too? Because that's what you're on your way to doing."

Bo-Kate said, "Stop trying to drive us apart. You want us to leave, we'll leave. But someday we'll come back, and—"

"See, that's what we're all afraid of," Rockhouse said. The clouds swirled, slow and majestic, above the crowd, and the faces within them grew more defined. "So we ain't gonna run you out. We're gonna *sing* you out."

Bo-Kate and Jefferson looked at each other in horror. "You can't do that," Jefferson said.

"Give me one reason why not," Rockhouse said.

"We're Tufa! We're almost purebloods, even! You've heard us sing and play!"

"Yes," Mandalay heard her voice say, "you are. That makes everything you've done that much worse. Did you need to kill that entire family? Children, even their dogs?"

"Nobody can prove I did that!" she snapped defiantly.

"This ain't a court of law," Rockhouse said. "And the wind is all the proof we need." He gestured up, where the half-visible cloud-faces now glared down in obvious anger.

"We do know what you did to Penny Hadlow," Mandalay's voice said. She glanced across the circle, where a teenage girl with a huge disfiguring scar on her face stood with her family.

"Penny started it!" Bo-Kate fired back. "If she'd kept her eyes off my prize, she'd be fine!"

"And Michael Finley?" Rockhouse added, looking at Jefferson.

"That was a fair fight," Jefferson said.

"Except that you kept smashing his head into the road even after you knocked him out."

Jefferson managed a slow little smile. "Didn't want him coming back someday when I wasn't looking."

Rockhouse looked over at Mandalay, who said, "And then there was Adele's baby."

"It's not mine," Jefferson said. "I swear, I never touched that girl."

"He's telling the truth," Bo-Kate insisted.

"That's beside the point," Mandalay said. "You were plotting to kill a *baby* because you took offense at a pathetic girl's desperate cry for attention."

"She was spreading lies!" Bo-Kate shouted.

"She was spreading wishes," Mandalay's voice said. "She just wanted to be noticed and not forgotten. She certainly didn't deserve to have her baby killed."

"Well, we didn't do it, so you got nothing on us," Jefferson said.

"We got all we need," Rockhouse said. "What you've done is bad enough, what you tried to do was worse, and what you might do is scary enough that we ain't gonna take any chances." He looked back at Mandalay. "Enough talk. Count us off, Ruby."

So now she knew. She was looking through the eyes of her immediate predecessor, Ruby Montana.

"No!" Bo-Kate and Jefferson cried in unison.

"One, two, one two three four . . ."

Mandalay snapped out of the vision.

She looked around her tiny room in the trailer. Her heart pounded, tight and hard in her chest. Sweat made her heavy winter clothes stick to her body. She knew about what she'd just seen, of course; like everything else to do with the Tufa, the memory was packed into her head, there to call up at will. But remembering it and *experiencing* it were different things. She remembered the words that were spoken, then sung; but now she recalled anew the fear in everyone's eyes, not just Bo-Kate's and Jefferson's. She remembered the smell of the air, charged with static and magic, as the night wind came forward to take an active hand, one of the few times in their ancient history it had done so.

She fell back on her bed and dug her fingers into the comforter, reconnecting with her present. She was where she was supposed to be. But then again, if some future self was reexperiencing this moment, would she even know it?

"Oh, good God," she sighed in disgust, looking up at the ceiling fan. A strand of cobweb stretched from one unmoving blade to the wall. Leshell would have her hide if she saw that. "We may live in a trailer," she said often, "but we don't have to *act* like we live in a trailer."

Mandalay dug her cell phone out of her school backpack and found Bliss Overbay's number. Bliss was her guardian, her adopted sister, her second-in-command, and the woman who came closest to understanding what it felt like to be Mandalay Harris.

Bliss worked as a paramedic, and so should always answer her phone, but many times she'd be stuck somewhere in the hills and hollers where cell signals didn't reach. This seemed to be one of those times, since the call went straight to voice mail.

Mandalay said, "Hey, Bliss, it's me. Something . . . Ah, never mind. I just had a thought, but it passed. Call me when you can. No hurry."

She hung up and thought who else she might call. She didn't want to discuss her vision; she just wanted to reconnect with the real world in some way. Her emotions were all skewed, half drawn in by her ancestor's fear, half the numb boredom of a girl at home by herself. She needed some immediate reality.

She looked at the tiple, still on the bed beside her. The last verse of "Paranoid" came to her:

You're making me nervous
Stop standing so close
Do I deserve this
Or is this a hoax
You're like a mystery
That's hard to avoid

"*Either you're out to get me,*" she whisper-sang, "*or I'm just paranoid.*"

She had the urge to run, but the snow outside was too heavy for her usual flight into the depths of the woods. Still, she couldn't just stay here, not with all these adult emotions surging through her twelve-year-old heart. She had to do *something*.

She grabbed her coat and ran outside. The snow was ankle deep, and each step seemed twice as difficult as it normally would. She didn't go into the forest, though; she walked down the road, then began to jog, running as much as the weather allowed. The cold air burned in her nose and lungs, and after a while the snow fell so heavily, she worried she couldn't find her way back.

A truck approached her, its lights on in the winter afternoon dimness. She stepped down into the ditch, crunching through the ice over the shallow water, and back up onto the bank. She held on to the fence there as the truck passed, its plume of snow and slush just missing her. If the driver saw her, he gave no sign. She didn't recognize the vehicle.

When it was gone, she climbed back onto the road and continued away from her home. Something called to her, with an urgency she'd never before experienced. It had to be connected to the recent vision, to that memory of Bo-Kate Wisby and Jefferson Powell being sung out of the Tufa, banished from both the community and from all music forever.

In her haste, she hadn't grabbed a hat, scarf, or gloves. And now one foot was soaked by icy ditch water. Her coat had a hood, but with the wind in her face, it just billowed around her head. And she wore tennis shoes, not snow boots. She was cold, and getting colder.

Still, if anyone in Cloud County was protected, it was Mandalay Harris. And if she was being driven to do something as apparently foolish as run through a snowstorm, then there had to be a reason.

4

Bo-Kate Wisby looked out the SUV's window at the mountains looming behind the haze of falling snow. Unable to stand the silence, Nigel said, "Did you know there's a place called 'Frozen Head State Park'?"

"Yeah," she said absently.

"How does a place acquire that name? Is someone's head truly held on ice, and displayed there? I mean, your country is certainly in touch with its barbaric side, but that sounds positively Romanesque."

"No, it's because the mountain's top is so high, it's always got ice on it."

"Ah. That's a relief. I thought perhaps your Davy Crockett's cranium was kept there in its original coonskin cap."

This brought her back to the moment. "How the hell do you know about Davy Crockett?"

"Television, my pumpernickel. I can even sing the song for you, including a delightful racial variant my lighter-skinned chums enjoyed singing to me."

"You're not old enough to remember the Davy Crockett TV show," she snapped.

He gave no indication he noticed her tone. "Your

original colonial rulers have embraced the concept of the syndicated rerun."

She sighed. "Sorry, Nigel. I have a lot on my mind."

"Chopping off fingers will preoccupy one, I imagine."

"There was a good reason for that." .

"I'd certainly hope it wasn't an idle impulse."

"That old man exiled me from my home, and my family."

"So you've said."

She paused and mustered her resolve. She'd never told him what she was about to. "He did worse than that, too, Nigel."

Nigel didn't look at her, but simply said quietly, "I suspected as much. I've known other women who were . . . mistreated as girls."

"No, not that, although he did grope my butt once. He . . . Have you ever wondered why you never heard me sing until recently?"

"One never hears *me* sing, either. I sound like a garbage disposal with silverware caught in its teeth."

"Oh, I've heard you sing along with your iPod, or something on the radio. I mean, you're right, that *is* what you sound like, but I *have* heard you."

He gave her a dour sideways smile. "You're such a charmer."

"But you never heard me, did you? Before three weeks ago."

"No, I suppose I didn't."

"And I sound pretty good, don't I?"

He nodded. "You do indeed, actually. I recall wondering why you never pursued music itself as a career, instead of concert promotion."

"It's because that old man . . . and others . . . took away my ability to make music. To sing, to play, to dance. All of it."

"And how did he, or they, do that?"

She looked away, out the window. "If I say magic, will you roll your eyes that way you do?"

"Indeed I will not. But I will ask, if it's not impertinent, *why* they did that?"

Bo-Kate did not answer. After several minutes, Nigel accepted that she was not going to.

Eventually she said, "You know, every time I see Cloud County again, it's like seeing it fresh for the first time. And every time that happens, I keep asking myself the same question." She turned and looked at Nigel. "How can I be so damn stupid to keep coming back here?"

"That's from a movie," Nigel said.

"So? It still fits."

"Indeed. You know, there had better be a good reason for you insisting I accompany you. The mountains are like roach motels for black people: We go in, but we don't come out."

"For a long time, people thought the Tufa were black. Hell, you thought I was half-black when you first met me."

"For an instant or two."

"Oh, yeah? What changed your mind?"

"There are subtle differences, my lady, that I cannot explain to you and still keep my eyes on these abandoned streambeds you refer to as 'roads.'"

"Don't worry about anything. As long as you're with me, nobody will bother you, even if you were plaid."

"You'll excuse me if I don't want to bet my life on that."

Bo-Kate grinned. Nigel might be her executive assistant and occasional lover, but they bickered like siblings.

"So will people here believe I, too, am a Tufa?" Nigel added.

"Not a chance."

"Why not?"

"Two reasons. One's your hair. You have real black people's hair. The curliest any Tufa's hair gets is mine." She pulled one strand down into her eyes, then let it go. It bounced back into place.

"And the other?"

"Like you said, subtle differences that I can't explain to you."

"Oh, more Good Folk magic, eh?"

She glared at him, and the anger he saw sent chills down his spine. "That's *enough* of that, Nigel. I don't care what you think about it in the privacy of your own head, but you keep a civil tongue in that mouth of yours, or somebody might just snatch it out."

She turned away and looked out the window at the passing trees. Everything around her ached with familiarity. The Tufa connection to the physical reality of Cloud County was so tangible, it was almost like an umbilical cord. When the original exiles had landed here, back when the Appalachians were as high and rugged as the Rockies, they had bonded with the rock and soil and trees just as they'd once done in their original home. The songs they brought with them became tunes about the land they now inhabited, and the original songs they composed sealed that relationship like the first marital kiss at a wedding.

Beneath this awareness, of course, was the memory of two strands of that cord being forcibly cut that day on Emania Knob. And beneath that, thumping along like the bass note in a techno remix, was the fury that drove her desire for revenge.

Nigel pulled the SUV onto the paved road, grateful for the relative quiet. He turned west, toward the tiny town of Needsville. The road was still winding and treacherous, with patches of black ice where the sun never struck, but their progress was much faster.

Bo-Kate gazed through the bare tree branches at the rolling mountains visible in the distance. Eventually the snow became too heavy, so Nigel turned on the windshield wipers. The rhythmic squeaking finally got to him, so he risked a question: "How long has it been since you've seen your family?"

"Longer than you can imagine. When they chased me out, I didn't plan to ever return. But . . . things change."

"That sounds delightfully enigmatic."

They topped the rise and came down into Needsville itself. The entire town fronted on the highway, with no real side streets. A lone traffic light flashed yellow, cautioning people about the crossroads at the center of town. There was a new-looking convenience store and post office building, but all the other businesses seemed ancient, abandoned, or both.

"There," Bo-Kate said. "That motel. The Catamount Corner. Stop there. I want to see somebody."

"What's a 'catamount,' anyway?"

"A bobcat."

"That's not any clearer, actually. Who is 'Bob'?"

"It's like a mountain lion, only smaller."

"Do they have those here, too, as well as giant flightless birds?"

"They have 'em."

Nigel parked in front of the steps leading to the porch. He saw the warm glow in the café windows and said, "May we eat here? It's after lunchtime, and I'm a bit peckish."

"No." The way she said it left no room for debate.

He took it in stride. "I'll just wait in the car, then. Maintain the vital communications link, as Marlin Perkins would say."

"And I know there's no way you remember Marlin Perkins."

"Actually, that's true. I got the DVDs from the library. Fascinating stuff. Jim and Stan really were idiots." He unwrapped a granola bar from the bag between the seats. "Have fun. I'll use this to stave off dissolution."

Bo-Kate got out and climbed the steps. How many times had she done that as a little girl, to get a free Co-Cola from Peggy or her husband, Marshall? As if to dispel the warmth of that memory, the snow blew almost horizontally, right into her face. She squinted through it and opened the lobby door.

Inside, the fireplace crackled in the corner of the empty café. There was no one behind the desk, so Bo-Kate rang the little bell and waited, reading the text beneath the framed picture of Bronwyn Hyatt, Needsville's lone celebrity.

WAR HERO'S TRIUMPHANT RETURN, the headline announced above the photo of a pretty dark-haired girl in an army dress uniform. A separate frame displayed another clipping that read, WAR HERO MARRIES LOCAL MINISTER; this time the photo featured the same girl standing beside a handsome, sandy-haired young man.

"Bronwyn," Bo-Kate murmured. She knew all about this girl, both from the news, where for fifteen minutes she was unavoidable, and from the innate sense all Tufa had of each other. Something warned her that Bronwyn Hyatt, now Chess, would be a formidable opponent.

Peggy Goins emerged from the back, where she lived with her husband. "Sorry, I was using the little girls' room. Can I—?"

Bo-Kate smiled and said, "Hello, there, Miss Peggy."

Peggy stared, then said, "Hello yourself, Bo-Kate. Been a long time."

"Has indeed. How's Marshall these days?"

"No different. How's the big city?"

"Nashville's Nashville."

Peggy straightened some of the tourist brochures in the desk display. She looked to be in her fifties, with immaculate black hair starting to go gray. She wore a sweatshirt with an image of a bear cuddling a guitar. At last she said, "You and I could exchange pleasantries all day, Bo-Kate, but I know damn well you ain't here just to visit. So tell me what you want."

She smiled. "I want Rockhouse's old job. He can't do it anymore."

"So you heard about that?"

Bo-Kate smiled. "Night wind blows all the way to Nashville, you know. I heard he got called out, his dirge got sung, and his inbred daughter ripped out his throat. Might've been easier for everybody if she'd just killed him outright, but that ain't the way it happened, is it?"

Peggy hid her surprise as much as she could. "So you can hear the night wind?"

Bo-Kate laughed. "That's all you've got to say, Miss Peggy? What about me taking over for Rockhouse?"

"Anything to do with Rockhouse and his people, you'll have to take up with him, and them."

"Oh, I have." She reached into her purse and pulled out the baggy. She placed it on the desk between them. Against the bright white paint, the bloody fingers looked even more ghastly.

Peggy gasped and looked up at Bo-Kate, eyes wide. "You didn't."

"I did. He's done, Peggy. He can't sing, and now he can't play. Believe me, I know how that feels. But I'm not just aiming for *his* job. I want it *all*. I want to bring us back together, one tribe, and I have some ideas about how to also bring us into the present. No more hiding, no more singing just for ourselves. What do you think of that?"

"I think you'll find that the other seat is still occupied."

"By that girl Mandalay? Please. That kid is even less of a problem than Rockhouse, and just as easy to fix."

"You're threatening a *child* again? You didn't learn a damn thing, did you?"

"I'm not threatening anyone. If she wants to step down and live here quietly, that's perfectly fine with me. I might even keep her on as an advisor. I'm just saying, I'll be coming for what I want, and if anyone gets in my way, no matter how old or young they are, they'll have to deal with the consequences."

"You are a vile woman, Bo-Kate Wisby," Peggy said. "Vile. It's the only word for it."

"Yeah, well, sticks and stones, Miss Peggy. You know 'Bonnie Annie,' right? I'll steal my father's gold and my mother's money,

just like the song says. But I don't need a sea captain; I'll make
myself a lady."

"Not if somebody stops you."

Now she laughed outright. "There's not a person in this town,
in this *valley*, who can stop me. Not you, and for sure not that
creepy-ass little girl. I'll see you soon, Miss Peggy." She turned
and strode out of the lobby.

Peggy Goins stared down at the baggy with the severed fingers.
The skin was cut clean, with the ends of the bones visible in the
stump. Blood pooled in one corner of the bag. One finger lay
nail-up, while the other displayed its pad. The distinctive finger-
print whorls were crisscrossed by tiny scars, and blocked in places
by calluses from more years of banjo playing that anyone could
imagine.

How many times had she, girl and woman, heard those fingers
in action? The old man was a vicious, lying, perverted bastard, but
he could make a banjo ring out like the bells of Christian heaven.
Now, even if his other fingers remained, that sound was gone;
no more would he create notes and chords only he could play.

Softly, she sang,

> *As I was a-walking down by St. James' Hospital,*
> *I was a-walking down by there one day,*
> *What should I spy but one of my comrades*
> *All wrapped up in flannel though warm was the day.*

She snatched a tissue from the nearby box and draped it over
the bag of fingers like a burial shroud. Something essential had
just died, permanently and irrevocably. It was like losing the rain.
And it left a vacuum into which the awful Bo-Kate Wisby hoped
to step.

She had to call someone. Mandalay was the obvious choice,

but something stopped her. It wasn't like Mandalay wouldn't know what had happened on her own, anyway. That girl knew everything. Instead she pulled up Bliss Overbay's number on the speed dial, but hesitated at the last moment. She couldn't go around spreading a panic.

So she went to the door to her apartment and hollered, "Marshall? Come on out here, and be quick about it, you hear me?"

Her husband emerged, yawning from his afternoon nap. "What's wrong?"

She told him. And then she showed him the fingers.

As Bo-Kate climbed back into the SUV, Nigel looked up from the game on his phone and said, "So, are we staying here at the Bobcat Arms?"

"No, I told you. We're staying at my family's house."

"I've seen pictures of houses in Appalachia. I'm not sure I know outhouse etiquette." He paused, then added, "So how did it go?"

"Delightfully. I left her speechless."

"You showed her the fingers, didn't you?"

"Didn't just show them. I left them with her. Now everyone in the county will know I ain't fooling."

"Won't the police come looking for you, then? I mean, I know this is the hills and all, but isn't taking body parts, even excess ones, frowned upon?"

"You just trust me, Nigel. What I've got in mind for this dump will blow your mind as much as it will theirs." She pointed down the highway. "Onward, sir. Our castle awaits."

Bliss Overbay awoke on her couch. She was confused for a moment, as the dream she'd just been experiencing was so vivid.

She'd been in an airplane, the small single-engine kind with a lone propeller, flying over the mountains at night. She could smell fuel, and sweat, and a kind of hair product once known as pomade, something she recognized from sitting on her grandfather's lap as he taught her chords on her tiple.

She hadn't been alone on the airplane, either. There had been a bespectacled young man, barely out of his teens, seated in the copilot's seat. He'd gotten up and come into the back passenger section to speak with the others. One of those was a middle-aged man whose shoes gleamed even in the dim lighting.

The other, in the cramped confines of the airplane, seemed to be a giant.

His face was broad and strong, with the kind of jawline that defined superheroes in the comics, and he wore a leather jacket that made him look like a thug. But his left leg held her attention—it extended straight out, with only the slightest bend at the knee, and she could see the mechanism of a leg brace under his jeans, and the metal heel loop wrapped with duct tape to keep it from scratching floors when he walked.

She couldn't hear what they were saying over the drone of the engine, but they were smiling, so it couldn't have been bad news. The fact that she was hovering like a ghost didn't strike her as unusual. She frequently had dreams like this, and often found that what they showed her turned out to be true, if you compensated for the malleable dream-language of the images. She once thought it might be astral projection sending her out into the world, but too many times there had been true dream abstractions involved. Now she believed it was like a TV channel that your antenna could pick up only for those brief periods when the atmospheric conditions were exactly right, and even then there was usually some sort of static or distortion.

Then she was traveling outside the plane, flying as a Tufa flew. The night must have been cold, since the bare spots visible on the mountains below were all covered with snow. But she felt nothing.

Then she was looping around the plane in great swirling arcs, coming within inches of the propeller blades. It was incredibly dangerous, because not only did it mean she might get caught on a wing or other protrusion, but the pilot might see her and panic, too. But there was no denying the glorious freedom, this sense of moving with impunity through an element denied to mere humans.

And then a gust of wind blew her sideways into the propeller, and she snapped awake just as the blades began to shred her.

She went to the bathroom, brushed her teeth, and started coffee in the kitchen. As she waited for it to brew, she thought back to the dream, wondering what it was trying to tell her. Had it been a true vision from the night winds, or just her subconscious's free-form choreography?

Just as she thought about calling Mandalay, the phone rang. "Hello?"

"Bliss," Peggy Goins said, sounding both tense and relieved. "Bo-Kate Wisby is back. And she's . . . You won't believe what she's done!"

Instantly Bliss put the dream aside. "Tell me what happened."

5

Marshall Goins wheezed with exhaustion, the cold air tightening his lungs with every breath. The hike up to Rockhouse's place was designed to discourage visitors, and he was definitely discouraged. But after seeing the severed fingers, he'd told Peggy he'd go up and check on the old man. So here he was.

He'd gone a secret way, and wandered into something that ended up taking a lot longer than he'd expected. Now he was back on track, and in the grand scheme of the regular world, he'd lost no more than a few minutes. But the Tufa ability to slip in and out of time always took a lot out of him, and lately he'd found the transitions harder and harder. He knew the reason: He'd lived in that regular world so long, and so thoroughly, that it had begun to rub off on him. The Tufa might not be entirely human, but they were close enough that mortality could hum in their ear in many of the same ways.

Then he heard whistling, and stopped to listen. It grew louder, and then Junior Damo appeared on the trail above him, coming down the mountain and jauntily twirling a stick.

He cut off in midnote when he saw Marshall.

"What are you doing, Junior?" Marshall asked.

"Might ask you the same thing," Junior shot back.

"Might, but I asked you first."

"Just taking a walk."

"Good God, Junior, that's the worst lie I've heard this week, and I had to talk to a state senator on Wednesday. But you can save me some trouble. How is Rockhouse?"

"What makes you think I've seen him?"

"There ain't a goddamn other thing on this mountain besides him that could get either one of us out here, that's what."

"Why do *you* want to see him?"

"Damn it, Junior, I'm not in the mood." He made a quick, decisive hand gesture, one that asserted his status in the Tufa hierarchy. "Now, *tell me.*"

Junior sighed. "He's been better." When Marshall glared at him, he continued, "Somebody done come along and cut off two of his fingers. Them extra pinkies he had."

Marshall kept his face neutral. "Somebody like you?"

Junior held up his own hands defensively. "Not me, man, I swear. Somebody got there before I did."

"Which brings me back to why you were there in the first place." When Junior still didn't answer, Marshall shook his head. "Junior, I don't know who'll end up taking Rockhouse's place, but it ain't gonna be you. You don't even scare *me,* and I'm almost as old as Rockhouse."

"Maybe it ain't about scaring," Junior said. "Maybe it's about pushing past where we been. Rockhouse wouldn't never even think about that. Maybe it's about time somebody did."

Marshall blinked in surprise. The same issues had come up among his half of the people, the ones governed by the First Daughters and protected by the Silent Sons. Bronwyn Hyatt, after her stint in the army and her now-famous rescue in the Iraq desert, insisted the Tufa could not continue the way they had for so many generations. And Mandalay seemed to sympathize with that idea, although she'd made no changes yet. "Damn, Junior. That's downright insightful."

Junior said nothing, but Marshall thought he blushed.

"But I still got to climb up there and see the old man for myself."

"He ain't much to see."

Marshall smiled wryly. "He never has been, has he?"

Mandalay climbed down the hill slowly, high-stepping through the drifts stacked by the wind. Whatever lay down in this hollow, just off Skunk's Misery Road and on land owned by the Somervilles, had been calling to her with an urgency that only grew stronger the closer she got. It pulled her off the road and into the forest despite the weather and encroaching evening. She couldn't tell what it was, though; it seemed to exist in a fog of perception, hiding from her by ducking out of sight whenever her mind's eye landed on it.

But now she could tell that it had a tune: "I'm Nine Hundred Miles from My Home." She recognized it from the few clear notes that cut through the mental and magical noise. She'd heard many versions and with many changes, but the one that always spoke to her most—and that this half-heard song seemed to mimic—was recorded by Fiddlin' John Carson back in 1924.

> *You can count the days I'm gone*
> *On the train that I left on*
> *You can hear the whistle blow a hundred miles*
> *If that train runs right*
> *I'll be home tomorrow night*
> *Lord, I'm nine hundred miles from my home.*

At last she had to stop, exhausted, and lean against a tree. Snow peppered her cheeks and eyes. When she looked around again, she realized she was totally lost: not only did she not know where she was going, but the blowing snow had already filled in her footprints. She couldn't even find her way back.

She dug out her cell phone but got no signal. She tried to listen to the wind, to hear its voice, but there was nothing. Suddenly she was *only* a twelve-year-old girl in the woods, underdressed and disoriented, and the fear that came with that realization threatened to choke her.

What had the night winds done to her?

She began to sing "Babes in the Wood," a song so spot-on, it made her smile despite the wind, snow, and fear.

> *Now the day being long and the night coming on*
> *These two little babies laid under a stone.*
> *They wept and they cried, they sobbed and they sighed;*
> *These two little babies, they laid down and died.*

She moved around to the back side of the tree to block the wind as much as possible. She stuffed her hands in her jacket pocket, wishing for the umpteenth time that she'd taken her gloves from her school backpack. There was not even a stone for her to crawl under.

She was in serious trouble, all right.

And then she heard a man's voice clearly singing, "I'm Nine Hundred Miles from My Home."

As he drove back toward town, Marshall Goins tried to ignore the pain in his back and legs. He kept glancing down at his cell phone, waiting for the NO SIGNAL message to go away. At last he got a single bar, and quickly hit the name DEACON

HYATT. After a few rings, the call connected, and a voice said, "Hello."

"Deacon, it's Marshall. Some shit's hit the fan. I'm on my way to pick you up."

"Which fan, and which shit?"

"The big fan, and some big shit. Somebody's cut off Rockhouse's extra fingers."

The line hissed in the lull, and then Deacon said, "That a fact."

"That's a pure-D fact. I just saw him. He's sitting in his gopher hole crying, Deacon. *Crying.* Blood everywhere. Tried to get him to let me drive him to the emergency room over in Unicorn, or at least have Bliss come up and give him stitches, but he ain't having none of it."

"Who did it?"

"He wouldn't say. But Peggy told me it was Bo-Kate Wisby."

Deacon let out a long, low whistle. "That explains why Chloe's been snapping heads off all day. All right, I'll call the rest. Where you want to meet?"

Marshall thought it over. Normally, they met outside, under the sky, but the weather wasn't conducive to that. He said, "I'll pick you up and we'll go up to the Catfish. Pass the word so somebody can bring a propane heater; that way our balls won't freeze off."

Deacon hung up the phone. His wife, Chloe, seated at the kitchen table working a sudoku puzzle, looked up and peered over her reading glasses at him. "What?"

"I have to go out. Marshall Goins's coming to pick me up. Somebody's done attacked Rockhouse Hicks."

Chloe's expression didn't change. "I know."

"That what you been whispering about on the phone all day?"

She nodded. "Peggy Goins told me."

"Did she tell you who did it?" he asked.

"Bo-Kate Wisby."

The name hung between them.

"Jefferson back as well?" Deacon asked.

"I don't know."

Deacon took his heavy coat down from the hook. "That's some bad news for everyone, ain't it?"

"It is. But there's worse. Mandalay's disappeared."

Deacon stopped in midmotion, one arm in a sleeve. "Disappeared?"

"Last anyone saw of her, the bus let her off after school. She ain't answering her phone. She ain't reachable the other ways, either. Bliss is out looking for her."

Deacon nodded. Normally these First Daughter matters would stay secret, not just to men but to any women not part of the group. But clearly neither the return of Bo-Kate nor Mandalay's disappearance could remain a First Daughter secret for long, and it was better to share the information than to risk something crucial getting missed.

"You want me to get the boys out to look for her?"

"Not until Bliss says so."

He scowled. "Might not do to wait. It's cold out there."

"It's Mandalay."

"I know, but . . . I mean, whatever else she is, she's also a little girl. A lot of bad things can happen."

"I know. But we have to do it the right way. If Bliss doesn't find her soon, I'm sure the word will go out."

He finished putting on his coat. "All right, if that's the way it is."

"Be careful," Chloe said as she stood. "It's awful messy out there, according to the Weather Channel." She kissed him, and he patted her backside.

"Get a room, you two," their teenage son Aiden said from the couch. If he'd followed the conversation, he gave no sign.

"I'll be careful," Deacon assured her. "But I reckon it's about to get a whole lot messier."

Mandalay pushed through the snow toward the song. "I'm Nine Hundred Miles from My Home" was not exactly a staple in the Tufa repertoire, and while a lot of folks might know it, its sentiment didn't really apply here where the Tufa lived; most of them stayed, and the ones who did leave came home one way or another.

Then a strong blast of wind made her duck behind a tree. When it passed, the song was gone, and she was more lost than ever.

How could this be happening? She was the leader of the First Daughters, the repository of their lore, history, and wisdom. Although it was difficult for her to access all that accumulated knowledge at once, in the past she'd always had the answer appear on its own, rising from her mind when needed. Now it simply didn't happen.

That meant one of two things. Either the night winds had taken it from her, which she knew they hadn't done . . . or what was happening to her now had no precedent in the entire history of the Tufa.

And that idea terrified her.

Before she could give in to that fear, another noise rose over the wind. A male voice, singing.

> *One morning, one morning, one morning in May*
> *I overheard a married man to a young girl say*
> *Arise you up, Pretty Katie, and come along with me*
> *Across the Blue Mountain to the Allegheny.*

Mandalay peeked around the trunk, toward the sound. A human shape emerged out of the snow, accompanied by a large dog.

She sang out,

I'll buy you a horse, love, and a saddle to ride
I'll buy me another to ride by your side
We'll stop at every tavern and drink when we are dry
Across the Blue Mountain goes Katie and I.

The shape stopped. The dog barked once. "Who's there?" the shape called.

"My name's Mandalay Harris. I reckon I'm lost. Who's that?"

"Luke Somerville. Lord a'mighty, girl, how'd you end up all the way out here?"

"Like I said, I got lost. Reckon I have a talent for it."

"You sure do." He came closer, and she could see his face. He was about the same age as her, black haired and big eyed. She'd seen him around school, but he belonged to Rockhouse's people, and they tended not to interact with her folks anywhere but the Pair-A-Dice. She wondered if he knew who she was.

"Well, you best come home with me and get out of this storm before you drop off into a gully and nobody finds you until spring. It'll be full dark soon."

She didn't realize he carried a rifle until he swung it up and rested it over his shoulder. She got a chill that had nothing to do with the weather.

"You could just point me toward the road," she said, trying to sound casual. No matter who she was or how many secrets she carried, a bullet would kill her just like anything else alive.

"The nearest road's two miles away," he said. "And you're fifteen miles from your house."

She blinked in surprise. Fifteen miles? She couldn't possibly have walked that far. Either she'd slipped into fae time without realizing it, which ought to be impossible, or the night winds had blown her here on purpose. Still, she thought wryly, better than nine hundred miles from home.

She held back her hair from her face and studied him. He didn't look dangerous, and she got no sense that he meant her harm. Perhaps he didn't. But his family, seeing the head of the First Daughters walk into their house, might feel otherwise.

"I know who you are," he said quietly, just loud enough to be heard over the wind. "In case you were wondering. But it's okay. My folks won't hurt you."

"You a mind reader, too?"

"I just figure that's what I'd be thinking if I was in your shoes."

"If you were in my shoes, you'd be wishing you'd worn boots," she said with a smile.

He smiled back. "Come on, let's get out of here. Mom'll make us some hot chocolate."

She followed him through the snow, the big dog dancing around them both.

6

The convenience store door closed behind Junior Damo as he stomped his feet to dislodge the snow. The old man behind the counter, dressed in the chain's bright orange and blue shirt, looked up from reading *Entertainment Weekly*. His name tag read TIRRELL.

"Junior, what're you doing out in this weather?" he asked. "Loretta finally kick you out?"

"Nah, I'm on my way home to her, that's why I need me some beer," Junior said. He went to the cooler, nearly knocked over the WET FLOOR sign, and pulled a twelve-pack of Miller Lite from the rack. "Hey, you ain't seen any of the Hickses around, have you?"

"We're all hicks, son," Tirrell said with a grin, displaying the gap where two of his bottom teeth were missing.

"Didn't you teach college once?"

"I did, but they don't give tenure to hicks."

"Well, I meant the Hicks family. Rockhouse, Stoney, Jewel, Mason, any of them."

"Well, you know what happened to Rockhouse.

"Of course," Junior said, trying to sound blasé. After all the time he spent on the road, he'd forgotten just how fast the Tufa telegraph traveled. In the time it took him to get from the mountain to town, everyone in the county probably knew about it. And ever since that Collins woman stabbed him in the dick two summers ago, Stoney just sits around moping. He weighs three hundred pounds these days, so he don't come to town much. Ain't seen Jewel since he got married. Mason got some gas this morning, but he didn't come in. Why you looking for them?"

"Just want to see about hunting some squirrels," Junior said as he ran his debit card through the machine. "You see any of 'em, tell 'em to call me."

"I ain't your message boy, Junior."

Junior scowled at him. "Really? That's your attitude? Somebody asks you to do something as simple as pass on a message if you see somebody, something that don't even require you getting up off that stool, and you cain't be bothered? No wonder you didn't get that ten-four or whatever the hell it was."

"Man, what bug crawled up your ass and died?" Tirrell said.

"You. And every single damn one of us. We don't do a damn thing to help each other out. We won't even pass on a fucking message if there's nothing in it for us."

"You turning into a socialist? Did you sign up for Obamacare or something?"

"Do you even know what a socialist *is*? 'Cause I don't." Junior turned to leave.

Tirrell laughed. "Actually, I do. And I'll tell 'em if I see 'em. But you're gonna owe me a favor."

"See?" Junior said as he went out the door. "That's what I mean. Nobody does nothing for nobody."

He got into his truck, started the engine, and took one of the beers from the cardboard case. The first beer he ever drank was Miller, when he was fourteen, and although he'd sampled others over the years, he kept returning to that familiar, icy tang. It represented to him what "beer" in general was supposed to taste like, and the freedom that came with it.

Of course, that freedom—like the beautiful girls, and the

fancy clubs, and the friends who always laughed at your jokes—
was just an illusion. No, actually, it was worse. It was a *lie.* Like
a woman saying she loves you just to get away from her parents.

In the side-view mirror, he saw the old man talking on the
phone, and smiled. He could make the Tufa telegraph work for
him, too. Whichever Hicks Tirrell was calling, the word would
get back to the one Junior actually wanted to talk to. Then things
could progress. Seeing old Rockhouse bloody, mutilated, and
afraid had opened up vast chasms of ambition in Junior, and he
saw no reason to wait to put his plan into action, especially with
Bo-Kate Wisby skulking around. But first he had to know what
might be in his path.

He put the truck in gear and pulled out onto the highway.
He turned on his lights, as it was getting dark. He passed four
cars heading the other way. Anytime he saw more than two vehicles together, he assumed they were on their way to a meeting
of the Silent Sons. Once he'd wanted more than anything to be
a member, but now he just saw them as one more obstacle.

Let them talk, he thought. *While they're flapping their gums, I'll
be* doing *something. We'll see who stands tallest when it's all done.*

It took almost an hour for Bliss to reach the Hyatt farm. The
snow was particularly slushy, and even her four-wheel-drive had
to proceed with caution. She saw an extra truck already there,
and realized Chloe had called her daughter, Bronwyn.

Ever since her marriage to Craig Chess and her move to his
home across the county line in Unicorn, Bronwyn had spent a
vast amount of time commuting back and forth. Even now, eight
months pregnant, she was as likely to be here as at her own place.
It signaled no trouble in her new marriage; she and Craig had
hashed all this out ahead of time, and he was, as always, even-
tempered and supportive. Bliss, who lived alone and probably
always would, envied them more than anyone knew.

But now First Daughter business had called the three of them together. She struggled up the slope to the front door, knocked, and was immediately let in. She stood on the rug and took off her boots and coat, then gratefully accepted the hot coffee Chloe offered.

Bronwyn sat at the kitchen table and didn't stand. On her slender build, the baby made her look like she'd swallowed the king of pumpkins whole, and her face was drawn tight with discomfort. She said at once, "Are you *sure*?"

"Good to see you, too, Bronwyn." She looked around. "Where's Aiden?"

"He's in his room," Chloe said. Her youngest child, thirteen and stereotypically sullen, interacted with the family less and less. "Playing *Minecraft*. That's all he does anymore."

"Never mind that," Bronwyn said, although she knew more about her baby brother than their mother did. She knew that he liked a girl from a farm down the road, and often snuck out to meet her. Since the girl also liked another boy, one who was older and had a motorcycle, Bronwyn also knew the source of Aiden's sulkiness. "Are you *sure* it's her? Did you see her?"

"I haven't seen her myself," Bliss said. "But Peggy has."

"It's been a long time," Chloe said. "She might've changed a lot. Maybe Peggy made a mistake."

"Could *you* mistake anybody else for Bo-Kate Wisby?" Bliss asked.

"Maybe one of them barracuda fish," Chloe said.

"I've been hearing about her all my life," Bronwyn said, shifting to find a better position, "but I thought she couldn't come back."

"She shouldn't be able to," Bliss said. "She was sung all the way out. It's the only time that's ever happened since we came here. She shouldn't even be able to *find* Needsville anymore."

"So how did it happen?" Bronwyn pressed.

"That's just one of the questions we have to find the answer to." Bliss's cell phone rang, and she looked at the number. "Well, shit."

"What?" said Chloe.

"It's Junior Damo."

"You going to answer it?" Chloe asked.

Bliss shrugged and put the phone to her ear. "Hello? Yes, Junior, I remember you. What can I do for you?" She paused to listen. "Is that a fact? I hadn't heard about that. What do you think she wants?" Again she listened, and her face hardened. "Well, that just ain't going to happen. So why are you calling to tell me this?"

This time she listened for a long moment. "I see. I'll pass it on, then. It ain't my decision. Yeah, I got your number. Goodbye." She turned off her phone and said, "Junior wants to meet with Mandalay."

"What about?"

"He figures we may all have to get together to get rid of Bo-Kate."

"She's just one woman," Bronwyn said. "If y'all want, I can—"

"No," Bliss and Chloe said together.

"What, you think we should just talk to her? Get all touchy-feely with her?"

"I think that may be a better first step," Chloe said.

"Yeah, well, I don't do touchy-feely. I do punchy-bleedy."

"I know," Bliss said. "That's why you're not the right person for this."

Bronwyn glared at them both. "It's because I'm pregnant, isn't it?"

"It's because it ain't your place," Bliss said.

"She's causing trouble. I'm the one who usually stops it when people do that."

"This is bigger than what you handle," Bliss said. "Junior confirmed what Peggy told me: Bo-Kate cut off Rockhouse's extra fingers. Now I have to go find Mandalay. Get the word out to the other First Daughters, if they don't already know. Which reminds me . . . either of you had any dreams about airplanes?"

Chloe and Bronwyn shook their heads.

"Nothing about flying around outside one of them old single-engine planes? Okay, guess it was just me. I'll be in touch. If I don't find her before midnight, we'll have to put the word out to everyone." She left and descended the hill to her truck. The snow had begun to fall again.

Nigel's voice vibrated along with the shuddering SUV as he said, "Your people's definition of 'road' is very fluid, isn't it?"

"This isn't a road," Bo-Kate said through clenched teeth. "It's a driveway."

"Does anyone ever use it to leave?"

"Not if they can help it."

It was early evening, and the mountain shadows made it dark for all practical purposes. The trees and terrain kept the house hidden until the very last minute, when the SUV rounded a bend and emerged into a clearing. The headlights raked dramatically across the front porch, illuminating the old, intact Doric columns.

Nigel frowned at the dilapidated house, two stories tall, with gables on the roof. Several windows were boarded up; the remaining ones were dark.

An rust-rimmed pickup and a gigantic, ancient Ford sedan were parked next to each other, and on the porch rested a worn, battered refrigerator and stove. As they parked, two nondescript dogs, one bigger than the other, appeared and barked warnings.

"Hush up, you two," Bo-Kate said as she climbed out. "Don't make me put a boot to your asses."

The smaller dog yelped once at the sight of her and ran off into the darkness. The bigger one lowered its head submissively and skulked forward until she could pet it. It whined, and eventually its big tail thumped the ground.

"Missed me, huh?" Bo-Kate said.

"You know this dog?" Nigel asked.

"Of course I do. This is Stinkerbelle. Known her since she was a pup. That little one that ran off is Cheeto-Bear."

"I thought you said you'd been gone from here for twenty-some years?"

Bo-Kate patted Nigel's smooth cheek. "Nigel, there's something you've got to realize about the Tufa, and I haven't told you about it, because there was no way you'd believe it sitting in Boscos on Twenty-first Avenue."

"And that's what?"

"Time doesn't work the same for everybody. And it works real different for us."

"Ah. So not only have you broken the laws of your country once today, you've now broken the laws of physics?"

"I just don't want you to be any more blindsided than you have to be."

There was something new in her voice, a kindness he'd seldom heard before. He bowed his head slightly and said, "Well. Thank you, then."

She turned to face the house. The SUV's headlights were still on, illuminating the faded wood. It might have been painted once, but the color had long since leached down to a slate-toned neutral gray. Except for the dogs, there was no sign of life. Then the headlights automatically clicked off, leaving them in almost-darkness.

"Chez Wisby," Bo-Kate sighed.

"This is where you grew up?" Nigel said. "I know you said it was poverty, but somehow I imagined something less . . . poor."

"No, this is it. Looks about the same, too."

"Did you play in that refrigerator, then?"

"Daddy keeps his beer in there. And his venison in the freezer."

"Venison is . . . Wait, don't tell me. . . ."

"Deer meat."

"Dear me."

"Ha."

"And the stove? Does it work, too?"

"What, you've never heard of a cook-out?" He couldn't see if she was smiling, but he felt her humor.

"And we're supposed to stay here," he continued. "Despite the, ah, rustic portico kitchenette, I hope we do get to sleep indoors."

"Yep."

"That was a perfectly pleasant-looking motel back in town, bobcat or no."

"It is perfectly pleasant, but I'll never stay there. It belongs to one of the others."

"Ah. The great schism you mentioned."

The humor left her voice, replaced by the hard steel he knew so well. "It's not a 'schism,' you pretentious jerk. It's a separation, one that's been around since the Tufa first came here."

"And you're here to heal it."

"I'm here to *end* it, smart-ass. That's different." She pointed to one of the gables. "That was my room. I'd crawl out the window and jump to that tree to go see my boyfriend, Jeff. He was one of . . . the others. I tried not to like him, and he tried not to like me. But it was no use."

"Your parents didn't approve of him?"

"That's putting it mildly."

"How very Romeo and Juliet."

"It's not a *joke,* Nigel. His parents would've shot me on sight, and mine would've done the same to him. You ever risked anything like that for love?"

"Then it truly was love?"

"It truly was a kind of love," she said, her voice distant.

"But not the kind that lasts."

She looked down at her boots in the snow. "I'm done talking about this."

"Of course," he agreed gently.

When she spoke again, her voice had its normal sarcasm. "So I should also warn you, my family *will* call you a nigger to your face."

His eyebrows rose. "Will they?"

"They will. They'll watch you like a hawk, and treat you like a Martian. They won't hurt you, because you're with me, but I just want you to be prepared."

"No worries. I've been called a Martian before."

This made her smile. "All right, then. Let's get this over with."

When they moved, the dog Stinkerbelle trotted around the side of the house and disappeared. On the porch, Nigel followed her example and stomped to dislodge the snow from his boots. Then she stepped to the door and firmly knocked. It rattled against the frame.

"Put your pants on, everyone, the prodigal has returned!" she called out. There was no answer. She opened the door.

Inside was an enormous room, made even larger by its singular lack of furniture. A semicircle of straight chairs was arranged around the hearth, where a tepid little fire fought the winter chill. Oil lamps burned on two small tables in the corners. Beyond this, bright electric light radiated from a kitchen where three people sat at the table. To Nigel, it was like standing in the nineteenth century and looking into the twenty-first.

On the wall was a large, strange painting of a baby, maybe a year old, standing on a chair. The baby's head seemed to float just above its body, with no neck to attach it. It was disconcerting, and to Nigel, a little creepy.

The two people visible in the kitchen, an old man and an elderly woman, turned to look. The man immediately jumped to his feet, his fists clenched, as if he expected a fight. He wore overalls and a John Deere baseball cap.

"Hey, Paw-paw," Bo-Kate said as she took off her coat and handed it to Nigel. "That Memaw with you?"

"Bo-Kate," the old woman said. She didn't stand up, but her whole body grew tense.

"It's Bo-Kate," the man said to the third person, who sat just out of sight. Only a pair of slender, feminine bare feet could be seen.

"Just toss 'em on a chair," Bo-Kate said to Nigel, and he draped their coats across the backs of two of the seats. Bo-Kate grinned, but didn't move any closer to her family. "Reckon y'all are surprised to see me."

"Surprised ain't the word," Paw-paw Wisby said. His given name was Beauregard, but even people unrelated to him called him Paw-paw. "Why don't you tell me why you're here."

Bo-Kate raised her chin and sang in a sweet, pure voice:

> *To thee I'll return*
> *Overburdened with care*
> *My heart's dearest solace*
> *Will smile on me there.*

For a moment, there was no response. Then the bare feet withdrew from sight, followed by the scrape of a chair across the floor as the unseen person rose.

Nigel gasped as the newcomer stepped into the doorway.

She was a staggeringly beautiful, dark-haired girl of about twenty. Despite the weather, she wore scandalously short denim cut-offs and a threadbare, tight T-shirt with plainly nothing under it. She leaned against the doorframe and said in a low purr, "And who's your friend, Bo-Kate?"

"You just settle down, Tain," Bo-Kate said. "He's mine."

"Yours? You can buy and sell niggers again? I sure didn't see *that* on the news."

"I warned you," Bo-Kate asided to Nigel. To the girl, she said, "I just mean he's with me. Keep your hands to yourself. And any other body parts that might be inclined to trespass."

"Let's not be too hasty," Nigel said, and stepped forward. With British formality, he said, "I'm Nigel Hawtrey. I'm Ms. Wisby's executive assistant."

"Listen to him talk all fancy," Tain said. "Where you from, boy?"

"Manchester, originally."

"That in England?" Tain asked. The word came out, *Aingland*.

"It is. A beautiful place." He looked her up and down appreciatively. "Though not as beautiful as some of the scenery around here."

"Stop it," Bo-Kate said to Nigel.

"No, let him keep going," Tain said. "I like the way he talks."

"Tain is my cousin," Bo-Kate said. "My folks took her in after she got into some trouble."

"What sort of trouble?" Nigel asked.

"Oh, not *that* kind," Tain said. "What can I say? The trouble with trouble is, it starts out as fun."

"Now Mom and Dad are trying to teach her the straight and narrow, to make up for me turning out like I did. Right, Memaw?"

"We took her in 'cause she's family," the old woman said, still seated.

"That's right," Tain said. She stood in such a way that her long legs and slender figure were highlighted against the bright glare from the kitchen. "But I'm not too straight, and I'm definitely not narrow."

"Don't make me throw a bucket of water on you," Bo-Kate warned. "Where are Snad and Canton?"

"They're around," Paw-paw said evasively.

"Snad is out trapping coyotes," Tain said. "Canton is tom-catting around with that middle Adams girl. I'm sure they'll come running when they hear their baby sister is back."

"Don't be telling her nothing, Tain," Paw-paw snapped.

"It ain't like it's a secret," Tain said.

"We're here to stay for a while," Bo-Kate said to her parents. "We'll take my old room. No need to do anything special for us."

"*Why* are you here, Bo-Kate?" Paw-paw said. "And don't bull-shit us by saying you missed us. The only way you'd miss us is if you were shootin' at us."

"I see where you get your wit," Nigel asided to her.

Bo-Kate ignored him. "Paw-paw, I'm here to do what Rockhouse Hicks never could: draw us all back under one pair of wings."

"That can't be done, Bo-Kate."

"Sure it can. It just needs a little outside perspective. And be-lieve me, I've got that now."

Memaw raised one gnarled hand and folded her fingers into a series of gestures. Bo-Kate raised her left hand and pretended to turn a crank on it with her right one; her middle finger rose. "Your signs don't mean a thing to me, Memaw."

"You think—"

"I think I've been on the road all day today, and I'm tired. Come on, Nigel, before Tain makes your dick bust out and go dancing across the room to her."

"Thank you for your hospitality," Nigel said to Paw-paw and Memaw. "Miss Wisby," he added with an extra nod to Tain.

"Stop it, before you boldly go where every man has gone be-fore," Bo-Kate said, and dragged him away from the kitchen.

"I see he's a *personal* assistant, all right," Tain called after them. "Y'all have fun. Try not to bust the bedframe."

Bo-Kate led them up a staircase Nigel hadn't noticed when

they came in. Nigel flashed a smile back at Tain as he followed. She was already watching for it, and simply nodded in response, like it was no surprise at all.

"Sharin' the same room?" Tain called after them with a mocking smile.

The second floor was dark, and Bo-Kate did not turn on any lights. Nigel could barely see to follow her as she made her way to one door and opened it. Only when they were both inside did she throw the switch.

The bedroom had a vaulted ceiling and a bed with a canopy. It was also pristine, as if the owner had left that morning, not a decade or more ago. Nigel stood holding their luggage, staring.

"This room is on top of the house we saw from outside?" he said. "Where exactly does it fit?"

"It's like that TV show, *Doctor Who*. It's bigger on the inside."

"Oh, how quaint. We share a cultural reference." But his humor did not mask his confusion.

And yet the strangest thing about the room wasn't its apparent freshness, but its decor. It looked as if it had come right out of the 1950s. Framed pictures of Elvis and other original rock-and-roll figures lined the top of the bureau, and magazine pages showing the same people were lovingly pinned to the walls. They weren't faded, but as fresh and glossy as if they'd been hung up yesterday. It didn't match up with the Bo-Kate he knew, who must, like him, have grown up in the '90s. Michael Jackson and Kurt Cobain belonged here, not Chuck Berry and Carl Perkins.

"How old did you say you were?" Nigel asked as he put down the suitcases.

"That's not a polite question to ask a lady," Bo-Kate said as she sat at the vanity and took off her fur-topped snow boots.

"I apologize for my rudeness, but either you were the biggest fan of *Grease* there ever was, or we're going to sleep in a rockabilly museum exhibit."

She chuckled. "I liked that kind of music when I was younger.

Especially him." She nodded at a photo on the wall. "Byron Harley. He died not five miles from here, did you know that? His plane went down right up on the mountain in the middle of the night. He burned up, along with Guy Berry and Large Sarge." She bit her lip as she looked at the picture. "God, he was gorgeous, wasn't he?"

"I'm not qualified to judge."

"Since when did you become an art critic?"

"Now that you mention it, my parsnip, who was that rather strange youngster in the painting downstairs?" Nigel asked.

"Ah, some relative or other."

"His head did not seem to be attached to his body. Was that an artistic style at some point, or another of your people's delightful quirks?"

"That was practicality, my Continental employee. Because the winters were so bad around here back before the Civil War, artists spent the cold months painting generic headless portraits, then when they got commissions in the spring, all they had to do was add the heads."

"This one didn't quite add it all the way."

"Well, there's good artists and bad artists, Nigel. You should know that by now."

"That's a cosmic truth," he agreed. Then he sat on the edge of the bed and said, "So: what now?"

In one motion she stood and peeled off her sweater and blouse, then unhooked her bra and let it fall. She kept her chin high and her eyes locked on his. "If I told you I was older than these mountains around you, what would you say?"

Nigel made no effort not to look her up and down. He placed the luggage at his feet. "I would say . . . why, Grandma, what lovely breasts you have."

She smiled. "All the better to silence you with, my dear. Now, get those clothes off and get your ass in bed."

7

The little room was silent except for the wind whistling around the door. Rockhouse ignored it, too traumatized even to consider trying to make a fire. The light around the door gradually faded and finally disappeared altogether.

He sat at his table, his hands before him. He couldn't bring himself to look at his injuries before he lost the light. It surprised him that it had been considerably less painful than getting his throat ripped out, but maybe that was just due to shock.

He couldn't believe what had happened to him. Not long ago, he had been the most powerful man in Cloud County, and now he was *this:* mute, crippled, and isolated. What had he done to deserve such a fate? He knew better than to ponder that question, because the answers always came to him with ease.

It began with that stupid bet with the Queen over his prowess with his axe. As the Feller in the Queen's Forest, he had a position of power and influence over all those who lived outside the royal city. To retain that power, he'd needed only to do his job and shut up. It turned out he could do neither.

When the bet was lost, he could have released his people from their vow of fealty to him. He could've accepted exile alone, and left them to live out their lives in peace among the earth and greenery of home. But he hadn't even seriously considered the idea. If he was going down, he was taking them with him.

And then, over and above the exile, there were the things he'd done to his own family. Seducing his sister with a combination of magic and intimidation so that she'd conceive a child of pure Tufa stock, to counteract the gradual intermingling of his folk, first with the Asians who became the Native Americans, then with the Europeans who eventually followed the Tufa's own route across the ocean. Then he'd seduced the child of that union, his daughter Curnen, in an attempt to intensify the pure bloodline even more.

But before any of his seed took hold in her, her husband—that annoying, smug bastard Brushy Dale—realized what was going on. On the night Rockhouse Hicks should have been enshrined as the newest star of the *Grand Ole Opry,* Brushy accused him before the other musicians, then beat him mercilessly.

Still, he got his revenge as he always did. He cursed Curnen to slow oblivion, and sent Brushy to spend eternity as a stone in the forest. And then he forgot about them both, which proved to be his fatal error.

Of course, none of the Tufa understood why he did those ostensibly terrible things. They had no idea what it was like to carry his burden, no concept of the rage and responsibility that motivated him. His goal was always the same: keep the Tufa together, under his hand, until the day the Queen regretted her actions and allowed them home. Allowed *him* home.

He clung to that single thought as the eons passed, even though he knew that day would never come. In all the timeless years of her existence, the Queen had never, ever changed her mind.

Suddenly something *moved* in the room behind him.

He felt its presence as it took slow, light steps across the floor. It also gave off a faint, foxfirelike glow. The air grew charged with anticipation as it moved, not closer, but simply back and forth. To see it, he'd have to turn.

He didn't want to do that.

But at last, he could resist no longer. Because he knew what he'd see.

He turned, the old chair squeaking as his weight shifted.

The woman wore a long black gown with immense hanging sleeves, all tattered and worn. She radiated the faint pale-blue light. A black veil covered her face, so he could not tell her age. But he knew her purpose.

He looked around for his electrolarynx.

"Don't seek that mechanical voice, Tigh-na-creige," she said, using the pure form of his name. "It'll do nothing for you now. Nothing you could say will change your fate. That's why I'm here."

She lifted the veil. Beneath it was a beautiful mature woman of about forty, with dark hair falling around her face in waves.

Rockhouse mouthed her name. *Radella.*

"Your day has ended, by your own vile hand," she said. Her voice had a distant quality, as if miles—or eons—separated them. "I am simply here to make it official."

She smiled then, a smile so vicious and cold that it made his eyes well with new tears.

She tilted back her head, opened her mouth, and emitted a wailing shriek that filled the little room as if it had a physical force, pushing the air toward the walls and out through the myriad cracks and openings. Rockhouse suddenly couldn't breathe, and he got to his feet to flee. But the abrupt movement, combined with his injuries, made him dizzy and he fell to the floor.

The sound continued, growing, if possible, even louder. It encompassed oceans of pain, sadness, and torment, a cry that had often heralded death among the Celtic peoples. But here it announced more than a simple passing from this world to the next. It told of cessation, nonexistence in a void that never ended and was all encompassing. It announced Rockhouse's doom.

He crawled to the door as the banshee continued to wail, and managed to get it open. Outside, snow trickled lazily down from the darkness like the cold, dry tears of antiquity. He had no time to grab a coat, gloves, or his electrolarynx. He got his feet under him and fled down the trail as fast as his aged, damaged body would allow.

In his former home, the specter of Radella was gone. But the cry continued to echo, merging with the wind to travel great distances and follow Rockhouse long after it should have faded.

Luke Somerville looked across the dinner table at Mandalay. Her face was still splotchy from the cold, and her black hair frizzy from static. Since her own were soaked with melted snow, she wore clothes borrowed from his older sister that were big on her and made her appear weak and helpless. She caught him looking, and her cheeks turned extra red. He quickly looked away.

"I called your mama," Luke's mother, Claudia, said. She was a big woman, the kind who put on ten permanent pounds with each of her four children. She had Tufa-black hair, but her skin was pale and almost shone in the kitchen's light. She put a big bowl of mashed potatoes down on the table with a loud slam. "She said your daddy'll be along to fetch you in about an hour. That'll give you time to eat, at least."

"Thank you, ma'am," Mandalay said. She tried to ignore the wonderful aroma rising from the food before her, reminding her with every whiff that she hadn't eaten in seven hours. But the Tufa rules about food and drink made it impossible for her to accept it, and they knew that, too. "But if I don't eat at home, Leshell gets real mad at me."

"You call your mama Leshell?" asked Luke's baby sister Ida Mae. She sat beside Mandalay, on a homemade booster seat of three Knoxville phone books duct-taped together.

"She's my stepmother," Mandalay said. "My real mama died."

"Wow," the girl said. "I ain't never met nobody whose mama died."

"Behave," their father, Elgin, said from the head of the table as he wrote "Insurance Payment" over and over in tiny print on a piece of stationery. "That ain't no way to talk to somebody."

"But it's the truth," Ida Mae said.

"It's the truth that you're gonna get an ass-whoopin' if you don't button that lip," Elgin said. He finished his writing, then folded the paper into smaller and smaller squares. He said to Mandalay, "Luke says he found you wandering in the woods. Is that right?"

"Yes, sir. I was bored and went for a walk, but I got kind of turned around."

"Went for a walk in a snowstorm? That ain't too bright, is it?" He chuckled as he tied a red string around the folded paper.

"Elgin," Claudia said warningly. "That ain't polite."

Mandalay said nothing. When the Tufa had arrived here, they'd been one group, united under the leadership of the one who'd gotten them into this mess in the first place. It didn't take long for that to change, though, and their society quickly became a mirror of the one they'd left: two groups, diametrically opposed in almost every way, with their own leaders.

Luke's family was part of the group that stayed under the Feller. And now they had the leader of the other group, Rockhouse's opposite number, seated at their table. If she ate or drank anything they offered, it might affect the extremely tenuous balance of power even more.

"Well, it's a good thing Luke found you," Elgin said. He got up and took the string-tied note to the counter, where a pile of medical bills waited. He tucked it beneath them, returned to his seat, then spooned mashed potatoes onto his plate.

Mandalay looked at Luke. "Yeah, it sure was. If I ain't said it yet—thank you."

"No problem," Luke said.

One of his sisters, older and with glasses, sat down with an accordion and began to play. The music was infectious, and it took all of Mandalay's self-control not to tap her foot along with it. The sound filled the kitchen, and Luke's older brother patted out a rhythm on the table edge.

Mandalay gripped the edges of her seat as tightly as she could. If there was danger in sharing food or drink, then there was a possible apocalypse for her if she joined in their music. The problem was, music was insidious—you could find yourself humming, or swaying, or head-bobbing along with it before you were aware.

Claudia sang in a high, keening way that blended seamlessly with the accordion:

> Well, you look so fine
> In that borrowed suede jacket of mine
> Now, cozy up behind the wheel
> Of an aquamarine automobile
> We'll just take it slow
> Listening to songs on the AM radio
> No particular place to go
> Valiant and Fury girls. . . .

Mandalay felt the music swelling in her, connecting her with the years—millennia—of songs of the Tufa. The song ached with loss, with friendship and love that once flourished and danced among the flowers in the rain, but was now old, and tender, and reaching out for comfort. She wanted to cry, and fought mightily as her vision blurred. To admit this intense an emotional re-

sponse to their music was to give them a level of power over her
that could easily spell her doom.

The family, except for Luke, harmonized on the next verse.

> *Well, the Valiant finally died*
> *And I sat and said my last good-byes*
> *I saved a hubcap for my walls*
> *Called the garage to make that haul*
> *Well, the tow truck guys were drunk*
> *And they complained it was a piece of junk*
> *Yeah, that junk was my life*
> *Valiant and Fury girls.*

Mandalay bit the sides of her cheeks until she tasted blood.
The song draped over her like a cerecloth shroud, the weight of
its ache as heavy and final as the pressure of that wax-dipped
funeral cloth.

Then Luke said, "Mama, y'all stop it."

Claudia stopped singing, and the accordion choked off with
a melodic wheeze.

"Luke, you apologize to your mama or you'll get the whip-
pin' of your life," his father said.

Luke stood up. His face was red, and his eyes shone with tears
of anger. "You can whip me if you want, Daddy, but it still ain't
right, what you're doing. Mandalay don't want to sing with us,
and that's fine. She's a guest in our house."

Elgin stood, grabbed the back of Luke's shirt with one hand,
and began to unbuckle his belt with the other. "Boy, I'll teach
you to disrespect—"

"You will not," Mandalay said quietly.

Everyone froze and stared at her.

She stood, her fingertips resting on the table. Her voice took
on a quality of ancient, unyielding power. "You will not lay a
hand on this boy. You will not punish him for standing up for

what he thinks is right." She said these things as simple statements, not orders. It was as if they were an already accomplished fact.

For a long moment, the only sound was the refrigerator's compressor kicking on. Then they all jumped at the sudden knock on the door. It was one lone pounding, and they sat immobile, waiting for more. But it didn't come.

Mandalay saw Claudia and Elgin exchange a look. It wasn't hard to read: Whoever or whatever was out there, it wasn't a guest expected for dinner. And it was far too soon for it to be Mandalay's father.

Elgin picked up a shotgun from the corner and walked to the door. "Who's out there?" he called.

They all listened. Over the wind, they heard what sounded like fingers scraping on the other side of the wood.

"Mommy," whispered Luke's other sister, Deetzy.

"Hush," Claudia said softly but emphatically. Still, she took the little girl's hand.

Mandalay moved slowly around the table. There were things, she well knew, that lived near the Tufa, unseen and unseeable except in rare instances. Most of them were harmless, but not all. Some were both terrifying and incredibly dangerous. Given who she was, Mandalay should have been able to sense what was out there, and thus know how to respond to it. But nothing came to her.

And of course, none of that would matter if, on the other side of the door, waited a fully human maniac who had randomly chosen to slaughter everyone in this particular house.

More scraping sounded through the wood. It couldn't be an animal; the sound was unmistakably fingerlike. And as she approached, Mandalay could tell the sound came from low on the door, from a small child's height. If a child were lost in this weather, as she had been—

"Open the door," she said.

Elgin looked back at her. The fear and weakness in his face almost made her angry. "No fucking way."

"Open . . . the door," she said, using the same tone she'd used to stop him before.

"Barton," Elgin said to Luke's older brother. "Hold this gun. If it's anything that looks dangerous, shoot it in the goddamn head."

"You think it's a *zombie*?" the boy asked. The gun barrel waved in his unsteady grip.

Elgin looked at Mandalay with mixed contempt and fear. "It could be. It could be anything."

He slid back the dead bolt, took a deep breath, and threw open the door.

It slammed into the wall. That startled Barton, who yelped and fired the shotgun. The noise was like standing right next to a thunderclap. The two younger girls screamed.

The blast went through the open door, harmlessly over the old man sprawled on the porch.

Elgin snatched the gun from Barton and slapped him so hard, it knocked him to the floor. "You goddamned retard!" he shouted, his voice cracking.

"Stop it," Mandalay said. She knelt by the old man and turned him onto his side.

They all gasped when they saw the face of Rockhouse Hicks.

None of them spoke. Only the wind made any sound, whistling through the door and moaning in the cold sky outside. It tousled the old man's disheveled white hair and sent ripples along his clothing.

"Is he dead?" Deetzy asked.

No one moved to check. At last Elgin said, "My daddy told me this story once. These three fellas were coming across the mountain going to Kingsport, and one of 'em got tired. He told 'em he was gonna sit down on this here stump for a while, but he'd catch up to 'em. They went on into Kingsport, and on their way back they found him still sitting on that stump, froze solid." He nodded at Rockhouse. "Just like that."

Then Barton said, "Y'all, look at his hands."

Mandalay lifted the hand that must have clawed at the door. The wound where his extra finger had been sliced away was scabbed and swollen.

He was too big for her to move on her own. "He's not dead," she said. "Get him out of the snow."

"No," Elgin said contemptuously. "He ain't nothin' to us now."

"He can't sing," Claudia agreed, "and now he can't play. We don't have to bow down to him no more." She pulled Deetzy close and grabbed Ida Mae's hand. "We don't have to keep our girls away from him."

"We can't leave him there," Mandalay said.

Elgin put his foot on Rockhouse's shoulder and pushed him outside enough to close the door. "The hell we can't."

Mandalay turned to Luke. She didn't have to say anything; the boy said, "Get out of the way, Dad," and took one of Rockhouse's arms. Mandalay took the other, and they dragged him into the living room. Mandalay shut the door.

Rockhouse rolled onto his back. Spittle frosted the corners of his lips. He wore no coat, and his clothes were stiff with frozen sweat and snow.

"How the hell did he get here?" Elgin mumbled. "And what's wrong with him?"

"He walked," Mandalay said.

"Down from the mountain?" Luke asked in disbelief.

"There's no night wind for him anymore," she said. "No riding it where he wants to go."

"Jesus," Claudia whispered. The climb down was treacherous on a good day, and in this snowstorm, with no coat or other protection, it would be a nightmare. He was luckier than he knew to reach this house alive.

Mandalay looked around at the Somervilles. "I know how you feel about him, but look at him. He's nothing now but an old man who can't talk, and who's seriously hurt. Claudia, can you get me a cloth soaked in warm water? And Ida Mae, fetch me a blanket or a comforter."

As they went to their tasks, Elgin said, "He ain't stayin' here. You can take him with you when your ride gets here."

"I will," Mandalay said.

Elgin spit, not directly on Rockhouse but definitely in his general direction.

Luke asked quietly, "Who do you think cut off his fingers?"

Mandalay shook her head. "I don't know yet."

Headlights raked across the front curtains, and the squeak of brakes came over the wind. Then a shadow passed in front of the light, and someone knocked firmly on the door.

Elgin opened it. Darnell Harris stood there, dressed in insulated coveralls, his bearded face guarded and wary. "I'm here for my daughter, Elgin."

"Right here, Daddy," Mandalay said from the floor.

Darnell stared down at her, at Rockhouse, and then around at the gathered Somervilles. "Looks like I missed the party," he said at last.

"Ain't no party," Elgin said. "Take your damn daughter, and take this sack of shit with you."

Darnell saw by the look in her eyes that Mandalay had already decided. He nodded and said, "All right. Hold on, I need to go get something." He turned and walked away.

"And hurry up!" Elgin called after him. "We're gonna have more snow in the damn house than we do in the yard!"

A moment later he returned with Bliss Overbay. Mandalay immediately stood and let the other woman, a professional EMT, kneel beside Rockhouse. She checked his pulse, examined the wounds on his hands, and brushed the hair back from his forehead. "We need to get him out of this cold," she said.

"Yeah, that's what I've been telling you," Elgin said.

Mandalay took her coat from the wall hook and stepped back into her still-damp tennis shoes. "Thank you, Mrs. Somerville. I appreciate y'all taking me in out of the storm. I'll get these clothes washed and give them back to Luke at school." At the door, she stopped in front of Luke and looked right into his eyes. This time he looked back. "Thank you," she said softly.

He nod-shrugged, and shyly smiled.

Then she stepped aside while her father lifted Rockhouse from the floor. The old man protested weakly, but he'd shrunken so much in recent months that it was no effort at all for Darnell to overpower him.

In the cab of the truck, Mandalay sat between Bliss and Darnell. Rockhouse was stretched out in the back, under the camper shell, wrapped in a heavy blanket. Falling snow spiked through the truck's headlight beams as they drove.

"Reckon we need to take him to the hospital?" Darnell said.

"No, just take us up to the fire station," Bliss said. "I can tend him there."

"He might need more than tending," Darnell said.

Bliss looked at Mandalay. She said, "It'll be all right, Daddy. Bliss knows what to do."

Darnell sighed, but nodded. As an afterthought, he pulled a tiny semiautomatic pistol from his pocket and handed it to Bliss. She put it back in the glove compartment.

"You brought a gun?" Mandalay said.

"Honey, when I found out where you were, you're lucky I didn't bring a tank."

"They were good to me," Mandalay said.

"That's because they were afraid of you." They drove in silence; then he said, "Bliss, if I drop all of you at the fire station, can you give Mandalay a ride home? I got to be somewhere in a little bit."

"Sure," Bliss agreed after seeing Mandalay's faint nod. They both knew where he was going. Darnell was a pure-blooded Tufa, just as they were, and thus he was a member of the Silent Sons.

8

Because the old Norfolk Southern Railway locomotive, parked on a long-abandoned side track, had white whiskerlike stripes painted on it, it was known as the "Catfish." A single boxcar was still coupled to it, emitting a faint glow through cracks in its sides.

A half dozen trucks and cars were parked along the track. By the time Deacon and Marshall arrived, music echoed down the pass cut through the mountain by the railroad gangs over a century earlier.

> *Along came the F15 the swiftest on the line*
> *Running o'er the C&O road just twenty minutes*
>   *behind*
> *Running into Cevile head porters on the line*
> *Receiving their strict orders from a station just*
>   *behind. . . .*

They left their vehicle and walked down the tracks toward the train. Deacon glanced at Marshall, who had to stop and catch his breath. "You all right?"

"Yeah," he said. "Cold air messes with my asthma."

"Didn't know you had asthma."

"Didn't know it myself until this year. One of the perks of getting old, I reckon."

Deacon continued to look at his friend. "Does Peggy know about this?"

"Does your wife know whenever you get sick?"

"Hell, she usually knows about it before the germs do."

"There you go." He pushed on past Deacon toward the train, stepping on the cross-ties between the old rails. In truth, it was more than asthma, as a tingling in his left arm always accompanied the shortness of breath, but Marshall wasn't worried, because Peggy wasn't worried.

Deacon watched his friend for a moment, until an owl hooted from the nearby trees. It broke him from his reverie.

Inside the boxcar a dozen men waited. The youngest appeared barely old enough to shave, while the oldest sat shrouded in blankets, puffing on a homemade corncob pipe. One, a thin man with a beard almost to the middle of his chest, continued playing "Engine 143," although no one was singing. A kerosene heater sat glowing in the middle of the floor.

"Damn, y'all, you'd think your mothers died, and your dogs ain't doin' too well, either," Deacon said as he climbed into the car. He helped Marshall up, and the two of them slid the door shut. Someone closed the opposite one, and the men all gathered at the heater like old-time hoboes around a fire.

All the Tufa knew about the First Daughters, the exclusive organization that provided guidance, a forum for grievances, and occasional discipline up to and including execution. The group's members were known, respected, and in the case of Bronwyn Hyatt Chess, feared.

But the Silent Sons were different.

To be a First Daughter, you had to be, well, a firstborn daughter. Both parents had to be pureblood Tufas, a trait that was getting harder and harder to find. But to be a Silent Son, you had to pass an elaborate, multi-part and sometimes multi-year ritual designed to test both your courage and discretion. Almost like the *Fight Club* cliché, you had to prove you could keep a secret before you were allowed into its ranks. And since its membership was the most confidential thing, no one outside the group was quite sure who was in it.

The man playing guitar stopped. In the stillness, the heater hissed, and the wind whistled through rusted chinks in the box-car walls. Marshall said at last, "Is there some reason we can't meet in somebody's house in the winter?"

"Tradition," a younger man with prematurely white hair said. His given first name was Conway, but he'd been known as "Snowy" since his hair went white in eleventh grade. "All about tradition."

"Yeah, well, tradition's about to freeze my damn balls off," another man said.

"Then let's get this over with as fast as we can," Deacon said. "Bo-Kate Wisby is back. Peggy Goins saw her. She visited Rock-house, and cut off his two extra fingers."

There was a long moment of stunned silence at this news, so simply stated but earthshaking. At last Snowy asked, "Is Jeff back, too?"

"Ain't nobody seen him," Deacon said. "I'll call his office in New York in the morning, just to check."

"He won't talk to you," the old man in blankets said. His name was Adecyn Condilia, and he tugged the blanket around his shoulders as he spoke. "Hell, I'm not sure he can. Getting sung out and all . . ."

"Don't need him to talk to me, just need to know he's there. Secretary can tell me that."

Adecyn coughed, spit to one side, and said, "We knew some-body was going to try to do this. Once Curnen Overbay silenced Rockhouse for good, we knew somebody, sometime, would try to take over his spot. We figured we could handle whoever it was, 'cause we thought it'd be somebody from the county, like Junior Damo. We shoulda thought harder."

"Bo-Kate shouldn't even be *able* to come back," said Macen Ward, a young man with an enormous mustache. "Ain't being sung out supposed to be permanent?"

"It sure is," Adecyn said. "I was there, remember? But it's the first and only time we've ever done it, and I reckon we didn't sing as good as we should have."

"Can *she* sing?" asked the bearded guitar player, known only as "Whizdom."

Everyone looked at Marshall. He shrugged. "Peggy didn't say nothing about it."

"Well, if she can't sing, then . . ." He trailed off.

"I don't think we can afford to wait to find that out," Deacon said.

"What do the First Daughters say?" asked Draven Altizer, the youngest of the Silent Sons.

"That don't matter," Adecyn said. "We ain't gonna wait until they decide what they're gonna do. We got to do something now."

"They won't like it," Marshall said. "Bliss won't. Bronwyn and Chloe won't," he said with a glance at Deacon. "Mandalay won't."

"What's that old saying?" Adecyn said. "Better to ask forgiveness than permission? Bo-Kate'll end everything. All the songs, all the sailing on the night winds. We'll be just what we appear to be: a bunch of old hillbillies and rednecks."

"Hey, I ain't old," Draven said with a snort. No one else laughed.

"How do you know?" Marshall asked Adecyn. The man was even older than he appeared—he'd been old when the Tufa arrived, and his knowledge, if not his wisdom, was ancient and encyclopedic. But even a Tufa elder's mind could begin to wander when it filled to the brim with memories.

"Because she wants revenge," Adecyn said. "And what better

revenge than to make the Tufa just like everybody else? That's what we did to her, ain't it?"

Again only the wind and the heater were heard in the boxcar. A coyote howled in the distance.

"We need to find her," Deacon said.

"She's probably at her home place," a short, stocky man said. "I saw a shiny new SUV driving down that way this evening."

"Can't do much while she's there," Whizdom said.

"Reckon Tain might help us?" Marshall asked. "She's got no love for Bo-Kate, that's for sure."

"She might," Snowy said. "I can talk to her."

"Do that."

"I'd go check to see if Eli's got anyone around his fire," Adecyn said.

"Why?" asked Whizdom.

"Fella sits in slow time long enough, strange things can happen. We don't need no more strange things."

"All right, I'll go up there tonight," Marshall said. "And the rest of you, remember: not a word."

In unison, the Silent Sons recited their motto, from the words of poet Christina Rossetti: *"Silence is more musical than any song."* Then, wordlessly, they all left the boxcar. The last one out, Whizdom, turned off the heater and grabbed the gallon can of kerosene.

Junior Damo hung up his coat, kicked off his boots, and walked to his kitchen. He opened the refrigerator and put the beer he'd bought inside. He took one, and closed the door.

They lived in the old Edelmen place, which he'd bought at a foreclosure sale knowing full well he couldn't pay the mortgage for more than six months. He'd bought it, though, because his wife insisted. And when Loretta insisted, it was either go along or be prepared to face the consequences.

He sipped the beer and looked around the living room. Their old, thrift-store furniture was cluttered in ways that told more about their lives than he probably realized. The couch was set at an odd angle so it would face the TV straight on, which was the only angle where the screen was bright enough to watch. The TV had to stay where it was because the cord connecting it to the cable outlet was only two feet long, and they could never remember to buy a longer one on the rare occasions when they went into Unicorn or Herrowton. And since they stole their cable, thanks to some fancy wiring by his wife's cousin, they couldn't call Comcast and have them come out to fix it.

Still, it was either this, or live with his in-laws. And this was infinitely preferable.

"Where you been?" a harsh female voice demanded.

He didn't look up from the beer as he popped the tab. "Up the mountain. Went to see Rockhouse Hicks."

"Why would you go to see him? He ain't shit anymore." There was a pause, and then an even harsher screech. "You answer me when I talk to you, Junior!"

At last he looked up. Loretta, his wife of six months, tottered her seven-months-pregnant form into the kitchen. She was clearly not happy, but that was no surprise. She hadn't been happy since the last time a white man was president. She waddled across the room and leaned against the wall, exhausted. She had not been a small woman to begin with; now she was enormous, and like air in vacuum, her temper expanded to fit the available space.

Junior said, "You're wrong, honey, he *is* shit. That means he needs to get flushed, and somebody needs to take his place."

"As head turd?" she snapped.

"As head of our half of the Tufa."

She snorted. "You?"

"Why not?"

"If you need me to tell you, then you're dumber than I thought."

He took another long drink of the beer. "How's the baby?"

"Kicking the shit out of me whenever he can." She turned away, but he heard her mutter, "Just like you, asshole."

Junior fought down the anger. Loretta's temper was on a constant simmering boil, so it surprised no one when she barked at them. His, on the other hand, exploded without warning, and often got him into trouble. He had no problem slapping a mouthy woman, but even he drew the line at striking one who was pregnant.

This wouldn't be his first kid, but it was the first one he'd taken an interest in. Loretta wasn't a pureblood, but her family was well connected among the Tufa by marriage and otherwise, and that meant *he* was well connected. If he really intended to take over their half the Tufa, he'd need those connections to both help him achieve his goal, and then keep it. So he tried his best to ignore her singularly unpleasant personality and, just like the night their child had been conceived, tried to stay a little drunk so he wouldn't have to think too much about what he was doing.

Before Junior could respond to Loretta's abuse, or even *think* of a response, his cell phone buzzed. He fished it from his pocket and saw a number he didn't recognize. When he held it to his ear, a man's voice said, "What?"

"What?" Junior said back, puzzled.

"You wanted to talk to me."

"Who is this?"

"Someone you wanted to talk to."

Junior frowned, then said, "Jewel?"

"You expecting someone else?"

Junior began to sweat. He had not really planned out his end of this conversation yet, and thinking on his feet was not his strong point. Jewel Hicks was as shifty as his cousin Rockhouse, as brutal as his cousin Stoney had once been, and as devious as a copperhead in a woodpile. Junior went outside on the porch for privacy.

"I went up the mountain to see your cousin," Junior said, praying his voice didn't shake.

"Plays guitar like a chain saw buzzin'," Jewel shot back. Junior didn't recognize the lyric. Jewel continued, "You gotta be more specific, slick, I got a hundred and fifty cousins that I know about close enough to hit with a stick from where I'm standing."

"Rockhouse."

There was a long silence. "Why'd you go see him for?"

"I needed to see how finished he was. And he was pretty gone. Somebody's done gone up there and cut off his extra fingers."

More silence. Then, "Who?"

"Bo-Kate Wisby," Junior said.

"Bullshit."

"You think what you want, but it's sure enough been done. So now he can't sing *and* he can't play, which means he can't ride the night wind, neither. That makes him useless."

"If you say," Jewel said.

Junior licked his dry lips. This next bit was crucial, and it was the part he'd hoped to plan out in more detail. If Jewel got the wrong idea, then it was all lost. "That means we need somebody to take over."

"I reckon."

"Rockhouse ever name anybody?"

Jewel laughed. "That sum'bitch thought he was immortal. He never even thought about naming anybody else. But that ain't news to anybody that knew him. Now, why you askin' all this, Junior?"

Junior grinned. He *had* suspected that, but he needed it confirmed, and now Jewel had done just that. All Junior had to do was end this phone call without tipping his hand. "If you'd seen him like I did, you'd be asking, too."

That seemed to satisfy Jewel. "I reckon. I'm sure we'll hear about it when somebody else takes over. That all you wanted? We're just sitting down to dinner."

"That's all I wanted."

Without a word of good-bye, the line went dead. Junior closed his eyes and sighed with relief. He took a long swallow of his beer and luxuriated in the way it slid down his throat.

When he went back inside, Loretta said, "What the hell are you so happy about? Unless you won the lottery, you ain't got a thing to smile about, you hear me?"

"Sure do, your voice carries." He couldn't wait for the baby to be born, so he could take his son from this harpy and send her to the hell she deserved, a mirror of the hell she'd made of his life.

At the fire station, Rockhouse lay on a cot usually used for firemen working overnight shifts. As a volunteer force, they weren't manned as often as they should have been, but by the same token, the Tufa were very seldom surprised. If a dangerous fire was on the horizon, the night wind made sure someone knew in advance—via a dream, a premonition, hearing "Burning Down the House" frequently on the radio—and the fire department would have time to assemble.

Mandalay stood idly while Bliss gathered the medical tools she needed. She was thinking about what happened when her father dropped them all off. Just before he left, she'd impulsively hugged him tight, as she used to do when she was a toddler. "I love you, Daddy," she said, and kissed his cheek. She loved the feel of his thick beard against her lips, and the musky smell of it.

"I love you, too, june bug," he said easily. He was not a man who felt admitting affection was unmanly.

"Tell Leshell I love her, too."

"I will." When she pulled away, he looked at her closely. "Are you all right? Do you want me to stay?"

"No. Bliss and I can handle this."

"I don't doubt that. But I'll still stay if you want."

She felt a fresh surge of affection. "No, Daddy, that's okay. I'll be home later. I can't imagine we'll have school tomorrow, so I'll be able to sleep late."

He gave her a tiny grin. "Yeah, enjoy that while you can. When you have a job, you don't get snow days."

"I know," she agreed.

Now she stood against the wall, hands stuffed into the pockets of her borrowed jeans, and watched Bliss begin to clean the wounds on Rockhouse's hands. The old man was buried under a pile of blankets; his face was gray and slack. But his eyes were open.

"This is pointless, you know," Bliss said.

"You can stop," Mandalay said.

"No. It's my job. I can at least make him comfortable. It's what I'd do for anyone."

Mandalay looked at the old man's face. How many times had she done that, wishing it were the last time? And now that it was, she found herself as numb as he must have been coming down the mountain.

Bliss said, "So what happened between you and the Somervilles?"

"Luke found me before I froze to death and brought me home."

"Did he—?"

She smiled. "He was a perfect gentleman. He *is* only twelve, you know."

"His father once cut the brake lines on Dan Yorty's truck. Sent him off a ravine and broke his legs. Lucky he didn't die."

"The 'sins of the father' isn't really a Tufa concept, Bliss."

"I'm just saying, they're not our people. They might not have had your best interests at heart."

"Well, they did ask me to stay to dinner."

"Did you—? No, of course not, I apologize for even thinking it."

"If one of us had Rockhouse at our mercy, then we might've tried the same thing. It would be easy enough to do, and to claim it was just hospitality. And maybe it would be."

"Do you think this was?"

She smiled again, suddenly older than the rocks beneath them, and Bliss got the chill she always got when Mandalay revealed her true nature. "No. But Luke stood up for me. He knew what they were doing and told them to stop."

"Why?"

"Not everyone is what you expect, Bliss."

"Well . . . like you said, he's just a kid."

"So am I."

She didn't look up when she asked, "Why were you out in the snow in the first place?"

"I just . . . I had to get out of the house. I can't explain it. The night winds wanted me to run."

"Away from something, or toward it?"

"I'm not sure yet." She almost brought up hearing "I'm Nine Hundred Miles from My Home," but decided against it. Whatever that had been, it was something she hadn't yet worked out for herself, and having other people's theories bouncing around her head would just create the kind of psychic noise that kept her from comprehending things. There *had* to be a reason, and she'd figure it out. Or the night winds would smack her over the head with it.

Bliss bandaged the stumps of Rockhouse's amputated fingers. He watched her in his enforced silence, his eyes gleaming with tears of frustration and rage.

Mandalay remembered the arrogance and smug hatred that

used to reside in the old man's face. Now, deprived of voice and music, he was pitiful.

But she knew he was still capable of being dangerous.

"Bliss," Mandalay said, "I need a moment alone with Rockhouse."

"I'm almost done," Bliss said without looking up.

"Now," Mandalay said in the voice that brooked no dispute.

Bliss looked up sharply, then nodded and quickly left the room. She closed the door behind her as she went into the garage where the lone fire truck was kept.

When they were alone, Mandalay looked down at the old man.

"Ain't this a mess," she said at last. "Here you are, tore to pieces, and here I am. Pretty soon everybody's gonna expect me to step up and do like you did, keep us all together. The thing is, everybody was afraid of you. You made sure of that, didn't you? Like when you killed your daughter's husband, or made Uncle Node drive off that curve? Hell, you even sent a mudslide down on that whole Waddle family, just because one of 'em stood up to you."

He watched her, his eyes glistening with new tears, although now she wasn't sure of the cause, except that she was certain it was not regret.

"I ain't like that, Rockhouse," she continued. "I just ain't. And if that's what it takes to hold the Tufa together, then we're just doomed to split apart, because I won't do it. You think that makes me weak, don't you? You've always thought I was. At first it was because I was a child, then because I was a girl, and now because I won't be as ruthless as you. But here's something you don't know: 'Weak' ain't the same thing as 'not evil.'"

Suddenly he grabbed her throat with his bandaged hand.

She met the old man's angry, spiteful gaze. His grip was feeble, even on her thin neck, and she knew she was in no danger. He wasn't even able to cut off her wind. She began to sing softly,

The Gypsies came to our lord's house,
And oh! but they sang bonny,
They sang so sweet and so complete
That down came our fair lady;
When she came tripping down the stair,
With all her maids before her,
As soon as they saw her lovely face,
They cast their glamour on her.

As her voice rose in volume and intensity, his hand fell away. Something changed in the room. Power was shifting, and the words of the song were telling a story completely unrelated to the fate of Johnny Faa and his highborn lady.

At last Mandalay finished, holding the last note in a pure, high voice that rang like a bell, or a choir. As it faded, Rockhouse's eyes closed and he let out a long, final sigh.

The room was silent for a long time, except for the fluorescent lights buzzing overhead. At last the garage door opened and Bliss stuck in her head. "Can I come back in?"

"Yes," Mandalay said.

Bliss had seen plenty of corpses in her time, and had no trouble recognizing one from across the room. "Is he dead?" she asked, already certain of the answer.

"As dead as he ever could be," Mandalay said. There was a cold determination in her voice that came not from the twelve-year-old girl, but from all the eons she'd existed before now. "And we're gonna bury him."

Bliss stood beside the girl and looked down at the old man's slack face. "It's going to be a completely different world without him in it."

"A better one, I hope."

"That'll be up to you."

Mandalay said nothing.

While Bliss went to arrange for a backhoe to dig the grave in the cold ground, Mandalay stayed with Rockhouse's corpse. She stuffed her hands back in her jeans pockets and regarded the lined, aged face now slack and lifeless on the gurney.

"Well, old man," she said, "we've had quite the run. You were right, as it turns out; none of us could touch you. You were invincible. It took something you couldn't have imagined to finally bring you down."

Her voice dropped. "But you know what? I fucking *hate* you still. I hate you for what you did to all my ancestors, for all the women who carried what I carry and wanted to use it. I hate you for all the girls you groped, and humiliated, and molested, and ruined. I hate you for what you did to your own daughter, and I can't tell you how happy I was when that flatlander sang your dying dirge. If ever someone deserved it, asshole, it was you."

She bent and whispered into his lifeless ear. "And I want you to think about all this while you lie in your grave, Rockhouse. While you hear the faint songs of everyone else, and know that you'll never sing along, that you'll never walk these hills, that you'll never fly on the night winds again. I want you to think about the look on all those agonized faces, the cries and begging, the sheer *pain* you brought to the world out of your own meanness and self-pity. As you rot, I want you to think about it. And I hope you soak the fucking world to its core with your tears."

She stood up as Bliss returned. "It's all arranged. We'll bury him up on Redford's Ridge."

Mandalay nodded. "Call Reverend Chess and ask him to come say a few Christian words, too. Be sure and tell him it's a private service, so not to spread the word."

Bliss's eyebrows rose. "Are you serious?"

"He's married to Bronwyn. Her daughter . . . Well, he's the kind of man who'll love that girl when she's born no matter how she was gotten on her mother. He's a good man, and being involved with this will make him feel accepted."

"Then I'll call Bronwyn."

"No. Call *him*. I want it to come from you."

"Why?"

"So he can refuse. He'd never turn down his wife."

"But you said—"

Mandalay smiled and held up a hand. "Bliss, I know a lot, but not everything. I want something good to come out of this withered bastard's death, and if it means we find out that Craig Chess really is worthy of helping raise Bronwyn's daughter— and I think he is, or I wouldn't suggest this—then I think we should take the chance. The worst thing that can happen is that he says no."

"How bad would that really be?"

Mandalay's expression hardened. "Well . . . it means we couldn't let him stick around."

Bliss said nothing. The thought of what *that* meant—and of forcing headstrong and obstinate Bronwyn to choose between her people and her husband—was something she couldn't really devote a lot of thought to at the moment. "Excuse me, then. I'll go call him. I suppose it's okay to explain all this to Bronwyn if he says yes?"

Mandalay nodded.

When she was alone with Rockhouse again, Mandalay said, "See, old man? Not only can't you do any more damage, you will actually be helping us do good. That must gall you no end." She softly sang the last line of his dying dirge, just as the flat-lander had done the year before to destroy Rockhouse's hold on power: "You can do no harm while ye be here." Then she kissed him on his forehead.

Reflecting the power dynamic in their relationship, Bo-Kate fell asleep almost immediately after they made love, an arm draped affectionately—or possessively, he wasn't sure which—across Nigel's chest. She snored lightly, and the gentle tang of her sweat filled his nostrils.

He stared up at the canopy over the bed. He was wide awake, the aftereffects of their typically terrific sex shooting through him like the heroin he'd tried once as a teen. He'd been able to walk away from that; Bo-Kate, though, was far more addictive. And, he mulled, much worse for him in the long run.

He hadn't noticed the canopy's design before, but it seemed to be some sort of forest scene; with the drapes drawn and no digital clock or other electronic devices to provide any ambient light, he couldn't quite make out the details in the darkness. If it echoed the decor of the rest of the room, it was probably something princess-y, possibly with unicorns and knights in shining armor. Then again, given what she'd told him about the Tufa, perhaps it showed fairies frolicking in the woods, cavorting with young men and leading them in dances that would while away years from their lives.

Eventually, he accepted that sleep would not come. The image of those severed fingers in a baggy, like some cannibal child's after-school snack, was just too nightmarish. He carefully slid out from beneath Bo-Kate's arm, then waited until he was sure he hadn't awakened her. He got up, pulled on his trousers and shirt, and slipped into the hall looking for the bathroom.

The house was eerily quiet; after so many years living in cities, Nigel had forgotten how quiet the country could be. No traffic noises, airplanes overhead, or trains passing nearby marred the night. Since it was winter, there weren't even chirping crickets. Just the ever-present wind, at the moment blowing so softly that it, too, might be asleep.

Then a long, low cry rang out. He recognized it as the hoot of an owl, probably in one of the trees right outside. As he stood there in the dark, it seemed to him like the sound of a lost soul looking for redemption. What was that Carole King line? *Like a fallen angel when rising time is near.*

He almost yelped aloud as a door opened and a shaft of light cut into the hallway. Tain stepped out and closed the door until only a sliver of illumination remained.

She wore a thin cotton robe tied loosely—*very* loosely—at the waist, and nothing else. If the robe gapped any wider, she might as well have been naked, but she made no move to close it when she saw him. If anything, she stood provocatively, enhancing its effect, and the indirect lighting cast shadows that accented every flawless curve. Certainly her smile revealed no shame.

"Well, if it ain't the executive assistant," she said quietly, and tossed her dark hair behind her shoulders. There was a throaty rumble in her voice, like a growl or a purr.

"Indeed. I'm looking for the loo."

"The what?"

"The facilities. The bathroom."

"You probably want to put your boots on, too, then. It's outside."

"Outside? As in, outside the house?"

"Yep. Go down the stairs, through the kitchen, and out the back door. Can't miss it. There's a crescent moon carved into the door."

"Am I to believe you people actually use an *outhouse*?"

"We do."

"I thought that was a cliché, like going barefoot and having bad teeth."

Tain raised one foot, which caused her robe to slide back and reveal the full expanse of one smooth leg. "I don't wear shoes unless I'm going to town for something. And even then only when I have to stop at the Catamount Corner, because otherwise Miss Peggy will yell at me." She lowered her leg. "And as I recall, you English got your share of bad teeth, too."

"True enough."

Tain smiled, showing her own perfect, even teeth. "Well, we ain't got to worry about that. You won't find a Tufa with bad teeth unless something's knocked 'em out." She tossed her hair again. "So you still going to the outhouse?"

"I suppose so, if that's the only available option. You are aware this is the twenty-first century?"

"Pipes freeze in the winter no matter what year it is. And time don't work the same for everybody. Ain't Bo-Kate explained that to you?"

"She mentioned that. I assumed it was a metaphor."

"What's that? Is that like Campho-Phenique?"

"Not quite."

Tain came closer. Her breasts swayed beneath the robe, thoroughly distracting him. "You know, ain't never been a nigger in this house before."

"And if you insist on using that word, there likely won't be again for a very long time." It took all his resolve to keep his gaze above her neck.

"What word should I use? Handsome? Studly?" She put a hand lightly on his chest. "Fine as frog's hair?"

He laughed. "That last might not be that good, either, although I appreciate the sentiment." He removed her hand. A gust of winter wind howled outside, and he said, "Aren't you cold in something so . . . flimsy?"

"I don't get cold." She ran a finger along the edge of the robe's lapel.

"Ever?"

"Hardly ever. I been told I run pretty . . . hot. Are *you* cold?"

"It's a bit brisk."

He could see her nipples through the thin fabric. She lowered her chin and looked up at him, "You know, Bo-Kate ain't the only . . . accommodating woman in this house." She lightly bit her lip, all at once demure and compliant. "Be awful bad manners to leave a guest cold on a winter's night."

Despite having just trysted with Bo-Kate, Nigel found himself ready again. There was a tingle in the very air, a kind of erotic ozone that he'd felt with certain women before; and those women had been among the most exciting experiences of his life. But with them, the charge had been faint, and subtle. With Tain, it was almost like a lightning strike.

It wouldn't do to jump into bed with the cousin Bo-Kate clearly didn't get along with, though. He tried not to think about untying the belt on that robe and said, "I appreciate the offer, but I don't think it would be very appropriate. Bo-Kate is very clear about which lines one should not cross."

"Has Bo-Kate already wrung you out?"

"Pithy, but accurate."

"Well, I bet I could get that motor started again."

"Again, probably accurate, but not appropriate."

Her little smile was as carnal as some women's orgasm face.

"She ain't never gonna know unless you tell her. And I promise, you won't regret it. It'll be a memory to keep you warm on the next cold night like this."

"You're certainly warming me up right now," he admitted. "But *I'd* know what we did, and I fear I couldn't look at myself in the mirror."

Tain's grin widened. "Ain't you the prize. Did Bo-Kate tell you the story about why she ain't been back here in so long?"

"I believe it involved a young man from a family of whom her parents did not approve."

Tain laughed. "Well, that's true enough. But that ain't near the whole story." Then she raised her chin, closed her eyes, and sang in a soft, pure contralto:

> *About eight o'clock, boys, our dogs they throwed off*
> *Beneath the Widow's Tree, and that was the spot*
> *They tried all the bushes but nothing they found*
> *But a poor murdered woman laid on the cold ground.*

Then she looked back at him. "She ever sang that song to you?"

"I don't believe so."

"You need to ask her 'bout that." Then Tain's eyes narrowed. "Wait . . . I bet she ain't really told you nothin' 'bout nothin', has she?"

"I don't feel it's my place to say."

"Ain't you the gentleman. Lots of white boys could learn a thing or two from you, you know that?"

"I have no doubt."

"Well, before you get too tangled up in whatever she's got in mind, you need to ask her 'bout Jeff."

"Ah, yes, the infamous old boyfriend she used to sneak out to see. What about him?"

"She needs to tell you." All the assurance and sexual arrogance left her. "Look, I done said a lot more than I should have. You *do* seem like a nice fella, and I don't want you to get hurt because of it. You have a good night." She turned, and the motion fully dislodged the belt at her waist. The robe swirled back like a cowboy's duster, but before he could even glimpse her bare flesh, the door closed, the light went out, and again Nigel was in darkness.

He stared after her, wondering if he should wake Bo-Kate to enjoy the arousal her cousin had engendered, or simply go back to bed and pull the covers over his head until morning. But now he really *did* need to pee, so he crept down the hall until he reached the top of the stairs. By then his eyes had adjusted and he was able to see enough to descend to the living room.

It was chillier downstairs, and he wished he'd brought his coat. He found his boots by the front door and carried them into the kitchen.

The room smelled of decades of dinners, and breakfasts, and the kind of good, heavy food that poor people the world over cooked to get by. His own mother had made amazing things happen with the simplest and cheapest of ingredients, and he recalled how her kitchen always smelled similar to this.

But something was missing here, and as he sat at the table and pulled on his boots, he realized what it was: warmth. Not physical warmth, but the warmth of laughter, and teasing, and occasional tears that his mother's kitchen always held. Here there was no remnant of the joy those meals should have brought to the Wisby family. This was just a room where food was prepared, not a real kitchen. Certainly not, in the broad sense of the word, a *hearth*.

If Bo-Kate grew up here, no wonder she kept her feelings guarded and locked away.

He peered out the kitchen door and, sure enough, saw the little outhouse about fifteen yards away, at the very edge of the backyard. The snow had been trampled flat between it and the house.

He stepped outside. The cold bit through his clothes to his sweaty skin, and finished off Tain's effect on his body. The half-full moon cast enough light for him to see. He expected to smell the outhouse, then realized that anything it held would, obviously, be frozen. That made him glad they hadn't waited until spring to visit.

When he reached the outhouse, he paused. Somewhere in the distance, he heard the plaintive sound of a lone fiddle. It didn't come from the Wisby place, but from somewhere beyond the forested hill that rose behind the outhouse. He couldn't make out the tune, but the feeling it carried was so sad, so lonely, that he choked up and almost wanted to cry.

Then the wind picked up, and the song was lost.

He stepped into the outhouse, did his business quickly, and stepped back outside. A male voice said, "Who the hell are you?"

He looked around in time to see a big man come down from the trees. He was dressed in camouflage, wore a ski mask, and carried a rifle. He stopped when he got a good look at Nigel.

"You're a nigger," he added.

Nigel looked at his hand and feigned surprise. "My God, you're right. And I believe the appropriate term for you is 'peckerwood,' if I'm not mistaken."

He didn't blink at the insult. "What are you doing here?"

Nigel realized who this man must be. "I'm accompanying your sister, Bo-Kate. Are you Canton or Snad?"

The man smiled. It wasn't friendly. "Bo-Kate cain't never come back here. Everybody knows it. Not even if she wanted to, and I cain't imagine that." He lowered the gun and held it loosely in both hands, not pointed at Nigel but clearly now a threat. He cocked his head back and looked down his nose. "How about you try again?"

"That might have been true about your sister once. But I assure you, we arrived this evening, and she is asleep in her old room right now."

He thought this over. "And they're making you sleep in the outhouse," he said at last. It wasn't a question, just a statement.

"No, I used it just before you appeared." He tried a smile. "I'm Nigel, by the way."

"Canton Wisby." He offered his hand in a big, well-worn glove. "Pleasure to meet you."

Nigel nodded at the gun. "And do you always creep about your yard with a gun?"

"Nah, I was just out in the woods. Never can tell what might slip up on you out there."

"Indeed you can't," Nigel agreed.

A light appeared in one of the house's upstairs windows. Canton stepped back into the outhouse's moon-cast shadow. He said quietly, "You got good timing, boy. The show's about to start. Get back here before she sees you."

"What show?" Nigel whispered.

"Just watch. Better'n Cinemax."

Nigel joined Canton in the darkness. Whatever the "show" was, it made Canton entirely forget any doubts about Nigel.

The illuminated, and apparently curtainless, window allowed them to see into a bedroom. There was a big mirror on the opposite wall, and a moving shadow on the ceiling told them someone was there. Then Tain Wisby appeared and raised the window all the way up despite the winter cold.

And she was naked.

"Now, that," Canton said, "is a sight that don't never get old."

Nigel agreed with the sentiment. Tain unclothed was as spectacular as he'd imagined she would be, every part in perfect proportion and firm with youthfulness, strength, and beauty. She let the cold air blow over her and showed not the slightest bit of discomfort.

She sang in a voice like Norah Jones crossed with Lauren Bacall's growl:

The winter it is past, and the summer's come at last.
The small birds are singing in the trees
Their little hearts are glad oh but mine is very sad,
For my true love is far away from me.

Nigel felt fresh goose bumps that had nothing to do with the temperature ripple along his skin. He glanced at Canton, whose face was as rapt as a devout Catholic's at Easter Mass. And honestly, that didn't seem unrealistic. Tain was so beautiful, so unencumbered by societal shame or self-consciousness, that in many ways it was like seeing a goddess. He remembered in primary school they'd covered the story of the goddess Artemis and Actaeon, the unfortunate hunter who'd accidentally glimpsed her naked while she was bathing. She was so angry, she turned him into a stag, and his own hunting dogs killed him. Nigel wondered if he risked a similar fate.

"That'll bring back the spring," Canton murmured. "Sure enough it will."

Then Tain put one bare foot on the sill and pulled herself up to stand.

"What is she doing?" Nigel asked.

Before Canton could answer, Tain crouched slightly, then jumped.

Nigel started to rush forward and cry out a warning, but before he could do either, Tain shot *upward,* into the night sky.

Nigel stared up at the stars, mouth agape. He blinked several times and shook his head. He looked at the snowy ground beneath the window, where Tain *must* have landed. But there was no sign of her.

"Great gosh a'mighty," Canton said in wonder but not surprise. He took off the ski mask and revealed a broad, soft face with big eyes and a tangled mass of black hair. It was curly, like Bo-Kate's, but cut shorter. "That girl's so hot, if they ever sent her to the North Pole, Santa would end up living on a raft."

Nigel said nothing.

Canton clapped him on the shoulder. "Well, if my sister's in there, I reckon I better get in there, too. Memaw's probably having a cow."

Nigel just nodded and looked back up at the stars.

"You seem like a decent boy," Canton continued, tightening his grip slightly. "I reckon you won't be telling people you saw me out here starin' at her titties, will you?"

Nigel forced his attention back to the moment. "You keep my secret, my friend, I'll keep yours."

"That's the right answer," Canton said. He shook Nigel once, demonstrating an immense physical strength, then released him and strode whistling toward the house.

Nigel continued to stare up at the sky. He thought he glimpsed a shadow, visible only where it blocked out the stars, of something that resembled a woman with enormous butterfly wings. But it was too fast for him to get a good look. Then, faintly, he heard the distant, plaintive fiddle.

He thought again about what Bo-Kate had told him of the Tufa. Suddenly it all registered anew with fresh seriousness, and more than a little fright.

What in the world—or in the Other World—had he gotten into?

10

Byron Harley listened intently as the old man John played yet another sad, mournful tune on his fiddle. There was something familiar about the man, yet Byron couldn't place it. He wasn't someone he knew, nor was he another musician he'd played with on one of his many barnstorming package tours. In fact, he wasn't really a very good musician at all. So how in the hell could Byron know him?

He shifted his bad leg and winced as the bent brace pinched him again. The pain momentarily cleared the haze from his mind, and he remembered anew what had happened to him that night. His urgency returned: he had to get to a phone, call the police, and most important, call Donna to let her, and sweet little Harmony, know he was all right. He didn't want them to hear about the crash on the news or, worse, when reporters started flocking to his house.

John saw Byron's grimace, paused in the middle of "Brandi Jones," and said, "Something wrong with your leg, son?"

"Yeah, got an iron on it," Byron said. He raised his foot to display the metal piece that went under his instep and took most of his weight when he walked. "Messed it up in a motorcycle accident a few years ago. Doctors wanted to cut it off, but I wouldn't let 'em."

"That's doctors for you," John said. "Sure enough, if they can't get your money by making it well, they'll try to get it by cutting it off."

Byron chuckled in assent. Without any conscious realization, the haze enveloped him again, pushing all urgency aside. Sure, he needed to get moving eventually, but for right now, there was nothing wrong with hanging out with these gentlemen, sipping rockgut and listening to good music. Now he only thought about how much he instinctively distrusted doctors, and between the VA physicians and the ones he'd been able to afford since becoming a star, that distrust had grown exponentially. "Reckon the plane crash bent the frame on the iron, and it's pinching me something fierce if I move wrong."

John slapped his own leg. "When I was a young man, I was messing around and shot myself in the right foot."

"What were you aimin' at?" Eli asked.

"My left foot," John said with a guffaw. "Anyway, it sure laid me up for quite a while, I tell you what. Still twinges when the weather's about to change. And you know something else? I work with a one-legged guitar player. He's got a wooden leg, so you can't really tell unless he tries to move fast, but he ain't got but one real one, I swear."

Byron bent down and opened his own guitar case. "Well, maybe there's something 'bout musicians that makes our legs act up. Sure explains Elvis, don't it?"

John looked blank at the name. "Who?"

"Elvis Presley. From Memphis. 'Hound Dog,' 'Heartbreak Hotel.' You know . . . Elvis."

John shook his head. "'Fraid not."

This made Byron pause, and the fog again withdrew. How

could anyone, no matter how isolated, not know about Elvis Presley?

He glanced at the other man, who idly scratched his dog's head. What was up with that guy, anyway? Why was he dressed like a beggar from one of those movies about Scrooge and Christmas? Why was he out in the woods on a cold winter's night? Why did he seem completely unsurprised by the plane crash, or Byron's appearance?

"What's going on up here?" a new voice said. "Eli, you getting people drunk on that paint thinner again?"

Another man strode into the clearing and sat down beside Eli, shaking his hand like an old friend. He was about fifty, with black gray-streaked hair and a big, white-toothed grin. He wore a thick coat made out of some plastic material Byron didn't recognize; THE NORTH FACE was sewn over his heart. "Hey, y'all. I'm Marshall."

"Byron," he said, and offered his hand. "This here is John."

"Always glad to meet a friend of Eli's," John said, and they also shook hands.

Marshall sat near the fire and unzipped his coat. "Sure glad to see that fire. My toes are turning into ice cubes. Reckon that jug could pass around my way?"

John handed it to Eli, and he passed it to Marshall. Byron couldn't place what it was, but something seemed off about the newcomer, some detail that didn't match up. Marshall wiped his mouth with the back of his hand and said, "So, how's everybody doing?"

"Can't complain," Eli said. "If I did, nobody'd listen."

"Beats working in a coal mine," John said.

Marshall turned to Byron and asked, "And what brings you up on the mountain in the middle of the night?"

"My plane crashed," Byron said, the words sounding strange in his ears. "Hit the mountain up thataway. Three people are dead."

Marshall let out a long, low whistle. "That a fact. Reckon you'll need the police, then."

"Yeah," Byron agreed.

"I done told him we'll take him down in the morning," Eli said. Byron thought he saw a look pass between him and Marshall.

"Well, that's a good idea," Marshall said. "I mean, they're dead, right? Hurrying won't help 'em, and if you fell down a gully, wouldn't do you no good, either, would it?"

Byron nodded, because it did make sense. But Marshall's very presence still seemed off somehow. What was it?

John scratched on his fiddle, idle notes that sailed through the cold night. "Anybody but me feelin' squirrelly havin' to sit still?"

Byron positioned his guitar across his lap. "Well, that corn liquor's sure got me loosened up. What should we play?"

"You know 'Old Dan Tucker'?" John asked.

"I reckon," Byron said. His own Southern accent was growing more pronounced; the years of living in the Midwest, then traveling in both the army and for his career, had almost driven it out, but the moonshine and the company were bringing it back.

John scratched out the tune, and Byron joined in. After a few bars, the older man cleared his throat and sang:

> *Old Daniel Tucker was a mighty man,*
> *He washed his face in a frying pan;*
> *Combed his head with a wagon wheel*
> *And he died with a toothache in his heel. . . .*

The two of them joined in the chorus.

> *So, get out of the way, old Dan Tucker,*
> *You're too late to get your supper.*
> *Supper's over and breakfast cooking,*
> *Old Dan Tucker standing looking.*

John nodded at him. "You pick 'er up now, son."

"All right," Byron said. "Here's how I learned from my grand-daddy.

Old Dan Tucker was a fine old soul,
Buckskin belly and a rubber asshole,
Swallowed a barrel of cider down
And then he shit all over town.

By the time he'd reached the end of the second line, Byron realized who the old man was, but the profane lyrics had them all laughing so hard, they could barely play. When they finished the song, Byron said in a mix of awe and surprise, "John, are you by any chance Fiddlin' John Carson?"

"I reckon I am," John said with a grin.

"Well, goddamn," Byron said. "I grew up listening to you. My daddy had a big ol' stack of your records he brought up from Georgia when he moved to Minnesota. If us kids touched 'em without asking, he'd make us go cut a switch and then tan our hides good." He extended his right hand. "It's a real pleasure to meet you, sir."

"Thank you, son," John said as he returned the shake. "Pleasure to be met."

"What are you doing here?"

"I'm on the Kerosene Circuit: whorehouses, moonshiners' stills, and roadhouses. Played at a place called the Pair-A-Dice just down the road. Now, I have to ask you, what are *you* doing here? You're not a half-bad picker yourself."

"I get by," Byron said. He felt shy, something he hadn't experienced since he turned professional. But he could only imagine how excited his old man would be to hear that he'd met Fiddlin' John Carson.

"You sure do make that violin sing, sir," Marshall said.

"Violin?" John said in mock offense. "Son, I play the fiddle.

See right here?" He turned it over and displayed the back of the instrument's neck, which was painted bright red. "That's how you know it's a fiddle: Just like me, it's got a red neck on it." He held his straight face for a moment, then busted out laughing. The others did as well.

Marshall said, "Well, I got to be going. Peggy'll kill me if I'm out too late. I'll give the police a call when I get down, all right?"

"Can I come with you?" Byron said.

"Best if you just wait here, especially with that bum leg of yours." He pulled on his coat. "Somebody'll be here around daylight, I imagine."

"Reckon so," Eli agreed. Again there was a look between the two that Byron couldn't interpret. He stared as the man waved and strode off into the night.

Byron turned to John, who positioned his fiddle under his chin. As he began to play, something nagged at the back of Byron's mind. He couldn't quite tease it forward, so he tried to ignore it. But it stayed there, mosquito-like, at the edge of his consciousness.

They played two more songs, old folk tunes that they both knew, and passed the jug again. As he handed it back to Eli, Byron remembered what had struck him as odd.

It was 1958. Fiddlin' John Carson had died ten years earlier. He remembered his father telling him. So who was this man here, clearly nowhere near that old, who nonetheless sounded exactly like the voice and fiddle from those scratchy old records, and in fact claimed to *be* him?

John caught Byron staring at him. "What, son? You look like you done seen a ghost."

"Maybe I have," Byron whispered.

11

Bo-Kate opened her eyes. Something had startled her awake. She faced the wall and lay still, getting her bearings. She wasn't in her Nashville mansion, she was . . .

Home.

She rolled over. The room was dark and heavy with cold air. "Nigel?" she said sleepily. "What are you—?"

"Ain't your nigger," a voice said.

She sat up straight then, jolted fully awake. Rockhouse Hicks stood in the room.

She barely made out his shape in the darkness, and she couldn't see his face. But there was no mistaking the silhouette, the atmosphere of dread he always brought with him, or that voice. She grabbed a pillow to cover her nudity. She thought of the gun and knife in her purse. They were across the room, though, and he was between her and them.

Rockhouse said, "I want to show you something."

He's speaking, she realized. *How can he do that?* She tried to keep her own voice steady as she demanded, "What are you doing here? How'd you get in here?"

He laughed. "Ain't no place can keep *me* out, Bo-Kate."

"But you . . . I mean, you're. . . ."

She still couldn't see his face, but she felt his cruel smile in his words. "Yeah, I am. Thanks to you."

Then she sorted it out. He wasn't real. He was dead, and this was a *haint*.

She scooted back against the headboard and gathered the sheets around her. She was more scared than she'd ever been in her life, but she wasn't about to show it. "What do you want?"

"To help you get what you want."

"And why would you want that?"

He stepped closer. "You reckon because you came after me like you did, I want to get back at you, don't you?"

She nodded.

"Well, I would. Except there's others I want to get back at worse. And one of 'em is that little snot-bitch Mandalay."

"I got no quarrel with her."

"Well, you should. You want to take over my half of it, but why not take over it *all*?"

Bo-Kate said nothing. Could he read her mind now?

"Ah, I see you're thinking about it. Well, let me tell you, it ain't just about getting rid of Mandalay. If that's all it was, I'd'a done that. You got to also make everybody else see that you're stronger than her." He chuckled. "Not just meaner."

"And how do I do that?"

"You need a secret weapon. Now, get your pants on and I'll show you where it is."

"Turn around first," she said.

He folded his arms. "Hell no. I intend to see this. You got nothing to be scared of anyway, my pecker ain't no more real than the rest of me."

She didn't move for a long moment, then crawled out of bed and gathered her discarded clothes. She watched his face, hidden in shadow, as she dressed. "Get an eyeful?" she said as she finished buttoning her blouse.

"You're a pretty girl, Bo-Kate. Always have been. Too bad you got sung out before we could get to know each other."

"I knew all about you that I wanted to."

"Now, don't be mean. I'm here to help you, remember?"

"Where is Nigel, anyway? What did you do to him?"

"He's out back with your brother and cousin."

"No way."

The haint shrugged. "Believe what you want. He ain't my problem. Now, come on." Even though she was looking right at him, she couldn't spot the point when he dissolved into the darkness around him.

Without his presence, she immediately wondered if she'd hallucinated him. But no, she was wide awake, and while she might have imagined or dreamed his ghost, she'd never have invented his offer.

He could be luring her to her death, she knew. But she couldn't pass up this chance. Even if she tried, nothing could stop him returning to her over and over. The only thing that dispelled a haint was letting it, or helping it, accomplish its purpose.

She opened the door and stepped into the hallway, and saw his barely visible form waiting at the head of the stairs.

She did not see Tain, sweaty and windblown, peek out from her darkened room, noting her cousin's departure.

When Nigel got back to the room, Bo-Kate was gone. He undressed and waited in bed, but she never returned. Someone moved around in a distant part of the house, making the ancient wood squeak, but he heard no voices.

He turned on the bedside lamp and looked up at the canopy. Now he could make out the scene: fauns and sprites dancing to a little fairy band playing lutes, flutes, and bodhrans. At any other time it would've been annoyingly twee, but after what he'd just seen, he kept going back to Bo-Kate's insistence that her family, that all the Tufa, were descended from fairies and could, if the parameters were right, assume their fairy forms, wings and all. Just as Tain had done.

He tried to conjure rational explanations for what he'd seen. It had been dark, and cold, and certainly he didn't entirely trust his perceptions in the middle of the night. Tain might have simply jumped onto the roof, not actually leaped into the air. Yes, she'd been naked, of that he was *totally* certain, but some people got off on the cold. The Polar Bear Club, after all, was quite well populated. And the creature he'd spotted flying could have been the same owl he'd heard earlier; some of those in the United States were quite large, he knew from watching Animal Planet back when it had shows about animals.

The problem with all this was, when it came right down to it, he could accept Tain as a fairy. There *was* something otherworldly about her, an attractiveness and compelling quality he could easily put down as "glamour." But Bo-Kate? Bo-Kate Wisby, his lover and employer, flying naked on gossamer wings?

Bo-Kate was one of the most ruthless concert promoters in Nashville, and that was saying something. She had the ear of all the major country performers, and could get them to agree to terms that should have made their managers laugh in her face. Her pushiness had made her rich and powerful, spoken of with awe in Music Row boardrooms and Second Avenue nightclubs. There was even a term, never used to her face, called being "Bo-Kated," which meant that you'd agreed to terms common sense should've prevented.

Under it all, though, there was something else, a rage and defensiveness that drove her more than money, power, or sex. Nigel had seen it before, and recognized it. Bo-Kate sought, above all, *revenge*.

Yet he always wondered—against whom?

Not her family. She never talked about them with anything stronger than annoyance, certainly never intimated that there had been abuse or mistreatment. She never mentioned any friends, either; perhaps that was it, but in Nigel's experience, folks driven to elaborate retribution couldn't keep their mouths shut about the target of their ire.

But now that he'd seen what he thought he saw, after spending the day seeing how ruthless she really was, he was pretty sure he understood. She wanted revenge against the people who'd cast her out, who had taken away the ability to spread wings and fly as he'd seen Tain do. She wanted vengeance against the Good Folk.

He got out of bed and moved slowly around the room, perusing its treasure trove of vintage decor. Here was an apparent capsule summary of Bo-Kate before she left home as a teenager. He tried to ignore the strange time disparity, and the sheer oddness of her parents keeping her room immaculate, and just concentrate on what the items told him about the girl who'd lived here.

There was jewelry in the box on the vanity, which softly played Byron Harley's "Hip-Shakin' Black Slacks" when he opened the lid. He quickly closed it, but not before glimpsing pearls and assorted faux diamond pieces. He spritzed some of the perfume, labeled MOONLIGHT MIST, and sniffed it. It did not smell stale, although the heaviness did make him regret his curiosity. The rest of the items could have belonged to any teenage girl, of any era. But then he saw the picture.

It lay on the floor beside the dresser, facedown. When he picked it up, shards of glass remained in place. It had either fallen or been thrown, and recently if the lack of a dust pattern around it was any indication. Then that phrase, "Time doesn't work the same for everyone," came back to him. Who knew when the picture had been broken?

It was a black-and-white photograph of a very handsome teenage boy. Like Bo-Kate, he had the Tufa dark hair, and wore an old-fashioned American football letterman's jacket. He leaned against a motorcycle, one hand casually on his hip, the other braced against the seat.

Since the glass was broken, one corner of the picture poked out. He gently pulled it free and turned it over. On the back, someone had written, *Jefferson Powell, senior year.*

Nigel's eyes opened wide. *Jefferson Powell.* Tain had mentioned a "Jeff," but Nigel hadn't put two and two together. *Jefferson fucking Powell.* It was a name he knew as well as his own, that everyone who worked behind the scenes in the music business knew.

He looked at the picture again. The Jefferson Powell he knew was older and, in every picture or video Nigel had seen, immaculate. Yet there was an undeniable resemblance to this youth with his jaunty grin, cocky stance, and mussed hair.

He tucked the picture back in the frame and replaced it on the floor.

His eye was drawn to another photograph. He recognized the style: an artist's professional publicity shot. It showed a young man with a guitar in mid-strum, eyes blazing over the microphone before him. Nigel moved close enough to see the name printed at the bottom: BYRON HARLEY, along with contact information for his official fan club. This was the one Bo-Kate had sighed over when they first arrived.

Something seemed to be smeared on it. He leaned closer, and saw that it was actually red lipstick; someone had once kissed the picture, right over the singer's face. Did teenagers still do that sort of thing?

If Bo-Kate had truly been a teen during the '50s, when Byron Harley was alive, then she'd be in her sixties or seventies now, which he knew was patently untrue . . . unless, of course, "time doesn't work the same for everyone." Whatever was going on here, whatever he'd been drawn into by his boss/paramour, it must be based in reality. The Good Folk wouldn't live in decrepit old houses; women clearly in their thirties hadn't grown up in the era of Elvis and Byron Harley.

He heard someone move somewhere in the house, and quickly returned to the bed and turned out the light. But Bo-Kate still did not appear.

Mandalay sat at her desk. The only light came from her computer screen, and the only sounds were the clack of keys and the soft moaning of the cold winter wind. She searched YouTube and found a video of the song the Somervilles sang at dinner.

The singer and songwriter, Lou Buckingham, stood before a row of abstract watercolors in what appeared to be a coffeehouse or upscale bar. She had soft brown hair, and held an acoustic guitar that was separately miked. She began to sing, and this time Mandalay did not try to stop herself from crying. When the singer reached the verse about the Valiant being towed away, Mandalay felt as if she'd rip open with grief for many other things than the car in the song. She fought to keep it quiet, so that her father and Leshell wouldn't come check on her. This grief was nothing they could share, nor did she think she could explain why she was crying over Rockhouse.

But to her surprise, that wasn't the last verse. She choked her sobs down to hiccups as the woman sang:

> But the Fury still runs true
> Though it's a few years older than you
> And life beats down like that southwestern sun
> Fading its finish but you're not alone
> We'll ride the Fury again I know
> Listening to songs on the AM radio
> With no particular place to go
> The Valiant and Fury Girls.

Now Mandalay laughed through her tears. The song wasn't sad at all; bittersweet, yes, but with the promise of life continuing with love and tenderness. She wondered if the Somervilles even knew there was another verse.

She couldn't keep this quiet, though, and someone knocked softly on her door. "Honey?" her father said. "You okay?"

"Yeah, Dad, I'm fine," she said, reaching for a tissue.

"Okay. You come get us if you need us."

"I will." She blew her nose, wiped her eyes, and shut the computer. For a long time she stayed there in the dark, listening to the wind. Then she got up and went out to do one of those thankless tasks that nevertheless had to be done.

She needed to collect the sin eater.

Bo-Kate's thighs and calves ached with the effort of climbing up a mountain twice in one day, as well as the added exertions of her romp with Nigel. Ahead, the haint of Rockhouse walked with the ease of someone no longer bound to the world. She could see him plainly now, and he looked like the mental image of him she'd carried all these years: gray hair, black eyebrows, wearing overalls and a flannel shirt. This was the way he'd looked that day when he touched her, and then suggested that such a pretty girl should learn to get down on her knees without so much trouble.

She heard the music before she saw the fire's glow. She stopped when she got close enough to make out the tune. "I'm Nine Hundred Miles from My Home" rang through the cold air, and the high fiddle notes seemed to shimmer around her. She leaned against a tree and listened.

> *I used to have a woman*
> *She would walk and talk with me*
> *Now she loves sitting*

On some other rounder's knee
And she done told him
What she won't tell me
And I hate to hear that lonesome whistle blow. . . .

Rockhouse spoke from just behind her. "Know who that is playing that guitar?"

Out of breath, she shook her head.

"Who's the last person you'd expect to see up here?"

"You."

He grinned. "Other than me. Who's your secret love, Little Miss Bo-Kate?"

She glared at him. "I don't have a secret love."

"Ah, that ain't true." He leaned so close that, had he been alive, she'd have felt his breath on her skin. She resisted the urge to turn around. He said softly, "Who died on this very mountain fifty-some-odd years ago?"

"Everybody knows that, Rockhouse. Guy Berry, Large Sarge, and Byron Harley. So what?"

"Uh-huh. And whose picture inspired you to learn to touch yourself down there?"

She turned angrily, but he was gone.

She leaned against the tree again, exhausted. Was she crazy? Had her desire for revenge driven her over the edge? Had she hallucinated Rockhouse's appearance, externalizing her own insanity in the image of the person she most hated?

The "secret love" bit was nonsense, but she knew exactly who had spurred her to her first sexual feelings. She was a charter member of his fan club, and every night she used to kiss his picture before going to bed. But Byron Harley was dead; he'd died in a plane crash sixty years ago on this very mountain.

Then a jolt of realization went through her. Yes, his plane had crashed, killing everyone on board and, known only to the Tufa, that impulsive idiot Tarvell Moon who'd caused the crash in the first place. But Byron Harley's body had not been found, and it was assumed to have burned up in the explosion and fire that followed. Forensics were not as advanced back then, and sifting the ashes for DNA was not done. But what if he'd survived the crash? People could get stuck here, sometimes accidentally, sometimes out of someone's malice. They could exist in here for untold amounts of time with no one, human or Tufa, knowing about it. Had Byron Harley been stuck like that? And more crucially, *was* he still here?

She heard footsteps approaching, crunching the frozen leaves. Rockhouse's haint made no sound, so it couldn't be him. She ducked behind the nearest tree and held her breath.

Marshall Goins passed obliviously by her. He looked worried, but not unduly so, which meant he had no idea what was really going on. He whistled as he continued down the mountain.

When she could breathe normally, she climbed higher and closer. At last she made out the three men around the fire, one playing a fiddle, another with a Jew's harp to his mouth. But it was the third one, with the guitar across his lap and one leg straight before him, that she gazed upon with a mix of disbelief and arousal.

He was huge, easily a foot or more taller than the other two men, with broad shoulders that reminded her of Steve Reeves in those old *Hercules* movies. His hair was delightfully disheveled and fell in his eyes, causing him to toss it dramatically. She remembered that from the times she'd seen him on television when she was a girl. He also smiled as he sang, something that so many self-important lesser performers never did.

It really was Byron Harley.

She stared for a long time. The reality that this, the first love of her young womanhood, was here, alive, exactly as he'd been back then, overpowered her. Six decades he'd been stuck in this little clearing, but to him, no more than an hour or two must have passed.

"Your secret weapon," Rockhouse said into her ear. She jumped and turned, but no one was there.

What did that mean? How did Byron Harley's continued existence qualify as a "weapon"?

She made sure Marshall had time to get far ahead, then headed back down the mountain, toward her house. She could not wait to see Nigel's calm, reassuring face.

Mandalay stood in the forest darkness, not hiding but certainly not drawing attention to herself. Both Marshall Goins and Bo-Kate Wisby went right past her, but never looked her way. When both were out of sight and beyond hearing, Mandalay continued up the mountain.

When she saw the glow, she stopped. Once again, as she had earlier before Luke found her, she heard someone playing "I'm Nine Hundred Miles from My Home." She smiled as she recognized the voice: Fiddlin' John Carson. He had toured through Cloud County one year late in the fall, playing at house parties and barn dances, including the Tufa barn dance held just at the edge of this special, mercurial space. It had taken no effort at all that night to lure him away from the barn with the promise of moonshine, and he'd been here at the fire ever since. Mandalay knew that when he finally did work up the wherewithal to leave, he'd find only a few hours had passed, and would return to a career that ended with him as the honored elevator operator at the Georgia State Capitol. But for now, he was just a working musician taking time out for a drink of home brew. And that was okay. She was here to summon Eli the Sin Eater for Rockhouse, anyway.

Then she heard the *other* voice.

This was unexpected. She knew she'd find Fiddlin' John sitting with Eli, but who else was there? She searched her memory, and could find nothing. Had something changed without her being aware of it? If it had, then the night winds had to be behind it, and also behind keeping her in the dark.

That worried her. A lot.

She licked her suddenly cold, dry lips. She had to see who it was.

Careful to make as little sound as possible, she got within sight of the fire. Many times in her life, she'd slipped out here to see who was caught in one of these little bubbles of existence, wandering lost through the woods, unaware of time or distance. Folklore said that some people could spend lifetimes there—Washington Irving's tale of Rip Van Winkle was a variation on that concept—but usually it was no more than days, enough to cause confusion but not attract that much undue attention. And, since alcohol was usually involved, those affected tended to blame themselves for any lost time.

But for someone to be pulled into faery time without the head faery knowing about it . . . that was unusual, all right.

She peered around an oak tree's trunk, through the winter-bare shafts of a briar bush, and saw him. He was impossible to miss, being twice as big as Fiddlin' John, and dressed completely differently from Eli. He had a guitar across his lap that looked almost like a toy in his big hands, but he handled it with ease. His hair was mussed and askew, the way it was back in the '50s when Brylcreem and its ilk were popular.

But that voice . . .

To quote her father Darnell, holy fucking horseshit. It was *Byron Harley.*

Byron Harley, Guy Berry, and Large Sarge had died in a 1958 airplane crash. Everyone knew that. It even inspired a song, "State of the Disunion," in the '70s, which referred to the crash as "the night the music flew away." But here he was, playing along with Fiddlin' John Carson, who had also died, but long before that day in '58.

She leaned against the same tree that had supported Bo-Kate

and felt the cold air going in and out of her lungs. What was going on here? Where did he come from? And what did Marshall Goins *and* Bo-Kate Wisby have to do with it?

They finished "I'm Nine Hundred Miles from My Home." Fiddlin' John's laugh rang out through the trees. "Boy, you sure can pick that thing," he said to Byron Harley.

"Thank you, sir," Harley said with a shy, polite nod. "I purely wish my daddy was around to hear you say that."

"Has he passed on?"

"No, he's . . ." Byron's voice trailed off, and he seemed to struggle to remember something. Eventually, he gave up. "He's out in California with the rest of my family."

"Well, you sure tell 'em I said howdy," Fiddlin' John said.

"Hey, how about something else," Eli said. "Y'all know 'Sugar Blues'?"

"Clyde McCoy?" Byron asked,

"That's the one."

"I know it. Saw him do it, even, in St. Louis. Called it the 'Sugar Blues Boogie.'"

"Well, you take us off, then."

"Hell, I ain't got no horn to play."

"Don't you know the words?"

"Never heard the words."

Eli looked at Fiddlin' John, who shrugged. "Heard the tune, that's all."

"All right, then, y'all about to get schooled." Eli picked a rhythm on the Jew's harp, Byron picked it up, and Fiddlin' John played what would've been McCoy's trademark trumpet line.

In a growly voice at odds with the jaunty music, Eli sang,

> *My lovin' mama, sweet as she can be,*
> *But the doggone gal turned sour on me.*
> *I'm so unhappy, I feel so bad,*
> *I could lay me down and die. . . .*

Mandalay eased closer to the fire. Her heart wanted to explode from anxiety. At last she stepped into the open. "Hello," she said.

They all stopped playing. "Well, hello, there, Miss Mandalay," Eli said as if he saw her every day. "What brings you out here at this time of night?"

"I need a word with you, as it happens." She looked at the other two. "Introduce me to your friends?"

"Mandalay Harris, this here's Fiddlin' John Carson, and that big fella is Byron. Never did get your last name, I don't think."

Byron stood, awkwardly because of his leg. "Pleasure to meet you, miss. You live near here?"

"Not too far off."

He seemed to struggle with his thoughts. "Listen, I . . . my friends and I were in an accident up the hill. I could really use some help getting in touch with the police."

Eli stood, stretched, and twisted until his back popped. "You just rest that bad leg, youngster. Marshall said he'd call the police when he got home and send 'em up here at first light. You stay here so you can lead 'em back up to the crash."

Byron seemed about to say something, but then thought better of it. He nodded and sat back down, his bad leg stretched out before him.

Eli shuffled over to Mandalay and, hidden from the other two, made a simple hand gesture of respect. Mandalay nodded. "Be back soon, gentlemen," he said, and followed the girl out into the darkness.

Byron watched them disappear, then turned to Fiddlin' John. "Seem strange to you that a little girl's out running around the mountains all by herself in the middle of the night?"

Carson shrugged. "People round here have their own ways, and the kids have to pull their weight pretty early."

"Yeah," Byron said, unable to shake the gnawing sense that something was wrong. Then the haze enveloped him again; he smiled and reached for his guitar. "Well, we might as well pick a few while we wait, what do you say?"

"Sounds like the right thing to me," John said, and tucked his fiddle under his chin.

When they were far enough away they wouldn't be heard, Eli asked, "So who's passed away?"

"Rockhouse Hicks," Mandalay said.

The sin eater stared at her. "Are you serious?"

Mandalay looked back at him. Her eyes shone the way an animal's might. "You really think I'd make that up?"

"Well . . . how did he die?"

"Of a broken heart." She did not smile when she said it.

"Where is he?"

"The fire station. Bliss Overbay's there with him. Can you make it?"

"Course. Made it a lot further in a lot worse weather."

"Then I'll head home." She turned, then stopped. She looked back with the seriousness of her office. "Do you know who that is sitting with you?"

"Fiddlin' John Carson. Don't worry, he'll go back where he belongs."

"Not him. The other one."

"Beats me. He just showed up. He was on a plane that crashed."

"The plane crash that killed Tarvell Moon," she said with sudden realization. Mandalay looked back up the slope, past the glow of the fire, and into the darkness where the plane's wreckage remained. Tarvell Moon had been a young Tufa man desperate to learn to ride the night wind, but never quite able to manage it. Then, one night, he leaped into the sky, unfolded his wings, and began to dance. In his giddiness, he flew acrobatically around a small airplane; unfortunately, due to his inexperience, he flew right into the propellers. He was killed, and the plane crashed.

Like the song said, it was "the night the music flew away."

"He should be dead," Mandalay said.

"Tarvell? He is."

Eli had no idea who the big man was, and that, for the moment, was a good thing. It gave Mandalay time to try to figure out why no one else knew about it. "All right, Eli. And thank you for seeing to Rockhouse." She made a hand gesture of her own, one of respect and appreciation for the sin eater's dedication.

He nodded formally, doffed his top hat, and bowed. "It's my job."

Mandalay worked her way down and emerged from the woods into her own backyard. She slipped into the house and went to her bedroom without waking her father or Leshell, but she did not sleep. Instead she lay awake listening for the night wind, which for one of the few times in her life, was absolutely silent.

That should have dominated her thoughts. Or the presence of a dead man where he shouldn't be. Or the return of Bo-Kate Wisby. But instead, the kind look in Luke Somerville's eyes kept coming back to her.

Luke was one of Rockhouse's people. Not one of hers. This was a line that could never be crossed without great damage being done. Only at the Pair-A-Dice roadhouse, neutral territory, could the two sides meet and socialize.

She made a decision then. But she'd have to wait until morning to implement it. And first she had to see Rockhouse into the ground.

12

A firm knock at the fire station's back door awakened Bliss. She looked at the clock: 12:30 A.M. She'd curled up on a cot beneath one of the heavy blankets used for shock victims, and her back and legs were stiff. "Just a minute," she called, her hazy mind not even dwelling on who it might be.

She opened the door. A lone stooped figure stood in the porch light's glare, and she stepped back until her brain cleared enough for her to recognize him. His odor was thick and musty, like a closet full of abandoned clothes.

"Hello, Bliss Overbay," Eli the Sin Eater said. "Sorry it took me so long to get here. Turned out to be a hell of a walk in the snow."

"Come in," she said. He entered, stomped his feet on the mat to dislodge the snow, then stood aside so she could close the door. He was shorter than her, and probably skinnier under his many layers of rags.

"So the story little missy told me is true?" he asked. "Rockhouse is dead?"

"As dead as he can be."

He smiled. His mustache was long and ragged, and

the ends trailed down past his stubbled chin. "Well, with you Tufa, that don't always mean much. Let me see him."

She led him into the room where Rockhouse's body waited. He lay in state on a wooden door across two sawhorses. Tradition called it a "cooling board," used to keep the corpse from contorting with rigor mortis.

A heavy rag soaked in camphor oil lay on Rockhouse's face; it would keep the flesh a normal color, at least long enough to get the body in the ground. Beneath that, his eyes were held shut by silver coins that, if an expert ever saw them, would confound him or her with their antiquity. They were one of the only concessions to the deceased's former status.

Eli put a hand on the old man's chest to check for breathing or heartbeat. Much like hunters who administered an extra head shot even after the big game had been felled, Eli believed in always paying the insurance. Satisfied, he said, "What have you got for me?"

Bliss gestured to the floor under the table. A plate of biscuits and a whiskey jug rested there.

"It's what I had to work with," she said with a shrug.

The sin eater smiled. He picked up a biscuit, sniffed it, then touched his tongue to it. Satisfied, he took a bite. "It's fine."

"I'll leave you to it," she said. "I need to pee and brush my teeth."

When they were alone, Eli paced three times counterclockwise around the corpse. He watched for the slightest movement, for any indication that Rockhouse was either faking or not entirely dead. He saw nothing. And more important, he *felt* nothing.

"Supposed to wait three days to bury you, old man," Eli said to the corpse. "Make sure your spirit ain't hoverin' around to do mischief. But I reckon everyone knows exactly where your spirit is, don't they?"

The "sin eater" was the work-around for the Judeo-Christian concept of judgment. He ameliorated the sins of the recently deceased before he or she traveled on to whatever awaited them. The practice was ancient, and those with the gift of it were both respected and feared. Eli's father, grandfather, and great-grandfather had all been sin eaters; one of Eli's sons would someday hear the call and join his father to learn the skill.

The process was simple. Food was left on or near the dead for a time, during which it absorbed a lifetime of misdeeds, untruths, and deliberate wrongdoing. The gift allowed the sin eater to consume the evil with the food, taking it into himself and then dispersing its energy harmlessly.

Now Eli nibbled slowly on the most toxic, sin-loaded biscuit he'd ever eaten. And he had a whole plate of them to get through before daylight.

"Goddamn, Rockhouse," Eli said through the mouthful. "I knew we'd have to finish up someday, but I never imagined I'd be sitting here eating *your* sins. I'm already queasy, and I ain't finished one biscuit yet."

He choked down the last few dry bites and took a swig from the whiskey jug. "You did some terrible things in your life, Rockhouse, but I'll give you one thing: You held your people together. Even when Radella split to lead her own band, you made sure she stayed close, so you were all in the same valley. Don't know what the Tufa'd be now if you hadn't done that." He chuckled. "Course, shame you had to do it by being such a goddamned asshole. Never heard that saying about honey and vinegar, I reckon, did you?"

He finished the second biscuit and started on the third. "And what you did to your sister, then your daughter and her husband, that's just plain terrible. You crossed a bunch of lines with that, you know. They all respected you until then; yeah, they were scared of you, but that was only part of it. After that, they just kinda despised you."

He drank some more whiskey, and accidentally choked himself. He bent over and coughed until he gagged, but didn't throw up what he'd eaten. *That* was something he never wanted to do, because he then faced a terrible dilemma—eat only what was left on the plate, and leave some sins unleavened, or consume his own vomit like some coonhound. He sat back and took several deep breaths until the nausea passed.

"Well, anyway, old man, your time is done. I hope you end up back home, and that your Queen is in a forgiving mood. Yeah, that's right—I hope she lets you back in. Not even you deserve to be left in a rotting corpse for all eternity."

He took another bite, then smiled. "Then again . . . if anyone *did* deserve it, it's you."

Bliss came in to check on him shortly before sunrise. She looked exhausted, and the day was only going to get worse. "How's it going?" she asked.

He shrugged. "It's going. Some things you can't rush."

"Ever had one as bad as this?"

He smiled. "You'd like me to say no, wouldn't you?"

"It's hard for me to imagine worse."

He held up one of the biscuits. "This old man turned mean out of shame. He tried to show off once, and failed, and got all the Tufa sent over here. His pride choked him to death, and the only way he could deal with it was to be mean."

"You make it sound like I should feel sorry for him."

"Your choice. But I've known lots of folks who were mean just because it was in their nature. Nothing bad ever happened to turn 'em that way, they just was. If you ask me, that's a lot worse than turning mean."

"Is that why it's taking so long?"

"Well, he did turn mean a long time ago. He's had more time than most to pile stuff up."

———

When the day dawned, Mandalay felt the time-immemorial childhood thrill of hearing Cloud County Consolidated School District mentioned in the closed list on the radio. A mass text sent to her stepmother's phone by the principal confirmed this. A snow day also meant that everyone could attend Rockhouse's funeral that afternoon. She quickly showered and dressed, then departed in the way only a Tufa can for the firehouse. She had a long day ahead and was working on far too little sleep.

The skies cleared shortly after sunrise, about the time Marshall Goins and Deacon Hyatt arrived at the fire station with Rockhouse's coffin. It was made from a single pine log, cut in half lengthwise and then hollowed out. It rested in the bed of Deacon's truck, since this wasn't the end of its journey.

The fire station's bell rang pure and loud in the cold air as Deacon backed into the driveway. The peal would travel to every ear that needed to hear it. Tradition held that it should toll once for each year of the dead person's life, but in the case of Rockhouse, it would be tolling for a week. So it was just going until the whole Tufa community knew of it.

"Who's ringing the bell?" Deacon asked as Bliss came out to greet them. He yawned and shook his head to wake up. He'd gotten the call about Rockhouse just after he went to bed, and preparing the coffin had taken most of the night.

"Mandalay," Bliss said. "She wanted to." She peered into the truck bed. "Is that it?"

"Hard to find a tree trunk straight enough and long enough," Marshall said to Bliss. "Every one we dug out of the snow was either rotten or too twisted. Almost like the whole damn woods wanted nothing to do with him."

"Can you blame them?" Bliss muttered, then instantly regretted it. Rockhouse could no longer defend himself; picking on him now was no different from the way he'd treated people in his life.

"Did Eli come see him?" Deacon asked.

"Just finishing up," Bliss said.

"I don't envy him his job today," Deacon said wryly.

"I never do," Marshall said.

Eli emerged, looking slightly nauseated. He brushed dust from his hat and put it back on, then burped loudly and tapped his chest with his fist. "Well, he's as ready as I can make him."

"Thanks, Eli," Bliss said, and made a hand gesture of respect.

He responded with a similar gesture for her. "Glad to do it, Bliss. Wait—that's not true. I hated every damn minute of it." He chuckled. "But we do our jobs even when we don't want to, don't we? That's how we know we're all growed up, right?"

"Right, I reckon."

He doffed his top hat to Marshall and Deacon, then turned toward the woods. He shuffled through the snow, humming to himself, and disappeared among the trees.

"By the way," Bliss said to the two men, "I need someone to take care of that." She pointed to a bucket beside the door.

"What is it?" Deacon asked guardedly.

"Rockhouse's blood. I drained it out of him."

Marshall and Deacon exchanged a look. Somehow, the death of Rockhouse had all felt rather abstract until now, as if its reality were a distant thing that didn't really affect them. But there was no distance, physical or metaphorical, from that bucket of blood.

Deacon said, "What do you want done with it?"

"Find somewhere to pour it out. Just make sure you do it downhill from Emania Knob. Wouldn't want him able to draw it back, would we?"

"You really think he could do that?" Marshall asked.

"I think anything he's able to do shouldn't surprise us. Including coming back from the dead. That's why I want to make it as hard as possible for him."

Marshall looked at the thick crimson liquid in the bucket.

"Who would have thought the old man to have had so much blood in him?" he muttered, and picked it up by the handle. "I'll take care of it. I'll walk it down the hill and pour it somewhere safe."

"Sing over it, too," Bliss added. "Sing 'Edward, Edward.'"

That song, Marshall knew, was about a man who murders his own younger brother and has to leave his family, including his children. "This ain't exactly a tragedy."

"It is to Rockhouse. And the more we ease his passage, the safer we'll all be."

Marshall couldn't argue with that. He set out down the road, avoiding the slick spots of ice.

Deacon said, "What can I do?"

"Go over to Emania Knob and light a fire to melt the ground enough to dig the grave," Bliss said. "Then come back so we can load up the body."

"Will do." He got back in the truck and drove off, leaving Bliss with only the tolling bell for company.

Shortly after the bell stopped ringing, the Gwinns arrived.

Holbert Gwinn, tall and skinny, with skin the consistency of old leather, wore a button-down shirt and dress khakis cinched at his waist. His wife Murlo, 250 pounds and almost as wide as she was tall, wore her only dress, which was old and permanently stained. The half-dozen children that piled out of the old truck's bed, including the adults like Tiffany and Mercantile, were dressed in what passed for their best clothes. They were mirror images of their parents, the girls large and round and the boys thin as pipe cleaners. Pieces of black cloth covered both side-view mirrors and the rearview mirror in the cab, mountain tradition that usually didn't involve vehicles. But since they were here to visit Rockhouse, it was best to take no chances.

Holbert made a gesture of respect, and Bliss reciprocated.

Tiffany glowered at her, hateful because of their shared history of conflict, but Murlo smacked the girl on the back of the head.

Holbert held up an envelope with a black border. It was the funeral announcement that he, and many others, had found slipped under their door this morning as a reinforcement of the ringing bell. That way, no one could claim they didn't know about it. "What time's the old man going into the ground?"

"This afternoon at three. Up on Emania Knob."

"Should we go there now, then?"

"Might be best. Marshall Goins is up there lighting a fire to melt the ground."

"I reckon I can take some wood for that, then."

"Much appreciated."

"Oh, come on," one of the skinny sons, Phelan, said. "We got to stay in these monkey suits all day?"

Hobart snapped around. "You do if you want to see the sunrise tomorrow, you disrespectful little shit."

"For Rockhouse? He was a son of a bitch!"

Tiffany slapped the boy so hard, he spun around and fell to the ground.

"*Ow!*" Phelan cried in pain and anger. "God*damn it,* Tiffany!"

"You watch your mouth," she said as she stood over him. "Uncle Rockhouse was our leader, and we'll show him respect."

"Tiffany," Bliss said quietly. It wasn't the first time she'd had to calm the big woman, although it might be the first time Bliss had ever seen her in a dress. "Phelan can feel however he wants."

"Yeah, well, he best keep his feelings to himself," Tiffany said, then folded her arms across her chest.

"That ol' Rockhouse was the only man I ever saw who could strut sitting down," Hobart said. "We'll be going. Back in the truck, y'all."

Bliss watched them pile into their vehicle and only then realized the bell had stopped tolling.

The little room with the bell rope was basically a closet. The rope went up through a hole in the ceiling, and there wasn't even a light switch, so to see what you were doing, you had to leave the door open. Mandalay was about to leave when a sudden gust of wind slammed the door in her face. She felt the room fill around her with the presence of something she couldn't put into words, but most definitely recognized. It wasn't the ghosts of her own past, or the haints of others. Rather it was something expansive, and terrifying, and greater than even her simple feelings could encompass. She held her breath and fought not to turn, not to see what was behind and around her, because she doubted her consciousness could contain it.

These were the ones who made the songs. These were the ones who made the night winds blow. If they had a name, only they knew it.

Because of who she was, she could hear them speak clearly where most caught only vague whispers. But she had never seen them. No one had. Or if they had, they never lived to tell about it. But now they were there, with her, hovering near the body of the old man whose hubris caused the Tufa to be sent away.

Music hovered with them, a conglomeration of tune and melody like something Ligeti might have infused into the universe if he were a god.

Mandalay forced herself to breathe. She had often idly wondered why the night winds continued to be so interested in a small band of outcasts thousands of miles from their ancestral home. Surely the Queen and her court, back beneath the island's green earth, gave them plenty to worry about. But they'd always been there for the Tufa, guiding and hinting and occasionally taking direct action.

But never had they been there like this. Never had their direct action involved their actual *presence*.

Mandalay, something said in her mind, in a voice different from her own inner one. *There cannot be a caesura.*

Her voice trembled like a child's frightened by a storm. "Wh-what do you mean by that?"

You have until the full moon to find your opposite number . . . or take the crown yourself.

"Crown? What crown?"

If you do not do one of these things, then we will leave you. And your people. Forever.

"Wait . . ." She wanted to look around so desperately, to see the faces of her deities, but she continued to fix her gaze on the blank surface of the door before her. "I'm just a kid, I can't—"

The last light of the full moon.

"Oh, come on," she said impatiently. The full moon, she knew, was coming up on the night of February 3, mere days away.

Things must go forward. Songs cannot be sung in reverse.

"Now, that's just—"

But she knew they were gone before she finished the sentence.

"—plumb crazy."

She warily opened the door. What had visited her had departed. But its words vibrated in her head like the reverberations from a massive subwoofer connected to God's own surround sound.

When Bliss went back inside, Mandalay stood beside Rockhouse's body. There was something different about her, a break in her normal enigmatic certainty. "You okay?"

"A little overwhelmed," Mandalay said. "While I was ringing the bell, something . . . really hit me. He's gone. The one who brought us here, who *kept* us here, is gone."

Bliss put a hand on the girl's shoulder. "And you're not."

"No, I'm here all alone now. Who am I without him, Bliss? I mean, for . . . for *forever,* I've used him as a reverse barometer.

If it sounded like something Rockhouse would do, I knew I shouldn't. If he thought it was a good idea, I knew it wasn't. Now . . ." She sighed, sounding old and tired and defeated.

"You're not alone, you know."

"Yes, I am. That's part of the job description. I know you mean well, but . . . from now on, I *am* alone."

Bliss said nothing. The ancient ache in Mandalay's voice, coming as it did from a twelve-year-old girl, reinforced the truth in the words.

Mandalay managed a smile. "Don't worry, though. Now . . . someone needs to go up the mountain and get Rockhouse's favorite banjo. And the axe. They need to be with him, wherever he is."

"Who do you trust?"

"You or Bronwyn, but I need you here and she's way too pregnant for the hike."

"Don't let her hear you say that."

Mandalay smiled again. "And the rest of the First Daughters will be getting their families ready. So who do you think?"

"One of the Silent Sons, then?"

"Yeah," Mandalay agreed. "Send Snowy Rainfield."

"Snowy? Why him?"

"I don't know," she said honestly. "He just popped into my head."

"Okay," Bliss said, took out her cell phone, and scrolled through her contacts.

When Snowy reached the top of the mountain and saw Rockhouse's door, he sat down on a fallen tree and waited to catch his breath. He was in pretty good shape, but the climb was deliberately rigorous. Even with Rockhouse dead, the spells and secret powers that protected the place remained in force. He looked around at the trees, but only a pair of big crows sat in the bare branches. They watched him implacably, and their caws had the ring of malicious laughter. He got a chill that had nothing to do with the weather.

As he sat there, another man came up the trail, leaning heavily on a walking stick as he, too, fought to catch his breath. He didn't notice Snowy at first, and when he did, he let out a yelp of surprise.

"Snowy Rainfield, what are you doing up here?" Junior Damo asked.

Snowy stood up. "Running an errand for a friend. What about you?"

"I was just . . . uhm . . . h-hiking, you know."

Snowy stood up. He was taller than Junior, younger, and more powerfully built. Driving a truck had done nothing for Junior's muscles. "Junior, you're the worst liar I know. Tell me why you're up here, or I'll beat it out of you. And you know I can."

Junior wanted to appear tough, but it wasn't his best skill, especially without a crowd watching. "Hell, Snowy, I just wanted to see what was left up in Rockhouse's home."

"Why?"

"Maybe I want a souvenir."

"Yeah, or maybe you're thinking about moving in when nobody's watching."

"And what about you?" Junior said with false bravado. "What are *you* doing here?"

"I'm here on official funeral business. You can come in and look around with me if you want, but don't touch anything, and don't try to sneak anything out."

"Well, goddamn, Snowy, ain't you a peach. Why you being so nice to me?"

"It's easier to keep an eye on you when you're underfoot."

Junior gestured for Snowy to precede him to the door. Snowy did, but said over his shoulder, "Try to hit me with that hikin' stick and I'm liable to shove it somewhere you won't like and turn you into a popsicle."

"Yeah, you've made your point, you know," Junior muttered.

Snowy pushed open the door and stepped aside to let the light shine in. The bloodstains on the floor were still shiny, and dust hung in the air from the earlier disturbance. Junior said, "Looks about like I expected."

"You ever been up here before?"

"No," Junior said. He waited to see if Snowy would acknowledge the lie, but either he didn't catch it, or he didn't think it worth mentioning.

"Well, I need Rockhouse's favorite banjo, and the Fairy Feller's axe."

"Reckon that's his favorite. That Fender Rustler there."

"Why do you say that?"

"Well, he had six fingers on each hand, and that's a six-stringer."

Snowy looked at the other banjos, all of which were five-string. "Good point. Hadn't thought of that." He picked up the banjo, half-expecting some kind of electric shock from touching the old man's stuff. "Do you see the axe anywhere?"

"Naw. Where you figure he'd keep it?"

"If I knew that, it'd be the first place I'd look."

There wasn't much to search. The furniture was very basic, and the little chest of drawers that held his threadbare clothes was the only thing that took any time to inspect. As they went through his pants pockets, Snowy said, "Junior, I'd be lying if I said I didn't know that you wanted to take over for Rockhouse. You're practically wearing a sign around your neck. If you were trying to keep it secret, you did a really bad job."

"I wasn't trying to keep it secret," Junior said, and again Snowy either didn't notice or didn't care about the lie. "Why should I? Somebody's got to take over, right?"

"There's a fair number of us who think we should all be under Mandalay now."

Junior laughed, then choked it off when Snowy glared at him. "Snowy, that ain't never gonna happen."

"Why do you say that?"

"What united us all under Rockhouse?"

"We weren't all under Rockhouse. Some of us—"

"Don't bullshit me. Rockhouse was the thing that we all agreed on. Whether we were part of his bunch or Mandalay's, we knew he brought us here, picked this spot, told us how to behave and how to interact with the other folks as they started to settle in around us. He was the thing we had in common. He was the one thing we was all afraid of. Mandalay cain't never be that."

Snowy stopped searching and looked steadily at Junior. After a thoughtful moment, he said, "Hell, you might have a point there."

This emboldened Junior. "So since Mandalay can't be the one to fill that, we need someone who can do what she does, but for my folks. And also work with her when it needs to be done, which Rockhouse never could do." His bravado left, and he said sincerely, "I can do that, Snowy. Nobody expects it, but I can."

Snowy smiled. "Might be, Junior. But you'll have to take it up with your bunch. And you best not forget that Bo-Kate's nosin' around, interested in the same job."

"Oh, I can handle *her*."

"Really? How?"

Junior grinned. "Now, Snowy, I can't be giving away all my secrets, now, can I?"

"I reckon not." He closed the last drawer on the dresser. "Well, that axe ain't here, is it? I bet Bo-Kate has it."

"Won't do her any good," Junior said.

"Well, that remains to be seen. I have to get this banjo down to the funeral. I assume you'll be there?"

Junior pulled out a small envelope edged in black, an old-style obituary notice. "Found this under my door. Wouldn't miss it."

"Well, we best get going." With the banjo in one hand and Junior's arm in the other, Snowy took them out the door. It closed on its own behind them.

13

It would have been the perfect time to break into almost any house in Needsville and Cloud County, because everyone, the entire Tufa community, gathered on Emania Knob to say good-bye to Rockhouse Hicks.

Well, almost everyone.

Bo-Kate and Nigel sat on the roof of her family house. He was terrified of heights in general, and the slanted, rough-shingled surface only added to his fright. Bo-Kate seemed not to notice, though; she stood astride the roof's peak, peering over the tops of the trees with binoculars she'd gotten from her father. They were old, and the rubber grips were cracked and dry-rotted, but they seemed to work fine.

"Would you look at that," she said. "I've only seen that many people on Emania Knob one other time." She held out the binoculars. Nigel took them without standing. "You won't be able to see anything sitting down."

"That's all right. You paint a vivid word picture."

"You'll be fine." She grabbed him by the arm and pulled him up. One foot skidded on the shingles, and he almost threw himself flat to keep from sliding off. Bo-Kate laughed.

He repositioned himself with as much dignity as he could. "Now, what is it I'm looking at?"

She pointed. "That way. The top of that flat hill."

Nigel looked through the binoculars. "My goodness. That is indeed quite a gathering. And all for the funeral of that old man you visited?"

"He was the cheese, that's for sure."

"Yesterday you said you didn't kill him."

"I didn't. But apparently he died anyway."

"I think you bear some responsibility."

Bo-Kate waved her hand dismissively. "There's not a person on that hill who's sad that the old bastard is gone."

"And that makes murder acceptable?"

Bo-Kate gazed at him in a way he'd never seen before. She had the look of someone debating whether to kill a pest or simply chase it out of the house. "Nigel, you've done nothing but criticize me since we got here. It's getting old. I've told you what I'm doing, and I've been honest with you. If you've got a problem with it . . ."

She let the unfinished threat hang between them.

Nigel sighed. "My apologies, Bo-Kate. This is all very new to me, and I'm unsure how to navigate this situation."

She looked at him for another long moment. Then, apparently satisfied, she took the binoculars and resumed watching the distant ceremony.

"Is your family there?" he asked.

"Oh, yeah. Mom, Dad, my brothers, and Tain."

"Why aren't we attending?"

"It's all about marketing, Nigel. This isn't the time for our product reveal. We don't want it to get all tangled up with funeral stuff in people's minds. When we unveil ourselves, I want the moment to be all about us."

He nodded and said nothing.

She grabbed the front of his coat and kissed him. "Now, come on. We have another important errand to run."

Rockhouse's grave was only three feet deep, thanks to the frozen rocky ground. Even with the fire that had melted the top layer of soil, they couldn't dig any deeper. But it was enough. Here on top of Emania Knob, there was no way Rockhouse could summon uphill the blood that Bliss drained from his corpse. And without that, he was, as his own song title said, chained to this spot. Or at least, everyone hoped he was.

The grave had been dug on an east–west line, and the body would go in with the feet pointing toward the sunset. The superstition was that, since the Summerlands and Isles of the Blessed were all to the west, the rising spirit would see them and know which way to go. But Rockhouse's spirit wasn't going anywhere.

Mandalay stood by the grave, dressed in a long-sleeved black dress, with her hair pulled severely back in a bun. She wore her puffy winter coat but still shivered with cold.

The log coffin lay beside the grave, ready to be rolled in when the ceremony was finished. Leather straps held the lid on. Inside, Rockhouse's mutilated hands were crossed over his chest, and the banjo Snowy brought was tucked in beside him, along with a copy of his only vinyl album. Mandalay had taken the news about the Fairy Feller's axe with equanimity; it wasn't exactly a surprise. It was, however, a problem that would have to be addressed.

For now, though, there was nothing to do but put the old man in the ground.

Noah Vanover, known to all as Uncle Node, stood as gatekeeper to the mountaintop. He checked that everyone who arrived was either someone he knew, or brought one of the black-edged funeral announcements. It was an academic screening, since no one would be able to find their way to the mountain if they weren't meant to be here, but in these community-wide ceremonies, it was important to observe all the proprieties.

Bliss stood with Bronwyn and the Hyatt family. The two men, Deacon and his thirteen-year-old son Aiden, were dressed in uncomfortable-looking suits. Chloe and Brownyn wore simple black dresses, and Chloe had added an appropriate black veil. Bronwyn looked miserable, and kept shifting her position, trying to find a comfortable way to stand.

Finally she said softly, "Y'all, I got to walk around a little. I'll be back when the service starts."

"And now where are we off to?" he asked as Bo-Kate drove them along the deserted country roads.

"To the home of Bliss Overbay," she said. "She's . . . What do you Brits call a person who fills in for a king when he's too young to rule?"

"That would be a 'regent.'"

"Yeah, well, she's the regent for the other half of the Tufa."

"And who's the king?"

"Not a king, a queen. Her name's Mandalay." She said the name with distaste. "But I'll deal with her when the time comes."

They drove vigilantly through the mountains. The snow was gone from the main highway, but once they returned to Cloud County's much less traveled roads, it became an issue. Bo-Kate handled the SUV with great skill, steering through the couple of times they skidded and continuing unerringly higher until they stopped at a battered old mailbox. The name OVERBAY was painted on it; the artist had misjudged the size, so the final *Y* was on a line below the rest of the word.

Bo-Kate put the vehicle in park, lowered the windows, and turned off the engine.

"What are we doing?" Nigel asked after they'd waited for several minutes.

"Listening," Bo-Kate said.

"For?"

"Any sign that Bliss Overbay isn't up at Emania Knob right now."

Nigel heard nothing but the winter wind and the occasional bird. Eventually Bo-Kate put the SUV back in gear and turned down the driveway. They picked their way over a rickety bridge above a creek, then emerged into a small valley.

Junior stood next to his wife, trying to ignore the great wheezing gulps of air she sucked in around her cigarette, a habit no doctor or husband could convince her to abandon. She clung to his arm as if he were all that held her up.

Above the heads of all the assembled Tufa, the bare tops of the trees waved in the wind. They seemed synchronized, like the hands of a crowd during the slow part of the encore. The clouds thinned enough for the sun to almost break through, making them luminous.

"You shoulda brought me a camp chair," Loretta said, as always picking the perfect time to break the spell of beauty and wonder.

"You shoulda asked for one," he said without looking at her.

"I shouldn't have to ask you for this shit, you should know it," she shot back.

He still didn't look at her. The thought of punching her in that fat, whining face was so vivid that he was afraid he wouldn't be able to control himself. Instead he remained calm, and stoic, and everything that was, in his mind, appropriate to a future leader.

She pulled on his arm. "Oh, Junior," she said, her voice weak, "I think I'm having a contraction. . . ."

He took as much of her considerable weight as he could on his arm. His aloofness vanished at once in his surge of concern. "Do we need to go get Bliss? Or Granny Rogen?"

"No," she sighed, "it's passing. Just . . . a false alarm, I think."

"You okay, then?"

"Yeah. I'm gonna go sit in the truck."

He held her hand tightly in his and kissed the top of her head. He hated himself for this weakness, but his sense of obligation, to both her and their baby, was something he couldn't seem to shake. He'd have to work on that to be the ruthless leader he wanted to be.

Bronwyn walked over to the row of vehicles parked along the edge of the mountaintop, went around to the far side where she'd be reasonably out of sight, and leaned heavily against the fender of the nearest truck. The baby was kicking her a lot now, dancing to the music running through their mutual blood. It was almost as if the little bozo was delighted that Rockhouse was gone. And maybe so, Bronwyn thought. She had to admit, it didn't bother her at all to imagine her daughter growing up in a Rockhouse-free world.

"You okay?" a voice said.

She looked up. Loretta Damo, just as pregnant, climbed out of the truck. She also leaned on the fender as they spoke.

"Hey, Loretta," Bronwyn said. "Yeah, I'm okay. You know how it is."

"I surely do," she said. "What are you having?"

"A girl. You?"

"A boy. Be just as worthless as his father, I reckon."

"Maybe not," Bronwyn said with a groan. She'd known Loretta all her life, and the woman was never happy about anything. Having a child probably wouldn't change that. "How's Junior handling it?"

"Him? He's always off working or hanging out with his friends or creeping around on one of his secret missions. I swear, you'd think he was damn James Bond, the way he acts sometimes. Did you know he thinks he can take over for Rockhouse?"

"I'd heard that."

"Yeah," she spat. "Let's see him take care of his own family first, I say."

Bronwyn remembered the way Craig held her hair while she threw up with morning sickness, kneeling right there on the tile with her and stroking her back. She hadn't wanted him there at first, but then she realized that nothing she could ever do—even vomiting like a woman getting over a three-day bender—would ever make him love her any less. The security of that was something she never expected to experience.

"When are you due?" Loretta asked.

"A month. Around the end of February. You?"

"First week of March."

"Well, good luck." Suddenly all Bronwyn wanted to do was be beside her husband. She pushed herself off the fender and walked—waddled, really—back toward the grave.

Nigel drank in the valley's spectacular view. Snow gleamed off the bare ground and powdered the vast forest. Ahead rose a big, old house beside a small frozen lake. The house, unlike most of what he'd seen so far in Cloud County, was beautifully restored and tended. The driveway ended at a circle outside the garage.

"What does this Bliss person do?" he asked.

"She's an EMT."

"I don't know that term."

"Emergency Medical Technician. Paramedic."

"Their union must be quite influential. Or she married very well."

"What, this? Nah, she inherited all this. And she'll never get married as long as she's looking after Mandalay."

She parked and got out so quickly, Nigel had to rush to catch up. She stepped up to the door and pressed the bell. It rang inside the house; after a couple of minutes, she tried again.

"It appears you were right," Nigel said, looking around again at the amazing scenery. "No one's home."

"Good," Bo-Kate said, stepped back, and kicked the door twice until it flew open. "Break on through to the other side," she said with a wry cackle.

"Jesus!" Nigel exclaimed, looking around. The noise echoed back at them. By then Bo-Kate had strode into the house, and he rushed to follow. "Bo-Kate, I must register my disapproval."

"The stakes are high, Nigel," she said as she looked into each darkened room. "People's lives are at stake." She paused and looked at him. "You likely want to remember that."

He knew that when her Southern accent came out so strongly, she was serious. He said nothing.

Bronwyn's husband, Reverend Craig Chess of the Triple Springs Methodist Church, stood at the edge of the shallow hole in his best suit and holding his Bible. Craig was young, handsome, and absolutely committed to his calling. He'd been sent to his current assignment, a small dying rural church just across the Cloud County line, with the unspoken goal of drawing the Tufa into it. But he didn't approach the mission the way so many others sent to his church had done: he didn't proselytize, berate, or harangue. He simply made the decisions he thought Christ would make, helped those who needed it whatever their beliefs, and as a result, he slowly gained the Tufa's trust. They still didn't beat a path to his door on Sunday, but he'd found his wife Bronwyn, one of their respected First Daughters, through his work, and that made every bit of it worthwhile. Whatever he knew of the

Tufa—and by this point, it was a lot—he understood that his part in today's funeral service was as a guest, and not a full officiant. He would let Mandalay orchestrate things.

When they first arrived, before the log had been closed and strapped shut, Bronwyn had wanted to see the old man a final time. But everyone, from her family all the way up to Mandalay, stepped in to block her.

"What the hell is this?" she demanded.

"A pregnant woman should never look at a corpse," Chloe Hyatt said.

"Oh, come on. I've seen plenty of corpses. I was in the army, remember? I served in the damn Gulf War."

"Maybe they're right," Craig said magnanimously. "This is a rather unique occasion, and that's a very . . . special corpse."

She glared at him. "Don't you start taking their side."

"I'm not taking anyone's side."

"Do you believe in superstition, then?" she challenged.

He smiled. "I believe that it's important to listen to people who might know more than you do. Like your mama."

She tried to stay angry, but her giggle burst out despite her best efforts. "You smug bastard."

"All yours," he said, and kissed her.

"Yuck," her brother Aiden said. "Isn't that how you got knocked up in the first place?"

Deacon smacked him on the back of the head. "You don't want to walk home, smart-ass, you better apologize."

"Sorry, Brownyn," the boy muttered, rubbing the back of his head.

"All right, fine," Bronwyn said. "I'll avert my poor virgin eyes. But you all better swear the old bastard's in there."

"He is," Mandalay said. "I promise you. And he'll stay in there."

Now Mandalay stood beside the coffin, waiting for the community to find its places in the circle around the grave. They divided naturally into the two Tufa groups, and the tension hummed through the air. There was a reason only the Pair-A-Dice roadhouse was neutral ground for all Tufa to meet: No one trusted anyone if they weren't either family or tribe, and preferably both.

Her father and stepmother stood at the front of the crowd. It gave her a special warmth to know that, even though neither of them could ever truly understand her, they loved her enough to be constantly watching out for her. She felt especially tender toward Leshell, who had no blood ties to her at all except those that bound all the Tufa. To love someone so thoroughly, for no reason other than genuine affection, made Mandalay feel lucky beyond belief.

Earlier, while the crowd gathered, the Oneys, part of Rockhouse's people, approached the coffin. Their even dozen children, including two sets of twins and one of triplets, stood behind the parents. "We'd like the kids to see him," patriarch Floyce Oney said.

"Of course," Mandalay said.

Floyce Oney lifted the coffin lid, and his wife, Audra, urged the children toward it. "No, Mama, I don't want to see no dead man," one of the girls said.

"You show some respect," Floyce said firmly. "You go up and give your uncle Rockhouse a kiss, every one of you."

The Oney brood exchanged looks. Mandalay expected half of them to turn and flee, but none did. The oldest, a girl, knelt on the ground by the log and peered in at Rockhouse's immobile face.

"Good-bye, Uncle Rockhouse," she said formally, then leaned down and kissed his dry, lifeless forehead.

One by one the others did the same, until it came time for the youngest boy, six years old, to do it. He stopped about three feet away.

"I ain't gonna," he said, and turned to run.

Floyce caught his arm and yanked him to the coffin. "You sure as hell are."

"I don't wanna kiss no dead person!" the boy almost shrieked. "That's gross!"

Floyce grabbed him by the hair on the back of his head and pushed him down toward Rockhouse.

"Mr. Oney," Mandalay said quietly, but in a way that always stopped people dead.

Floyce looked up. "What?"

"If the boy doesn't want to do it, you shouldn't make him. It won't matter to Rockhouse, and it *will* matter to your son."

Floyce seemed about to argue the point, but Mandalay's steady gaze shut him down. He released his son, who turned and ran toward the crowd.

"I don't like allowing him to be disrespectful," Floyce said.

"You and I have very different ideas of respect, Mr. Oney," Mandalay said.

There was nothing unusual about Bliss Overbay's house, at least not to Nigel. It was simple, and warm, and filled with the detail of long habitation. The air smelled of recently cooked food. He stood ready to run, in case a dog like the ones at Bo-Kate's house appeared.

"Help me look for the door to the cellar," she said as she searched. "It's got to be here somewhere."

"Is that where they keep the moonshine?"

"That's where they keep the most precious thing they have. And I want it."

"What is it?"

"You'll see. You ever heard of the Fairy Flag of Dunvegan Castle?"

"I have."

"There's a similar relic here."

"Ah. Instead of a fairy flag, perhaps some fairy pantaloons?"

She ignored his comment and continued to search. But they found no door that led down to a cellar. She tore into all the ground-floor closets, looking for hidden access behind clothes, musical instruments, and canned vegetables. She also grew angrier and angrier.

Eventually she stood in the kitchen, staring around at the shiny surfaces and immaculate shelves, her face red from exertion and fury. "God damn it," she said, speaking each syllable distinctly. "Where the fuck is it?"

"Perhaps there is no cellar?"

"Oh, it's here. It's just hidden. Well, fine, Miss Bliss. You want to play it that way, we will." She rifled the kitchen drawers.

"Now what are you looking for?"

"This!" she said, holding up a box of matches. She sang, "Three hun-dred six-ty five de-grees."

He recognized the lyric from a Talking Heads song, and his eyes opened wide. "Burning down the house?"

"Exactly." She struck a match and held the flame to the little lace curtain over the sink window. It failed to catch, and the next three did as well. She stared at the curtain, which certainly looked flammable.

"Perhaps," Nigel offered, "if this place is so important, it's protected by magic spells or some such."

Bo-Kate looked up sharply, then smiled. "Nigel, sometimes you're a genius." She struck a final match, and as she touched it to the lace, she sang:

> Fire on the mountain, run, boy, run,
> Sal, let me chew your rosin, son. . . .

It caught at once. Leaving Nigel standing in surprise, she rushed from room to room, lighting everything that looked like it would burn while continuing to sing. Every fire alarm in the place was screaming at them, and air grew opaque with smoke.

She tossed the matches aside and headed for the door. "Come on, we're done here."

Nigel followed her outside. Somewhere a window shattered from the heat. They climbed into the SUV and spun gravel as they headed back toward the road. In the side-view mirror, Nigel saw smoke billow from an upstairs window.

"Bo-Kate," he said, feeling a bit sick. "What have we done?"

"We didn't start the fire," she said happily.

"Yes, we did!" he yelled in outrage. "We most certainly did!"

"Nah, it was always burning," she laughed. "Since the fucking world's been turning."

"Stop that!" he practically shrieked. "What if someone was in there? We didn't go upstairs to see if maybe someone was asleep, or—"

"You stop it," she snapped. "You sound like a panicky cheerleader. This is war, Nigel. And that was Fort Sumter." When Nigel continued to stare, clearly not getting the reference, she added, "The first battle of the Civil War."

"Your Civil War, I assume. We've had many."

"Ours ended with one country under one flag, one leader, one song. And you know what? So will this one."

At Emania Knob, others came up to say their final good-byes to Rockhouse, or just to make sure the old man was actually dead. Most of them were his people, and very few of them seemed truly sad. At most Tufa funerals, there were at least a couple of people who broke down in wailing sobs, and usually someone jumped in the grave with the deceased. But that didn't happen here.

Now all the good-byes had been said, and the coffin was

sealed. When everyone was quiet and still around the grave, Mandalay said loudly, "I've asked Revered Chess to say the words to send Rockhouse on his way. Reverend Chess?"

Craig stepped up and smiled. This was by far the biggest crowd he'd ever preached before, and although he had a prepared text, he abruptly second-guessed it. What was needed here was not comfort for the friends and family of the dead; no one, including Craig, would truly miss the old man. But the ceremony was important nonetheless, as a way for the whole community to put Rockhouse behind them once and for all.

He opened his Bible to 1 Timothy, where his notes were tucked. Silently he prayed, *Lord, don't let me make a fool of myself in front of my wife and in-laws, and help me say the right thing for the right reasons.* Then he began.

"Almighty God," Craig said, "into your hands we commend Rockhouse Hicks." Usually this was followed by, "in sure and certain hope of resurrection to eternal life through Jesus Christ our Lord," but in the case of a Tufa, especially one as despised and feared as this one, he didn't know enough about what they really believed to include that. Some preachers might consider omitting mention of Jesus as a betrayal of his own faith, but for Craig, his ministry was about building bridges, not burning them.

"This body we commit to the ground," he continued. "Earth to earth, ashes to ashes, dust to dust. For we brought nothing into this world, and it is certain we can carry nothing out . . . except a song."

He saw Bronwyn look up sharply at this. It was an impulsive addition to his text, but he could tell by her expression that it was exactly the right thing to say.

He closed his Bible and looked at Mandalay. "Would you care to lead us in a song?"

Mandalay gazed across the clearing. In front of the crowd stood three women only she could see, all dressed in ways very different from anyone around them. There was Radella, and

Scathac Scaith, and Layla Mae Hemlock: all now part of her, yet still existing as themselves in a contradiction every bit as deep and puzzling as the Christian trinity. Other women in the chain of her past milled about as well, all unseen by most, all waiting to see Rockhouse Hicks in the ground.

"Mandalay?" Craig said again.

Mandalay nodded and gave him a little smile of approval. She raised her chin and began:

> *Of all the money that ever I had, I spent it in good*
> *company.*
> *And of all the harm that ever I've done, alas, was done*
> *to none but me.*
> *And all I've done for want of wit, to memory now*
> *I cannot recall.*
> *So fill me to the parting glass. Good night and joy be*
> *with you all.*

At first she was the only one singing, but by the end of the first verse, almost everyone joined in, including the specters of her former selves. The song was a traditional Irish good-bye, usually interpreted as the dead saying farewell to his friends. But on Emania Knob this day, it was a community saying a relieved good-bye to the one who'd brought them, formed them, and kept them together, while simultaneously making them miserable, frightened, and afraid.

When the ceremony ended, people couldn't disperse fast enough. They tore the black coverings from their vehicle's mirrors and spun dirt and gravel away from Emania Knob. In short order there were only a handful of people left: Mandalay, Bliss, Marshall Goins, and Snowy Rainfield. Marshall and Snowy held shovels, waiting to fill in the grave.

Stoney Hicks, once Rockhouse's favorite nephew, was also present. He had been the local John Mayer, seducing any girl at will and leaving them brokenhearted and often suicidal, until one girl finally struck back by stabbing him repeatedly in the groin. Whatever physical damage had been done was nothing compared to the psychological trauma of having his legendary dick hacked. It left him a shadow of his former self: now fat, his hair thinning, and needing one of those carts to get around the Walmart in Unicorn.

Stoney watched his cousin Dorcas back up his huge Dodge Ram pickup to the grave. In the bed was a chair-sized rock with an inscription carved on it.

Mandalay, who wasn't quite tall enough to see into the bed, said, "What does it say?"

"Something I reckon we can all agree on," Stoney said.

Bliss looked at the stone and snorted. "Yeah, I think you're right."

Mandalay climbed onto the bumper and looked over the tailgate. The inscription read:

HERE LIES THE BODY OF A MAN WHO DIED
NOBODY MOURNED, NOBODY CRIED
HOW HE LIVED, HOW HE FARED
NOBODY KNOWS, NOBODY CARES

The wind picked up, blowing cold and sharp across the mountaintop. Mandalay looked at the clouds now gathering overhead.

"More snow's coming," she said. "Let's get him in the ground."

"I'll take you home," Bliss said. "I need to go clean up the fire station, anyway."

The two women left, leaving the men to attend to the grave. A half hour later, they'd gotten it halfway filled when Marshall stopped, pointed to a column of smoke rising in the distance, and said, "Hey, what's that?"

14

After dropping Mandalay off at her family's trailer, Bliss finished cleaning up the fire station, eliminating all traces of the events of the last days. No one would ever know that a body had been here. It was highly unlikely that any law enforcement types would come by, but it paid to be careful. She didn't want to have to disinter Rockhouse because some bureaucrat got hung up on missing paperwork.

She poured herself a cup of coffee, stirred in the creamer, and watched the pattern of the swirl. Some people could tell the future by these things, but not her.

The front door burst open and Duncan McCoy entered. Without taking off his boots, he said, "Bliss, your house is on fire."

It took a moment for the words to register. "What?"

By then Duncan had already pulled on his turnout coat. "We tried to call you, but you didn't answer. Everyone's heading up here to get the fire engine, but . . ." He paused before adding, "you better be prepared. I don't think there's much we can do."

Bliss stared at him, unable even to find words. She

pulled out her phone; sure enough, it was dead, the charge completely gone.

There was just no way her house, the house that had been in the Overbay family for generations, the house that protected one of the Tufa's most precious artifacts, could just burn down. Not unless—

"Bo-Kate," she said.

But before she could say more, other men rushed into the station and donned their firefighting gear.

The column of deep gray smoke rose into the clear sky. Cloud County's lone fire truck idled in the circular drive, its intake hoses trailing down to the little lake, where a hole had been chopped in the ice along the edge. By the time the volunteer force got ready to aggressively battle the flames, though, the house was destroyed.

Bliss stared at the remains with the same numb shock she felt when, as an EMT, she arrived at a fatal accident and realized she knew the victim. There was no need for her skills, at least; no one was in the house when it burned down. No one, that is, but her family's ghosts, and they were immune from fire, if not loss.

Deacon Hyatt came over to her and took off his fireman's helmet. He looked exhausted; he'd been up all night working on Rockhouse's coffin and then had rushed to the fire station with the rest of the volunteer force. His face was stained from sweat and smoke. "Ain't nothing we can do, Bliss," he said sadly.

She nodded. "I understand. Is there . . . Can you tell where it started?"

"It looks like all over the downstairs, honestly."

"Like it was deliberately set?"

He nodded.

"So it was arson."

"Well, you knew that, anyway, didn't you? I mean, it had to be, right?"

"Yeah."

He pulled off one heavy glove and put his hand on her shoulder. "I'm real sorry, Bliss."

She patted his hand. "Thank you, Deacon. Tell me, did it spread into the cellar?"

"Can't tell until we get the hot spots out. But . . ." He trailed off, leaving unspoken what they both thought. The slightest spark would've sent the tapestry up in an instant. He turned and went to rejoin the others.

She leaned against the fender of her truck. What Bo-Kate had done to Rockhouse was awful, but it was hard not to think the old bastard deserved it. That, she knew, would be the general consensus among the Tufa on both sides.

But this . . .

This was more than just burning down someone's house. If that bitch wanted a war . . .

The tapestry in her cellar was older than this country, older than the mountains around them. It was a touchstone of the Tufa's shared collective history, and had been in the Overbays' charge since . . . well, since the night winds first blew them here. If Bo-Kate Wisby had destroyed it, then she'd gone a long way toward destroying the Tufa, because without these common symbols to bind them, they would dissipate and fade even more than they already had.

Bliss stood alone in the center of the storm of activity, her rage making a bubble around her that no one else dared to penetrate. She balled her hands into fists. It had been barely two days; what would Bo-Kate do by the end of the week?

Bo-Kate sat on the picnic table at the scenic overlook and watched the column of smoke rise over the valley. She sipped from a beer and felt a level of contentment she'd never thought she'd again experience. It wasn't quite like riding on the night winds, but it was close.

She looked over at Nigel, who stood by the SUV, arms folded. He was a delicious bit of man, all right: tall, muscular, handsome in a lean way, and sophisticated. He knew books, music, and art; he was a loyal employee and a ferocious lover. It would be a shame when she had to kill him, but she knew before she started that there would come a point when he would stop being useful.

She just didn't think it would be so soon.

He joined her on the table. "What now?" he asked morosely.

"Oh, come on, Nigel, I didn't murder anybody," she said. "I just burned down an empty house."

Nigel said nothing, but he remembered the particular way some strange knicknacks had been arranged on a shelf, around the photograph of a young couple dressed as people did in the '60s. It was a little family shrine, and it spoke of love, and kindness, and the type of family who called each other on birthdays and got together for holidays. He'd always envied families like that, and for some reason the idea that he'd helped injure their sense of security made him feel especially bad.

"You still haven't told me," he said, "what you were looking for?"

"A tapestry. Something woven in the old country and brought over when the Tufa first came here."

"And why is it important?"

"It's a symbol, that's why. If I'm going to unite the Tufa under my hand, then the old symbols have to go."

He nodded. They watched for a bit longer as the smoke column grew thinner and more wispy against the dimming sky. At last she climbed down, brushed off the seat of her jeans, and said, "Okay, back to the salt mines. We have to go find a young woman named Carolanne Pollard."

"And shall we kill her, then?"

She laughed. "No, she's always been resentful of the status quo, and she's a smart, resourceful girl. I want to recruit her."

Nigel nodded, but she could sense by his tightly wound silence that his usefulness really might come to an end even sooner than she thought. She hoped she'd get one more night out of him, but if he had to go, then he had to. Sacrifice was necessary for every worthwhile endeavor. Besides, there were plenty of handsome young men among the Tufa, and soon she would have her pick of them.

Carolanne Pollard sat looking at her laptop screen. It was the latest exam for her online college course, and it made her head hurt. A lot of things in her major came naturally to her: behavioral psychology, primate biology, even history. But calculus was like learning a language that had no words in common with her own. Like Finnish, she thought, which had only the word "sauna" in common with English.

Her house was on a winding dirt road up on Walden Mountain, one of the smallest peaks in Cloud County. In fact, it was bisected over the top by a row of power lines, like a metal mohawk across the top of a skull. But the leases for those towers paid for her college, so she learned to choke down the sense of violation she felt every time she saw them.

Besides, soon she'd be out of here. Once she got her undergraduate degree, she would begin to look for master's and Ph.D. programs. She knew that Tufas who left Cloud County often met with disaster, but that was only if they meant to never come back. She had every intention of coming back, triumphantly, as a goddamned full-fledged symphony conductor.

That'd show those damned First Daughters.

She was a firstborn daughter. But because she wasn't also a pureblood Tufa, they'd turned up their collective noses at her.

That rejection had fueled her determination, but it also broke her heart. It meant she'd never really belong.

A knock at the door made her jump. It was nearly dark, and there was snow everywhere. Her father and brother had run out to help fight a fire, her baby sister was spending the night with a friend, and her mother was at her sewing circle. Who would brave this weather just to come see her?

She opened it to see a Tufa woman in her thirties and a handsome black man standing at the bottom of the steps. She did not know either of them.

"Can I help you?" she asked.

"I'm Bo-Kate Wisby, and this is Nigel Hawtrey," the woman said. "You're Carolanne, right?"

"Yeah," she said guardedly. Her father kept a loaded shotgun beside the door, and she placed her unseen hand on the barrel. "If you're selling something, you're wasting your time. My folks ain't home, and I'm in college, so I'm broke."

"No, we're not selling anything. I want to talk to you about something."

"Me?"

"Yes, you."

"I'm nobody."

"That can change."

"What do you want to talk about?"

"The First Daughters."

Carolanne's eyes narrowed suspiciously. "I ain't one of them."

"I know. They wouldn't let you in, despite you learning so much of their ways."

Carolanne said skeptically, "Now, how would you know that?"

"Does it matter? Look, can we come in? It's cold out here."

"You can, but not him. My mama would have a conniption if she knew I let a colored man in the house."

The black man raised one eyebrow. Bo-Kate turned to him and said, "Wait in the truck, Nigel. This won't take long."

"As you wish, my dear," he said, and trudged through the snow back to the vehicle.

Bo-Kate took off her boots by the door and hung her coat on an empty hook. The old house was smaller than the Wisby farm, and considerably more modern. A laptop, thick textbooks, and piles of paper were scattered on the kitchen table, while a fifty-inch TV dominated the living room. "Your parents aren't home?"

"No." Then she added quickly, "But they'll be back any minute."

"You don't have to be afraid of me, Carolanne. I'm not going to hurt you. I want to offer you something."

"What's that?"

"Pretty soon, everything's going to change. The Tufa are going to stop being split, and come together under one leader."

"Mandalay Harris?"

Bo-Kate smiled. "Me."

"And who are you?"

"I'm the woman who's already taken Rockhouse Hicks permanently out of the equation. And I'll do the same to that Harris girl."

"That still doesn't tell me who you are."

"I'm what this backwards-ass county needs. I'll bring businesses and money and the fucking modern world here. We won't be folktales and myths anymore, we'll be out there on the radio and downloads where we belong. I know the music industry like I know the sound of my own voice, and it's time for us to take it back from the Simon Cowells of the world."

Carolanne considered this. "Okay," she said, still guarded, "so what do you want from me?"

"Information, sweetie. I haven't been here in a long time, and I need to know who's doing what to who."

Carolanne smiled. "Gossip? You want gossip?"

Bo-Kate grinned back. "I want the most valuable thing in the world, honey: *secrets.* Bring the dish."

15

More snow fell that night, and the next day was another no-school day. Mandalay had to learn about it from the radio in her father's truck, since the snow and ice had snapped the power and phone lines somewhere, and all the family's cell phones had gone dead. Luckily they heated with a woodstove, so they stayed warm.

She had a gnawing sense that something was wrong, but couldn't put her finger on the source. She was also incredibly, inexplicably preoccupied.

She stood in the door in just her long T-shirt despite the cold wind and watched her parents depart in her father's big truck. Alone, she padded the length of the house and retrieved her guitar. Once again, the first song that came to her was Alice Peacock's "Paranoid." As she played the last chord, the power came back on, startling her.

She reset all the clocks, then waited until 9 A.M., the unofficial time it was okay to call someone for a non-emergency reason. Then she dialed the number for Luke's house.

On the third ring, he answered it himself. "Hello?"

"Hey, Luke," she said with false casualness. It amazed her that despite the accumulated Tufa wisdom and experience rattling around in her head, she could still be nervous talking to a boy. "It's Mandalay. Mandalay Harris. You know, from the other night."

"Yeah."

"Watching it snow?"

"Nah, eating breakfast."

"I should do that. Our power was out until about twenty minutes ago. Your parents working?"

"Yeah."

"Mine, too. You think you can make it down to the Pair-A-Dice around lunchtime?"

There was a long pause. "Why?"

"Thought you might bring your guitar and we could play a little."

Another long pause. "Are you serious?"

"Well, I can't invite you to my house, and you can't invite me to yours, can you?"

"Reckon not."

"So?"

She heard other voices behind him, no doubt his brothers and sisters. They didn't seem to have noticed he was on the phone, or have any ideas whom he was talking to.

"I might can catch a ride with my uncle Andy," he said. "He usually heads to town about then."

A warm thrill ran up her neck and cheeks. "Well, I'll be there anyway. Maybe I'll see you."

"Maybe you will."

She hung up, threw herself on the couch, and stared up at the ceiling. Memories and sensations of so many Tufa women attracted to so many men filled her, things she could neither comprehend nor understand yet as a twelve-year-old girl. She closed her eyes and gritted her teeth against it. *I am Mandalay Harris, not any of you,* she said to the ghosts trying to command her attention. *You've had your fun. This is all about me.*

At that moment, the house phone rang, her cell phone beeped with a text, and her laptop chimed to announce she had e-mail. All the messages concerned the fire at Bliss Overbay's the previous evening.

Tain Wisby looked out at the Hang Dog Diner's empty tables. The snow had effectively killed their business this morning, with men concentrating on getting to work, and women stuck at home with children out of school. Only three people needed her attention, all elderly retirees with nowhere else to go. They barely even noticed her in her scandalously tight waitress uniform, with her legs bare and top button undone. That indifference annoyed her more than the weather.

The Hang Dog was located on Highway 7 just past the interstate, outside Cloud County. There weren't many non-agricultural jobs in the county itself, so the non-farming Tufa had to look a bit afield for gainful employment. Once again Tain wished she'd kept her pants on that night at the convenience store, when her boss had discovered her and Shelby Renfro doing the deed in his office. Now Lassa Gwinn had her old job, and seemed determined to keep it until she was too big to get through the doors, like the legendary moonshiner Great Kate Gwinn.

"Little top-off here, Tain?" one of the old men said, and raised his cup in her direction.

She picked up the carafe and poured with a sigh of boredom. "Here you go, Mr. Lytle."

"Not too exciting this morning, is it?" he said as he sipped.

"It sure ain't," Tain agreed.

"If I was forty years younger, I might show you something a little exciting," he said with a grin and a wink.

"If you were forty years younger, Mr. Lytle, I'd sure enough let you." And she meant it.

Headlights swept through the gloom as a truck pulled into the lot. She didn't recognize the figure that got out, but her brief excitement was diminished when she saw white hair above the face half-hidden in a scarf. *Another geezer,* she thought to herself. *Yay.*

When he came in the door, she recognized him. "Snowy Rainfield," she said, genuinely pleased to see him. She knew he worked construction, and in this weather he couldn't be on his way to a job. "What brings you out on a day like this?"

"If I say it's to see you, will that get me a slap or a kiss?" he said as he took off his coat and sat at the counter.

"It'll get you a cup of coffee," she said, winking.

Snowy leaned his elbows on the Formica and watched her as she moved to get his cup. Tain always knew when men watched her; it wasn't so much a sixth sense as a simple certainty that, if there were men around, they would *always* watch her. And it didn't bother her—she liked *all* men, up to a point. Past that point, though, only very select men would do.

As she poured she said, "How are the roads?"

"All right, where the sun hits 'em. Lots of black ice out there, though. You better be careful going home."

"I didn't know you cared."

"You're being coy," he said as he sipped his cup. Then he looked around and saw that they were reasonably alone. Quietly, he said, "Can I ask you something?"

"Sure. No promises I'll answer it, though."

"What's Bo-Kate up to?"

Tain started, and banged the glass carafe against the edge of the counter, but luckily it didn't shatter. She composed herself, then said, "Would you believe me if I said I honestly don't know?"

"If you look me in the eye when you say it." Even more softly, he added, "Tain, this could be bad news for everybody. Both sides. She flat-out shouldn't be here. She shouldn't be *able* to be here. And she's already done a couple of pretty horrible things."

"Like what?"

Snowy dropped his voice even lower. "She's the reason Rockhouse died. She cut off his extra fingers. And yesterday, while we were burying him, she burned down Bliss Overbay's house."

Tain stared at him, waiting for the smile, the sign that it was all a joke, but it never came. She had to clear her throat before speaking. "I really don't know what you mean, Snowy."

Snowy leaned back and looked at her skeptically. "Is that right," he said flatly.

This time she leaned close. Softly she asked, "Snowy, you know where the Wildwood Motel is?"

"Yeah."

"Meet me there at three o'clock. Ask for me at the desk, they'll tell you which room."

Snowy grew even more skeptical. "You setting me up, Tain? Who's going to be there waiting for me? Snad and Canton, maybe? With a couple of baseball bats?"

"Just me, I promise. If you want to talk about this, we'll need privacy."

He knew what she meant. She knew that he knew. She also knew that he, like just about every man she knew, couldn't possibly resist.

Yet he said, "No thanks, Tain."

She put the carafe aside and stood with her hands on her hips. "Snowy Rainfield, are you serious?"

"*This* is serious, Tain."

"Your memory must be shorter than some other things I could mention."

He grinned. "Good one. And my memory's just fine. But this ain't about us."

She blew a stray strand of hair from her face. "What kind of assurance do you need that I'm not going to have my cousins hiding in the closet to beat the snot out of you?"

"I'll take your word for it."

"I *promise* I am meeting only you to tell you what you want to know."

He made a gesture with the fingers of his right hand, then touched his heart. With an annoyed sigh, she did the same, sealing the meeting with vows of honesty that went back further than most spoken languages. "Believe me now?"

"See you there," he said.

As he drove back to Needsville, Snowy couldn't keep the memory of previous trysts from his mind. He and Tain had fooled around a dozen times over the years, and it had always been spectacular. Each time, he convinced himself that his memory of the previous encounter had been enhanced by time and wishful thinking, then found out that, no, it *was* as good as he remembered. Tain was uninhibited, afraid to try nothing, and most attractive of all, always let him know when she liked something he did.

He shifted uncomfortably as his physical response to those memories asserted itself. He checked his watch—eight hours until three, when he'd see her. He hoped nothing came up that required real concentration, because he doubted he could manage it.

He turned on the radio, set to the oldies station. Chaka Khan sang, "Tell Me Something Good." Her sexy, carnal voice didn't help his concentration at all.

"Rise and shine," Bo-Kate said. "We're burning daylight."

Nigel opened one eye and winced against the glare from the window. "I never imagined Americans actually said that."

"We invent all sorts of clichés." She was dressed in tight-fitting layers that accented her curves, and he considered for a moment how long it might take to undress her. Then he saw the look in her eye, which said, *I know what you're thinking, and stop it.* With a sigh, he threw back the covers and swung his feet onto the icy wooden floor.

He started to pull on his pants. She said, "It doesn't matter. We're the only ones here."

"Your cousin's not skulking about?"

"She went to work. Mom and Dad went wherever they go. My brothers are passed out, or never came home from the wake, I don't know which. We've basically got the whole house to ourselves."

"And this is how you want to spend it?"

"Not now, Nigel. Big things are afoot."

"They could be."

She slapped him, lightly but not playfully. "Eyes front, soldier. Get cleaned up so we can get going."

"Aye, mistress," he said, and followed her out of the bedroom.

Within an hour they were back in the SUV, out of the woods, and on the paved highway. It was still messy after the snow, but mindful driving kept them from any calamities. "Where are we going?" he asked.

"You'll see. Just stay on this road until I tell you differently."

"That's essentially my job description, isn't it?"

She looked out at the trees passing on the passenger side. "There—see that extra-tall tree there?"

"Yes."

"That's the Widow's Tree. Women who have lost their husbands or lovers go and carve messages on it. It's got to be a couple of hundred years old by now."

"Any messages from you on it?"

"Ha! Not likely."

"No?"

"No. My only real Tufa love was lost . . . differently."

"You must spend vast amounts of time working out ways to hint at things without giving away any actual information."

"As a matter of fact, smart-ass, we're on our way to get some information right now."

"Indeed? What sort?"

"Tactical. Then you'll understand who the players are in this little war."

"You could just tell me."

"Then you might not believe me."

"And this will convince me?"

"No, of course not. All in all, this is just another brick in the convincing wall."

"How can I eat my pudding if I don't have any meat?"

She smiled, then resumed looking out at the forest. "We have one stop to make first, though. Just outside town. Time to announce myself properly."

16

Snowy dropped the load of debris from the backhoe's bucket and swung around to scoop out another one. Bliss deliberately didn't look at what tumbled out, not wanting to see her family's heirlooms burned, dropped, and discarded into the big green Dumpster. She was having a hard enough time accepting that the old homestead, which had stood in one form or another since the Tufa arrived, was now gone.

Orpheus Carding stood watching. The backhoe belonged to him, but he wasn't able to run it since losing his arm five years before. "That sure is a mess," he said over the noise.

"It is," Bliss agreed.

"Reckon we'll need about six or seven Dumpster loads to get everything cleared out."

"Reckon."

"Then we'll all pitch in and build you a new place. Just like they used to in the old days, you know? Lots of music, lots of hard work."

"Thanks." She knew they would, too. She'd have a new house as good as, if not better than, the old one. But it was like those logging companies who claimed they'd plant one hundred trees for every one they cut down. They simply didn't understand that you could regrow *a* forest, but not *the* forest.

Snowy dumped the latest load, then leaned out of the cab and yelled, "I think you can get to it now! Watch for hot spots, though!"

Bliss pulled on a pair of fireman boots and gloves, then picked her way through the debris along the path that Snowy had cleared for her. When she reached the stairs that led to the cellar, she shone a flashlight down into the darkness. Smoke and dust hung in the air, but not so heavily she needed a breathing apparatus.

"Want to tie a line to yourself in case there's fumes?" Carding called.

"No," Bliss answered. "It'll be fine."

She carefully descended the stairs. The wooden steps went from singed to water damaged to untouched just before they changed to solid rock. These ancient stone steps were as dry as if they'd been under a protective bubble—which, in a sense, they had.

She walked past the rows of shelves along the stone corridor, to the door at the far end. The only footprints visible in the dust were her own, from the last time she'd visited. She unlocked the door and shone the flashlight inside.

The tapestry still hung as it had for longer than most could imagine. Just the sight of it made her sigh with relief. It was a relic of the Tufa's old country, brought when they crossed the ocean to the jagged mountains that had since become the rolling, soft-sloped Appalachians. Stitched into the ancient fabric were the faces of the original Tufa, many of which could still be seen, if you knew how to look, on current residents of Cloud County.

She closed the door, locked it again, and then leaned back wearily against it. This was great news for the Tufa, but it did nothing at all for her. It didn't replace the Overbay family history, which had gone literally up in smoke. It didn't bring back Rockhouse, and it didn't send Bo-Kate Wisby back into exile. The enchantment protecting the tapestry had worked, but the magic that was supposed to protect the Tufa had been proved fragile and insubstantial when the threat came from within the community itself.

She wanted to cry. She could always blame it on the acrid, smoky air. But this wasn't the time. The Tufa's greatest artifact was safe, at least, and would remain so. Now she had to protect the Tufa themselves.

She ascended the stairs and waved to Snowy and Carding as soon as she saw them.

"Everything okay?" Snowy asked as she approached.

"It's fine," she said. "But we need to close the cellar off with a door or something. Something we can padlock. I don't want to take any chances."

"Surely she ain't gonna try again," Carding said.

"I have no idea what she might do," Bliss said as she took off the boots. "I just know we have to be ready for anything."

She turned around, and Mandalay stood behind her. The girl wore a heavy coat and snow boots, and carried a guitar. "If you'd excuse us, Orpheus, I need to speak with Bliss privately. Thank you for coming out in this weather to help."

"Always a pleasure, never a chore," Carding said with a nod.

Bliss followed Mandalay down the hill toward the frozen pond. When they were out of earshot, she said, "I just heard. The storm knocked out our power last night, and all our cell phones were dead."

Bliss nodded slowly. "Mine, too. Someone had to come tell me at the fire station."

"I assume it's still okay?"

Bliss nodded. "She didn't find the way down."

"I don't have any words of consolation for you. I don't know what happened. I can't imagine why we were cut off like that, except that the night winds wanted things to proceed without anyone interfering. That's small comfort, I know."

"I don't want comfort. I want Bo-Kate Wisby's head on a platter."

"That's not going to solve the problem, either. We have to know what she wants, and why she came back. And how she came back."

"Why?"

"Yes, exactly."

"No, I mean, why do we need to know these things? She was cast out once, for just cause. Isn't that reason enough to cast her out again? Or even something more permanent?"

Mandalay saw something in Bliss's eyes she'd never seen before: hatred. It both frightened and saddened her to see this steadfast woman so badly wrenched asunder. "Bliss, it may come to that. And when it's over, you may have every reason to scream at me for not acting sooner, or with more force. But for right now, I really feel we need to know more. If we were meant to just stop her, then we would've done it yesterday."

"If you're reading it right."

"There's always that."

Mandalay continued to look steadily up into Bliss's face, until the taller woman blinked and turned away. "All right. I won't ever go against you, you know that. You always have my loyalty."

"I know, and I treasure it."

"But I'm very angry."

"So am I."

They were silent for a moment; then Bliss nodded at the guitar case. "Where are you off to?"

Mandalay couldn't repress a little smile. "Would you believe . . . I have a date?"

———

Mandalay walked into the Pair-A-Dice roadhouse and propped her guitar case by the door. Even at midday, the place was fairly full, mostly with old men still gossiping about Rockhouse's funeral and the arson at the Overbay place. They looked up when the door opened, and a wave of surprise spread through the room, silencing all conversation. The young inheritor of the Tufa legacy did not often show up unaccompanied and unannounced.

The Pair-A-Dice was a rectangular cinder-block building, windowless and with only one visible door, set back from the highway in the center of a gravel parking lot. Two enormous cutouts of dice on the roof were the only signage. Like many things to do with the Tufa, the place could be found only by those meant to find it. Unlike other things, the roadhouse could be found by outsiders, usually musicians who, for one reason or another, were open to the magic that dwelled in music, no matter what the source.

Most of those present belonged to Rockhouse's group; the old bootlegger's cave they used for their meeting place was inhospitable during the winter, so they had to gather elsewhere. The few women still wore mourning black, but no one seemed terribly sad.

The kitchen was in full swing for lunch, and the smell of fresh burgers filled the room. Mandalay hung her coat on the last remaining empty wall hook, then went to the small stage in the corner. An old Yamaha speaker was the only thing on the wooden platform. She sat the edge of the stage, took out her guitar, and idly noodled on it.

She couldn't believe that news of the fire had not reached her until that morning. She wanted to berate people for not driving out to get her, or using one of the other ways open to the Tufa. But she'd realized after talking to Bliss that something deliberately kept the news from her, just as Bliss's own cell phone had been drained of energy. And by waiting until now to let her know, it had given her time to rest and clear her head.

Well, sort of clear her head.

Even as she gazed down at her fingers, though, she felt all her watchers. Conversation returned, but people spoke in whispers. She heard the unmistakable click of cell phone cameras, and that made her angry: What the hell was so interesting about a girl playing guitar, a girl they all knew and had known all her life?

She raised her eyes and saw a dozen heads snap around, looking anywhere but at her. That made her smile, so she did it twice more.

Arshile, the head cook, came through the crowd with a cup. He placed it on the stage beside her, then stood back and made a quick, complex gesture with his right hand. He said, "Thought you could use some hot chocolate, it being so cold and all."

She smiled. "I sure won't turn it down. Thank you, sir. How much do I owe you?"

"On the house. I only make it for myself, nobody else drinks it."

"Much appreciated." She noticed a Band-Aid on his forehead. "What happened to you?"

"That? Oh, got it at Bliss's house yesterday. Beam nicked me when it fell." He paused, uncertain, then blurted, "Is something going on here today?"

"Like what?"

"Like . . . something to bring you here. I mean, after the funeral and the fire, and all . . ."

"I'm meeting Luke Somerville."

"Elgin Somerville's oldest boy?"

"That's the one. We're gonna play a little. Hang out."

"Nothing . . . bigger going on?" he asked apprehensively.

"Nothing bigger."

Arshile nodded thoughtfully. "I reckon that's all right."

I reckon I don't need your permission, Mandalay thought but didn't say.

He nodded, made another hand gesture, then went back to

the kitchen. If he thought that someone so important to the Tufa should have better things to do with her time, he was smart enough to keep it to himself.

Mandalay strummed a few chords, inevitably segueing into "Paranoid." She wondered why that particular song suddenly obsessed her. Then again, she practically felt the rumors running through the crowd, all speculations as to why she was here, now, alone. Maybe it was just the right song at the right time.

The front door opened again and Luke entered. He was thoroughly wrapped against the weather, and only his distinctive, lanky walk identified him until he started removing layers. Static made his black hair stick out in odd directions. He banged his guitar case on chairs and people's legs, and muttered, "Excuse me, sir," as he crossed the room. He dropped his coat and gloves on the floor and sat down beside her on the edge of the stage. "Hi."

"Hi."

"I, uh . . . don't know any of the hand signals I'm supposed to use to show respect."

She looked away as she felt her cheeks flush. "That's all right. I invited you, remember?"

"Yeah. That must've been quite a walk from your place. Did you get a ride?"

"No."

It took him a moment to get the implication. "Ah. I guess . . . I ain't never been able to do that. Had to get my uncle to drop me off. In his truck, not . . . the other way."

"You're young. It'll come. Just keep listening and playing."

"Why didn't you do it the other night when you were lost, then?"

"I didn't need to. You came along first." She looked back down at her guitar once more, blushing again. Suddenly she was entirely twelve years old, and sitting beside a boy she liked, the *first* boy she liked "that way."

Luke looked away as well, but he smiled. He took out his own guitar, an old Sunburst with a cracked body. He positioned it across his lap and said, "What you want to play?"

"You pick."

"How 'bout 'Lost Highway'?"

"The Hank song?"

"Yeah."

"The way he played it, or like Jason and the Scorchers?"

"I ain't never heard that, so I reckon like Hank."

"You need to hear Jason. But you picked the song, so you start."

He did, strumming the chords with big nervous strokes. She picked a simple lead, trying very hard not to show him up. He was a beginner; she had more musical experience to draw on than he could possibly imagine.

He sang with a plainspoken earnestness that more than made up for any problems with his still-changing voice. Somehow even at his tender age he found a way to connect to the aching sense of doom Hank put in the song.

Mandalay knew that Hank had once played that song on this very spot, when he got lost driving between gigs and had no money to pay for his drinks. The people here hadn't believed it was him until his voice echoed off these same walls; then they'd listened, rapt, aware that this was one of those times that would be passed down through generations, each teller tasked with bringing it to life for the next listener.

Luke couldn't know that, of course, except maybe by rumor. The Somervilles hadn't been present that night, and even if they had, she doubted old Seaton Somerville, Luke's grandfather, was open enough to take in what had happened. He would've only seen a drunken, prematurely old man with a twisted spine, not the angel that Hank became when he sang.

"Not bad," Luke said when they finished.

"No, it almost sounded like a song."

"You can sure pick a little, for a girl," he teased.

"And you sing pretty good, for a boy. Want to try something I like?"

"Sure."

"I need the piano. Come on."

She led him over to the piano in the corner, beneath the big industrial heater that hung from the ceiling. Since the air blew out and away, it was actually cooler there than in the rest of the stuffy room. It was also much dimmer, since the light fixture that hung beside the heater always blew its bulbs in winter.

The piano was an old Schiller upright, the finish worn in places and the white keys stained from decades of use. The instrument's workings, though, were pristine; at the Pair-A-Dice, instruments simply didn't wear out. Mandalay sat on the bench, lifted the cover from the keys, and positioned her feet on the pedals. Her big snow boots made it awkward at first.

With no preamble, she began to play. Although she'd never played this song on the piano, she had a flawless ear, and could pretty much re-create any song she'd heard. Her hands pressed the keys firmly but gently, creating a rolling sound that propelled the melody.

When she got to the last verse, she realized at least one reason why this song haunted her. She couldn't look at Luke as she sang:

> *You're making me nervous*
> *Stop standing so close*
> *Do I deserve this*
> *Or is this a hoax*
> *You're like a mystery*
> *That's hard to avoid*
> *Either you're out to get me*
> *Or I'm just paranoid. . . .*

When she finished, she sat back and waited for Luke's reaction.

"What's that called?" he asked.

"'Paranoid.'"

"You write it?"

"No. Woman named Alice Peacock, from over in Nashville."

"Never heard of her."

"She's probably never heard of you, either."

He laughed, and she felt an unexpected rush at the realization that she could *tease* him. It was something she'd always wanted but never found: a friend unintimidated enough to accept teasing, and give it right back.

"Where'd you hear it?" he asked.

"On YouTube. They got a channel on there where a bunch of women songwriters have to write a new song every week for a year, based on what they call a 'prompt.'"

"That don't sound like too much fun."

"You ever written a song?"

"No."

"Well, then, you don't know, do you?"

"I figure you cain't write a song until you're in the right mood. And I know a good song when I hear it."

"I hope so, because this is a good song."

He sighed. "Yeah, it is."

"Does it bother you to admit that?"

"Well, we've been taught that everything from Garth Brooks on ain't real music, it's just commercials to sell you things."

"Rockhouse's idea?"

"Yeah, but my daddy bought the program. He won't let us listen to the radio because of it, we have to play CDs or even old records he's still got."

She looked at him seriously. "That's *not right*, Luke. There's good music everywhere, from every time. Sure, it may take a little work to find it now, since the radio don't play anything good anymore, but it's out there." She paused, aware that her next words would irrevocably change her relationship with Luke. "Would you like me to burn some stuff off on a CD for you?"

Luke shrugged as if it were no big deal. "Yeah, sure. Whatever." But he blushed.

She felt yet another blush creep up her cheeks, too. "Okay, I will."

Bo-Kate looked out the passenger window as they approached the Pair-A-Dice. The place looked no different than it had the last time she'd seen it, so long ago. A few of the vehicles parked out front were newer, but many were not; and when they got out and walked across the frozen gravel parking lot toward the building, she heard the music bleeding through as always: someone playing the old piano with skill and heart.

"Are we to burn this down, too?" Nigel asked dryly.

"Ha. No, smart-ass, we're just here to visit."

How long will this take?" Nigel asked.

"Not long. Just need to start announcing myself to people, now that Rockhouse is off the stage."

"Don't you think they know you're around by now?"

"But they don't know *why* yet."

"What if they don't like your announcement?"

"Is that what you're worried about?"

"Not entirely. I'm also worried if it's safe for a gentleman of my complexion to enter this place. I see no windows, and only one door."

"Are you the fire marshal?" she shot back.

"No, I'm a black person in the American South walking into a bar most likely filled with Caucasian people from the lower echelons of education and socioeconomics. It's not exactly Morehouse College."

She laughed and kissed his cheek. "Ten minutes, loverboy. I promise. Just be quiet and look pretty."

The door squeaked loudly as they entered. Instantly they were struck by heat, and the smell of accumulated bodies and unwashed clothes. It was a musty, distinctive odor, and Nigel recalled something similar from his visit to a homeless shelter soup kitchen when he was a teen living on the streets. It brought back feelings he tried very hard to keep buried: the helplessness, the gnawing hunger, and the determination to make his life better. He liked people to think he'd always been the way he was now.

Coats were hung three deep on the hooks just inside. Bo-Kate took off hers, but Nigel kept his brown leather jacket on. If he didn't smile, it made him quite intimidating, and he was sure he'd need as much of that as possible.

He observed the crowd seated at the tables talking and drinking. They all had the same black hair and dusky complexion, like part of some giant extended family. When they all turned to look at Bo-Kate, the resemblance was even more pronounced. He'd always assumed the rumors of inbreeding in the mountains were just that, rumors. But he might have to reevaluate.

Like a slow wave, quiet spread through the crowd. Even the cook and two waitresses stopped serving. The only sounds were the hum of the big heater in the corner and the squeak of chairs as people shifted their weight.

"Well, ain't y'all a big scary bunch," Bo-Kate said loudly. "All of you staring and glaring at me. Reckon I should pee my panties and run away, Nigel?"

"I don't . . . reckon you should," he said, the unfamiliar word awkward on his tongue.

"Nah, me, neither. In fact, I think I need to stay around. How would y'all feel about that?"

No one replied.

She pulled an empty chair away from a table and propped one foot on it. "I suppose y'all know I've been busy since I've been here. We won't get into that; what's done is done. Here's my offer. We've been two tribes forever. And as a smart guy named Frankie said, when two tribes go to war, a point is all that you can score. All the skirmishes, all the fighting and feuding, where has it gotten us? I mean, *look* at us. Most of us are on food stamps, ain't got no insurance, drive cars older than our children, and farm this damn rocky-ass soil just to stay alive. Shouldn't we be able to do better?"

"We do just fine," someone muttered.

"Because we've never thought we deserved any more," she said emphatically. "When y'all kicked me out, I had to make my own way. I saw the world, more than any of you ever have. I saw what I was capable of, and what *all* the Tufa are capable of. Every damn one of you could be as good a session musician as anyone in Nashville or L.A. And once we start spreading out to those places and word gets around, we'll be able to bring the big names *here,* to work with *us.* Just like Muscle Shoals."

She paused to let that sink in, and watched confusion give way to guarded consideration.

"Come on, you know I'm right," she pressed. "Remember when the Blair Family used to travel around singing in the summer? Everybody for a hundred miles in any direction would be sorry to see them go, because when they left, they took the music with them. We can do that to the whole damn *world*. And I only ask one little thing of you."

She let that settle. The worried expressions delighted her. She continued, "It's a real treat to see you shiver with antici. . . ." She looked back at Nigel.

". . . Pation," he finished flatly.

"So you want to know what it is?" she asked.

No one nodded, but they all watched her intently.

"I want you to change the name of this town from Needsville to Scarborough."

Everyone sat back and looked around, startled by this unexpectedly arbitrary request. Even Nigel was taken aback; she'd never mentioned *this* to him.

Bo-Kate glanced back at Nigel and winked.

Hidden in the dark corner in the shadow of the heater, Mandalay clenched her fists in anger. She realized Bo-Kate had no idea she was there.

Luke asked softly, "Who is that?"

"Bo-Kate Wisby."

Luke did not seem to know the name. "Is she important?"

"She's trying to be."

"You gonna stop her?"

"Not while she's Blofelding," Mandalay said. It was her father's term for villains who told captured heroes all their evil plans. "Might as well find out what she's got in mind."

He nodded, and scooted closer to her on the bench. She found the gesture both comforting and oddly empowering.

"Think about it," Bo-Kate said. "Nobody's going to come to a town with 'Needy' right there in its name. But Scarborough: 'Are you going to Scarborough Studios?' That would work on T-shirts, flyers, banner ads online, key chains, anything. We could get anyone to come here. Even Garth Brooks."

"Garth Brooks," the crowd repeated reverently. To many, he was the last true country singer star, one whose physical appearance didn't matter, only his music.

"I've got the industry connections. I've got the wherewithal to make the initial investment, and the marketing savvy to get out the word. That's why I want to take over for Rockhouse. More than that, I want to be in charge of all of Cloud County. I shouldn't have to run all my decisions by some tween girl, should I?"

There were murmurs of assent. Then Junior Damo said loudly, "Maybe we got someone already in mind."

Bo-Kate laughed contemptuously. "Who's that, Junior? You?"

"Why not let Mandalay take over everything?" Whizdom said loudly. "Least she wasn't never sung out because she was dangerous as a rabid coral snake."

"She's a *child*, that's why," Bo-Kate said, ignoring the insult. "She's a *little girl*. She might have more history in her head than a dozen of us put together, but all she's got to filter it through is some little kid's brain filled up with *The Hunger Games* and One Direction. What sort of decisions will that let her make?" She walked over to Whizdom and looked down at him in his chair. "Admit it, my idea sounds good." Then she turned and looked straight at Mandalay in the shadows. A slow, predatory smile spread across her face. "Doesn't it, Mandalay?"

Mandalay felt a sudden jolt of an unfamiliar emotion as her gaze met Bo-Kate's: terror. Her heart thudded, sweat trickled down from her hairline, and she could hardly catch her breath. She had been worried in the past, even apprehensive, but never this thoroughly *scared*. And despite everyone turning to look at her, she couldn't get a word out in response.

Luke saw it, too. He knew exactly what she was feeling. Fear was an old friend to him, the first emotion he remembered feeling, and the last one he expected to feel before he died. He reached down, took her hand, and squeezed it once.

The connection to the boy sent a grounding, cooling sensation through her. The terror receded, and she rose from the piano bench fully in control once again. She stepped out of the shadows and said, "Bo-Kate, the last time you were here, you left a trail of dead behind you. Planning to do that again if you don't get your way?"

Bo-Kate bowed her head in a mocking gesture of respect.

"Mandalay, that was a long time ago. A *long* time. I was impatient and immature. Since then, I've grown up, mastered both myself and the world. And now . . ." She grinned, showing off her perfect Tufa teeth. "I'm perfectly willing to accept your surrender in front of these people."

Now everyone else was frightened, looking from the woman to the girl and back. No one came to the Pair-A-Dice expecting to be caught between Armageddon and Apocalypse, yet here they were.

Mandalay was calm. "I'm not a warrior, Bo-Kate. I can't 'surrender' to you. I have a job, and I'll keep doing it until my time is done."

"And if your time is done now?"

"I don't think it is. And I'd know."

"Because you're so damn smart?"

"Yes."

"Smarter than me?"

"I see farther than you. And I always will."

"Maybe that's why you can't see what's right in front of you."

"Good thing I can, then," a new voice said. "And I *am* a warrior."

Everyone turned. Bronwyn Hyatt and Bliss Overbay stood just inside the doorway. Both women were angry, but only Bronwyn gave her fury voice.

"I see a murdering, treacherous bitch," Bronwyn continued. "One who was lucky to walk out alive when she got in trouble before, when she should've been finished once and for all. And that kind of luck doesn't strike twice."

"Careful, darlin', don't get *too* wrought up," Bo-Kate shot back. "With that belly, you look like you're about to shit a pumpkin."

Bliss moved between Bronwyn and Bo-Kate. "Say something to me, Bo-Kate."

"I've got nothing to say to you."

"Really? I just assumed, since you burned down my house, you might have a few choice words. I know I do."

Bo-Kate showed no sign of fear. "Let's hear them, then."

"Go home, Bo-Kate. Pack your stuff and go back to Nashville where you belong. This all needs to stop."

"But I don't want it to stop, Bliss," she taunted. "I want it to keep going, until this adorable little Munchkin sees the light and steps aside. It doesn't have to affect you anymore, or Miss Fertility there at all; when my plans all work out, I'm sure the new stores will need salesclerks. And cocktail bars can always use waitresses, if she gets her figure back."

"That's generous of you," Bliss said evenly, through clenched teeth. "But it's not going to happen."

Bo-Kate shrugged. "Then I'll just have to find people more loyal. Shouldn't be too hard, once folks realize how much better off they'd be. And remember that, everybody. Nobody has to be poor. There's a way out, and I've got the map. Think about it."

She turned and winked at Mandalay, then took Nigel by the arm and led him out. As they passed, Bronwyn and Nigel exchanged a look. Bo-Kate did not see it, but Bliss did.

After they were gone, Mandalay joined Bliss and Bronwyn at the door. "What was that about?" Bliss asked Bronwyn.

"What?"

"The way you and that black guy looked at each other."

"I don't know. I just wanted to intimidate him, so I gave him the hairy eyeball. But I don't think he's as much into this as she thinks he is."

"He's having second thoughts," Mandalay said with certainty.

"So what do we do?" Bronwyn asked.

"I have an idea," Mandalay said. "But I need to think through."

"Just so you know, being pregnant doesn't affect my shooting," Bronwyn said.

"I think your hormones are affecting your judgment, though," Bliss said with a little smile. "And if anyone has a right to wipe that little smirk off her face, it's me."

"My judgment is just fine," Bronwyn said. "It's getting my ass kicked from the inside that makes me want to kick a little ass on the outside."

Mandalay turned around and looked for Luke, but he was gone. He couldn't have gotten out the front door past them, so he must have slipped out through the kitchen. He'd taken his guitar, too.

She choked at the realization, and something burned in her eyes, but she pushed it down before Bliss or Bronwyn noticed. She had huge, possibly world-shaking issues on her mind—so why did this little crush feel just as important, and far more urgent?

"You need to say something to them," Bliss said quietly.

Mandalay looked around at the other Tufa. The ones who weren't staring directly at her were talking in low tones among themselves. They weren't angry, or even upset; to them, Bo-Kate's offer sounded eminently sensible. Hell, on the surface, it did to Mandalay, too.

But she was too choked, physically and otherwise, by Luke's departure to manage any sort of leadership. She said, "I've got nothing to say. You two can go."

"I don't think we should—"

Mandalay made a fierce, unmistakable gesture with her fingers, one that asserted her authority in a way that left no room for discussion. Bliss and Bronwyn exchanged a look, then replied with gestures of respect, and departed.

17

"Well," Nigel said as he looked around an hour and a half later, "were one to look up 'quaint' in the dictionary, one might find an illustration of this place."

They got out of the SUV, the only vehicle parked at the visitors' center. Cricket, Tennessee, was what remained of a Victorian-era plan for an isolated Utopia of creative minds and hard workers. A dozen small, elaborate buildings lined the highway, all built in an unmistakably English style. They were painted in colorful pastels and connected by wooden sidewalks. Now, in the winter, there were no tourists visiting the café or shops, and apparently no workers, because the center's doors were locked. Nigel rattled them again to make certain, then peered inside. He saw the dim shapes of various rustic exhibits, but no sign of movement.

"Well, it appears our drive was for naught. What did you want to show me?"

"Oh, I'll still show you. Come on." She led him past a restored schoolhouse, through a break in the trees, to the front porch of a green building with a bell tower.

"Is this a church?" Nigel asked.

"It's a library," Bo-Kate said. "All the books in here are at least a hundred and fifty years old."

Again he rattled the locked door, which gave a bit. "You'd think they'd have better security."

"Wouldn't matter," Bo-Kate said. She stepped back and kicked where the double doors met. It took three tries, but eventually they sprang open.

Nigel looked around. He saw no sign of anyone else, and no alarm sounded from within. "Uhm, Bo-Kate, my delight, is this—?"

"Come on," she said as she strode inside. He followed.

The Roy Howard Library consisted of one big, high-ceilinged room. Tall windows rose on both sides, shuttered with heavy wooden louvered blinds. Books were displayed on the reading table. The air smelled musty and exceptionally dry; Nigel assumed a dehumidifier was responsible. Shelves lined the walls, and there were two freestanding shelf units as well.

Bo-Kate pulled a small halogen flashlight from her purse and shone it around. She strode straight to the back of the room, to the end of one of the standing shelves. "Stop gawking," she said. "You've never seen a library before?"

"I've never broken into one, no."

"Come here. This is what I brought you to see."

He joined her at the back of the shelf, where a small painting in a thick, heavy frame hung. A group of fairies stood among flowers and weeds, watching the figure in the middle of the throng. This subject's face was hidden, but he wore an odd cap and raised a double-bladed axe above his head. A hickory nut at his feet seemed to be the blow's target.

"What's this?" he asked.

"Ever seen it before?"

"It looks vaguely familiar."

"It's called 'The Fairy Feller's Master Stroke.'"

"Ah," he said dryly. "Fairies."

She ignored his tone. "I want you to look at some of these faces. Try to remember them."

"Why?"

"Pay attention, Nigel. This is Bliss Overbay, who you saw at the Pair-A-Dice. And this is her sister, Curnen. Up here is Marshall Goins. And this is Snowy Rainfield, before his hair turned white."

"And this gentleman in the middle with the axe?"

She laughed. "I visited him on top of that mountain." She reached into her purse, pulled out the tiny axe, and held it up to the painting. It was identical in shape and size.

"So someone painted a bunch of locals into this?"

"Not exactly. This was done in 1864."

"I don't understand what you're telling me, then." He kept glancing at the still-open door, expecting guards or police, or at least an irate librarian.

She shone the light on a particular part of the painting. "Who does this look like."

He bent close to see. "You."

"That's right."

"So you knew the artist?"

"No. I just saw him when he sketched this."

"A hundred years ago."

"Time doesn't work the same—"

"—for everybody, as you keep saying."

"All these people are *here*. You're likely to meet them. You need to know what they really are."

"Fairies?"

"That's one word."

"That's the word you keep using. What's another?"

"Tuatha de Danaan. But that's a mouthful, so over time it got shortened to 'Tufa.'"

He indicated the man in the center. "So to clarify: this old

man with the axe is the same old man you visited and disem-
fingered."

She slapped his hand away from the painting. "Don't touch
it!"

"Well, why isn't it under glass?"

"You don't put glass over an oil painting, you doofus."

She took out a nail file and, with four quick swipes, scratched
off the head from the Fairy Feller. Then she walked away, whistling. Nigel took out his phone and snapped a couple of quick
pictures of the painting, then rushed to catch up.

Snowy Rainfield lay naked on his back on the bed at the Wildwood Motel while Tain Wisby, also naked, straddled him. Despite the snow outside, the room was hot, and both of them
gleamed with sweat. The dim afternoon light bled in around the
closed curtains, and the only sounds were the wind and their
own exertions.

"Snowy, why don't we do this more often?" Tain asked, brush-
ing her bangs back from her face.

"Your dance card's usually pretty full," Snowy said, lifting
her with his hips.

"Yeah, but I'd always work you in."

He laughed as much as his heaving chest would allow. "That's
mighty considerate of you."

"When I was born, the night winds told me I could either
have a great memory, or be a great lay." She frowned in pretend
confusion. "Aw, shoot, now I forgot what I was going to tell you."

He laughed. She bent slowly and kissed him until they both
had to break for air. "Working you in is the best I'll ever be able
to do, Snowy, you know that," she said. "I am who I am."

"I know. It doesn't bother me."

"Really?"

"Really. And you and I both know that if I hung around too much, you'd get bored with me."

He reached up and cupped her breasts, at which she sighed and moved her hips against him. He gasped and gritted his teeth, but he knew she wasn't ready to let him finish. She would hold him right here, on the edge, until she got what she wanted. That had been the danger of this rendezvous, and while it certainly had its attraction, he also knew how thoroughly in her power he'd placed himself. Tain had the talent of being whatever the man with her wanted her to be, and at this moment, she was the most beautiful and arousing thing he'd ever seen. And he wanted to finish in her so bad, it was almost agony.

Still, he'd experienced it before, and he was a Tufa like she was, so his life and soul weren't in danger. Men from outside Cloud County, with no Tufa blood in them, found themselves so obsessed with Tain that her subsequent disinterest in them led to broken marriages, shattered families, and suicides. Tain had a body count higher than most people knew, but she remained blithely unconcerned. Her conscience was clear; she never seduced anyone who didn't make the first move.

Snowy rose on his elbows. "Can we talk now?"

"Talk?" she said with a sensual laugh. "Sure. You want me to tell you what it feels like to have your cock inside me?"

"Honey, I'd like nothing better. But I mean about your cousin."

She lowered herself so that her breasts were in his face. He took one hard nipple between his lips and sucked. She hissed at the sensation and rotated her hips against him. "You sure that's what you want to talk about, Snowy?"

"I'm sure," he said, his mouth still full.

She sat up, put her hands on his chest, and pushed him flat on the bed. "What do you want to know?"

"How did she get back here?"

"I don't know, honestly. She just showed up and moved back into her old room with her boyfriend."

"Boyfriend?"

"Some black English guy."

"What did she say?'

"Nothing, really. You know how she is. She talked a lot, but it was all just . . . snark."

"What did they do today?"

"Beats me. I've been at work."

"Is there a way to stop her?"

"Shoot her in the head like a zombie? Other than that, I don't know of one."

"And you don't know what she's up to?"

"No, I swear. But she went somewhere alone last night."

"Without her boyfriend?"

Tain nodded. Then she bent and kissed him furiously, crushing their lips, mashing their teeth against each other. His hands slid to her hips and pulled her hard against him as he rose beneath her.

He kissed around to her ear and whispered. "You must have some idea where she went last night, Tain."

She pulled his hand between their bodies to cup her breast. "She's family, Snowy. I can't rat her out."

He gently pinched her nipple, and enjoyed the shudder that went through her whole body. "She's not family anymore. She was sung out. And if she's back, it's bad for everyone."

She sat back up and slid her hand between them, to stimulate herself. "I do know that when I went outside to ride the night wind. . . ." She sucked in air and yanked her hand away, not wanting to come yet. "I didn't see her."

He watched her face wrench into what might have been a desperate grimace of pain as she fought to hold back. He had to concentrate with all his might to follow her implications. He used his thumb to pick up where she left off. "She went into slow time?"

"Oh, God . . . oh, Jesus," Tain said. She grabbed his wrist, but couldn't bring herself to pull his hand away. "Yes . . . I think so. I think there's . . . something or someone hidden in there . . . waiting for her. . . ."

And then they couldn't resist any longer, either of them. Their mutual cry would've summoned the police or at least the guests in the adjacent rooms, if the woman who ran the motel hadn't known all about Tain and put them far away from anyone else.

Later, exhausted, they lay entwined on top of the covers, the musky smell of their bodies enveloping them in something neither of them really expected.

Snowy kissed Tain's shoulder. "I could fall in love with you pretty easy, Tain."

She didn't move. The words hung in the air, echoing like a scream or a song.

"I'd be a terrible wife, Snowy," she said at last. "And a worse mother. I'm not meant for just one man. I've always known it. And the thing is, I like it."

"I know. I'm trying to decide if I can live with it."

She rose and looked at him. In the low light, his white hair looked silver. "I can't be with someone who can just 'live with it.' You'd start to resent it sooner or later. If you want to be with me, you have to like it, too."

"Like that you go out with other men all the time?"

She nodded. "And like that I stay home with you."

He looked into her eyes. They had known each other since they were children, and watched each other grow up. Snowy had seen Tain move among all the Tufa boys and many non-Tufa ones, leaving broken hearts and secret smiles in her wake. He had the same Tufa nature as she did, but Tain had it in a special way, and there was no changing it. She was meant to be a fairy lover, immune to love herself but inspiring it with all the men who crossed her path.

"Do you say this to every man who sticks around after you're done?" he asked.

She smiled a little. "Sometimes. If I think it's what they want to hear."

"And you think it's what I want to hear?"

"You brought up love."

He ran his fingers through her black hair as much as the tangles allowed. "You almost had me there, Tain. Almost."

"Oh, Snowy, I can have you whenever I want." She kissed him, nipping at his lower lip. "See?"

He looked down and saw that he was, in fact, ready for action again. "Well, look at that," he said. He rolled atop her, and they slowly moved their bodies together, no urgency this time, just a lazy, mutual enjoyment.

Leshell Harris came into the Pair-A-Dice and waited for her eyes to adjust. She heard murmuring and whispers, and at first thought they were directed at her. Then she saw her stepdaughter seated on the piano bench, staring at the keys but not touching them.

Parenting a girl who could, at any time, switch from being a typical preteen to the leader of her entire people was challenging, and at times like this, only the immense affection Leshell felt for the girl kept her from running screaming into the woods. She worked her way around the room.

Mandalay had been less than a year old when Leshell and Darnell started dating, barely two when they married, and so by all rights, Mandalay should think of Leshell as her only mother. Yet even as a preverbal child, at times Mandalay would look out at the forest or sky and Leshell knew she was seeing things no one else could. As the girl grew, Leshell found those moments more and more unsettling, contrasted as they were with times of normal childhood activity. And although she didn't do it any-more, for a time Mandalay had prefaced statements with, "Mommy told me . . . ," and Leshell knew she hadn't meant her. The spirit world spoke to the girl, and everyone knew it.

She skirted the wall until she reached the piano. "Who called you?" Mandalay asked before Leshell could speak.

"Bliss. She told me about the scene with Bo-Kate. She was . . . concerned."

"She should be." Mandalay continued to stare at the keys. "I'm lost."

Leshell sat down on the bench beside her. "I assume you don't mean like the other night."

"No." She trembled as if she wanted to say something, but couldn't decide where to start. "I'm lost just sitting here."

Leshell stroked the girl's hair. "Because . . . ?"

"Because the ancient me and the current me are both out of their depths."

Leshell scooted closer. "I can't speak to the ancient, but I might know something about the current." When Mandalay didn't con-tinue, Leshell guessed, "Is it about a boy?"

Mandalay half smiled. "I'm that much of a cliché, huh?"

"Is it a cliché to fall down when you're learning to ride a bike? We all do it, and it's pretty damn scary the first time for every-body."

Mandalay turned and looked at her. The ache in the girl's eyes shot straight to Leshell's heart. "He ran out on me," she said softly. "He didn't even stay to see how things turned out."

"He's a child."

"So am I."

"Not in the same way. Imagine if you didn't have all that time in your head, that instead you had only twelve years to pull ex-perience from. That's what he has."

The girl's eyes shone with unshed tears. "So it's always going to be like this? I'm going to be this different to every boy I meet?"

"I can't speak to that. I'm just saying, him being scared makes sense. Only you can decide how it changes what you feel about him."

Mandalay put her arms around Leshell. Her stepmother hugged her tight. "You'll be okay, baby girl," she said softly.

And Mandalay felt, for that moment, that she would be. Then she remembered Bo-Kate. And not even Leshell's hug could help with that. It was time for Mandalay to get over herself and get back to work.

18

An hour later, just after sunset, Bo-Kate strode into the Catamount Corner as if she owned it—which, of course, was part of her plan. She whistled cavalierly as she looked around at the excessive countrified decorations, imagining the bonfire all that lace and pastel-painted wood would make. Nigel locked the front door behind them and stood with his back to it, again in "intimidating black guy" mode.

Peggy Goins came out of the stairwell that led to the second floor holding a bundle of towels. She froze when she saw the other woman.

"What do you want here, Bo-Kate? Planning to burn me down, too?"

"Is something on fire?" Bo-Kate asked innocently.

"You best get on the road," Peggy said, putting the towels on the front counter. "'Bout the only thing that'll save you is to not be here when they come lookin'."

"When who comes looking? The First Daughters? The Silent Sons? Some other inane secret club? Maybe the Boy Scouts or the Brownies?"

"Get out, Miss Wisby," Peggy said. She now stood defensively in front of the counter, feet apart and fists clenched.

"Peggy, I'll give you one last chance to make this civilized. Agree to sell me this place right now, and nobody important to you has to get hurt."

Peggy made a sharp gesture with her right hand, followed by a complicated one with her left.

Bo-Kate laughed. "Good God, Peggy, you still believe in that nonsense? When you kicked me out, all that went with it. None of it has any effect on me anymore, if it ever did."

"You'll get this place over my dead body, Bo-Kate," Peggy snapped.

Bo-Kate shrugged. "That's not really a problem."

"Stop," a new voice said calmly.

They all turned. Mandalay Harris stood in the entrance to the café. She hadn't come through the front door where Nigel stood guard, or any of the other entrances behind Peggy. She'd simply appeared, in jeans and a heavy winter coat, her black hair peeking out from under a knit cap.

"Let's talk this all out," the girl said, "before anyone else—"

Bo-Kate blinked in surprise, then reached in her purse, withdrew a small revolver, and fired at Mandalay from ten feet.

"Bo-Kate!" Nigel shouted just before the shot rang out.

Mandalay vanished. Peggy screamed.

The gunshot echoed in the room, and all three stared at the spot the girl had just occupied. The weapon in Bo-Kate's hand did not shake. "Fuck me," she gasped, both astounded and delighted at her own impulsive act.

"Indeed," Nigel said. He took the gun from her fingers. "Perhaps we should—"

Bo-Kate grabbed the gun back and pointed it at Peggy. Her voice giddy, she said, "Say you'll do it, Peggy. Or I'll shoot you, then—"

But in the few moments Bo-Kate had been distracted, Peggy grabbed her own weapon, a shotgun she kept behind the counter, and had it leveled at Bo-Kate. "I may not know your dyin' dirge, Bo-Kate Wisby, but I bet this buckshot does. You sing your song, I'll sing mine, and we'll see which one gets an encore."

The smell of gunpowder lingered around them. Nigel leaned close and said, "I have to say, she has the upper hand. You might wound her, but her weapon will make an Italian mess of you. And possibly me, since I seem to be standing right beside you."

There was no amusement in Bo-Kate's face when she returned her gun to her purse. "All right, we'll call this one a draw, Peggy. But just remember, nothing you have it safe."

"As long as you're around? Maybe we should fix that, then."

Bo-Kate said nothing, just remained still until it was clear Peggy wouldn't shoot her in cold blood. Then she turned and walked out the front door. Nigel quickly followed.

Almost as soon as the door shut behind them, Mandalay said, "There's no reasoning with her, is there?"

Peggy looked over. Mandalay stood where she had before, in the doorway to the café. There was no sign of any injury from the gunshot. "No, there is not," Peggy said, and propped her shotgun against the nearest wall. She lit a cigarette with trembling fingers. "That bitch needs to be put down."

"You may be right. Hell, you *are* right. But who can do it? You just had the chance, and you couldn't."

"It's Bronwyn's job."

"Bronwyn's too pregnant right now."

"Then Bliss?"

"Killing Bo-Kate isn't the answer, Peggy. How did she even come back? We have to know. Otherwise, if we ever sing anyone out again . . ."

"And how do we find that out?"

"Tell the First Daughters to meet here tonight, at midnight. And . . ."

She looked down. Peggy, mistaking the look for fear, said, "Lord a'mighty, Mandalay, are you crying?"

Mandalay looked up with a wry smile. "No, Peggy," she said in that voice that rang with all the ages of the mountains around them. "I was actually about to laugh."

"About what?"

"About the look I imagined on your face when I tell you to call the Silent Sons, too."

Peggy fought to keep her expression neutral. "What can *they* do for us?"

"Not just for us, Peggy. For all the Tufa."

Bo-Kate drove the SUV ferociously around curves, skidding as she did. They were headed back to the Wisby place, or at least that seemed to be the general direction to Nigel.

"You took a shot," he said at last, "at a little girl."

"Hell, what lives in that little girl is the oldest thing in these hills."

"Perhaps. But I suspect that, had your shot found its mark, only the body of a little girl would've been found there."

She glared at him. "Are you questioning me again, Nigel?"

He was glad she couldn't see his hands tremble. "I have to on this one, Bo-Kate. There are simply some lines in the world, and cold-blooded child murder is one of them."

"Lines that you won't cross?"

"That I hoped you wouldn't, either. But no, I won't cross it."

Suddenly the gun was in her hand, the barrel an inch from his face. "Then what the fuck use are you?"

Nigel licked his lips. "I'd like to think my charm has value."

Bo-Kate's eyes flicked from the road back to him, and then she put the gun back down. She held up her own hand, which now trembled as much as his. "Goddamn, Nigel, that was a close one."

"It certainly was."

"That little girl you're so worried about isn't even human. She's . . . Fuck, I don't know *what* she is, really. I'm not sure anyone does, including her. But you saw her appear and disappear. Could a real human being do that?"

"You have a point."

She let out a long sigh. "But you're right, I shouldn't have tried to shoot her. It was pointless, and I knew that. It's just that when I saw her, I . . ."

"Lost it?"

She chuckled. Her temper was notorious among the venue owners and band managers she worked with, but Nigel understood that it was mostly an act, a buffer to prevent real trouble later on. This was something different, though.

"So," he said, hoping the storm had passed, "Where are we going now?"

"Back home. I found something in the woods the other night, and it's time to bring it out."

I know dark clouds will gather round me
I know my way is rough and steep
Yet golden fields lie just before me
Where God's redeemed shall ever sleep
I'm going there to see my father
He said he'd meet me when I come
I'm only going over Jordan
I'm only going over home

Byron and Fiddlin' John looked up as the sin eater entered the clearing. "That didn't take long," Byron said.

"Nope," the sin eater agreed as he took his spot.

"You looked kinda peaked," John observed.

"Must've been something I ate. What'd I miss?"

"'Bout three songs and four ounces," Fiddlin' John said.

Eli grinned. He understood where he was, and was one of the few non-Tufas who were able to slip in and out of fairy time at will. He did notice that his thoughts got fuzzier the longer he stayed, which meant that whenever he came back, he noticed things he hadn't before.

And this time, he noticed Byron Harley. And remembered Mandalay's confusion. Now, he was confused as well. Who *was* this big guy?

"Come on, then, let's keep it a'goin'," Fiddlin' John said, and led them into another chorus of "Wayfaring Stranger."

When they finished, Fiddlin' John held up his hand for silence. The only sound was the fire's crackling. Then the others heard it: a sobbing woman.

It grew louder, along with footsteps through the damp leaves. Byron stared into the darkness, and saw one shadow detach itself from the others and approach. As the firelight reached her, he saw that it was a young woman with red hair, without a coat or gloves, arms wrapped around herself against the cold. Her sobs had the weary, ragged quality of those that came after hours of crying.

Byron got to his feet and limped over to intercept her as she reached the clearing. "Hey, honey, you're okay now," he said, and draped his jacket over her shoulders. "Sit down and join us."

She put up no resistance as he guided her to the log and sat beside her. She was pretty, except for the way her eyes were swollen from crying.

"My name's Byron, honey. What's yours?"

"Stella," she whimpered. "Stella Kizer."

"Where're you from?"

"Michigan."

"You do know you're in Tennessee, right?"

She nodded. "We were staying in Needsville. My husband and me." At the mention of her husband, she began to sob anew.

Byron put one massive arm across her shoulders and drew her

close. He had three sisters, so he knew how emotional women could get. "There, honey, it's all right. We'll get you back to him."

She jumped up and wrenched away. "No! I can't go back. You don't know what I did, what I did to *him*!"

"Whatever you did," the sin eater said in a calm and knowing voice, "it wasn't your fault."

She choked out a sob that seemed to come from so deep inside her, it made them all ache in sympathy. "You *know*?"

"Yes, I do." Eli recognized her as one of the normal people who occasionally ended up in slow time after a major emotional trauma. And he knew what had happened to her at the Pair-A-Dice with Stoney Hicks, back when the boy had been a magnet for women. "If you want, I can take you back."

"No. I can't face my husband, not after . . . after what I did." She shrugged Byron's jacket off her shoulders and ran off into the woods again before any of them could stop her. In moments, her footsteps and sobs were gone.

Byron turned to the others. "Fellas, my leg ain't up to chasin' her, but one of you two should—"

"Doesn't matter," the sin eater said. "She's not going anywhere."

"She's pretty much going down the mountain," Byron said, annoyed. "And in the dark, without a coat, in the middle of winter. You keep telling me how dangerous it is—"

Eli reached for the jug. "Tell me something, Byron. You ever read 'Rip Van Winkle'?"

"I ain't much of a reader."

"Do you know the story?"

"He's someone who falls asleep for a long time, right?"

Eli nodded. "He met up with some supernatural folk, took a drink of some of their magic beer, and time stopped for him. It didn't for the outside world. That's what's happened to that girl."

"That's plumb crazy," Byron said, but something in the way Eli spoke made it sound plausible. And for the first time since he'd stumbled into the clearing, Byron felt the same rush of the fear and sorrow he'd felt up the mountain, at the site of the plane crash. He sat down, overwhelmed, and felt his eyes burn with tears.

"Here," Eli said, passing the jug. "You look like a fella whose wife just left him, and his dog ain't doin' too well, either."

Byron took a long swallow, luxuriating in the burn down his gullet and into his stomach. The emotions overwhelming him seemed to recede, leaving a kind of numbness that was different from simple drunkenness. But whatever it was, he was grateful for it. He passed the jug to Fiddlin' John and said, "You're being awful quiet."

"I think I want to get on down the mountain, too," he said quietly, as if worried he might disturb some delicate balance. "My daughter Rosa's likely to be worried about me."

"Your daughter comes with you?" Byron asked.

John nodded. "She calls herself Moonshine Kate."

Byron smiled. "Well, I'll be. I figured that was your wife or girlfriend or something."

"Nope, that's my baby girl."

Byron picked up his guitar and put it across his lap again. He started strumming, "My Man's a Jolly Railroad Man," which he knew by heart from one of those old scratchy 78s his father used to play. John smiled, too, and began to play along. Eli pulled out his Jew's harp and picked an occasional note, but he mainly watched the darkness in the direction the woman had disappeared.

He would lead Fiddlin' John Carson back down the mountain in the morning, because he knew that the man had years of life left to him. But he also knew Stella Kizer would not emerge from the forest for another twenty years, although mere hours would have passed to her. And as for Byron . . .

What the hell *was* he doing here? And where was he supposed to go?

19

Dinner at the Wisby household was tense as only family gatherings can be. Nigel grew up as one of two children, in a small row house with his mostly unemployed dad and bitter housewife mom, so he knew a thing or two about the dynamics at work. But nothing in his family compared to the animosity Bo-Kate brought out in everyone.

Memaw and Paw-paw regarded their only daughter with the same sideways suspicion you'd show a snake that slithered into your house. Is it poisonous? Should I chase it back out, or just kill it outright? Paw-paw slopped gravy with bits of crumbling biscuit, his actions loud and wet, while his wife daintily cut corn from the cob before eating no more than three kernels at a time with her fork.

Tain, once again dressed in skimpy summer attire despite the snow and wind outside, sipped her iced tea and kept trying to catch Nigel's eye. He understood that she wasn't interested in him particularly, just in "the new guy," who happened to be an exotic black man from a strange background. Despite her beauty, it

creeped him out a little, counteracting most of—but not all—
the desire her blatant carnality inspired.

Bo-Kate's other brother, Snad, slouched in his chair half-
awake, scooping up mashed potatoes and slowly raising them to
his mouth. He hadn't said a word, and Nigel was unsure whether
the passivity was his natural state, or if he was stoned out of his
mind.

"You hear about that country singer, Raylon Dupree?" Bo-
Kate's father said between bites.

"What about him?" his wife asked.

"They say he ran off with a policeman's horse in New York.
He was all drunk, and somebody in some bar said he wasn't a
real cowboy, so he had to show 'em." The old man shook his head.
"That'd been you or me, we'd be sitting' in jail right now. He
just got a slap on the wrist and a pat on the back."

"That's always the way," his wife agreed.

"Them big shots in Nashville, they think they eat roses and
shit sunshine," the old man added.

Tain turned to Bo-Kate. "Hey," she said, drawing out
the syllable. "Doesn't your old boyfriend manage Raylon
Dupree?"

Bo-Kate looked up sharply. "Shut up, Tain."

She leaned her elbows on the table and blew a loose strand of
black hair from her face. She grinned, taunting. "Yeah, I'm pretty
sure he does, I read that on the CMT website. You ever hear
from him?"

"Shut . . . up . . . Tain," Bo-Kate said warningly.

"She never did tell you about Jeff, did she?" Tain said to Nigel.
"They were Romeo and Juliet, or Roseanna McCoy and Jonce
Hatfield. Nothing could keep them apart."

"I mean it, Tain," Bo-Kate said.

"*You* shut up, Bo-Kate," Tain said with sudden ferocity.
"Who the fuck are you to come barging back in here, fucking

everything up again?" Nobody wants you here. Whatever song you've managed to steal, it ain't yours and never fucking will be."

"Language, young lady," the old man snapped.

"Come on," Tain taunted Bo-Kate, "tell your colored boyfriend here all about Jeff. How handsome he was, how much you loved the way he fucked you in the bed of his truck, how when he killed that Spicer boy because you told him to, you fucked him right there beside the body. Ain't that true, Bo-Kate?"

Bo-Kate leaped to her feet and snatched up the big fork used to serve the pork roast. "How about I kill *you,* Tain, and do every man in three counties a favor?"

Tain jumped up as well. "Bring it, bitch."

"Language!" the old man roared, and slapped the table so hard, the silverware jumped. "If you two can't be civil, you can just get the hell out of my house!"

"It's my house, Daddy," Bo-Kate said, still glaring at Tain. "It's *all* going to be mine before I'm done, so enjoy it while you can." She rammed the fork into the wooden surface hard enough that the tines stuck in the wood, then turned and stalked from the room. Nigel rose to follow, but she said, "No, Nigel. You just stay here and be ready to go when I get back. It's time to bring on the headliner." She snatched her coat from the chair by the heater and went outside.

She glared at Tain from the doorway. "And you, Little Miss No-Panties. I'm going to sing you to a place where no man will ever touch you again. You'll be all alone, for the rest of your miserable slutty existence. You think about that."

When she was gone, Nigel let out a breath he hadn't realized he was holding and said, "I apologize. She's not herself today."

"I don't know who you think she is, then, because that's my damn daughter, all right," Paw-Paw said. He took another biscuit from the bowl.

Nigel glanced at Tain, then did a double take. Tears poured down the girl's cheeks. When she realized everyone was staring at her, she jumped up and ran upstairs.

"Goodness," Nigel said. He felt ridiculously uncomfortable now, alone with the elder Wisbys and the mute, dissolute brother. "I hope we didn't hurt her feelings too badly."

"It's not her feelings," Mewmaw said. "She's part *glaistig*. She can't stand the thought of never having men around."

"Now, you don't say that," her husband said.

"What's a 'glaistig'?" Nigel asked.

"Nothing," Mrs. Wisby said. "I spoke outta turn. She's just a girl who likes men a lot, ain't nothing wrong with that no matter what them Christians say."

Nigel sat quietly after that. The two old people continued to eat, eyes downcast, not speaking. The noise of their chewing and swallowing was almost deafening. Snad finished his mashed potatoes and stared at the residue on his plate. Nigel wondered where Bo-Kate had gone, and how long he was expected to sit here, trapped by politeness.

Junior Damo walked into the Fast Grab convenience store with the forced saunter of someone trying to appear casual. Behind the counter, Lassa Gwinn looked up from the tabloid she was reading and said, "Evening."

"Evening," he said back. He slapped the counter harder than he meant to—so hard, it made Lassa jump. "Keepin' you busy?"

"I'm only busy close to closing," she said, "when everybody comes in to get beer."

He nervously tapped the counter until she added, "Can I help you?"

"What? No." He leaned on one elbow. "What's going on over at the Catamount Corner? Looks like everybody and their mother is there tonight."

"Beats me. Nobody came in here for anything."

"Did you happen to see if Mandalay Harris was there?"

Lassa gave him a look. "No idea, Junior. Why are you so interested?"

"I just don't like things going on that I don't know nothing about. With Rockhouse being dead and all, whatever they're talking about is likely to be important."

"If it is, they'll tell us." She resumed reading her magazine.

"Really?" Junior said in disbelief. "You think so? We got nobody in there to advocate for us, Lassa. They could be deciding we were all more trouble than we're worth."

"You're paranoid," she said without looking up.

"Well, I think we need somebody to stand up for us now that Rockhouse is gone. Somebody that gives a shit."

This got her attention. "You?"

"Yeah . . . maybe. Why not?"

"Junior, you ain't never done a damn thing for anyone but yourself. You know, though, maybe you would be a good follow-up to ol' Rockhouse, after all."

"Maybe the reason I ain't been no great philly-anthropist is because I ain't never had the chance, I been working too hard just trying to make it. You ever notice how Mandalay's folks all help each other out, and we just bitch and snipe? Slash each other's tires, shoot holes in each other's roofs, shit like that? It ain't no good no more, Lassa."

She thought this over. "You might have a point."

"Damn right, I got a point."

Then she scowled. "Luckily that Peterbilt cap covers it."

"Fuck you, then," Junior said. "I'll remember this, Lassa Gwinn. It might come back to bite you."

He stomped out of the Fast Grab. He didn't look back and see that Lassa was still thoughtful.

———

The café at the Catamount Corner Motel was packed. Women, young and old, sat at all the tables while the men stood with their backs to the wall. Some sipped coffee while others held beers or spit tobacco into old Coke cans. And all of them, with the exception of those whose hair had turned white, had the same jet-black hair, olive skin, and enigmatic expressions. To an outsider, it would've looked like the gathering of an extended family; to those familiar with the Tufa, though, it was clearly a conclave of the two most powerful groups in the community, the First Daughters and the Silent Sons.

The two organizations were meeting to discuss their common fate, and what should be done about Bo-Kate Wisby. Without Rockhouse to speak, all eyes fell on Mandalay. She was the smallest person in the room, and physically the youngest, but there was no contempt or doubt in the faces watching her. Everyone accepted her wisdom as genuine, and as a gift from the night winds.

"We have a real problem," Mandalay said. "For those who haven't heard, Bo-Kate Wisby is back. We don't know how yet, but however she managed it, it shows that she's got access to things we don't know about. She's also determined to do as much damage as possible. She killed Rockhouse, burned down Bliss Overbay's house, and took a shot at me earlier."

"Then let's just go kill her," suggested an older man with a beard halfway down his chest. There were murmurs of assent.

"I don't know that we can," Mandalay said.

"Worth a try, anyway," someone else said, to a few chuckles.

"That was my idea, too," Bronwyn Hyatt said, shifting uncomfortably in her seat.

Mandalay faced the man who'd spoken. "You think? What if that's what she's trying to provoke? You may not understand what we're up against here, so let me tell you: In all of Tufa history, we've sung out exactly two people. One now lives in New York. And the other is Bo-Kate Wisby. She wouldn't be here just to say hello to her family. She's got an agenda, and we don't know what it is. She's got abilities we've never seen before. And she hates us all."

At last Peggy Goins said, "So . . . what do we do?"

"There's only one person who might have a clue in all this," Mandalay said. "Jefferson Powell."

There was a long silence, broken only by the gurgling of the coffeemaker.

"He's in New York," Mandalay continued. "So someone will have to go get him."

"Why can't we just call him?" Whizdom said.

"He couldn't hear us. That's part of what happened to him. The only way to reach him is face-to-face."

"I'll do it," Bronwyn said.

"Is it safe for you to fly?" asked Delilah, a sad-eyed middle-aged woman.

"Are you being sarcastic?" Bronwyn shot back.

"She'll be fine," Bliss said.

"But she won't go alone," Mandalay said.

"Why the hell not?" Bronwyn said, and tried to stand. It took a couple of tries for her to heave her pregnant self upright. "Oh, fuck it, never mind. Who's coming with me, then?"

"I will," a new voice said.

Junior Damo stood in the door, still in his coat and boots. He smiled, all faux innocence. "What? Y'all got a problem with that?"

"You're not supposed to be here," someone said.

"Yeah, well, things change. I don't want Bo-Kate here any more than the rest of you highfalutin' purebloods do, either. And if someone's gonna go fetch the cavalry, they need to represent all the Tufa, not just you."

Murmurs went through the crowd. Junior kept his eyes on Mandalay.

"You have a point, there, Junior," the girl said at last.

"You've got to be kidding me," Bronwyn said. "You expect me to go all the way to New York with him? I wouldn't trust him to lead me across the street."

"You ain't got nothing to worry about with me," he said. "In fact, it might be best for everybody. My wife's pregnant, too, so I know how you'll be."

"And just *how* will I 'be,' Mr. Damo?" Bronwyn challenged.

Mandalay held up a hand. "Calm down, Bronwyn. You'll be in charge, in my name. Is that clear, Junior?"

He nodded and made a hand gesture of respect.

"You'll deliver the message I give you, and you'll decide what to do based on his response. He's been gone a long time, and he's likely to be . . . reluctant."

"And pissed off," Junior added.

"Very likely. But he gets one chance, one offer. If he turns it down, then come back. We're not going to him on our knees, remember."

"All right," Bronwyn agreed. "And I'm in charge, right?"

"Yes."

"Anything you say," Junior said to Bronwyn, all smiles.

"Good. And remember, whatever differences you have here, you've both got the same goal on this trip, so help each other out."

Junior nodded. Bronwyn shrugged.

"In the meantime . . . everyone else, keep an eye out. If you see her, call someone. Try not to be alone with her."

"What about that nigger-boy she's got with her?" Macen Ward said.

"He's not our problem," Mandalay said. "And Macen? Remember how people used to talk about *us* before you use words like that."

"Sorry," Macen said, chagrined.

"Get him here as fast as you can," Mandalay said to Bronwyn. "If you need help, call Bliss."

"We won't," Bronwyn said.

"He'll come," Junior agreed.

Bliss drove Mandalay home. The radio was off, and the only noise was the steady thrum of the truck's tires on the pavement.

At last Mandalay, still looking straight ahead, said, "Bliss, if we're not careful, there's going to be a war. And everyone in power, on both sides, will be in real danger. That includes you and me."

"Which side are the night winds on?"

"They're still. Silent. Waiting." She smiled a little, the way an ancient, ageless crone might when contemplating the follies of mortal men. "They want us to settle this ourselves."

Later, Bronwyn Hyatt Chess sat with her back against the head-board while her husband Craig rubbed her feet. The baby in her stomach moved contently, stretching and curling, feeding off her mother's own contentment. The child would be special, and not just because her parents loved her so much. She embodied the future of the Tufa, however it ultimately manifested.

"I have to leave for a few days," Bronwyn said at last.

Craig looked up in surprise. "Really? When did this happen?"

"Tonight. It's First Daughter stuff. Three days at the most, I think."

"You think?"

"I'm sorry."

"They *do* know you're pregnant, right?"

"I think they noticed. But damn it, I'm not incapacitated."

"Don't get defensive. Can you tell me about it?"

"Being pregnant?" she deadpanned.

"The *trip,* you goof."

"Not really."

"Are you going by yourself?"

"No, a friend is going with me."

"Bliss?"

"No. Junior Damo. You don't know him."

"'Him'?"

She snort-laughed. "This is, like, the most useless time *ever* for you to be jealous."

"I'm not jealous, I'm concerned."

"Well, don't be. I'm still a trained soldier, you know."

He crawled onto the bed beside her and kissed her. "Will you call me?"

"I will."

"And you think it'll only take three days?"

"I think so. It better not take much longer."

He put his hand on her stomach, and the baby moved toward it, as if sensing that the man outside would be a major part of her life.

20

Byron Harley flexed his bad leg. The numb places along his skin tingled now that the brace straps weren't tied around them, but otherwise the deep, constant ache remained the same. He looked again at his watch, but it had stopped at the time of the crash; the hands under the shattered glass were frozen at 1:23 A.M.

"You thinkin' hard, there, Byron?" Eli said.

"Just wondering what time it was. Whether it was close to morning yet. It's gonna be a busy day, I imagine, what with the police and everything. Plus I got to call my wife and let her know I'm all right first thing, so that she don't hear about it on the news."

"We'll get you there."

"I reckon I need to get back as well," Fiddlin' John said. "My daughter's likely to be worrying about me." He frowned a little. "Hey, ain't we talked about this before?"

"We talked about a lot of stuff," Eli said.

"But no, we done had this exact same conversation . . . ain't we?"

The sin eater held up the jug. "Reckon you need some more of this to clear your head, don't you?"

"Reckon I do," Fiddlin' John said with a chuckle, and reached for the jug.

Byron said nothing, but tried to puzzle through events. They *had* gone through that exact conversation earlier, hadn't they? Because that's when he found out Moonshine Kate was John's daughter, not his wife or girlfriend . . . right?

Before he could get any further, there was more frantic rustling from the woods. They watched as an overweight young man clutching a thin gray piece of metal or plastic staggered into the clearing. He was so out of breath, he wheezed, and like the red-headed woman earlier—there *had* been a redhead, right?—he was dressed all wrong for the weather. He leaned against the tree and managed to squeak out the word, "Help."

"Sit down, son, you look plumb beat," Eli said.

The man did, apparently grateful for the fire. He coughed as the smoke blew over him, then rubbed his bare arms. The strange gray box rested beside him on the log.

"Wh-where are we?" he asked. "Are we anywhere n-near N-Needsville?"

"Not too far away," the sin eater said.

"Those fucking Tufa bastards," the man said, muttering as he waited to warm up. "They ran me off into the woods, can you believe it? I asked them for help, and they got me even *more* lost!" He took out a small, flat device and held it up. The front of it glowed. Then he said, "Damn it, *still* no signal. Anyone got a phone that works out here?"

The other three looked at him blankly. He sighed and said, "All right, whatever. Can one of you take me to the nearest place with Wi-Fi, then?"

"What the hell is 'Wi-Fi'?" Byron asked, suddenly annoyed by all the strangeness. "Is that some kind of food or something?"

"You don't know what Wi-Fi is?" the man asked in disbelief.

"Don't get smart with me, pudgy," Byron said. He hated it when he felt stupid or inferior. "What's your name?"

"Fred Blasco. I'm a blogger. You might've heard of me? I do *Fred, White and Blue*?"

He waited eagerly, but the other three just stared blankly.

"Son, I don't even know what a 'blogger' is," Fiddlin' John said. "Is that got something to do with cutting down trees?"

Blasco sighed. "No. It's . . . like a news commentator. I give people the right perspective so they can evaluate what the liberal media throws out at them."

Fiddlin' John chuckled and said, "Well, whatever it is you do, welcome. I'm John Carson." They shook hands. "Care for a snort?"

Blasco stared at the jug. "Is that *moonshine*?"

"It sure ain't turpentine," Fiddlin' John said, and passed the jug.

Blasco awkwardly tilted it, took a swallow, and nearly dropped the jug as he choked. Fiddlin' John guffawed and reached to take it. Blasco coughed and sputtered, the veins on his forehead standing out. It took him several moments to catch his breath again.

"Just take your time," Byron said, suddenly sympathetic toward the young man. "I'm heading down the mountain at daybreak. You can come with me."

Blasco sputtered to a stop, nodded, and croaked out, "Thanks. What's your name?"

"Byron Harley."

Blasco smiled. "Nice to meet you, Buh—" He stopped in midword and stared. "What did you say your name was?"

Byron smiled. He was used to fans. "Byron Harley. Pleased to meet you."

Blasco continued to stare. "Byron Harley? The musician?"

"Yes, sir."

Blasco swallowed hard. "That can't . . . You can't be him."

"It is kind of a weird place to find me, I'll admit."

"No, it's . . . Byron Harley is *dead*."

"The crash is already on the news, huh?" That meant Donna knew about it.

"Well . . . yeah. It's legendary."

Byron reached for his leg iron. He had to get to a phone, to tell Donna he was okay. She was an emotional wreck on a good day; this would send her off the deep end. And she had little Harmony to care for. "It ain't just legendary, my friend, it's myth-ological. Fellas, I need to get down this mountain now. I don't care if it's dark. I've got to call my wife and let her know I'm okay."

Eli said lazily, "Can't leave till sunup, I done told you that."

"Well, we're damn sure doing it!" Byron roared.

They all jumped.

Blasco said, "Wait—what year do you think it is?"

"Year? It's 1958. Why?"

Blasco picked up the flat metal box and opened the lid. A TV screen came to life on it. Byron stared.

"Hold on, I have this saved in a file," he muttered. There was a typewriter attached to the screen, and Blasco typed something on it. "I've been fascinated by Cloud County and the Tufa for a while now. Not sure what the government's got in mind, but they *have* to be involved in anything this secret. 'Don't know where they come from,' my ass. And they think they can get rid of me by just chasing me off into the woods?" He looked up at Byron. "The plane crash in '58 was the biggest thing to happen here until Bronwyn Hyatt came home."

"Don't get no Internet out here," Eli said.

"Screw the Internet," Blasco said. "You think I trust storing things in the cloud? The NSA has copies of all that shit. I keep my crucial stuff right here where I can put my hands on it, be-hind a firewall no government agency can ever breach."

The screen lit up with pictures of Byron, Guy, and Large Sarge. Beneath them was a newspaper headline that said, PLANE CRASH KILLS THREE STARS.

"What the hell is that?" Byron asked.

"It's the newspaper from the day after your plane crash."

Byron's fuzzy brain rushed to catch up. "It's . . . what? Tomorrow's newspaper? On TV?"

Blasco looked at him with an odd mix of awe and pity. "This," he said slowly, as if talking to a child, "is a computer. They're much smaller now. And more powerful."

"Now? What does *that* mean?"

Blasco licked his lips. "Dude, you're not gonna believe this, but . . . it's the twenty-first century. You've been dead for over fifty years."

Byron stared at him. He should laugh, he should smack the guy, but something in the man's voice was more convincing than it should have been.

"What you saying?" Fiddlin' John said.

"He's just messing with you," Eli said, and stood. "Come on, you two, I'll take you both to Needsville."

"Fuck you!" Blasco said, and jumped up. "You're a Tufa, I'm not following you anywhere!" He looked back down at Byron. "You don't believe me? Look at this."

He fumbled with the small computer, awkwardly trying to hold it, work the keys, and keep an eye on the sin eater. Then he turned the screen and said, "There. Is that not your wife and daughter? That was taken ten years after you died, at a tribute concert."

Byron choked. There on the screen was Donna, but she was old now, and heavy, and looked somehow sadder than he'd ever thought possible. The girl he'd married, the firecracker in bed and the delightful companion on the road, was completely gone from her. And yet it *was her.*

And next to her . . .

Harmony. His daughter. Tall now, and awkward, a teen wearing some sort of strange, wide-bottomed jeans and a blouse with a strange design, a stick-figure triangle inside a circle. She had a thick band around her head, like some Indian in a Western.

The caption read, *The widow and daughter of Byron Harley.* With the date, *June 1968.*

And again, he had no doubt. This was *her.*

He felt like he wanted to vomit.

"And wait, I've got . . . here."

Another newspaper article appeared. It showed an old woman with gray hair, but an unmistakable smile. Harmony. Then the story around it registered.

It was an obituary notice.

Harmony was dead. The little girl whose giggle could make him forget all about the constant pain in his leg was gone. She'd lived an entire life without him, while he sat here drinking and playing music.

He managed to skim the article. She'd been married three times, arrested for drugs, and killed by her latest husband, who also took his own life and the lives of their two children—Byron's grandchildren, a boy and girl.

His chest ached as if it might explode.

He turned to the sin eater. "What the hell—"

He was gone. And so was Fiddlin' John Carson.

He looked around. There was no sign of which direction they'd gone. For all he could tell, they might've gone straight up. He grabbed Blasco's arm. "You're staying right here, fat boy."

"You don't need him," a woman's voice said.

They both turned. Bo-Kate Wisby stood at the edge of the clearing, casually leaning against a tree, her hands in her coat pockets.

"Who the hell are you?" Byron demanded.

"Your way out. I can take you back to the world, if you promise to help me, too."

"Oh, yeah? You from the future, too? You going to take me to the twenty-first century?"

"I don't have to, Byron. You're already there."

He laughed. This all had to be some weird-ass hillbilly joke. "What's in it for me?"

"I'm *from* the twenty-first century," Blasco said desperately. "Can you take me back, too?"

"Sorry," Bo-Kate said, and touched him with the lipstick Taser. He let out a rippling cry of pain and collapsed beside the fire.

"What the hell was that?" Byron said, and limped away from her.

"Magic," she said. "Come on."

"No fucking way, whoever you are."

"Byron, do you want to get revenge on the people who took you away from your wife and daughter? If you do, I can take you to them."

He looked at her. His mind was clear, but overwhelmed with what he'd seen. He wanted to doubt her, but something told him that everything he'd heard was true, including her offer to put those responsible within his grasp.

"Wait, I have to put on my leg brace," he said. He quickly took off his jeans and strapped the brace around his withered left leg. His bad leg was much smaller than his other, the muscles atrophied and stringy beneath puckered, scarred skin. When he finished, he said, "Okay, which way?"

"Wait," she said, and walked over to him. She snuggled close and held up the phone. He saw both their faces on the screen. "Say cheese," she said, and smiled.

He didn't. The flash made him blink, but he did glimpse the picture before the little screen went blank.

"What the hell kind of camera is that?" he asked.

"You'll see lots of things like this," she said. "And can I ask you a favor? Give me that pick you've been using."

"Why?"

She smiled, shy and seductive. "Because I'm a huge fan of yours, Byron. I bought all your records. I even ordered 'The Girl Won't Stop' from Germany when they wouldn't release it here for being so 'suggestive.' I'd love to have a real pick that you once used."

He took the pick from his jacket pocket and gave it to her. She put it away and said, "Now. Follow me."

"Which way?"

She grinned. "Downhill. It's all downhill from here."

Bo-Kate looked at the sleeping form of Byron Harley, sprawled on his back in one of the old guest rooms. He was drunk, and the special valerian root she'd slipped into the moonshine had made certain he quickly passed out. She needed him out of commission while she decided her next step.

"So now that I've got you," she said softly to herself, "what do I do with you?"

"You really can't figure that out?" a familiar voice said almost in her ear.

She didn't turn. "He's famous, and everyone thought he was dead. Am I supposed to claim I resurrected him?"

Rockhouse chuckled. "Good thing I'm sticking around to help you out. What makes this big ole sum'bitch valuable is that he's a *secret*. Nobody knew he was there 'cept me, ole Eli, and Marshall. And them other two never quite figured out who he was. I never had any particular need for him, so I just left him alone. But you? Hell, play it right, and nobody'll stand in your way, not even that little bitch Mandalay."

"And how do I play it?"

"First, you make sure anyone else who knows about him won't talk. Then you trot him out as proof that the night winds are on your side, because look what they done brought to you."

"I ain't heard shit from the night winds."

"Don't matter. All that matters is what everyone else thinks. You got some good ideas, and people know that. This'll tip the scale in your favor. You just have to make sure nobody knows them other two knew about him."

"How do I do that?"

"You need me to lead you by the damn hand?"

She turned, but no one was there. She knew what he meant, and as she stood there gazing at Byron, the logic of it grew more and more irrefutable. If she wanted what she said she wanted, it was, in fact, the only choice. She'd promised Byron his revenge, after all.

"Sleep while you can, Byron," she murmured. "You're about to get your hands bloody."

21

On an upper floor of the Flatiron Building in Manhattan, Jefferson Powell sat behind his desk, chin in his hand, listening to the distant voice of Rhett Carrington demand to be moved further down on the bill on a "new country" package tour.

Rhett was sex-symbol gorgeous, six foot two with sculpted abs that his unbuttoned shirt made certain were visible from the stage, especially after deftly applied spray-on highlights. He was from Arkansas, so when he sang of trucks, beer, and girls, he knew whereof he spoke. But he was both dumb as a tire and cocky as a Kardashian, which made him insufferable and explained the frequent turnover in his stage band. He had no concept of what made a song good or bad, could barely tell which end of a guitar was up, and took everyone's advice except the people who truly had his best interests at heart.

When Carrington finished his tirade, Jefferson said coolly, "Done? Are you done? Because I counted thirty-three uses of 'motherfucker' in five minutes, and I don't want to stop you if you're going for a record."

"Fuck you!" came the reply on the phone speaker.

"I'm twice as popular as Blake Gilbert, I shouldn't have to go on before him."

Jeff looked at his assistant Janet Ling. She was Asian, whip-smart, and surprisingly sexy for a woman who never spoke in public. But in private, she provided a valuable service by calling him out on his bullshit and suggesting solutions he had never considered. If half of being a good boss was surrounding yourself with brilliant people, then Jeff was the best boss in Manhattan.

Now Janet made a face and rolled her eyes. She and her boss shared the same opinion of this particular cash cow.

"You're right," Jeff said. "I can count Blake Gilbert's fans on Homer Simpson's fingers. But he's handled by Creativity Incorporated, and they also handle Miranda Quick, so they're a package. I can't get them to move Blake even if I wanted to." He rubbed his temples and said wearily, "You know, this is simple stuff, I would've thought you'd understand it by now."

"I understand you ain't doin' shit for me," Carrington said.

"Really?" Jeff laughed without any real humor. He was getting mad, and that brought out his own Southern accent. "You don't deserve me, you know that? I should really just cut you loose. Do you realize what you have the chance to do here? Not only make it impossible for Blake Gilbert to follow you, but to show Miranda Quick that you should be her opening act on her solo tour this summer. If you put some of that piss into your show that you've been using to cuss at me, you might just find yourself in a better place. That ever occur to you?"

There was a pause. "Naw."

"I know. *That's* the shit I'm doing for you."

"Sorry about that," he said like a guilty teenage boy. Which, Jeff knew, he basically was, and would be until he stopped being a star.

"No worries, Rhett. How's rehearsal going?"

"Great. I nailed two of the backup singers at the same time two days ago. Got 'em both in the shower."

Jeff sighed. "I meant the *music,* Rhett. How's the music going?"

"Aw, it ain't nothin'. It's all good."

The band's drummer was a veteran touring musician who'd played with everyone, and whom Jeff paid to send reports back to him without Rhett's knowledge. He already knew about the two backup singers, which was no big deal to him; but Rhett was also blowing off the rehearsals, showing up drunk and high and then with an entourage of Arkansas rednecks who told him how awesome he was.

"Yeah, well, it better be," Jeff said. "This is your chance, and if you blow it, it's nobody's fault but yours. Not mine, not the band's, not Blake Gilbert's. We clear on that?"

"Yeah."

"Good. Get back to work. I'll be in touch later in the week. Maybe I'll fly down and sit in."

"Want me to set you up with one of them girl singers?"

"Hell no, I want 'em both, just like you."

They both laughed, but when Jeff hung up, his laughter shut off like a tap. He rubbed his eyes, then got up and went to the window. Below, and above, Manhattan surged with life and vibrancy.

"Janet," he said at last, "do you ever actually listen to Rhett Carrington?"

"I've heard him."

"Yes. But do you *listen* to him? I mean, if he comes on the radio, do you turn it up or change the station?"

"Nobody listens to regular radio anymore, Jeff. They either stream it online, or use Sirius."

He rubbed the bridge of his nose. "Janet, I'm just asking, however you listen to music, do you listen to Rhett Carrington?"

She thought about it. "I don't really know. I mean, I'm sure I've heard him, but he just kind of blends in with everyone else. One more Chippendale in a cowboy hat."

"Uh-huh," Jeff said. He always wanted the truth, and Janet always gave it to him. Of course, he had to factor in her professional determination to essentially take over his job one day, which meant she might try to deliberately mislead him to hasten his own demise in the industry. But in this case, she confirmed what he already knew: Rhett Carrington had peaked and, barring a miracle, was already on his way down. It would be time to unload him soon.

Janet went into the front room to type up her notes from the phone call. Jeff went back to his desk. He sat down, tried to get comfortable, but something made him edgy. It was a kind of gnawing uncertainty that he couldn't pin down to any particular cause, but it was impossible to ignore. Was it an omen? If he was still connected to the Tufa, he'd know, or at least know whom to ask about it. But that had ended a long time ago, leaving him with the psychic equivalent of a phantom limb.

His phone buzzed. "Sir," Janet said, "your ten o'clock is here."

He looked at the schedule. It was Krystal Bradbury, whom he'd heard during a trip to Austin a month ago. He'd flown her up here, put her up in the Ritz-Carlton overlooking Central Park, and generally sought to impress her with the world in which he operated. She had two essential things he wanted in a client: a great voice and a great figure. With those two things, he could get three solid years out of her, five if she didn't crap out like so many of them did. And who knows? She might be that rare one who had a sustained career.

"Send her in," he said, and stood. If nothing else from his childhood remained, he still had his Southern manners.

Jefferson stopped at Your Mama Don't Dance, his usual watering hole. He kissed Violetta, the greeter, on the cheek as he went in and made his way to his usual small table, which a RESERVED placard held for him. He sat with his back to the corner, checked his phone for messages one last time, then smiled up at the waitress.

"Hey, Cassidy. How's it going tonight?"

"Busy as a fuckin' beehive," she said in her harsh Irish accent.

"Are you the queen bee, then?"

"Ha! I wish. No, I'm just another drone."

"Drones are males."

"Really?"

"Really. They have one job, then they die."

"Huh. That's sounds fucking brilliant."

He smiled. "Anyone asking for me tonight?"

"Just the usual desperate fucking losers, Mr. Powell."

"Well, tell them they've got five minutes. And bring me some of that 1958 Glenfiddich you keep locked away."

"Why you always ask for that year, Mr. Powell?"

"It was a very good year," he said, almost singing the words in a Sinatra voice.

Cassidy sauntered off. She was very attractive, and probably had a dozen Jersey gym rats vying for her attention. Her window of beauty was wide open now, but within three years would likely close with the addition of a husband who believed she slept around, kids who complained constantly, and in-laws who knew their boy could do better.

Almost at once a skinny young man with tousled hair and a soul patch came over. He was barely five and half feet tall, and wouldn't make eye contact. He sat down and said to Jeff's shoulder, "Hey. Nice to meet you, uh . . . sir."

"What's your name?"

"Johnny Bryan."

"Is that your real name?"

"It's two of 'em. Last name is Yosonovich."

"No."

"Yeah. The latest in a long line of Yosonoviches."

Jeff smiled. "That's tough. You made the right call. So you've got five minutes—tell me why I should give a shit about you."

"Can I play you something?"

"No, I want you to talk to me. I'll take it as a given that you can sing, and play, and maybe even write songs. If I'm going to put my time into you, I need to know what kind of person you are." He smiled again. "Whether or not you're a real Yosonovich."

"Okay. I'm from Michigan, and I've been playing down at the Billy Bristol's on off-nights, just me and my guitar. I'd like to put together a band, but I don't know the scene well enough yet. And I'd like to get a record deal."

"Why? Cut your own, sell it online, keep all the money yourself. Why do you need a label?"

"Because it's my dream. I wouldn't be here if I didn't have a dream, would I?"

"It can become a nightmare pretty damn fast."

"That's why I need a good manager. Like you."

Cassidy delivered the whiskey, and it was like a smooth sizzle down his throat. He said to the boy, "Nicely done, Johnny. You worked the suck-up organically into the conversation."

He smiled, and for the first time looked directly at Jeff's face. "I've been coming here for over a week, waiting to get up the nerve to talk to you. If that waitress hadn't told me to come over, I'd probably still be sitting at the bar, watching you drink."

"That's creepy, Johnny."

"I know. But what can I do?"

"What'd you think of her?"

"Who?"

"Cassidy. The waitress. You must've checked her out. Or are you into guys?"

"No, I'm straight. I mean, I don't care one way or the other what you are, but I'm straight." He looked back at Cassidy. "Well, she's cute enough. But that voice is kind of like sandpaper. And

I get the feeling she's just trolling for a husband. What do you think of her?"

"I don't," he said. "I just wanted to see if you noticed things."

He sat back with a frown. "You're not like the other managers I've talked to."

"You mean the ones that turned you down?"

He smiled. "Yeah. Them."

"Well, I am different. I do this for reasons I'm not going to explain, because you'd never understand. You know where my office is?"

"Yeah."

"Send me a demo. Three songs. Your best one, your favorite one, and the one everyone else tells you is your best."

"What if those are all the same song?"

"Then you don't have enough."

"I have plenty."

"I'll take a listen, and be in touch if I think I can do you any good."

They shook hands. The boy sauntered off, and Jeff sipped his whiskey. He'd already classified the boy as a two-year wonder at the most; after that, the kid would be past his sell-by date. But for those two years, Jeff could make him one of the most popular figures in entertainment.

As long as his demo didn't totally suck.

He waited, but no one else approached. After half an hour, he motioned Cassidy back over and ordered his dinner.

"How come you never bring a wife or girlfriend in here?" Cassidy said when she finished writing his order.

"Maybe I'm gay."

"You're not gay," she said with a knowing chuckle. "I've seen how you watch me and the other girls."

"Maybe I'm just very, very hard to live with."

"Maybe. I'm guessing you have a broken heart, though."

"And what makes you say that?"

"Most guys, when they stare at my ass, they look like they do when they get their steak. You look like you're remembering the best steak you ever had."

He gazed at her with surprise. "That's a very perceptive thing to say."

"Thank you," she said, and went to put in his order. He finished his whiskey and watched the TV, muted but with the closed captions on, mention the latest political snafu threatening to ensnare local politicians. But his mind was a million miles away, soaring on night winds.

He arrived home a little before midnight, tipsy and sad and annoyed. His cat Cecil purred around his ankles as he turned on the lights, locked the door, and tapped the touch pad to bring up his laptop screen. He glanced at his e-mail, decided nothing needed his immediate attention, and dropped heavily onto the couch. Consuela had been in today, and everything was neat, tidy, and smelled like potpourri.

His cell phone buzzed. He recognized the number. "Hello?"

"Hey, baby," Lisa said. "You still awake?"

"Still, but not for long."

"I wanted to let you know, I saw that preacher on the subway again."

"The Diana Ross one?"

"Yes."

Jeff smiled. The oddities of New York never ceased to amaze him, such as this subway preacher who kept muttering, in some thick accent, "Jesus and Diana Ross." It had become a great inside joke for him and Lisa, a phrase that never failed to reduce them both to giggles like small children. They'd spent endless hours parsing out the possible meaning, to no avail. "He's still at it, huh?"

"Yes, but I figured it out tonight. We had it all wrong. He's not saying, 'Jesus and Diana Ross,' he's saying, 'Jesus died on the cross.'"

Jeff barked out a surprised laugh. "No way. How did we miss that?"

"I know, right? It's so obvious." They both laughed, and then Lisa added, "Do you want some company tonight?"

He sighed. "I'm sorry, Lisa. It's one of those nights. One of those crazy, crazy nights."

"I'm sorry, too," she said, missing the Eagles reference, which didn't surprise him. "Want to just talk?"

Lisa was a librarian at the local branch, who helped him track down old CDs and albums from other far-flung institutions. She thought they were for some kind of professional research. She'd never believe the truth, of course: that he sought for the lost pieces of his soul that resided in this old music, and that even though he knew it was futile, he could never stop trying. "Nah, thanks, though. I'll see you."

"Okay," she said, disappointed. She was a pretty woman in her thirties, with that angular Manhattan attitude that was both attractive and, to a country boy like Jeff, also off-putting. He could never quite shake the sense that she was laughing at him, even though he was a powerful music executive and she was a lowly librarian.

He stared at the black TV screen for a long time before he stretched out on the couch. Cecil crawled up onto the small of his back, and in moments, both of them were asleep. The cat dreamed of mice, which he'd never seen; Jeff dreamed of wings, which he'd never see again.

22

Jefferson jumped as the phone on his desk buzzed. He nearly spilled coffee on his lap, which would ruin his Earnest Sewn jeans. He knew he didn't have any appointments this early. He pushed the response button and snapped, "What?"

"Touchy," Janet said. "Stay up late last night?"

"Just the usual."

"Uh-huh. How many fingers of vodka am I holding up?"

"Did you actually want something?"

"There's a couple of people to see you," Janet said. Her voice sounded odd.

"They have appointments?"

"No."

"Then tell them to make one and come back. Jesus, I nearly poured hot coffee all over my balls."

"I think telling me that counts as sexual harassment."

"My balls would certainly think so."

"I think you might want to see them, though."

"Why?"

"Well . . . I think they may be relatives."

"Of mine? I don't have any relatives."

"Well, they have the same skin and black hair."

Jefferson's head cleared at once, and he felt a surge of both panic and, far worse, hope. "What are their names?"

"Bronwyn and . . . Junior."

He frowned. He didn't know either of them. But then again, he couldn't be sure that losing the memory of specific Tufa wasn't one effect of his exile. Many of those consequences had revealed themselves only over time, such as the subtle magic that kept people from noticing that he didn't age. It diffused through everything connected with him: pictures, videos, interviews, personal relationships. Even people who were now elderly didn't register that he looked exactly the same as he had decades ago.

He opened his desk drawer and positioned the gun he kept there. It was usually merely for show, but in this case, he was glad he kept it cleaned and loaded. He had no idea what this was about, but if two Tufa had come all the way here, after all this time, he wasn't about to be caught undefended. "Okay," he said. "Send them in."

The first thing that registered was Bronwyn's near-term pregnancy: her belly preceded her, and she had the pained, slightly annoyed look he'd seen on lots of heavily expectant women. For an instant, he wondered if this was all a paternity shakedown, but when he looked at her face, he realized he truly didn't know her.

The man with her was tall and handsome, with unruly black hair and a permanently suspicious glint in his eye.

"It's okay," Jeff said to Janet. "These are people from back home."

Janet nodded, rolled her eyes a little, and closed the door.

He stepped around the desk. "I'm Jefferson Powell."

"Junior Damo," the man said, and they shook hands.

"Mrs. Damo," he said to the woman.

"Bronwyn Chess," she corrected. "I used to be Bronwyn Hyatt."

"I know the Hyatts," Jeff said; then the name registered. "Bronwyn Hyatt. Deacon Hyatt's daughter. You were a war hero, weren't you?"

"I was in the army, we'll leave it at that," she said.

"So you two aren't a couple, then?"

"No," they said in unison.

"That's not what we're here to talk about," Bronwyn added.

"So this isn't a social visit?"

"No." She looked around. "Excuse me, but I have to sit down." She lowered herself into one of the guest chairs.

"Can I get you anything?" Jeff said.

"A can opener," she said wryly. "No, thank you, I'm fine. I'm supposed to feel like this, apparently." She settled into the chair, then said, "We need to talk to you about Bo-Kate."

Jeff jumped as if he'd touched the subway's third rail. It was a name that hadn't been uttered aloud in his presence for longer than he cared to remember. Of course, it sounded in his head every day, and he would often wake from dreams of being with her, calling her name in his mind if not actually aloud. But this wasn't a dream, or a memory.

"I haven't seen her or spoken to her in longer than you can imagine," he said. "Well, okay, *you* can probably imagine it, but it's still been a long time. The last I heard, she was in Nashville. I have no idea if she's still there."

"We know where she is," Junior said. "She's back in Needsville."

They all waited as this registered. Finally Jeff said, quietly and deliberately, "How is that possible?"

"We don't know," Bronwyn said. "But she's already killed Rockhouse Hicks. She burned down Bliss Overbay's house. And she wants to kill Mandalay Harris and take over as leader of all the Tufa."

"We need your help dealing with her," Junior said.

Jeff just stared at them, letting this information sink in, un-

able to believe at first what he was hearing. He wasn't even sure
which bit appalled him the most: Bo-Kate being on a murder-
and-arson spree, that she'd somehow been able to return to Cloud
County at all, or that the Tufa had asked for his help. At last he
said, "I appreciate you letting me know what she's been up to,
and I'm real sorry to hear about Rockhouse, but to put it simply . . . you motherfucking sonsabitches can do your own dirty
laundry. You kicked me out, remember?"

"We know," Junior said. "But we're still your people."

He wanted to laugh at them, to throw them out of his office,
but he'd negotiated with too many lawyers, agents, and promoters not to see where this was going. "All right, I'll nibble. What
makes you think I can help?"

"You know her better than anybody," Bronwyn said.

"I haven't seen her in a coon's age. A very long coon's age. How
could I know her anymore?"

"Because she hasn't changed that much," Junior said.

"In that case, your best bet to stop her is to shoot her on sight."

"That was my suggestion," Bronwyn said. "I was overruled."

Jeff leaned back in his chair, using body language that
conveyed his total dominance of the situation. It worked with
musicians, and often with lawyers. He had no idea if it would
with Tufa, but he figured it couldn't hurt. "So you need me so
that no Tufas will get their hands bloody, is that it? I'm like the
hired gun who comes in, does the job, and then gets run out on
a rail by the hypocritical townspeople."

"It won't be like that," Bronwyn assured him.

"Uh-huh. What have you got to trade?"

Junior and Bronwyn exchanged a look. Bronwyn said seriously, "Amnesty."

"Nice word. Explain exactly what it means."

"You get to come back."

Luckily Jeff had many, many years' experience keeping his
emotions off his face, so he didn't show the volcanoes that went

off inside him. "What makes you think," he said deliberately, "that I *want* to come back?"

Bronwyn said, "Because I know a little of what you feel. I was in Iraq, and I thought I was going to die there. That terrified me. The thought of never riding the wind again, singing, or playing, of never being *home* . . . those things scared me a lot more than the thought that I'd actually die."

He laughed. "And you think that's how I feel?"

"Isn't it?"

"You want to know how I feel? I loved that woman more than either of you will likely love anyone. I did horrible things because of that love, but I never felt more alive than when I was with her. Then you banished us from Cloud County. That was okay, I could live with that. But you also banished us from each other. Yeah, you didn't know about that, did you? I don't know if it was an accident, or if ol' Rockhouse just threw it in to fuck with us that much more. But we couldn't be with each other out in the world. We couldn't find each other, contact each other, or anything. If I tried to call her, it wouldn't go through. If I sent her a letter, it disappeared. If I went somewhere I knew she'd be, we couldn't connect. Oh, we could hear about each other. I knew she was a big promoter in Nashville, I even represented some of the artists she promoted. But we could never communicate directly."

He looked distant, and anguished. "We were both at a Beyoncé concert, both of us backstage, in the same goddamned room, even. But we couldn't see each other, or hear each other, or *find* each other." He smiled coldly and shook his head. "You know what? Fuck you both. Bo-Kate is your problem, not mine. And my life is here now."

"Selling musicians instead of being one?" Junior said.

"Now you're insulting my profession? You really don't know how to motivate people, do you?"

Bronwyn put her hand on Junior's arm. "Let's go. I'll leave

my cell number with your secretary. We'll be in town until to-morrow morning. Call me if you change your mind."

Bronwyn pushed herself up from the chair with a grunt of annoyance. They had just reached the door when Jeff said, "Let me make sure I understand your offer. I help you deal with Bo-Kate, and my exile is over, whatever the results of that. I mean, you're getting my best effort, not a guaranteed result. Are we clear?"

"Yes," Bronwyn said.

"And I'm allowed back unconditionally and without any res-ervation. It's like it never happened. Right?"

"Right."

"So I'll be able to sing, and play, again?"

"Yes."

Something struck him. "Can Bo-Kate sing and play?"

"She can. We have no idea how."

He nodded. "I'll think about it. But don't get your hopes up."

They left, and Jeff went to the window to stare out at Man-hattan as he thought of mountains and guitar strings beneath his fingers.

"What are you doing?" Melanie said sleepily, and stretched on the bed. Her long legs slid against the sheets, inviting his gaze with their linear perfection. One thing about a model, Jeff thought: they knew how to present themselves in every situation. "Wishing we'd bought that weed from those guys at the club?"

Jeff sat on the edge of the bed, gazing out the window. "It's not a good idea to buy weed from strangers, especially in Manhattan."

"They're not strangers. They're our new friends with weed."

"If you're so desperate, look in the top drawer."

"I'm more desperate to know why you're still wide awake. Usu-ally you're fast asleep before I stop breathing hard."

"Thinking," he said. "About my hometown."

"Down South?"

"Yeah. Some people from there came by today and invited me to come back."

She smiled the same half smirk that teenage boys masturbated to all over the world. "That explains it."

"Explains what?"

"Why your accent was so strong tonight. You must've said 'y'all' a dozen times."

He slapped her bare behind. "I'd mock *your* regional culture, if you had any."

She play-pouted at him. He kissed her. Then he walked to the window and gazed up at the starless city sky.

"I thought you said you didn't want to go back," she said as she sat up.

"I said that because it was better than the truth. Until today, I thought I *couldn't* go back."

"So that's good news, right?"

"Maybe. They also said my ex-fiancée is causing trouble, and they want me to help get her back under control."

"Why is that your problem?"

"I'm not sure it is. That's part of what I'm thinking about."

She got out of bed, unself-conscious as only the truly beautiful can be when they're naked, and came up behind him. She put her arms around his neck and kissed his shoulder. He felt her breasts against his back. "Tell me about it."

"About what?"

"Well . . . about her."

"Her name is Bo-Kate."

Melanie laughed. "That's an unusual name. What does she look like?"

"A lot like you—tall, slender, with dark curly hair and a great pair of tits."

"So you have a type, then?"

"I do." He turned and kissed her again. "We met when we were little kids, but we didn't start dating until we were teenagers. You can't imagine how beautiful she was then, all smooth and soft, like something on a vine just at the right point of ripeness. The first time I saw her naked, she was coming out of a pond where she'd been skinny-dipping. It was like seeing something elemental."

Melanie nipped at his earlobe. "I see it's a vivid memory."

"Well, to be fair, you're adding to the 3-D effect."

"Tell me more about her."

"We couldn't keep our hands off each other. Every chance we got, we'd get together. We skipped school, we ignored our friends, we ignored our families. That was a mistake. You see, we came from opposite sides of our community. We weren't supposed to fool around, let alone fall in love."

"A blood feud, like the Hatfields and McCoys? Mmmm, that's kind of hot."

"You can joke about it if you want, but believe me, it's pretty fucking serious when you're in the middle of it. And it wasn't just our families. It was the whole Tufa community. Nobody wanted us together, and we couldn't stay apart."

"So what happened?"

He looked back out the window. This high, it was almost—almost—like riding the night winds. His voice grew heavy with unaccustomed emotion. "They . . . banished us, I guess you'd call it. They told us never to come back. And we lost . . . we lost a lot of the things that were important to us."

He fought to hold it back, but the emotions were too strong. There was no one way to describe to this beautiful woman the things he'd lost. How did you tell someone what it was like to hear music, to feel it and be around it constantly, yet be unable to make it? To have hands that once mastered the intricacies of twelve-string guitars now useless when any instrument was placed in them? To never be able to harmonize, to hear pitch accurately, to stay on beat?

And there was simply no way to describe Tufa flight to a non-Tufa.

Melanie turned him to face her, and wiped the tears from his cheeks. "Wow, Jeff. I'm sorry I brought this up, I didn't meant to upset you." She paused, then asked, "Do you still love her?"

"No," he said without hesitation. "She's a monster."

"So what are you going to do?"

"I don't see as I really have a choice. And they know that, which pisses me off. I don't like being manipulated."

"Because you're a manipulator?"

He looked down at her and smiled. "Do I manipulate you?"

"I'm a model, it's my job to be manipulated."

"You think you're on the clock when you're with me?"

"I think that I'll do whatever you tell me. Because I want to make you happy, if I can."

"What if I want to make *you* happy?"

"Hm. I can think of a couple of ways that might happen." She put her hands on his shoulders and firmly pushed him down to his knees. Then she draped one perfect, world-famous leg over his shoulder, her smooth thigh against his cheek.

But even as he paid attention to Melanie, Jeff pondered and fumed over what the two Tufa had told him about Bo-Kate. Not only had she killed people, but she now wanted to destroy the careful balance that allowed the Tufa to continue to exist. She did have to be stopped. But how would he do it? He couldn't just ask her to come back to him, not after the way things ended. And he didn't want that. He wanted to put his hands around her neck and choke the life out of her.

He also, he hated to admit, wanted to do to Bo-Kate exactly what he was doing to Melanie. Because no matter how much time went by in the human world, or how many beautiful women he seduced with his power, influence, and money, she was still the best he'd ever had.

At the Holiday Inn on Twenty-ninth Street, Bronwyn sat in one of the padded chairs noodling on her mandolin. She missed Craig, and her parents, and everything about her home, even though she hadn't been gone twenty-four hours yet. She'd never felt like this when she was in Iraq, and put it down to one more thing the baby in her belly had changed about her.

There was a soft knock at the door. "Bronwyn? It's me, Junior. You awake?"

She opened the door and let him in. She wore a man's undershirt and flannel pajama pants, and the shirt didn't quite cover her belly. He was barefoot, in jeans and a T-shirt.

"Excuse me for sitting back down," she said, and plopped heavily on the bed. "What can I do for you, Junior?"

"I was just passing by on my way to the ice machine and heard you playing." That wasn't entirely the truth; he'd actually stood with his ear to her door until he caught the strains of her mandolin.

"You can hear me in the hall? I'm surprised the front desk hasn't called up with a complaint," she joked. In a Yankee accent, she said, " 'We don't allow that kind of redneckery, folks.' "

"This is New York City, they'll just send up some Eye-talians."

She laughed. "You might as well sit down, too. There's nothing on TV, and I'm not up to wandering around Manhattan like a tourist."

"Me, neither, and I ain't even pregnant." He settled into one of the padded but uncomfortable hotel chairs. "How do you think it went today?"

"Oh, fine. I can't imagine he won't say yes. Can you?"

"Does seem unlikely."

"Then we can only hope he's up to the challenge."

After a moment, Junior said, "Did you hear what Bo-Kate said the other day at the Pair-A-Dice? About her plans?"

"I heard *about* it. I got there too late to hear it firsthand."

"It's sure had me thinking. It doesn't sound like it would be that bad, does it? Everybody making money, everyone having jobs. What's bad about that?"

"The cost."

"Changing the name of the town?"

"Not that. It'll cost us our identity. Junior, when I was in Iraq, I wasn't a Tufa, I was just Private Hyatt. There was nothing special about me. I had a good job, and a secure future if I wanted it. If we change everything the way Bo-Kate wants, then yeah, we'll all maybe be a little more comfortable and secure, just like I was. But we won't be Tufa. We'll be way too entangled with the world to ever ride the night winds again. There won't be anything special about us."

"Then why does she want to do it?"

"Because she hates us for what we did to her, and to Jefferson."

"And he doesn't hate us?"

Bronwyn said nothing. The question was unanswerable until it was too late. They had to trust him.

"I reckon," he said, "that's something only Mandalay knows."

She looked at him seriously. "Junior, tell me. Do you *really* want to step in for Rockhouse?"

"I know what you think, Bronwyn. It's what everybody thinks. I ain't smart enough, I ain't sophisticated enough, I ain't scary enough. But you're all wrong. And you know, the proof's sitting right here." He patted his chest. "I got myself in on this trip without too much trouble, didn't I? And this is some important shit."

"It is," she agreed. "And you're actually doing a good job, Junior. I'm impressed."

Junior could handle criticism without blinking, but he had no idea how to react to compliments. To change the subject, he nodded at her stomach and said, "How's your little pea pod doing?"

"She didn't like the flight much. But she's okay now. I think she's sleeping."

He looked away, out the window that showed a view of another nearby building. "My wife's pregnant, too."

"I know. I saw her at Rockhouse's funeral."

"It ain't bringing out her best qualities."

"It's a hard thing for some women, Junior." She winced and wriggled in the chair. "Ow. Guess who's awake now?"

"Did we make too much noise?"

"Probably just me getting wrought up."

"I'm amazed my baby ever sleeps, then," he said a little bitterly. "Loretta is always wrought up."

Bronwyn had no problem seeing Loretta acting that way. She'd always been a whiner, even when they were children, and it was doubtful that bearing a child had made her any nicer. "Sorry, Junior. Maybe she'll stop taking it out on you when the baby's born."

"She was doing it long before the baby came along," he muttered.

Bronwyn picked up her mandolin and began to pick, precise little notes that didn't really develop into anything. Junior fished a harmonica from his pocket.

"You don't sing?" Bronwyn said.

"Whenever I have a problem, I sing. Then I realize my voice is a lot worse than my problem."

He patted the harmonica against his palm a couple of times, then put it to his lips and blew soft, mournful wails in counter-point to what Bronwyn played. If anyone had heard, they would've been moved to tears. But no one did.

23

"Tell me," Jeff said seriously, "exactly what you expect me to do. I mean, exactly. I don't want any misunderstandings."

They were in the hotel's little continental breakfast café, seated at one of the faux-rustic tables. Bronwyn leaned as close as her belly allowed and said, "We want Bo-Kate stopped, and back out of Cloud County. However you need to do that. If it means killing her, that's all right, too."

"Wow," Jeff said. "That escalated quickly."

"It's always been life and death."

"So how did she manage to get back in the first place?"

"We don't know," Junior said. "She just showed up, with this black guy in tow, and the shit hit the fan. She cut off Rockhouse's extra fingers, and he died that night. She gave them to Peggy Goins to show she meant business."

"Who's the black guy?"

"He seems to just be an assistant," Bronwyn said. "He's certainly not the one in charge. And he's British, if that means anything."

Jeff sipped his coffee. He hadn't touched his bagel. "Okay. As far as I know, as far as I can tell, I'm still banished. How do we fix that?"

"It's fixed," Bronwyn said.

"Just like that?"

"Just like that."

"So I'll be able to find Cloud County again?"

"Like you never left."

"How did you manage that?"

She shrugged. Truthfully, even though they weren't 100 percent certain he would agree to help them, they had followed Mandalay's instructions and asked the night winds to listen to them sing "Take Me Home, Country Roads," an inane and obvious choice but one that embodied the right spirit. Even in New York City they were heard and their wish accepted. She only wished every request could be that simple.

"The question is, what will you do?" Junior asked.

"First I'll find her, then I'll talk to her. Then I'll make it up as I go."

"That's not much of a plan."

"You haven't given me much to go on. And you forget, I haven't seen her in a very long time. I'm a different person now; I have to assume she might be, as well."

"Meaning . . . ?"

"Meaning that I don't know how she'll react when she sees me. She might kiss me, she might take a shot at me."

"That's your risk," Bronwyn said.

"Yes, I understand that," Jeff snapped. "And when this is over, whatever the outcome, I get to stay. Right?"

"Yes," Bronwyn said.

"That's it? No dramatic pause? No exchange of a surreptitious glance?"

"No. You're back. You're a Tufa again."

"So . . . I can sing?"

"Just like before."

He sat back, sipped his coffee again, then softly:

> *As I wandered through the townlands,*
> *And the luscious grassy plains,*
> *Who should I meet but a beautiful maid,*
> *At the dawning of the day.*

When he finished, he sat silently for a long time. At last he said, "Well, damn."

"Welcome back," Junior said.

"I have some things I need to do today," he said. "Loose ends to tie up before I leave. I'll be in Needsville by tomorrow night, Thursday morning at the latest. Will my parents know I'm coming, or will I need to stay at Peggy's motel?"

"I'm sorry," Bronwyn said. "Your parents passed away some time ago."

He said nothing, and kept the emotion off his face. "Well . . . it has been a while. My brothers and sister?"

"They're still around. They'll be glad to see you."

"I'm not sure about that. But I have to start somewhere." He handed them each a business card. "My cell's on here. I'll see you both down South."

When he was gone, Bronwyn took a bite of her eggs and said, "This is awful."

"He knows what he's getting into."

"I mean these eggs."

Junior scowled at her. "Ha ha. Do you really think he'll be able to stop her?"

"I don't know. We have to trust that Mandalay's right."

"Yeah. We have to do that a lot, have you noticed?"

"It's the way things are. She's never been wrong."

"Well, there's that. But Bo-Kate killed Rockhouse. We never thought that could happen, either."

"That's an even bigger reason to do what Mandalay tells us."

"So you think she is right?"

"I think she knows more than we do, and so we can't help but be wrong if we second-guess her decisions."

"That sounds a lot like the way Christians like your husband talk about their God."

Bronwyn smiled at the irony. "Yeah, it does. Guess a lot of things work in mysterious ways."

"Hey, man, what're you doing here?" Hector Jacob, leader of the band Meat Raffle, said as Jeff walked into the recording studio. The place smelled of dope and cheap wine, with a slight under-taste of fast-food grease.

"Wanted to see how my favorite band was getting along," Jeff said. The band was in its second week of recording its third album. Drug use was rampant but not affecting performance, and Hector's tendency to get drunk by three in the afternoon was accommodated by having him record all his vocals first. Jeff nod-ded at producer William "Little Bill" Paul, the man who had quickly sorted out how to get the most from the band in the least amount of time.

"We're making the grade," Hector said. "Getting ready to re-hearse 'She's Like a Flower.'"

Jeff knew that one from the band's original demo. He stood before a PRS Custom 24 guitar in its stand and rested his fin-gertips lightly on the head. "Mind if I play along?"

"Okay with me," said Johnny Pigsty, the sullen guitarist.

"You play?" Hector said, surprised.

"I've been known to pick a song or two."

"Sure," Hector said with a shrug. The rest of the band said nothing, but they all watched as Jeff shrugged the strap over his shoulder and plugged into the amp.

"If you get lost," Jeff said, "just go to G and wait for me there."

LONG BLACK CURL   271

The drummer counted off, and the band slammed into the song, which was upbeat, cheery, and had an incredibly catchy chorus. Jeff found the chords easily and felt the eyes of the other band members on him, watching with surprise and appreciation.

When it came time for the instrumental bridge, Hector said, "Take it, Jeff," and Jeff did. His fingers slid expertly up and down the strings, squeezing high, rapid notes out of the instrument with the skill and dexterity of the best session guitarists. But there was something else, a desperate, plaintive quality that worked perfectly against the overall vibe of the song, adding a depth to the simple party tune that no one expected. When he nodded at Hector to begin the final verse, Jeff saw open mouths all around.

The song crashed to an end, and as the last notes faded, Hector said, "Little Bill, please tell me you were recording that."

The intercom clicked open. "Sorry, guys, thought it was just a jam session. Damn, Jeff, I had no idea you could do that. Why have you been hiding it?"

Jeff took off the guitar, put it reverently back on the stand, and took a deep, satisfied breath. He wanted to cry, but figured that would be even more difficult to explain. "I just putz around. I'm better at arguing with people than I am at playing."

"Then you must be the best arguer in the world," drummer Cap Hathstone said. "Glad you're on our side."

Jeff smiled. "Thanks for letting me jam, guys. I'll let you get back to work." He shook hands and slapped high fives all around, turned down an offered joint, then went into the control booth to speak to Little Bill. When the door shut, he said quietly, "You did record it, didn't you?"

"I record everything, you know that."

"Thanks for not telling them."

He shrugged. "I want to keep working with the bands you handle. And it wouldn't be fair to put a solo on the actual album that none of them could play."

"Oh, I wasn't that good."

"You're telling *me* how to listen to music?"

Jeff chuckled. "Can you send me a copy?"

"Sure."

"I'll be out of town for a few days. Have to go home for some family business. Just e-mail it, and I'll get it that way."

"Will do. Where's home, by the way?"

"Tennessee. Up in the Smoky Mountains."

"Beautiful country."

"It is that. Haven't been back there in a long time, so I'm really looking forward to it."

"Well, have a safe trip."

Jeff left the studio and walked down the crowded sidewalk with a lift in his step, whistling "She's Like a Flower." He hadn't truly realized how hollow he'd been until now, when that space was once again filled by music.

24

The plane ride to Nashville had been uneventful, and the rental car was comfortable and rode smoothly up the interstate. Jeff sang along with Sirius's Bluegrass Junction station and pondered what he'd learned.

Earlier that day, after leaving the Nashville airport, he drove into the city. The enormous BellSouth Building, with its batlike silhouette, dominated the skyline. He merged from I-40 to I-24, then exited and crossed the Cumberland River into downtown.

He found Bo-Kate's office with no trouble. He casually entered the waiting room, where posters of various concert package tours lined the walls. There were all kinds: rap, country, pop, and has-beens. A black secretary with a big Afro sat typing behind the desk. "Yes?" she said coolly when she looked up.

"Is Ms. Wisby in?"

"I'm afraid not. Can I take a message?"

"No, I was just in the neighborhood. Bo-Kate and I grew up together in Needsville, I thought I'd stop by and say hi."

"Oh, yeah, I can see the resemblance. Same hair and teeth."

He laughed. "Don't let her know you said that."

"She checks in a couple of times a day. I can tell her you asked about her."

"Nah, that's all right. What's her assistant's name? Jerome?"

"No, Nigel. Nigel Hawtrey."

"Nigel, that's right," Jeff said, snapping his fingers as if it had been right on the tip of his tongue. "English fella, right?"

"That's him."

"Is he here?"

"No," she said with exaggerated seriousness. "Bo-Kate takes him everywhere. A lot of what he does for her isn't covered in the employee handbook, if you know what I mean."

"Really?"

"But you didn't hear it from me."

"Hear what?" he said with a grin. He looked around at the office, all gleaming and new. "Looks like she's doing pretty good for herself." He noticed a framed tour poster on the wall, displaying the face of a young woman with a '60s-style hairdo and extreme eye makeup. "Well, except for that whole thing with Naomi Barden."

"That was tragic," she agreed. "But when a girl's got demons, only she can chase 'em out. And she didn't want to."

Jeff remembered the girl's most successful song, an anthem for her right to keep partying no matter what. The chorus was:

> *I won't sober up*
> *I won't dry out*
> *I won't make amends*
> *I'll always dance and shout.*

"But someone else will come along," the receptionist said. "Bo-Kate has a knack for knowing who's going to be the next big thing."

"That's a good knack to have. Wish I had it."

"Me, too," the secretary said, smiling at last.

Jeff said, "Can I leave her a note for when she comes back?"

"Sure." She handed him a notepad, with Wisby Tour Management's logo across the top.

Jeff wrote, "Listen to the mandolin rain and the banjo wind," signed just his first name, and folded it up. He had no illusions that the secretary would leave it unread, but that was okay. The message would mean nothing to anyone but Bo-Kate, and she wouldn't read it until after he'd dealt with her, one way or the other.

Now as he drove west on Interstate 40 past Cookeville, his adrenaline faded, replaced with the kind of dread only someone doomed to see an old lover can feel. But in his case, it was more than just "old lover": it was coconspirator and evil genius. What he and Bo-Kate had done in the name of their love now appalled him, and he hardly knew the young man he'd once been, who was capable of such atrocities.

No, that wasn't true. He *did* know him. Because the thing he truly hated to admit to himself was that what they'd done felt *good*. When they'd torn into each other afterwards, biting and clawing and fucking until they both couldn't move, it had been the grandest, biggest thing he'd ever felt. His main worry was that, when he saw Bo-Kate, that feeling would return. He wasn't sure he was strong enough even now to resist it.

It was midafternoon when Jeff topped the hill and saw Needsville in the valley below.

He pulled to the side of the road and sat, trying to calm his physical self as well as his emotions. His heart pounded, sweat trickled down the back of his neck, and his chest tightened. He was astounded at how little the town had changed in the unbelievable years he'd been away. There were some new things: Wires ran down the highway, streetlights gleamed in the winter dimness, and a new convenience store beckoned. But everything else was the same. He felt like there should be horses tied outside the buildings instead of parked cars.

"Remember what year it is, dumb-ass," he whispered to himself. "And remember why you're here." He put both shaking hands on the steering wheel, and pulled back onto the highway.

He stopped in front of the Catamount Corner, alongside three other vehicles with out-of-state plates. He got out and went up the steps before he could talk himself out of it.

The lobby was a lot like he remembered it, although the knick-nacks for sale were now extraneous decorations, not useful sundries. In the little café, a couple sat talking in low tones, their eyes not leaving each other. He went to the desk and tapped the bell.

Peggy Goins emerged and said cheerily, "Yes, sir, how may I help?"

"You can help by saying hello, Miss Peggy."

It took her a moment. "My God. Jefferson Powell."

"I'm your god? That's flattering."

She laughed. "I'm sorry, it's just . . . I mean, I knew you were coming, but to see you there, just standing there like nobody's business . . ."

"It's a surprise to me, too. You're looking well."

"I'm feeling great. Especially now that you're here to deal with that girlfriend of yours."

"She's not my girlfriend, Miss Peggy. She hasn't been for a long time."

"Well, she's got everyone stirred up here, that's for sure."

"Any idea where she is?"

"No, I'm afraid not. The last time I saw her, she was standing right there, took a shot at a twelve-year-old girl and then ran off. As far as I know, no one's seen her since."

"A twelve-year-old girl?"

"Mandalay Harris. She carries the songs."

"Ah. I suppose I need to talk to her, then. Where does she live?"

"Out across Jury Creek. In a house trailer with her dad and stepmom."

"Reckon she'll be expecting me?"

"Probably." She smiled. "It's good to see you, Jeff. Thank you for coming to help. I know it couldn't have been easy after what happened."

"No, but Bronwyn Hyatt made me an offer I couldn't refuse."

"She's good at things like that."

Simultaneously down the street, Peggy's husband, Marshall, sat behind the desk in the closet-sized office that served as Needsville's city hall. Marshall had been the mayor for a decade, and no one seemed inclined to challenge him. It was not a job with many perks. As he stuffed property tax bills into envelopes, he thought about how many times he'd done this, and how in a couple of weeks he'd have a high percentage of overdue notices to send out as well. He disliked doing that even more.

There was a knock at the door. He said, "It's open," and looked up.

A woman with black curly hair entered, followed by a limping giant. Sun from the door backlit them, hiding their faces.

Marshall stared. He didn't recognize either of them. "Can I help y'all?"

The woman turned to the giant. "Recognize this gentleman?"

"Yeah," the giant rumbled. "He was at the fire."

Marshall realized whom he now faced. "What do you want, Bo-Kate?"

"Me? Nothing at all. Byron here . . . he's got a bone to pick with you."

She stepped aside so that Byron could loom over Marshall's desk. His leg brace clanked with each step.

"You were there," Byron rumbled. "You sat down with us like it was no big deal. You *knew* I'd been stuck there for sixty years, and you didn't lift a finger to help me."

"I couldn't help you, man. I'm not important enough. I'm—"

"My little girl *died*!" Byron roared, and swept everything off the desk. Tax notices went everywhere. "And my grandchildren, who I never met! If I'd been there, I could've changed things!"

Marshall jumped to his feet and backed against the wall. "Call him off, Bo-Kate. This won't help anyone."

"It'll help him," she said with a malevolent grin.

Marshall could tell by the giant's expression that he'd have to talk fast to get out of this. "Friend, I swear to you, there was no way I could—"

The giant grabbed Marshall by the hair and slammed his head down hard into the desk. Stunned, Marshall staggered to his feet, and the giant punched him in the chest. Marshall felt the impact down through his toes, and fell back into the wall. The giant roared and grabbed him around the throat.

Bo-Kate stepped up to the giant. "Sing the song I told you," she said, then smiled with such evil that Marshall knew he was doomed.

The giant began to sing, his rage making the words bite:

In Oranmore in the County Galway
One pleasant evening in the month of May
I spied a damsel, she was young and handsome
Her beauty fairly took my breath away.

She wore no jewels or costly diamonds
No paint or powder, no, none at all
She wore a bonnet with a ribbon on it
And around her shoulders was the Galway shawl. . . .

Marshall's chest felt crushed, as if bands of metal tightened around him. He couldn't breathe now, the huge hand around his neck, and he felt the giant lift him off his feet, dangling him like a small child's toy.

"You son of a bitch," the giant snarled at him. "How many of you damned Tufas knew I was sitting up there while my baby girl suffered and died? If I could kill all of you, I would."

But he didn't have to do anything else. The song, coupled with Marshall's own weakness, combined to drain the life from him, and what the giant dropped to the floor of the city hall was only a shell for the spirit that had departed.

"And that," Bo-Kate said with satisfaction, "is why it pays to learn as many dying dirges as you can."

Byron looked down at the dead man. He should've felt something other than seething fury, but each time he started to simmer down, the memory of his little girl came rushing back and restoked his anger. He said quietly, "I suppose we should leave now."

Bo-Kate smiled down at Marshall's body, also thinking of the past, specifically the time on the hilltop when Marshall looked her right in the eye as he joined in singing her out. Marshall had been much younger then, and Bo-Kate suspected that he had a thing for her; certainly he and Jefferson had no love lost between them, having been rivals since forever. Every encounter between the two of them had led to a competition of some sort, and Bo-Kate had been merely the latest bone of contention. Jefferson won, but Marshall had the last laugh.

Until now.

"Yes," she said. "We should get out of here. Don't worry, unless you squeezed his neck so hard it left bruises, it'll just show he died of natural causes. Probably a heart attack, judging from the way he was clutching his chest."

"I don't care," Byron growled. He kicked Marshall's body with his bad leg, wincing at the pain but glad to feel the impact.

Bo-Kate turned him to face her. "Byron, don't shoot your anger wad all in one place. We're just getting started."

He glared at her. "Where did you learn to talk, girl? I was in the army, and we didn't swear as much."

"The world's different now. Just come on."

They went outside to the SUV, where Nigel waited behind the wheel. He stared straight ahead, not even looking as they climbed into their seats. The vehicle shifted as Byron settled his weight. Nigel said flatly, "Where to now?"

"Back home. Already accomplished a day's work, haven't we, Byron?"

"Hmph," he said.

As they waited to turn onto the highway, a pickup pulled into the post office parking lot. Bo-Kate frowned as the man who got out sauntered over to them and tapped on her window.

"Afternoon, Ms. Wisby," Junior Damo said. He nodded at Nigel and Byron. "Gentlemen. How goes the campaign? Trying to get the mayor on your side?"

From the backseat, Byron said, "You want me to—?"

"No, Byron, that's all right. You two wait here for a minute."

She opened the door, forcing Junior to jump back. When she stepped out, she saw by his deferential body language that she had all the power, and it took all her self-control not to laugh. She said, "You been following me, Junior?"

"Nope. I been out of town. Just got back and happened by."

"Uh-huh. At the Pair-A-Dice, you said you'd be better than me at leading the Tufa, right?"

"Yeah, I do say," he said, not meeting her eyes.

"Well, let me ask you something. If you had the chance to shoot Mandalay Harris in the head, would you do it?"

He looked up sharply. "What?"

"Would you shoot her in the head if you could? She's your true rival; she represents everything you're against. She leads the other side."

"She's just a *kid*."

"See? That's the difference here. I don't care about that. Hell, I tried to shoot her once, but I missed. Next time, I won't." She patted him on the cheek. "You want to see what a real leader does? Go in the city hall and look around." Then she turned on her heel and got back into the SUV.

As he watched her drive off, Junior realized he was sweating, and shaking. He wondered if she had noticed. For the first time, he had real second thoughts about his plans. There was something in her eyes that was more terrifying than anything he'd ever imagined. And he doubted that even Jefferson Powell could handle her.

He looked back at the city hall door. The thought of seeing whatever Bo-Kate had left was too much for him, and he got back into his truck. He turned the radio up as loud as it would go, not caring that it made the cracked speaker buzz. His tires squealed as he tore out of the parking lot and turned in the opposite direction from Bo-Kate, heading out of town and up the hill toward the county line.

He wasn't ready to give up, though; he simply knew he had to change tactics.

25

Jeff knew he'd be meeting a little girl, but the reality still took him by surprise.

Mandalay Harris was not quite five feet tall, and slender with the first hints of teen curves. She had a small mouth, narrow chin, and long neck, with her black hair down past her shoulders. But it was her eyes that held him: he saw the great distance in them, the unmistakable sign that this was, indeed, the psychic descendant of Ruby Montana, the woman who'd led the song that banished him and Bo-Kate.

He made a complex gesture of respect and subservience. She returned a sign of acknowledgment.

"Come in," Mandalay responded.

He entered the trailer. Two adults, whom he took to be Mandalay's parents, sat at the kitchen table. Neither stood or spoke. "Hi," Jeff said. They both nodded.

Mandalay said, "Follow me."

He trailed her down the hall to her room. It was hard not to watch her minutely, knowing as he did what she really was. She closed the door behind them and said, "Have a seat, if you'd like."

He pulled out the desk chair. She sat on the edge of

her bed. Jeff looked around at the typical tween girl decor. He pointed at a band poster and said, "I manage them."

"Really?"

"Yeah. They won't be around for long. The only real talent in the group is the drummer. The singer's letting himself get fat, and the guitarist can't even play 'Smoke on the Water.' "

"It must be hard to make them sound so good."

"Nah. With Auto-Tune and session players, anybody can sound great. Then they just lip-synch on tour."

A long silence settled between them. Finally Jeff said, "So I'm here. At your command, I understand."

"My suggestion. How does it feel to be back?"

"Strange."

"I bet. Have you seen Bo-Kate yet?"

"No. I haven't even been home yet."

"Do you know about your parents?"

He nodded. "But my brothers and sister are still around, right?"

"They are." She stood and walked to the door, then stood with her back against it. The maturity and grace of her movements, contrasted with her preteen form, made her seem even more alien. She said, "I'm putting a lot of faith in you, Jefferson. Many people think it's misplaced. They remember what happened before."

He had to swallow hard before speaking. "I'm not like that anymore."

"I hope not. Bo-Kate is. She mutilated Rockhouse and took a shot at me. It's only a matter of time before she flat-out kills someone, if you don't stop her."

"I understand. But if she's so dangerous, why didn't *you* stop her?"

Mandalay looked down. "This will sound absurd to you. It does to me, honestly. But . . . I'm too weak." She met his eyes. "I have more knowledge and memory than you can imagine,

Jefferson, but I'm still . . . I'm a kid. Bo-Kate tried to kill me, and probably will again. That terrifies me. I haven't told anyone else this, so I'm trusting you. I can't stop her, because I'm too scared."

Jeff said nothing. He tried to imagine Ruby Montana, with all her bluster and certainty and profanity, admitting that she was scared. The image just wouldn't come.

"I have no idea how she was able to overcome her banishment and return," Mandalay continued. "The idea that she might be more powerful than Rockhouse, than me, than *any* Tufa is just . . . terrifying. And I'm also too scared to send any of my friends to deal with her, in case something happens to them."

"But you're not too scared to send me?"

"No." She went to the window and looked out at the snowy yard. "Do you have a plan?"

"Not really. I suppose I'll find her and try to talk to her first."

"And when that fails?"

"How do you know it'll fail?"

"Because I've seen her. You haven't."

"Well, if it does . . . I'll take whatever action is necessary."

The implication hung in the air. "You can do that?" she asked.

"I can do that."

She turned back to look at him. "There's a deadline, you know."

"No, I didn't. Nobody mentioned that."

"Tuesday. The night of the full moon. On that night, the future of the Tufa will be decided."

"You or her?"

"It appears so."

"Majority vote?"

"Or something like that. Whatever the people want."

He stood. Despite the winter chill, he was sweating with nervousness. "Then I guess I better get to work." He made another complex gesture, which Mandalay returned. "I'll be in touch."

"No need. I'll know if you're successful."

He nodded. She opened the bedroom door and preceded him down the hall.

Icarus Holmes found Marshall two hours later. He rushed to tell Peggy. Peggy called Bliss at the fire station, where she was staying until the insurance on her house was settled. Bliss called Bronwyn and Mandalay, then called in another EMT so they could take the ambulance down into town.

Peggy then called the police. Cloud County did not actually have a sheriff, so State Trooper Alvin Darwin, a one-quarter Tufa who had the distinctive black hair and dusky skin, responded. Bliss and the other EMT took Marshall's body back to the Catamount Corner, where a spare trundle bed was set up in the café for him. He lay in state, covered by a quilt, as Peggy sobbed in a chair beside him. Darwin patiently asked her the questions he would need answered to close the official investigation.

Bronwyn stood in the café door, out of breath from climbing the steps. Her husband, Craig, stood beside her.

"You should leave," Bronwyn said softly.

"Okay." He kissed his wife on the cheek and said, "Call me if you need me."

Bronwyn nodded. She knew Craig only wanted to help, and certainly his training as a minister, plus his innate goodness as a person, would be very welcome. But more than comfort was needed here.

Bliss joined Bronwyn and helped her take off her heavy coat. Bronwyn asked quietly, "I'm guessing Bo-Kate was behind this?"

"I don't know," Bliss said. "He looks like he had a heart attack. I've seen enough of those to recognize the signs."

"Come on. You don't really believe that, do you?"

Bliss shrugged. "Not really."

"Did anyone see her around?"

"No. No one saw anything. Icarus said he just stopped by after getting his mail because he saw the light on. Without Rockhouse sitting on the post office porch all day, hardly anyone sticks around, they just get their mail and go."

Bronwyn suddenly winced and leaned against the wall. At Bliss's concerned look, she said, "The baby's learning to clog dance, I think. I just don't know how she got hard-sole shoes in there." She took several deep breaths, then said, "Where's Mandalay?"

"On her way."

"Someone should be with her. Protecting her. I'm too fucking big around right now to be much protection."

"She'll be fine."

"Are you saying that because you're sure, or because you want it to be true?"

Bliss turned in surprise. There was a bite to Bronwyn's words that she hadn't heard before. "What are you so angry about?"

"You mean besides Marshall being dead, Rockhouse being dead, and your house burning to the ground?"

"Is it because you can't take a more active hand in all this?"

"That *does* piss me off," she admitted.

Bliss put her hand on Bronwyn's belly. "What you're doing is just as important. Maybe even more so. She's the future."

"I *know* that. I'm just aggravated that the future is taking so long to get her ass out here."

Darwin left Peggy and joined the other two women. "I've got what I need. You'll sign that it was heart attack, natural causes, right?"

Bliss nodded. It didn't matter what the actual cause was on the paperwork; the important thing was to fill it out and file it in such a way that no one thought to come around snooping. The Tufa had mastered the skill of avoiding official notice.

LONG BLACK CURL   287

"Then I'll be heading out." He looked back at the body, and at Peggy crying beside it. "That's a damn shame, all right. Marshall was a good fella."

"He was," Bliss agreed.

Darwin put on his coat and broad-brimmed hat before he stepped out into the cold evening. He held the door for two more women, both First Daughters. They nodded at Bliss and Bronwyn, but said nothing.

Bronwyn said softly, "So have you seen Jeff since he got back?"

"No."

"Me, neither."

"Then how do we know he's even here?"

"I've seen him," Peggy said, her voice ragged. They hadn't realized she was listening. "He came by this afternoon. I was probably talking to him when Marshall . . ." She trailed off and began to cry again.

"At least he's here, then," Bronwyn said.

"What do you think he'll do?" Bliss asked.

"I hope he'll walk up to her and put a bullet in her head. Someone should, and I wish to God I was in a condition to do it myself."

"That's not the way to handle it," Mandalay said.

They turned. She stood right behind them, bundled in her winter coat, with the fur-lined hood around her face. She pushed it back and added, "We still need to find out how she was able to come back without being pardoned. And any justice she faces, needs to come from someone in the right position to dispense it."

"You saying I'm not the right one?" Bronwyn said. "It's my fucking *job*."

"But it's not the job we need done right now." She said it with the certainty that was usually comforting, but now just pissed Bronwyn off more.

"And what do we need done, then? Wait until—"

"We wait until Jeff Powell does what he can do. If he fails, then perhaps your solution will be best. But until then, we leave it to him."

"Have you even met him?" Bronwyn challenged. Then she winced as the baby kicked her again.

"I don't think you should let yourself get so upset," Mandalay said.

"You might have a point," Bronwyn said through gritted teeth.

"Are you all right?" Bliss asked.

"I think the little shit cracked a rib," Bronwyn said. Her face grew red from pain.

Bliss and Mandalay helped her sit in one of the lobby's overstuffed chairs. After a few moments, the pain subsided, and her color returned to normal. Other First Daughters arrived, milling about the lobby, allowing Peggy her time alone with Marshall.

Then Peggy began to sing, an ancient song that used the same tune as "For He's a Jolly Good Fellow."

> *Marlbrook the Prince of Commanders*
> *Is gone to war in Flanders,*
> *His fame is like Alexander's,*
> *But when will he ever come home?*

Bronwyn and Bliss exchanged a look. The song was lighthearted and rollicking, a silly song even though it was about death and loss.

Mandalay walked into the café and stood beside Peggy, her hand on the older woman's shoulder. They sang together:

> *Perhaps at Trinity Feast, or*
> *Perhaps he may come at Easter,*
> *I swear he had better make haste or*
> *We fear he may never come home.*

The other First Daughters joined them, draping their coats over chair backs or tossing them atop tables. They gathered around Marshall, and all joined in.

> *For Trinity Feast is over,*
> *And has brought no news from Dover,*
> *And Easter is passed moreover,*
> *And Malbrook still delays.*

Bliss helped Bronwyn stand at the back of the little group, and they joined the others. Many were smiling, and some chuckled as they sang,

> *Milady in her watch-tower*
> *Spends many a pensive hour,*
> *Not knowing why or how her*
> *Dear lord from England stays.*

Now the group grew more somber.

> *While sitting quite forlorn in*
> *That tower, she spies returning*
> *A page clad in deep mourning,*
> *With fainting steps and slow.*

In the break between stanzas, someone sniffled. A few voices quavered with emotion.

> *Oh, page, I pray, come faster!*
> *What news do you bring of your master?*
> *I fear there is some disaster,*
> *Your looks are so full of woe.*

As the song detailed the end of Malbrook, the singing grew serious, and a few voices dropped out to cry. Bronwyn had to sit in one of the chairs, still wincing at the pain in her side, Mandalay continued to rest her hand on Peggy's shoulder, giving her the strength of her presence and the full weight of generations of Tufa women who'd lost lovers.

It didn't make her cry any less.

26

Jeff got out of the truck and sank up to his ankles in the snow. There was always a drift in this spot, and apparently the contours that guided the wind had not changed in all the years he'd been away.

Plenty of other things had, though. The old Powell home place was mostly gone; the brick chimney remained, and the stone foundation, but the wooden structure had vanished. He wondered if it had simply fallen or been deliberately taken down, but there was no way to tell from the old driveway. He pulled on gloves, wished he'd brought real boots, and trudged through the snow to the remains.

He tried to see it as it was now, not as it had been, but the memories were too strong and fought their way around any mental barriers he erected to stop them. Here was the corner of the porch where Sandy the old hunting dog liked to hide from the sun; over there was the maple tree with the swing made out of a tractor tire that was too heavy for any of the kids to move on their own. His dad's old Ford Model 79 flatbed was always parked in the shade right there, and the chickens would shelter under it from the rain.

Here had been the front door. There was still a two-inch piece of doorjamb protruding up like a hangnail from the rock foundation, and he remembered the way the old hinges squeaked when anyone entered the house. Inside the foundation, the snow covered a layer of accumulated leaves and twigs that crunched as he walked over to the fireplace.

How many times had his mama called them all to supper from the window beside that hearth? How often had the smell of burning wood led them home from deep in the forest? He put his hand on the old bricks and closed his eyes, letting the memories come, hearing the voices and cacophony of the Powell home come to life around him, the songs that they would always sing on cold winter evenings just like this. . . .

He forced himself back to the moment. There was no sense in mourning. His parents were long dead, and his siblings had gone to their own respective lives, where they no doubt had children and grandchildren of their own now. Only he remained alone.

He took out a pocketknife that he'd bought at a convenience store in Nashville and wedged it in around a particular brick. The mortar's seal was already broken, but the ice that coated it needed to be chipped away before the brick slid out. Once it did, he took off his glove, reached inside and felt around until his fingers snagged the old chain.

He pulled it out slowly. A girl's high school class ring hung on it, and he held it up to the light. The words around the birthstone read CLOUD COUNTY HIGH SCHOOL.

He smiled, put it over his head, and tucked it into his shirt. The icy metal stung against his chest. He put back the brick and picked his way out of the ruins.

He had almost reached his rental truck when a voice said, "That's far enough. Who are you?"

Jeff smiled. "It's your big brother."

He turned. Holden Powell stood beside the fireplace, having

emerged from the woods, with a shotgun leveled in Jeff's direction. He was middle aged, heavy jowled, and unshaven. Unruly gray hair stuck out at odd angles from beneath a wool cap.

"Good God A'mighty," Holden said, and lowered the gun. "What the hell you doing here, Jeff?"

"I done got me some special dispensation," he said wryly. "They want me to figure out what Bo-Kate's up to and get her to stop before anybody else dies."

"So you done heard about Marshall Goins, then?"

Jeff caught his breath. "No. What happened?"

"He's dead. Everybody figures it was Bo-Kate."

"Shit fire," Jeff sighed. He and Marshall went way back, and once they had contested for Bo-Kate's affections. Jefferson won; he wondered how different things might have been had he lost. "Guess I'm too late for ol' Marshall."

Holden crunched through the leaves and snow and put one boot on top of the foundation stones. "So how does rootin' around in our old home place help you deal with Bo-Kate?"

"Needed a souvenir of old times. Figured it'd still be here."

"Was it?"

"Yeah." After a moment, he continued, "So . . . how's everyone?"

"Everyone who?"

"Bascom, Nadine, Milgrom. You."

"Bascom's fine. He's on disability from hurting his back. Nadine lives over in Asheville; she runs one of them New Age witchy stores, and spends all her free time drumming with the hippies in the park. Milgrom's still farming."

"And you?"

"Ain't no news with me. Married Edney Hemphill, we got four kids now. Youngest one's a sophomore."

"Done pretty good for yourself."

"Yeah."

They both paused, trying to decide if the bonds of family still existed after what had happened. Jeff looked at his younger brother closely. "You ain't gonna rat me out, are you?"

"To Bo-Kate? Why would I?"

"'Cause of what happened."

"That was a long time ago."

"Yeah, I know that. I also know that around here, grudges tend to hang in the air. Especially family grudges."

"We're both grown men now, Jeff. I got a family. If anything happens to me, nobody to take care of them. You got a family?"

"I have clients. They take more care than families."

Holden chuckled. "You always wanted to go somewhere big."

"Yeah, well . . . it wasn't all it was cracked up to be. You gonna keep this to yourself, little brother?"

"Sure thing, big brother. I'll even act surprised next time I see you." And with that, he turned and walked back into the woods.

Jeff watched him go, remembering the little boy who used to trail after him to the swimming hole. Back then his black hair had been impossible to comb, his little torso had been lean and muscular, and his feet were so black with dirt, he looked like he was wearing shoes until he wiggled his toes. Now he was a heavy-set, middle-aged man with graying hair, stubble, and worn-out clothes. Did he remember his big brother with the same vividness, Jeff wondered?

Jeff went back to his truck, fastened the seat belt, and touched the ring against his chest. He recalled the day they exchanged them, lying naked in the back of his father's old pickup, the air around them damp and still with the heat of summer and their recent exertions. He'd never felt more certain of anything in his life: He knew he wanted to spend the rest of his existence, and for a Tufa that was saying something, with the girl beside him.

Now he had to face her again after all these years, all this time—both regular time and Tufa time—and get her to stop what she was doing. He'd never been able to get her to stop anything before—and sometimes, that had been amazing. But now, people were dying.

Of course, people had died before. That's what got them banished in the first place.

As they drove back to town through the heavy winter evening, Nigel kept glancing in the rearview mirror. Byron's huge frame almost filled his field of vision, and the man stared out at the night with the pensive seriousness of someone pondering weighty things. Nigel wasn't sure what to think of this big man: either he was mental, a modern man who believed he was a vintage rockabilly singer, or he was the real deal, and Nigel's whole view of the universe had to change.

And then there was Bo-Kate. He had no idea how to feel about her now. The things she'd done—and done with smiles, and laughter, and joy—appalled and terrified him. And he had no idea what she might do next.

"Drive past the motel, Nigel, and look for a place to pull over," she said. "Then kill the lights."

The motel parking lot was full of other vehicles, and lights blazed from within the café. People stood on the porch smoking and talking. Nigel thought he heard music as they passed, but it was faint and uncertain.

They topped a small rise and he pulled off the road onto a wide section of the shoulder. He turned off the lights and turned to Bo-Kate. "Now what?"

"We do a little hiking," she said cheerily. She turned to Byron. "Your leg up to it?"

"My leg is fine," he growled. "What will this accomplish, though?"

"Well, we're going to meet another old friend of yours, someone I think you'll be glad to clear the air with, just like you did with Marshall."

Bo-Kate led them through the forest. If there was a trail or path, Nigel couldn't see it, and instead followed Byron's broad back. They went down into a gully, then up the other side until they found themselves on a hillside, looking down on the Catamount Corner from the back. They couldn't see into any of the ground-floor windows, but they heard the music clearly now: plaintive, aching tunes of love and loss. Nigel's eyes started to burn with sympathy, and only the cold kept him from crying.

If Bo-Kate noticed, she didn't let on. "Watch the edge of the woods below," she said. "That's where he'll come out."

"Where who will come out?" Nigel asked.

"You'll see," Bo-Kate said almost gleefully.

They sat in the cold night for what seemed like hours but, according to Nigel's cell phone, was only about thirty minutes. By the time Bo-Kate said, "There!" and pointed, Nigel's feet were numb.

A shambling, zombielike figure emerged from the woods. It paused to look around and listen to the music coming from inside. Then it shuffled over to a back door and picked up what, at this distance, appeared to be a plate of food that had been left there.

Without a word, Byron started down the hill at a trot, using the trees as supports. He moved with surprising stealth for a man so big, and with a bad leg. "What's he going to do?" Nigel asked softly.

Before she could answer, Byron reached the other man and, with no preliminaries, laid him out with a wild roundhouse punch to the head. The plate flew into the motel's brick wall and shattered.

"They'll hear it," Nigel said.

"Not over the music," Bo-Kate said with certainty.

Byron pulled the man to his feet and punched him again. The other man attempted to crawl away, but Byron stood over him and kicked him in the side with his good foot.

"Are you going to let him kill him, too?" Nigel asked.

"No," Bo-Kate said as if it were the most casual thing in the world, "but I want the big guy to work off some steam."

"Who *is* he, Bo-Kate? I mean, I know who he apparently thinks he is, but that can't be, can it?"

"What was one of the first things I told you about the Tufa, Nigel?"

"That time doesn't work the same for everybody."

"Exactly. Believe it or not, that *is* Byron Harley, the real one, the one who supposedly died in a plane crash sixty years ago. To him, those sixty years passed in a single night."

"But, Bo-Kate, that . . . that isn't possible."

She grinned. He was beginning to hate that smile. "It is here, my little Brit."

They watched Byron pummel the other man for a few more minutes; then Bo-Kate led Nigel down the slope. When they reached the others, Byron was breathing heavily, and the other man groaned and held his ribs.

"Enjoying yourself?" Bo-Kate said.

"Just getting warmed up," Byron growled. "This son of a bitch owes me a life."

"You're not cashing that check today," she said. "He's actually very important to the Tufa community, and we need him alive."

She knelt beside him. In the glow from the motel's security lights, Nigel saw that he was an old man, with ragged whiskers and a dirt-smeared face. His clothes were oft-repaired rags, and his boots were held together with duct tape.

"Well, if it isn't the scariest man in Cloud County," she said. "Not so scary now, are you, Eli?"

The sin eater said nothing. He groaned deep in his throat.

"Oh, you'll be fine, old man. Just some bruises and cuts. Nothing you can't sweat out. Now, I want you to listen to me very closely. Are you listening?"

The old man nodded.

"Other people are going to die. You'll have plenty of sins to eat very soon. But once that's done, once everyone agrees that I'm in charge, things will be peaceful again. And this time, there won't be that undercurrent of tension between that six-fingered old bastard and a damn little girl. This time the peace will be solid."

The sin eater said nothing. He just looked into her eyes, and Nigel noticed that Bo-Kate looked away, unable to hold his gaze. She got up, wiped her hands on her jeans, and said, "Come on, gentlemen. Back to the truck. Places to go."

Byron bent down and said, "You have no idea how lucky your sorry ass is tonight." Then he kicked the man once more and followed Bo-Kate up the hill, into the woods. Nigel brought up the rear, fighting the sick feeling that now roiled inside him.

In the truck, Nigel drove with his hands tight on the wheel. When Bo-Kate put her hand on his arm, she said, "Wow, what's with the death grip?'

"I'm in new moral territory," he said without looking at her. "I'm learning my bearings as I go."

"You having second thoughts?"

He risked a glance at her, but her face was shadowed. "Second thoughts about your reign of terror? Of course not. I'm still on your payroll."

"And in my bed?"

"Of course."

"Good." She leaned close and said softly, "Although you might have to share me with Byron. How do you feel about that?"

"I don't own you; therefore, I cannot share you."

She laughed. "You always know what to say, Nigel."

He smiled. But he thought to himself, *If only that were true.*

27

Bo-Kate rose on the bed and pushed her hair out of her eyes. She was naked, and so was Byron Harley, his big body stretched out on the guest room bed. He'd dragged the sheet over his bad leg, although truthfully she didn't mind it at all. But he was not rising to the occasion despite her best efforts, and that was starting to bug her. If she knew anything, it was how to give a blow job, both metaphorically and literally.

"What's wrong?" she asked, trying not to sound impatient. She'd wanted to make love to him since she was twelve, and to have him this close but apparently uninterested was not something she could tolerate.

He didn't look at her. "Just got a lot on my mind."

"Feeling guilty about beating up those two guys? Look, they—"

"It's got nothing to do with them."

Suddenly she understood. "Your wife?"

"Her name is Donna. And yeah. Her, and Harmony."

"You can't tell me you haven't fooled around on her before. You're a musician, for God's sake."

He glared at her, and his face turned red. "I don't think you want to get into this."

"Byron, she's not around anymore. You can do what you want."

His massive right hand tangled in her hair and jerked her face close to his. "What do you know about it?"

She gasped, though not from pain. She loved the sense of being overpowered, because it happened so seldom. "If it'll make you feel better to hit me, go ahead."

He shoved her away to the end of the bed, almost toppling her onto the floor. "I don't want to hit you. I'm sorry, Bo-Kate, it's just . . . I mean, when I cheated on her before, I always told myself I'd make it up to her when this whole rock-and-roll thing ran its course. I'd be the best husband in the world, the best father. Only now . . . I'll never get the chance. So cheating on her, on *them,* actually feels worse now that she's gone. Does that make sense?"

Bo-Kate knelt on the bed. "It does. You're a good man, Byron. You don't deserve what happened to you."

"Tell me about it."

"But you also have to move forward. You can't reach back in time, you know. Not even the Tufa can do that." She sat back on her heels and arched her back, presenting herself to him as submissive and feminine. "Let me help you. Let me show you what this world has for you."

He looked her up and down. Out of the corner of her eye, she saw him begin to respond.

She slowly, gently cupped her breasts, barely touching the skin, and closed her eyes. It had no effect on her, but she knew very few men who could resist it. Then she slid one hand down between her thighs.

Through her eyelashes, she saw him now fully aroused. When he reached for her, it was all she could do not to laugh in triumph.

———

When it became clear that Bo-Kate was not returning anytime soon—and the sounds that bled through from across the hall left no doubt—Nigel slipped out of bed, dressed quietly, and went out into the hall. He thought seriously about jumping into the SUV and fleeing this whole disturbing scene, and if he'd been certain it would free him from Bo-Kate's wrath, he might have done it. But of course he could never be sure of that. If what she told him was true, on top of the things he'd seen for himself, the only place he could ever be safe was by her side, doing her bidding. That thought terrified him the most.

He saw light at the bottom of the stairs and went down to find Tain seated at the kitchen table, drinking a cup of coffee and reading a romance novel. As always, she seemed dressed for a hot summer's day.

She looked up with a little half smile. "What are you doing up at this hour?"

"One could ask the same of you."

"I have to be at the diner by five."

"May I join you?"

"At the diner?"

"At the table."

"I reckon. Bo-Kate asleep?"

"She's entertaining her other guest."

"And she didn't include you?"

"I'm not sure a threesome is in my job description."

"Mm, too bad. So what did you do today?"

"We drove around and met some people."

"Marshall Goins, I assume. Heard he turned up dead."

Nigel had not been in the city hall, and so hadn't seen what occurred. Still, he suspected, and now it was confirmed. "He did?"

Tain nodded. "Heart attack. They say, at least."

Nigel felt a flood of relief. Natural causes were no one's fault. "That's unfortunate."

"But not a big surprise, not when Bo-Kate's around."

"Do lots of people drop dead of heart attacks in her vicinity?"

Tain did not smile when she said, "Lots of people die around her, yes."

Nigel looked at the scratched, ancient tabletop. "I'd appreciate you keeping this between us, Tain, but I'm having serious second thoughts about our purpose here."

"Don't have the stomach for a shock-and-awe campaign?"

"No, not really. My skills are administrative and logistical. And my relationship with Bo-Kate was founded on beliefs that have proven not to be true." He paused. "I admit an attraction to powerful women, and when we first crossed that line between business and personal, I found it incredibly exciting. And surprisingly easy to maintain. But now . . ."

"You're in it up to your neck, aren't you?"

"I am. And I fear I may drown in it. And that isn't something I want."

"I wish I could help you, Nigel. You seem like a nice guy."

"For a 'colored boy'?"

She took his hand sympathetically. "No, you seem like a nice guy, period."

"Thank you. But I fear that is no longer the case. And I truly fear things may get worse."

She bit her lip thoughtfully. It was one of the sexiest things Nigel had ever seen any woman do, ever. Then she said, "I know someone who might be able to help you."

"And who is that?"

"I can't say. I need to check with this other person first. But if I'm right, I'll connect the two of you."

"It will have to be soon. Whatever Bo-Kate ultimately has planned, it's coming to a head. One can't accumulate too many bodies without attracting attention."

"I'll get back to you later today. What's your cell number?"

LONG BLACK CURL   303

He took a card from his wallet and slid it to her. "If I sound a bit nonsensical when I answer it's because your cousin is listening and I want her to think it's a misdial."

"Gotcha."

"Thank you."

She bit her lip again. "I wish we had time for you to do that properly."

28

The Hang Dog Diner was packed with its usual morning regulars, and Tain stayed busy refilling coffee, taking orders, and avoiding impulsive butt-grabs. The other waitresses—heavyset, dour matrons already tired of life and love—looked at her askance, but knew better than to say anything. Tain wasn't deliberately courting this attention; it just came to her, especially from the non-Tufa men who didn't understand what she was. The women may not have known either, but they did realize it wasn't deliberate, she didn't encourage it, and however annoying it was, it wasn't her fault. Certainly the girl worked as hard as they did.

Tain watched the door for Snowy. She needed to connect him with Nigel as soon as possible, but he hadn't returned either of her calls, and she didn't have a computer to discreetly e-mail him. He had every reason to suspect she was calling for a repeat of their afternoon at the motel, and was clearly avoiding her. That made her sad, and a little angry, but she kept reminding herself that it actually wasn't *about* that.

"Hey, hot stuff," a voice said as she picked up the

coffee carafe for another round of refills. She looked to see Junior Damo seated at the counter.

"Hey, there, Junior," she said neutrally. "Want some coffee?"

"Only if you stick your little finger in it to sweeten it."

"Junior, I'm really busy. What is it you want?"

"Your cousin's staying with you, ain't she?"

"Which cousin is that? I'm related to damn near everyone in the county, including you."

"You know which cousin I mean. Who's that big ol' muscle man she's got with her?"

"Some musician, that's all I know."

"I doubt that, but it ain't important. Tell her I want to talk to her. Alone, without André the Giant."

"Why would anybody want to talk to you, Junior?"

"Just tell her."

"If I see her."

He stood up and headed out the door. He passed Snowy on the way in, and they each nodded a greeting.

Tain came around the counter and quickly grabbed Snowy by the arm. "Sit at the counter, I need to talk to you."

"Okay," he said.

She made her round with refills, cleaned up a few plates, and brought him a cup of coffee. She leaned close and said, "That black boy with Bo-Kate wants to talk to you."

"Why?"

"He's finally caught on that she's crazy."

"Or he's doing exactly what she told him to do."

"I don't think so, Snowy. He's scared."

"Or he's a good actor."

"Do you not trust my ability to tell when someone's lying?"

He'd never seen her so nonsexually serious. "No, I trust you."

"Then will you just *talk* to him?"

"Sure, but somewhere neutral. Have him meet me at the Pair-A-Dice tonight around seven."

"I'll do the best I can. Thank you."

She put her hand lightly atop his. They both looked into each other's eyes, each feeling the same thing but not realizing it. Then he got up and left. Tain gazed after him until one of the other waitresses nudged her roughly in the back. Then she made her way to the kitchen, where she took out her cell phone and dialed the number on Nigel's card. Junior Damo's message to Bo-Kate would be the excuse she needed to tell Nigel to meet Snowy.

When Junior got back home, Loretta threw open the door and yelled, "Some woman called here looking for you!"

"Yeah? What'd she want?"

"That tiny little pecker of yours, that's what, ain't it? Who is she, Junior? Is she knocked up, too? How many little bastards you got running around by now?"

Junior pushed roughly past her and went into the house. He turned on the radio in the kitchen, loud, which made Loretta screech that much louder.

"I won't have your whores calling the house, Junior! You want to see them, you make arrangements on your cell phone, not here! You hear me?"

"They can hear you in China," he said as he dropped into a kitchen chair. Coming home now reminded him of how it felt to be smacked in the head with a two-by-four, which had happened to him when he was fifteen.

Loretta leaned on the counter and clutched her belly. Junior said, "Are you all right?"

"What do you care?" she snarled through her clenched teeth.

The radio played "50 Ways to Leave Your Lover."

"You need me to call Granny Rogen?"

"Is that all you can ever ask? No, it ain't time yet, he's just kicking me because he knows I'm mad. He gets mad, too, when I do."

"That'll be great," Junior said, anticipating a lifetime of everyone in the house always yelling at him.

The phone rang again. He picked it up before Loretta could and said, "Hello?"

"I hear you're looking for me, Junior Damo," a woman's voice said.

"Is this Bo-Kate Wisby?"

"Who else? I tried calling earlier, but your wife or sister or hound dog for all I know started calling me names. I'm not even sure what some of them were."

"She gets going. She's eight months pregnant."

"Well, congratu-fuckin-lations. My slutty cousin says you wanted to talk to me. So talk."

Why did she always corner him when he was off-balance? He'd worked out the perfect speech in his head, but he couldn't do it with Loretta glaring at him. "Not over the phone. Meet me at the Pair-A-Dice tonight."

She snorted, "Why the hell would I do that? What could you possibly have to tell me that I need to know?"

"You'll find out when you get there," he said.

"I might see you there, then. But don't get your hopes up."

He glanced at Loretta. "I haven't had any hopes in a long time."

The call ended. He turned to look at Loretta, expecting another vicious tirade, but instead she just stared at him in half amazement and half horror. "That was Bo-Kate Wisby?"

"Yeah," Junior said.

"What are you doing talking with her?"

"Maybe I'm going to fuck her," he said impatiently.

She grabbed him by the arms, and all the contempt and spite were gone when she said, "Junior, please, don't get messed up in this. We're gonna have a baby in less than a month, I can't do it alone."

He pulled her hands off. "Nothing's going to happen to me."

"Don't you know the stories about what all went on before? And look at what happened to Marshall Goins. That woman is a monster."

"Well, I'll wear a rubber, then."

"This is no joke! I know you ain't screwin' around on me, and I know you ain't meeting' her to screw *her*. That's—"

That set him off. "If you know it, then why the hell have you been giving me all this shit about it?"

She began to cry. "Look at me, Junior. I'm the size of a god-damned Volkswagen. I'll end up looking just like my mama, and she weighs two hundred pounds. Then you *will* start screwin' around on me." She sank into a chair.

Junior just stared at her and numbly took a seat at the table. All the weeks of her accusations and viciousness had left him unable to comfort her, so they sat in their chairs, him slumped, her sobbing, neither making any real effort to reach out to the other.

Bo-Kate went into Byron's room. He sat on the edge of the bed, his leg brace on the floor beside him. He was strumming idle notes on his guitar. He looked up when she entered.

"When do we leave?" he said.

"Not today. Today we just stay around here. Let the word spread. Then tonight, I have to go meet somebody. He's an idiot, but he'll be useful. It'll get word to the right people without me having to spend days driving around."

"Can't you use those magic phones?" he said dryly.

She laughed. "Believe it or not, a lot of the people around here are more primitive even than you."

"I could take that personally."

"Aw," she said, and reached out to touch his cheek.

He grabbed her wrist. She winced and pulled back her hand, but couldn't get free. He said, "Don't *patronize* me, Bo-Kate. I'm out of touch, not a moron. I *will* catch up to this world."

"I know you will," she said, and tried again to pull away. "Let me go, Byron. Please."

"I'll sit in this room today. But tomorrow, you better have something for me to do, or I'll hitchhike into town and take care of business on my own."

"I will, Byron, I promise."

He glared at her, then let go. She jumped out of reach as she rubbed her wrist. It was one thing to manhandle her in bed, but a whole other thing to do it like this. Venomously, she said, "Don't ever do that again, Byron."

"Or what? You'll kill me?" He snorted. "You Tufa have already done that. I'm a fucking ghost, I just haven't dropped over yet."

"Don't talk that way. You can start over here. Make a new family. No, you won't forget your old one, but it'll make you treasure this one that much more, right?"

"With you?"

"Maybe."

"You think it's that easy?" he said, and gazed back down at his guitar.

"I didn't say it would be easy. I just said it was possible. I was an exile, too. I know a little of how you feel."

He looked up at her. "Did you ever have kids?"

"No."

"Then you have no damned idea how I feel."

He hummed along with his song, a tune Bo-Kate didn't recognize. She backed out of the room and closed the door. When she turned in the hall, Tain was standing right there. Bo-Kate jumped.

"Dammit, Tain!"

"What was the shouting about?" Tain asked coolly.

"He's got a little cabin fever. Maybe you should go in there and take his mind off it."

"You're not my pimp, Bo-Kate. I fuck who I want, when I want."

"Shouldn't you be at work?"

"My shift's from five to one."

Bo-Kate's expression changed as something occurred to her. "Tell me something, then: Who have you been fucking since I got back?"

"What difference does it make? I haven't touched your British boy toy, or that lummox in the guest room."

"Makes a big difference if you've been pillow-talking about me."

"You're not that interesting," Tain said with a humorless grin. As she started to walk past, Bo-Kate suddenly grabbed her by the hair and slammed her face-first into the wall. She twisted one of Tain's arms behind her and pushed it up painfully until Tain let out a cry.

"Your arm may break, or just come out of its socket, I don't know which," Bo-Kate hissed. "And I don't care. Answer my question."

"Fuck you!" Tain said, and struggled to escape, but Bo-Kate pulled her head away from the wall and then slammed it again. Blood trickled from her nose.

"That's not the answer I'm after, Tain. Try again."

"Let me *go!*"

A door opened, and Byron stepped out. He was shirtless, and seemed larger than a human man should be in the old house's corridor. "What the hell's all the caterwauling about?"

Bo-Kate released Tain with a final shove into the wall. "Nothing. Just cousins being cousins. Go back inside."

"I will when I feel like it," he rumbled. To Tain he added, "Are you all right?"

"Why? What do you care?" She wiped the blood from her nose, leaving a smear on her arm. "I hope you rot in hell, Bo-Kate. I hope you get buried up to your neck and covered with honey near an anthill. I hope you live to see your children die."

Bo-Kate smiled. "I had no idea you had such strong feelings for me, Tain."

Tain's eyes grew wet, but she turned and stomped off downstairs before she actually began to cry. Bo-Kate crossed her arms and considered going after her, but figured the results wouldn't be worth the effort. Whatever Tain might've passed on, it couldn't possibly upset her plans at this point. It might even help.

"That how you all treat each other?" Byron rumbled. "All you Wisbys?"

She faced him. "Shut up, Byron. Get back in your room and wait for me."

He looked at her steadily for a long moment, then went inside his room and closed the door.

Snowy was asleep on his couch when the doorbell rang. He sat up and looked at the clock; it was barely eight thirty. Who would be at his house on such a cold, miserable evening without calling ahead?

He opened the door. Tain Wisby stood at the bottom of the steps, a battered old suitcase in her hand. She'd been crying, and her nose was swollen and bloody. "What happened?" he said in alarm.

"Bo-Kate beat me up," she said. "Want a roommate for a while?"

He stepped aside so she could enter. While she sat at the kitchen table, he got some ice in a sandwich bag and wrapped it in a dish towel. She put it on her nose.

"Thanks," she said.

"So why did she beat you up?"

"Because I wouldn't tell her about you."

"Tell her what about me?"

"That I've been telling you about her."

He nodded thoughtfully. "You want a beer?"

"Good God, yes."

He got them each a bottle, opened them, and handed one to her. He leaned against the wall beside her as she drank. She asked, "So can I stay here?"

"For how long?"

"How long do you want me?"

"Are you proposing to me?"

She shook her head. "No. But . . ."

"What?"

"I like other men a lot, Snowy. I like the variety, and the adventure, and the sense of new countries to explore. I'm not going to give that up just to keep a roof over my head."

"Yep, that's definitely not a proposal," Snowy agreed.

"No, let me finish. I . . . I'll live with you, and I'll help you, and I'll—" She took a deep breath to muster her courage. "—I'll make you first choice. But if you're busy, or working, or not in the mood . . ."

"How hard did Bo-Kate hit you?"

She laughed and clinked the beer bottle against her teeth. She put it down, and the laughs morphed into tears and from there to hard sobs that started her nose bleeding again. Unsure exactly how much comfort to offer, Snowy got her some tissues and waited until she calmed down.

"I'm sorry," she said at last, holding the blood-soaked tissue to her nose. "It's been a stressful day."

"Just so I can be clear . . . you're asking me if you can live with me despite us being from two different groups, but still go out with other men when they attract your attention."

She nodded.

"Why? I mean, I know why you're here right now, and of

course you can stay until this blows over, but why turn this into something semipermanent? Why not just say you need a few days to get back on your feet or something?"

Her look didn't waver. "Do you remember that day in the motel?"

"Oh, yeah."

"You know what the hardest thing was that day?"

He laughed. She realized what she'd said, and she laughed, too. "No," she said, "not *that*. It was not telling you I loved you. And that I've loved you since the day we met."

"We met when we were seven."

She nodded. "Yep. I know."

He couldn't look away from her piercing, steady gaze. She normally looked straight at you, but that was always with a kind of superior amusement, as if she knew exactly what you were thinking. And she usually did. But this time, there was an openness and vulnerability that he found impossible to resist.

The Wisbys and the Rainfields were from opposite groups. Just like Bo-Kate and Jefferson had once been. In fact, this happened fairly often, since people never wanted anything so badly as something they'd been told they couldn't have. Usually it ended with the partners realizing it was only a temporary infatuation. Occasionally, as with Bo-Kate and Jeff, it left a trail of death and destruction.

He nodded and said quietly, "It was hard . . . *difficult* for me not to say it, too."

She smiled, then turned serious again. "I love you."

"I love you, too."

She stood, left the ice pack and tissue on the table, and came into his arms.

29

Jeff looked up at the ten-foot cutout of dice atop the Pair-A-Dice's roof. The sign was faded, and the lights that once glowed in the dice's holes were out. Still, the parking lot was half-full even on a cold winter after-noon, which said something about its popularity among the Tufa.

Although bars in Tennessee were supposed to be off-limits to those under twenty-one, in Cloud County the rules were a bit difficult for the state to enforce. For one thing, simply finding the place could be impossi-ble for the average non-Tufa officer. As a result, Jeff, like every other child in the county, was brought to the Pair-A-Dice as soon as he became proficient on his instru-ment of choice, the guitar. He was eight, and he'd been so nervous, he'd almost been unable to move his hand along the guitar neck. But before the night was over, he was totally at ease, and totally aware of what music *re-ally* meant to a Tufa.

He put his gloved hand on the door handle, but had to take a deep breath before working up the nerve to push it open.

The smell of the place instantly brought back memories he'd long since suppressed, since not doing so would have made his banishment that much worse. But now he luxuriated in it, momentarily forgetting the reason he was here and just letting the memories flow over him.

There weren't many people here, and most of them just glanced up and then returned to their greasy burgers or bottles of beer. He walked over to the bar and took a seat on a stool. A beautiful girl in a tight tank top that accented her broad shoulders said, "What's your pleasure?"

He gave her a blatantly appreciative look, but said only, "Miller, on draft if you got it."

"We run out of Miller, we might as well close the doors," she said as she poured.

"My name's Jeff."

"I'm Rachel."

"Always loved that name."

She smiled with just enough shyness that it made her adorable. "So you from around here?"

"Originally, yeah."

"You don't live here now?"

"No, I haven't for a long time."

"That must be why I don't remember ever seeing you before. Where *do* you live?"

"New York, but I get back . . . whenever I can."

She put the glass before him and then almost knocked it over when she started. Almost whispering, she said, "Wait . . . you're Jefferson Powell, then?"

"Yeah."

She looked as if something had punched her. "I . . ."

"Don't worry, I'm not here to cause any trouble."

She genuinely looked terrified. "I don't . . . I didn't mean to insult you, I hope you won't take it personally."

"Rachel, please. I did some regrettable things when I was younger, and I *do* regret them. I'm certainly not going to repeat any of them today. I'm just going to sit here, drink my beer, and wait for my friend. Okay?"

"Well . . . I mean, yeah, of course."

Jeff smiled. If nothing else, he knew how to smile in public and make it look sincere. He'd used the talent on venue owners when musical acts were too stoned or drunk to appear, on musicians when they were being overruled by their record companies, and on wives and girlfriends so dumb or naïve, they were surprised by what their men got up to on the road. Now he used it on Rachel, and saw the tension leave those gorgeous shoulders.

"Sorry, Mr. Powell."

"No worries, Rachel. And call me Jeff."

She smiled again, then scurried off to do whatever else she had to do.

Jeff turned and surveyed the room. Conversations murmured all around, and he caught no one stealing glances at him. Maybe they didn't recognize him after all this time? No, he knew better than that. One Tufa never forgot another Tufa's face, even after eons. More likely, they knew why he was back and didn't want to get into the middle of it.

His gaze fell on the small stage in the corner. It was completely bare except for a microphone stand. He smiled at the memories of all the great musicians who had graced that wooden platform over the years. If Bo-Kate took over, then this place would likely wither and die. Then the chain of greatness that twined around that stage would be broken, never to be restored.

He swung back around and rested his elbows on the bar. Rachel watched him surreptitiously from the other end, and he smiled when he caught her doing it. By the third time, she smiled back, shy and embarrassed.

Inwardly, Jeff laughed. He knew all about young women from his time on the road, and even though he was considerably older, with a little effort he could probably seduce that tank top right off her. But whom would that help? Not him, not really. Certainly not her. At this point in his life, seduction was like camping: The best you could hope for was to leave as little trace of your presence as possible.

"What it is, what it was," a new voice said at his elbow.

He turned. Junior Damo sat there with the kind of quick insincere smile Jeff knew very well. "You again," Jeff said.

"Me again."

"What can I do for you?"

Junior leaned close. "Well, your old girlfriend has been saying some interesting things, you know. Real interesting."

"Like what?"

"She wants us to change the name of the town, and open the place up to anyone who wants to come here. She's talking about building studios and turning us into a new Muscle Shoals. A lot of people don't like that."

Jeff wasn't surprised. He knew Bo-Kate's plan had to be suitably epic. "I bet a lot do."

"That's true, that's true. But things worked for an awful long time the way they were, and some of us don't see the need for change."

"Does this change what you want me to do?"

"Naw, but it does kick the mule a little harder. You might need to deal with her sooner than you thought. Don't you think?"

Jeff took a swallow of his beer. Junior was really bad at the kind of phony confidence Jeff saw every day, and it was hard for him not to smile. The main reason he didn't was that, beneath the phoniness, there was sincere element of danger. Junior might be slow and unsophisticated, but then again, so were brown recluses, and they could sure fuck you up. "Junior, what I think has nothing to do with you."

"Well, that's true right now. But when you take Bo-Kate out, that'll leave a vacuum, just like it did for her when Rockhouse died. I figure I'm as good a person as any to step into it."

Before Jeff could reply, a cell phone rang. The ringtone told Jeff it wasn't his. Junior fished it from his pocket and said tiredly, "Yes, honey?" He listened for a minute. "Okay, fine. I'll get it on the way home. Well, I'm talking to somebody about something important. Yes, of course I think you're important." Jeff could hear the shrill voice, if not the exact words, at the other end. Junior listened for a moment, then whisper-yelled, "I will get . . . your goddamn chocolate . . . when I get done here!" Then he vehemently pushed the END CALL button.

"It was always more fun to slam down those old-fashioned phones, wasn't it?" Jeff said.

"Ah, the woman is eight months pregnant, and it's doing bad things to her temper, which wasn't exactly great to begin with." The phone rang again, and this time Junior just turned off the ringer before stuffing it back in his pocket. "So—where were we?"

"You were telling me why you were the logical successor to Rockhouse. And I was telling you I didn't care."

"Well, it ought to be clear that—"

"Oh, *fuck*," Rachel said, louder than she'd probably intended.

Jeff and Junior turned. A tall, elegant black man stood just inside the door. It had to be Bo-Kate's assistant, the Englishman named Nigel. But why was he here?

And then everything, every sensation in Jeff's body, every thought in his head, even the beating of his heart stopped. The moment froze, suspended like a fly in amber.

Nigel had moved aside, and now Bo-Kate stood in the door. Looking right at Jeff.

30

Jeff wondered if all over Cloud County people stopped what they were doing and glanced in the direction of the Pair-A-Dice. Certainly if anything could cause that level of psychic disturbance, it would be the convocation of the only two people to ever be excommunicated from the Tufa.

Bo-Kate looked just as surprised to see him, which he guessed was roughly equivalent to the look the captain of the *Titanic* gave that iceberg. She also looked beautiful, and he couldn't repress the memory of the body beneath her heavy winter coat. And there it was—that lone, long black curl that always fell in her eyes, the one that transfixed him with its trespassing from the first day he saw her when they were children.

Bo-Kate glided through the tables with a grace that he recalled from their dances together. Those watching, many of whom had been there for her prior visit, couldn't believe the look on her face. All the arrogance and certainty had fallen away, leaving a look of such longing that even those most terrified of her felt a deep pang of sympathy.

She stopped before him. "Jeff," she said. She didn't whisper, but the word came out on a single choked breath.

"Hello, Bo-Kate." His deeply ingrained manners tried to force him to stand, but he couldn't move.

She looked beautiful. There were other words that could describe various aspects of her appearance, but the totality of it could only be expressed by that one, lone word. Her black curls fell around her face, which still had the high cheekbones and full lips she'd had when they'd both lived here. Beneath the heavy coat, he could tell that her body was still as exquisite as it had been when they'd been awkward teenagers first learning how the other sex felt beneath their hands.

"I heard you were coming back," she said.

"And I heard you were making waves."

"I have some ideas that might help drag this place into the twenty-first century, yeah."

Jeff got to his feet and gestured to the empty stool beside him. "Will you join me?"

Still looking nowhere but at him, she slid gracefully onto the barstool. Rachel appeared, and her voice trembled as she asked, "C-can I g-get you something, ma'am?"

Bo-Kate looked at her and smiled a little. "Did you hear that? 'Ma'am.' Could make a girl feel old."

"I'm sorry, I—"

"She's just yanking your chain," Jeff said gently.

"I'd like a Goebel. Do you still have those?"

"We d-do."

"Put it on my tab," Jeff said. Rachel scurried off.

"Thanks," Bo-Kate said.

"Least I can do."

"That's probably right."

They both chuckled. Rachel delivered Bo-Kate's beer, then rushed away to wait on people at the tables.

"So," he said. "I guess you know they asked me back to put a leash on you."

"Oh, you have to buy me dinner first if you want to do that."

"What'll that beer get me?"

"You can scratch behind my ears and I'll kick my leg."

They realized no one else was speaking. In fact, everyone in the place studiously looked the other way and pretended they weren't listening, when obviously they were. Bo-Kate said, "Want to go for a ride?"

"With you?"

"Yeah."

"I'm not sure that's a good idea."

"Why? Don't you trust me?"

"Maybe I don't trust me."

"You can't get close enough to snap on that leash from all the way over there."

"I suppose that's true." He stood and gestured at the door. "Your car or mine?"

"Oh, mine. There's something I want to show you."

They left, aware that every eye followed them. Just before the door shut behind them, Rachel dropped a beer glass from her shaking hand. The shattering sound was the last thing they heard.

Junior sidled over to Nigel. "You ain't going with 'em?"

"I can't imagine they would want my company."

"Think he'll kill her?"

Nigel looked at him. "You sound rather eager for that to happen."

"Nah, I just . . . I mean, that's what he's here for, ain't it?"

"I wouldn't know." But Nigel did know that he wished he could have met with Jeff alone before Bo-Kate took him away. If the plan was to let Byron handle Jeff the way he'd done with the others, then Jeff didn't really have much of a chance. And if Bo-Kate intended to take care of it herself, then Jeff had no chance at all.

He looked around for the white-haired young man Tain had described, who wanted to meet with him. He almost yelped out loud when a voice spoke practically in his ear. "I reckon you must be Nigel," Snowy said softly.

Nigel turned, and did a slight double take at the other man's white hair and paradoxically young face. "Ah. Now I understand. 'Snowy.'"

"Nicknames tend to be obvious."

"Indeed."

"Well, we seem to have a few minutes. Shall we chat?"

Nigel looked around. Many eyes were on him, none of them friendly. "Here?"

"Follow me. Nobody'll bother us."

"Nobody will bother *you*." But Nigel followed him through the crowd and into the kitchen.

Arshile looked up from the grill. "Snowy," he acknowledged.

"We're just going into the pantry to talk," Snowy said. "If anybody looks for us, you ain't seen us."

"Who said that?" Arshile deadpanned.

When the door was mostly closed—he wanted to be able to hear if anyone did approach—Snowy said, "Your boss is out to destroy us, Nigel. The whole Tufa community. That may sound a little melodramatic, but it's true."

"No, it sounds perfectly reasonable to me," he said.

"I understand you're having second thoughts about it."

"I assume you heard this from Tain?"

"Doesn't matter. Are you?"

Nigel realized that Snowy stood between him and the door. "I did not comprehend the depth of her acrimony until I saw some of her actions once we got here."

"So what does she really want?"

"She wants what she says she wants. To be totally in charge, and to wreak as much havoc as possible."

"And she's willing to do anything to get that? Including killing people and changing the town's name?"

Nigel hesitated, then nodded.

Snowy paused while he absorbed this. Then he said, "There's a deadline. For reasons that wouldn't make any sense to you, it's all going to be decided Tuesday night. We know she's got something planned. What is it?"

Again Nigel hesitated, though not from fear of betraying Bo-Kate. "If I tell you . . . there's a great chance, percentage-wise, that you won't believe me."

"Try me."

"She's found . . . someone. A man who should have died sixty years ago. She plans to present him as proof of her power."

"Why should some old man—?"

"You misunderstand me. He's not an old man. He's exactly as he was sixty years ago. He looks no older than you, if that old. That's what she thinks makes him special."

"Who is he, then?"

"He's . . . Byron Harley."

It took a moment for Snowy to recognize the name. "Wait, the Hillbilly Hercules? From the '50s?"

"That's him. And it's no exaggeration. He's huge."

"And she brought him back from the dead? That's not possible."

"Orpheus believed the same thing. But I assure you, it's happened. I've seen him and spoken to him. He's no impostor."

Snowy nodded thoughtfully. "Well . . . that complicates things. Tell me: Will you help us?"

"In what way?"

"Our own secret weapon is off with Bo-Kate right now. If he doesn't work out . . ."

"Are you asking if I'd be willing to kill her?"

"Well . . . yeah."

Nigel was speechless, although the idea had been rattling around in his mind. The look of sheer glee she got when Byron was beating up those two men was a side of her he'd never seen before, and it left him a little sick. But to kill her outright . . .

"No. I can't do that."

"Are you going to tell her we talked, then?"

Again Nigel thought before speaking. "No. I won't. I must be Switzerland in this conflict."

Nigel waited to see if Snowy would move aside or try something harsher. Snowy seemed uncertain as well. Then he sighed, opened the door, and gestured for Nigel to precede him.

"Remember what you said," he warned as Nigel passed. "Neutral. You ain't got a dog in this fight."

Nigel nodded, grateful that he did not have to speak, since his mouth was bone dry. He wondered what Bo-Kate and her long-lost paramour were doing just then.

Jeff couldn't stop staring at Bo-Kate's profile as she drove. She kept her eyes on the road, but he could sense the same tension within her.

She said, "Where to? The old elementary school where we met? The creek where we made love for the first time? The high school where you killed Jesse Spicer for trying to rape me?"

Each option send a jolt through him, bringing back emotions with an immediacy that shocked him. It was like all the intervening years had never happened, and he was in danger of falling back into the same thoughts and feelings she had always inspired. And that way, he knew, lay madness. He said, "Only one place we should go, Bo-Kate. Emania Knob."

She snorted. "You're so predictable, Jeff." And he realized that's where she'd been heading all along.

The trees cast mottled shadows on the road as they took the

winding path up the mountain. Over the road noise, he said, "They tell me you're here to take over for Rockhouse."

"Who tells you?"

"Bronwyn, Bliss. Some guy named Junior. Mandalay."

She snorted. "You do what a little kid tells you to now, Jeff? That's not your reputation. You stopped representing that little Annie Hawk like a hot potato the first time she took naked pictures of herself that ended up on the Internet. Everybody said you were crazy, but sure enough, six months later, she was starring on a reality show, and a year after that she was dead."

"Annie wasn't anything like Mandalay, BK."

The snarky superiority left her voice, replaced by almost a choke. "Nobody ever calls me that."

They drove the rest of the way in silence until the SUV burst into the open on the snowy flat mountaintop. She put the vehicle in park but left the engine running.

Jeff nodded at the mound in the middle of the opening. "That where they buried Rockhouse?"

"It is."

"Did you come to the funeral?"

"No. I watched it from the roof of my parents' house."

He laughed. "That must've been a sight. The whole county turned out, I bet."

"They did. I was surprised they didn't have a line to go up and pinch him, to make sure he was dead." Again they were silent, until Bo-Kate added, "I didn't kill him, Jeff."

"You didn't exactly help him out."

"No, I didn't. I cut off his extra fingers to get him out of the way for good. But I swear, when I left him he was still alive. That seemed a lot worse than killing him, to be honest. Do you believe me?"

He looked at her. The planes of her face, the way the light caught her eyes, the texture of her lips . . . all those details had been exiled to his dreams, refused admittance to his conscious thoughts. The rise of her breasts against her blouse, the curve of her hip and waist . . .

"I don't know," he said honestly. "I want to. I want to believe you're at least a little different."

"Are you?"

"Yeah. What we did was terrible, Bo-Kate. We wiped out an entire family. We hurt everyone. Most days I can't believe we did that, but then it comes back to me, and I can smell the blood, and hear the screams, and I know we did."

"You enjoyed it at the time, Jeff."

"That's the worst part. I know I did."

She reached across the seat and took his hand. It was like she'd completed a circuit that had been humming for eternity, waiting for the inevitable connection. His body responded to her touch the way it always did, and it took everything he had, every single bit of strength, to sit still.

"Jeff, I want to bring this county into the modern world. I want us to be the new Nashville, or at least the new Bakersfield, California. We can do it, too. We change the name, we start getting the word out about the great musicians here, and it'll work. And if in the process, we get a little revenge, then so much the better."

The certainty left her voice on the last word, and Jeff understood that their reunion was throwing her own emotions askew just as it did his. He felt the last thing he ever expected to feel about her again: tenderness. He pulled his hand from hers, reached over, and stroked her cheek.

"Why did we fall in love?" he asked, his voice raw.

"For me, it was your laugh," she said so softly, he could barely hear it. "What was it for you."

"This," he said, and pulled one long black curl into her face. "I saw you with this falling into your face. I've never seen anything more beautiful, before or since."

"One curl did it?"

"One curl."

They gazed at each other, and all the years seemed to withdraw, leaving them both the same lovesick, aching teens they once were. His hand cupped her cheek, and she closed her eyes and leaned into it with a sigh. He moved closer, and their lips almost touched. Then they both stopped.

They opened their eyes.

"Let's stretch our legs," she said. He did not argue.

They got out of the SUV. Neither seemed inclined to walk toward the grave, so they went to the edge of a sixty-foot cliff that overlooked a deep gully. The tops of the trees below, where the sun never penetrated, shone white with snow and ice.

"How did you get back here?" Jeff finally asked.

"It's not a pretty story."

"I really didn't expect it to be."

"Do you remember Naomi Barden?"

"The singer who overdosed?"

"Yeah. I promoted her last tour, and we got to be friends. Could you hear it in her voice?"

"What?"

"She was Tufa."

"No way."

"Oh, yes. It went back to her great-grandmother, a full-blood directly related to Rockhouse, so what made it down to Naomi was thin, but she could access it like throwing a switch. That's why people loved hearing her sing. She had no idea, of course. She just thought it was cool and exotic, like being part Cherokee or something."

"And?"

"And . . . I killed her."

The wind was the only sound for a long moment.

The class ring around his neck seemed to burn against his skin. "Why?"

"I got her some heroin that was a lot more pure than what she normally used."

"That's 'how,' not 'why.'"

"The 'why' is easy: I saw a way back, and I wasn't about to let it pass. As for the 'how' . . . when she was unconscious, I cut out her heart and ate it."

"You *ate* her *heart?*"

"Yes. While it was still warm. Still beating, or at least twitching." She looked at him steadily, her chin defiantly raised.

"How did you . . . ? Good God, Bo-Kate, what made you even think of that?"

"Lydia."

"Who?"

She laughed. "It's a band. Lydia, out of Portland. Bunch of slackers with more beards than talent. They did a song called 'Eat Your Heart Out.'" She walked to the edge of the cliff. "I don't know, Jeff. I just looked at her one day and saw the spark. Maybe it was the shadow of her wings, so faint, they were like pollen in the sunlight, but . . ." She sighed. "Anyway, I just knew what I had to do. To overcome what they did to us, I had to be willing to do something awful, something I couldn't undo or turn back from. So . . . I did it."

"Wow."

"Don't waste any sympathy on her. She was a stuck-up, entitled little bitch. She would've died before she was thirty anyway. At least I made sure she got into the Twenty-seven Club with Cobain, Joplin, and Morrison."

"Yeah, but still—"

"Oh, come on, Jeff!" Her voice echoed out of the gully below. "You killed Jesse with your bare hands, remember that? You beat him to death for putting the move on me. I didn't kill Naomi, I . . . well, hell, I *sacrificed* her. She was a waste of skin with the voice of an angel, that's all. There's one of her in every other nightclub in Nashville. I gave her the only immortality her kind can ever achieve: a death at their peak."

Jeff started to say more, but the look in her eye stopped him.

Not because it frightened him—although it did—but because it was familiar. He'd seen that look before, when they were committing the crimes that got them banished. In the intervening time, he had come to regret what they did, truly and deeply regret the pain and hurt they'd inflicted. He realized that Bo-Kate had not, and never would.

She seemed to read the thoughts as they passed through him. "What's the matter, Jeff? Feeling sorry for those people? Sorry for Adele Anker and her family? Let me tell you, not a one of them would've been of any account even if we hadn't burned down their house with them in it. No one who knew them, missed them."

He said nothing. They stood right at the edge of the cliff, and it would've taken very little to push her over, into the treetops below. That would've settled things between them once and for all, and stopped the coming troubles. And yet . . .

"Thinking about pushing me over, Jeff? Sending me to my death? Getting to stay here for good if you do it?"

"No. Thinking about this." He pulled the class ring from his shirt and let it fall outside his coat.

She stared at it, then back at him. "What does that mean?"

He still said nothing.

"Are you saying you still love me?"

Part of him—a larger percentage than he liked to admit—wanted to scream, *Yes!*

"Or," she said, stepping close to him, "are you going to go over the cliff with me? The two great lovers, falling to their death to escape a world that won't let them be together?" She raised her arms above her head. "Come on, Jeff. Wrap me in your arms one last time. Hold me close as our souls fly to earth."

"Bo-Kate," he started to say.

She snorted. "Coward." And then she pushed him off the cliff.

31

Jeff had time to think, *I should've seen* that *coming;* then he hit the first treetop.

Luck was with him, though—he slid off the side of the topmost spire, then bounced down through the branches. He finally stopped about halfway down the big pine tree, splayed across two limbs and gasping from the blow across his back that had knocked the wind from him. Cold, powdery snow drifted down onto his face, dislodged by his passage.

Above, through the branches, he saw the gray sky and the side of the cliff. He couldn't see Bo-Kate.

She tried to kill me, was the first thought that solidified in his head. *She pushed me off the fucking cliff and tried to kill me.* Then he remembered pondering the exact same move, but being unable to do it. All he wanted to do, really, was pull her into his embrace, kiss her, and tell her everything would be okay if they just turned around and left Cloud County for good.

And when the wind tousled one long black curl into her eyes, he almost wanted to cry.

What had she called him as she pushed him off? A coward? He realized she was right. He'd been afraid to

take her in his arms, to tell her the things in his heart, because
to do so meant he might once again become the Jefferson Powell who had done those horrible things.

He could breathe more easily now, and he managed to roll
over enough to look down. The tree, due to its position at the
bottom of the ravine, had branches only near the top, where they
could reach the sun. The last twenty feet were bare trunk all the
way to the rocky, still-sloping ground.

"Great," he wheezed.

He rested a bit longer, then started the treacherous descent.
Without gloves, his hands quickly grew cold and numb. His grip
failed him, and he slid more than he climbed. At last he sat on
the lowest branch and contemplated the drop to the slanted,
rocky ground below.

A real Tufa, a *true* Tufa, would be able to drift down as lightly
as a falling leaf. And while Bronwyn had sworn he was wholly
reinstated, he hadn't tried to fly on Tufa wings in longer than
most people could remember.

Still, the choice was try, or take bets on which leg he'd break.
And a broken leg out here, even for a Tufa, was the same as death.

He closed his eyes. He tried to remember his boyhood, when
taking to the night winds had been second nature. But he needed
a song to ride, a tune to bolster his wings. *Think, you moron.
Surely you must know one song that will work. . . .*

And then he smiled. The first song that came to his mind was
actually a song he hated for its inane rhymes and self-important
seriousness. But it was still a song, and he knew it by heart.

He began singing the chorus to Steve Miller's "Fly Like an
Eagle."

He didn't. Fly like an eagle, that is. He flew like a badly made
paper airplane, but he still flew, and although he hit the ground,
it wasn't hard enough to break anything. He again knocked the
wind from his lungs and lay atop a pair of protruding rocks until it returned.

When he sat up, a large black bear watched him from less than five feet away.

Neither he nor the bear moved.

"Shouldn't you be hibernating?" he croaked at last.

The bear made a noise between a snuffle and a grunt.

Then Jeff noticed the change. All around him grew weeds, bushes, and vines. Grass sprouted in the cracks between the rocks. He looked up, and saw blue sky tinged with purple dusk along one edge. The air he pulled into his battered lungs no longer had the chill bite of winter.

"Oh, fuck," he said as he realized what had happened. Bo-Kate didn't just push him off the cliff—she pushed him into slow time. Faery time. The exile from which he might emerge, but there was no telling where, or when.

He got to his feet. The bear backed up and growled. He looked it right in the eye and said loudly, "Shoo!" The bear turned and waddled away downslope.

His heavy winter coat was now too warm for the humid air. He took it off and tied the sleeves around his waist. He looked back up at the sky, which was already fading to night. Still, there was enough glow for him to determine which direction was west, and therefore he knew he should travel east—toward the night, the darkness and the uncertainty ahead, as well as toward Needsville.

But with each slip over treacherous rocks, each unseen tree limb that slapped his face, each mosquito that buzzed in his ear, he grew angrier and angrier: at himself, certainly, but also at Bo-Kate, for not being what he'd needed her to be. Next time—and there would be a next time—he would not hesitate.

It was an hour later before he realized what he'd thought was the oncoming night was actually the dawn. So he'd been traveling the wrong way.

He sat down with a heavy sigh of annoyance and defeat. *Okay,* he thought, *I've been fucked with yet again. Now what?*

The forest looked the same in every direction. He could turn around and head toward the sunrise, but there was no guarantee that was right, either. Without some guide, some indication of the right direction, he simply couldn't know what he was supposed to do. Was this really how people felt when caught in fae time?

Then he heard a voice.

At first he wondered if it might be another trick, a siren call to keep him wandering. But what choice did he have? He got wearily to his feet, listened hard, then walked toward the sound.

As he got closer and it grew plainer, there was no doubt it came from a real person. The only surprise was, he realized the voice was a child's.

A child calmly singing meant a family nearby, and that meant relief, if not truly rescue. He had no idea where, or when, he was. It could be ten minutes or ten years later, and the world that waited for him outside these woods might be so different, he couldn't conceive of it.

He crept forward until the shape of a big house loomed up through the trees. There was something familiar about it, but then again, all the old houses in Cloud County resembled each other. His own family dwelling looked a lot like this before it fell to pieces.

He reached the edge of the yard and stayed out of sight. There was indeed a little girl, no more than five or six, singing as she ran around in circles. She wore a faded little dress and no shoes, and a small puppy played at her heels. She sang:

> *There was a man lived in the moon,*
> *Lived in the moon, lived in the moon,*
> *There was a man lived in the moon,*
> *And his name was Aiken Drum.*

Jeff stepped out into the yard. "Hi," he said, trying to sound as friendly as he could. "Could you tell me where I am? I'm kinda lost." He gave her the smile that usually made musicians fall all over themselves to sign on the dotted line.

The girl stopped singing and stared up at him.

Jeff's whole sense of the world collapsed.

The little girl was—without a doubt, without even the *possibility* of a doubt—Bo-Kate Wisby.

32

Until the little sparks appeared around the edges of his vision, Jeff didn't even realize he'd forgotten to breathe.

The girl's eyes were unmistakable. The little chin had the first hints of the strong, powerful jawline she would possess as an adult. The lips, though tiny, held the promise of the ones he would one day know so well. And the curly hair, held back by a handful of tiny ribbons, would one day entangle his fingers.

They looked at each other for a long moment. The only noise was the high-pitched barking of the tiny dog.

At last the little girl said, "Are you a fwend of my daddy?"

"I know him," Jeff managed to croak out.

"He's not here. He went to help someone round up some pigs that got out. In fact, ain't nobody here but me."

"Where's your brothers?"

"Snad's out chasing girls, Canton's out chasing Snad."

Jeff forced himself to sound casual as he asked, "What's your name?"

"Beauregard Katherine, but everyone calls me Bo-Kate. What's yours?"

"Jeff."

"This is Stinkerbelle," she said with a nod at the puppy.

Jeff knelt and patted the dog, who puppy-nipped at his fingers. He looked around at the house, which was almost exactly the way he remembered it. Even the old outhouse was still there.

"You can wait if you want," the girl said. "Do you want to sing with me?"

Jeff nodded. What the hell else was he going to do?

He sat on the grass as she resumed running around, and joined her as she started the song over.

> *There was a man lived in the moon,*
> *Lived in the moon, lived in the moon*
> *There was a man lived in the moon,*
> *And his name was Aiken Drum.*

> *And he played upon a ladle,*
> *A ladle, a ladle*
> *And he played upon a ladle,*
> *And his name was Aiken Drum.*

His brain danced, too, but far more frantically than the little girl before him, the girl he now knew was Bo-Kate Wisby. He had gone back in time. *Back* in fucking *time,* to the era of his own childhood. Somewhere nearby, at this very moment, he also existed as a totally separate, unaware entity.

Time was essentially linear, and the Tufa could dance in and out of it as they liked, but going back—returning to events already passed, already experienced—was reserved for only the purest of the purebloods. Certainly not someone like him. But if anyone, anything could manage it, it was whatever drove the night winds, whatever directed the Tufa's destiny, whatever had picked him up as he fell and deposited him here.

For a reason.

And then he knew.

And his hat was made of good cream cheese,
Of good cream cheese, of good cream cheese,
And his hat was made of good cream cheese,
And his name was Aiken Drum.

He looked around. A long, sharp scythe stood against the out-house wall between a post-hole digger and a shovel. The flat of the blade was rusty, but its edge gleamed in the sunlight. Jeff got to his feet and walked over to it.

And his coat was made of good roast beef,
Of good roast beef, of good roast beef,
And his coat was made of good roast beef,
And his name was Aiken Drum.

This was it. He was here to stop Bo-Kate before she did any of the horrible things she'd done, and was planning to do. Penny Hadlow would not be scarred. Adele Anker and her family would not be burned to death. Jesse Spicer's brains would not decorate the floor of the girl's dressing room. Rockhouse Hicks and Mar-shall Goins would still be alive.

All if Jeff could find it in himself to kill a child.

He picked up the scythe, disturbing a pair of yellow jackets that had begun a nest on the underside of the outhouse eave. The distinctive smell, particularly ripe in the heat, made him try to mouth-breathe. A black racer snake skittered along the edge of the building and shot through the grass into the safety of the nearest patch of weeds.

This blade would do the job, all right; that little head would separate from the diminutive neck with one good, strong swing.

He'd used one of these countless times in his youth, and the muscle memory was still there. He turned back to the girl.

And his britches were made of haggis bags,
Of haggis bags, of haggis bags,
And his britches were of haggis bags,
And his name was—

She stopped dancing when he took the first step toward her with the scythe.

The dog yapped twice, then turned and ran off toward the shelter of the back porch.

Jeff stopped in front of the girl. She stared up at him, her face blank. With her chin raised that way, her neck was a perfect target. One quick blow, and a whole universe of death and violence would never exist.

This was what he was here for.

He drew back, turning at the hip. The weight of the scythe swung easily.

And then he froze.

One long black curl came loose from a clip and fell into the little girl's face.

He couldn't breathe. He couldn't blink. The long black curl mesmerized him, as it always had. As, he realized, it always would.

Her lower lip trembled a little. "Mister?" she said in the tiniest voice imaginable.

He tossed the scythe aside and fled back into the woods.

Jeff ran as hard as he could, his eyes blinded with tears, his chest thundering with emotions he couldn't contain or even identify. He slammed into trees and felt branches slash along his arms and legs. He kept going until, exhausted, he could go no farther and fell to the ground. He sobbed harder than he'd ever done in his life.

A female voice said, "What happened?"

He jumped, turned, and looked around. The first thing he noticed was that there was once again snow on the ground. Then he saw Mandalay Harris leaning against a tree, her hands stuffed in her pockets.

He sniffed and wiped his nose. "I c-couldn't do it."

She cocked her head slightly. "Do what?"

"What you sent me to do!"

"I didn't send you anywhere. The night winds did it, and they've stopped talking to me."

"Then how did you know I'd be here?"

"I didn't. I just went for a walk."

Jeff sighed. "They sent me to Bo-Kate when she was a little girl. They wanted me to kill her."

"And you didn't?"

"I couldn't. I *couldn't*."

Mandalay nodded, then looked off into the distance. "She'll never be that vulnerable again."

"I don't c-care. I couldn't."

"You've killed people before."

"Not little children."

"You mean not looking at them."

Jeff felt the words like a scythe to his own neck. She meant Adele Anker and her family, one of whom, little Boone, was no older than the child Bo-Kate. He'd killed them in the metaphorical heat of his passion for her, and in the literal heat of a fire he set, but not, as Mandalay said, looking at them. "You're right," he choked out.

Mandalay's voice grew hard. "I know."

He sobbed some more. The memory of that curl falling into her little face sent another shock of anguish through him.

"You've doomed your people, Jefferson," Mandalay said. There was no anger, no rage, just sadness. "You had the chance to do something no different than what you've done before, and you couldn't do it. *I* can't defeat her. I may have the wisdom of centuries, but I have the courage of a twelve-year-old. You were our last hope."

"Just shoot her in the head!" Jeff roared. "Surely someone would do that for you."

Mandalay smiled sadly. "It's not that easy. People have to want me to lead them, or I'm a tyrant like Rockhouse. Just killing a rival wouldn't do that." She smiled, and it was the saddest thing Jeff had ever seen. "Good-bye, Jefferson. Keep going like you're going, and you'll find your way back."

"Are you banishing me again?"

"What's the point? The night winds gave you the chance. You didn't take it. On February 3, it all ends. That's it."

"What happens on February 3?"

"It's the night of the full moon. Everything changes. Bo-Kate wins."

"So you're giving up?"

33

After he calmed down, he put on his coat again and did exactly as Mandalay said. He continued walking through the woods, stumbled around a little, then emerged once again directly behind the Wisby house. Only he knew he was back in his own time.

Of course I'm right back here, he thought with grim humor. It wasn't really a surprise—the night wind was known for its perverse sense of humor—but he hadn't expected it, after what had happened here just minutes—or was it years?—before. He sorted through memories of the geography, to plot the quickest way back to the Pair-A-Dice, where he could retrieve his rental car and get the hell out of town.

Before he could, though, the back door opened and one of the biggest men Jeff had ever seen emerged. He was so large, in fact, that Jeff wondered if he'd actually tripped into some parallel universe where he would be considered a midget. But no, the door and windows were the normal height; this was just a huge guy.

He walked along the path to the outhouse in his shirtsleeves, hands in his pockets. He had a pronounced limp, and Jeff heard a faint metallic squeak with every step. When he passed through the glow of the moon, Jeff saw his face and almost gasped aloud. He'd known it, of course, but the reality had a weight he didn't expect.

It was Byron Harley, the Hillbilly Hercules, who had died sixty years before. This was no ghost or apparition; this was flesh-and-blood reality. He'd certainly heard enough of the man's music, and recalled all the pictures Bo-Kate pasted to her walls. All the connections clicked: the date of the concert synching with the date of the legendary plane crash, and now Byron Harley mere feet away, after Bo-Kate had resurrected him . . . but for what?

Byron went into the outhouse and shut the door. Jeff made a sudden decision and crept up behind it. He heard Byron settle down on the seat.

"There's a scattergun aimed at your back, son," Jeff said quietly, with as much drawling menace as he could muster. "It'll go right through this wood and give you a 12-gauge enema. You just sit there and answer my questions, and you may get out of this alive."

Harley did not respond.

"I'm gonna tell you something, and then I'm gonna go away. I expect you to acknowledge it. Are you listening?" He leaned close to a gap in the planks. "Do not help Bo-Kate Wisby take over the Tufa. You understand? Do not."

"Why not?" Harley growled, and the intensity in the voice made Jeff jump.

"Because it's not right. The Tufa—"

"You Tufa stole my whole fucking life. My wife and little girl are dead. My grandbabies are dead. You want to shoot me in the back while I'm on the crapper, you go right ahead. That's how Tufa courage works, ain't it?"

Jeff had never heard such venomous hatred. This man wouldn't be dissuaded unless he was killed, and if Jeff really had a shotgun, he might've used it. But he didn't, so he said, "All right. But come the night of February third, you better be watching over your shoulder."

"Yeah? Or what?"

But Jeff had already crept away into the woods, toward Donal Road, where he hoped he could hitch a ride back to the Pair-A-Dice and pick up his car.

When he went back into the house, Byron stomped up the stairs and banged on Bo-Kate's door so hard, the wood cracked. When she opened it, he said, "Somebody knows all about the little cotillion you got planned." Then he told her about the incident outside.

Bo-Kate grinned. "That's called free publicity, Byron. If they're that worried, then they'll definitely show up to see what happens."

"If they don't stop us first."

"Byron, they can't stop us. The guy could've blown your head off, but he didn't. He was too afraid of me. So just go back to your room and relax."

"I'm tired of my goddamn room."

"Just a little bit more, I promise you." She leaned up and kissed him on the cheek, then whispered, "I'll come visit you as soon as I can."

She saw the anger leave his face, replaced by something equally violent, but quite different. "I'll be waiting," he said.

Bo-Kate looked at Nigel on the bed, propped up on his elbows. "What was that about?" he asked.

"Byron just had a case of the jitters," she said. "He'll feel better when he beats up someone else."

"That's a comforting thought."

She shrugged. Nigel was attentive and considerate in bed, and she supposed at some level she loved him for it. But Byron *took* her, using his weight and strength to pound into her so hard, she worried he might crush her in his fury. And at the same time, she enjoyed the feminine submission he demanded from her by his treatment. Most men, Nigel included, were content to follow her lead and subsume their own desires to hers. But not Byron.

She slipped back under the sheets and turned off the bedside lamp. "Now, where were we?"

"You were, I believe, on your back. I was—"

"I remember exactly where you were," she said as she assumed her previous position and pushed his head down her body.

Mandalay lay in bed wide awake. Illumination from the security light by the road reflected off the snow onto her ceiling, through which the shadows of bare tree branches waved in the night wind.

She had two pressing problems: whatever Bo-Kate had planned, and whatever was going on between her and Luke Somerville. The first was clearly the most important: the entire future of the Tufa rested on it. But it was the second felt so urgent that she wanted to scream.

She couldn't be in love, not really. She was a child, and one advantage of holding so much inside her head was that it gave her a perspective far beyond childhood; hell, far beyond the span of a regular human life. With a little effort, she could see the patterns of history stretching out behind the events of the day, and could make a far better guess about what the future held than the average person. But the turmoil in her heart over Luke shorted out all that insight and left her as adrift as any other twelve-year-old girl nursing her first serious crush.

Does he like me, too?

Does he think I'm pretty?
Does he want to kiss me?

She rolled onto her side and punched her pillow in annoyance. Luke was from the other side; that made things even more complex. There was nothing stopping them from getting together, of course—the days of the real blood feuds were long over, and in fact, there had already been several couples quite happily married across that divide. But in those cases, their Tufa blood was diluted, mixed with human strains and not subject to the same urgent call. It was impossible for anyone to be more Tufa than she was, and Luke was certainly tied firmly into his people.

Some of her predecessors had been wives and mothers. Many had not. Each bore the burden in her own way. But none of that had any real influence on her life, and her decisions.

She wasn't deluded that she'd found the love of her life. But she wondered how, if this first infatuation felt so strong and incapacitating, she'd survive anything worse.

No, damn it, concentrate. Bo-Kate's going to make her move soon, and you have to be ready. Jefferson blew it, so now it's all up to you.

Jeff walked through the woods to the road, and caught a ride with a farmer driving two horses somewhere, for some purpose; the old man didn't talk much. It was almost dawn when the farmer dropped him at the Pair-A-Dice, and from there he drove to the Catamount Corner. He expected to have to ring the bell to be let in, but the door was open; apparently her grief had caused Miss Peggy to abandon the habits of a lifetime.

He went up to his room and dialed Janet Ling back in New York.

"It's me," he said.

"It's you," she agreed sleepily. "What time is it?"

"I don't know for sure. An hour later than it is for you. Listen, sweetie, I may . . . There might be some unforeseen problems with me getting back."

"Like what?"

"I don't know, if I did, they wouldn't be unforeseen. But I just wanted to tell you that you've always done a great job, and on some days you've been the single bright spot. And I regret that I never saw you naked."

Janet giggled. "Wow, Jeff. How drunk are you?"

"Not a bit. Hopefully I'm just being melodramatic, and you can feel free to tease me unmercifully. But just in case . . . I love you, Janet. Like a sister, or a daughter. You've been more loyal to me than any of my family, and I just wanted you to know that in case—"

"Aw," she said, clearly believing he *was* drunk despite his protestations. "I love you, too, boss."

He hung up, took off his coat, and collapsed onto the bed. Gray winter light was already filtering through the curtains. He was asleep at once, and dreamed of a long black curl.

The roads were clear enough for school on Monday and, in fact, all of Cloud County resumed its normal routines, despite the ominous forecast. The only one who didn't was Peggy Goins, who still sat in her living room, staring at the floor, occasionally sniffling. Processing the absence of Marshall would take her a while.

There were only fifteen kids in the sixth grade at Cloud County Consolidated Schools, so there was no way Mandalay and Luke could really avoid each other.

Monday was a busy day, as Mrs. Welch struggled to make up for lost time, especially in English. The class was reading *Wuthering Heights,* and the discussion of star-crossed lovers sent shards of metaphoric glass into Mandalay's heart. She wondered if Luke also felt the parallels.

Yet neither made eye contact, nor spoke before class, and Luke shot out of there so fast at the end of the day that Mandalay had no chance to speak to him. Which was okay, because she could only think about Tuesday night, under the full moon, when Bo-Kate Wisby might very well kill her.

Jeff awoke around eleven that morning, went across the street to the Fast Grab, and bought a case of beer. He returned to his room and drank until he fell asleep again. There was nothing he could do, and he just wanted to blank out the rest of the day, and his life. And the image of that curl falling into a little girl's face.

As darkness fell, Bo-Kate stood naked at the window in her bedroom, looking out at the snow. The sky was purple and pink in the west, and its whimsicality seemed totally at odds with the impending darkness, both outside and in her soul.

"Nigel," she said casually, "I think I'll kill Bronwyn Hyatt first. She's the real threat, even in her delicate condition." She said the last two words in a cold, mocking way.

Her casual tone frightened him more than anything. "Bo-Kate, I think that perhaps you're being a bit rash. Why not wait and see how your evening goes tomorrow night?"

She turned to him, and her nakedness did nothing to dim her intimidating intensity. "Nigel, this is it. Fish or cut bait. Shit or get off the pot. I've haven't kept secret what I planned to do here, and I need to know I can count on you."

Nigel gathered the sheets around him as nonchalantly as possible, feeling suddenly as vulnerable as a Stradivarius beneath a hanging anvil. "Bo-Kate, you can count on me, of course. But part of my responsibility to you is to make sure you don't do something exceptionally foolish."

"Are worried about the law? There's no law here. You could send every cop in the state, and they'd never find me. This place isn't like anywhere else."

"So I understand."

"The only law is the one that's always bound the Tufa to this spot. Everything else is negotiable."

"Even murder?"

She walked over to the bed, putting an extra sashay in her movements. "Nigel, if I could do it with a damn drone strike like those soldiers everyone calls heroes, I would. But I can't; I have to get my hands dirty."

Nigel chose his next words carefully. He'd promised Snowy that he'd remain neutral, and God knew he wanted to, but he couldn't let this pass without at least trying to convince her to change her plans. "She's *pregnant*, Bo-Kate. Extremely pregnant. You'll be killing her and an unborn baby. Doesn't that count for anything?"

"It's unfortunate, yes. But I can't be sentimental about any of this. That little girl is sentimental, and it's going to cost her her life. Eventually."

She slid her hand under the sheet. "Come on, Nigel. Let's make two minutes fifty-two seconds of squishing noises. It'll all be worth it in the end, I promise you."

He tried not to wince at the touch of her fingers. "I think I'm fucked out, Bo-Kate. Perhaps your teen idol is ready for another round."

She stood up. "Okay, Nigel. You've cast your vote." She took her robe from the door and put it on, cinching the belt tight. He just had time to notice the heavy object in her pocket before she pulled out the revolver.

He had time to think, *Well, damn. Here I thought I was the nice guy who'd get the girl in the end, but it turns out I'm the black guy in a horror film.*

Then she shot him twice in the head. The echo of the blast stayed in the room much longer than he did.

The door flew open and Byron burst in. He had to hold on to the frame to stay upright, since he didn't wear his leg brace. His sudden appearance and great size made Bo-Kate gasp and drop the gun, which clattered loudly on the wooden floor.

"What the—?" Byron started. Then he saw.

"You scared the hell out of me, Byron," Bo-Kate said.

He looked at her with nothing but contempt. "I doubt that, Bo-Kate. I bet there's plenty of hell left in you."

Byron withdrew, and she heard his door close. A familiar voice said in her ear, "That was the right thing to do. That nigger wasn't on your side anymore."

"I know," she said, her voice choked a little.

"Don't be getting sentimental on me," Rockhouse's ghost said. "You still got work to do. You got a plan?"

"Can't you read my mind?"

"Not from where I am, hot stuff. Y'all been readin' too many spook stories."

"Yeah, I got a plan." She picked up the gun, put it back in her purse, then went to the bedroom door, and hollered, "Snad! Canton! Y'all get up here!" She looked back at Rockhouse, who was a transparent, wavering form in the darkest corner of the room. "But I ain't telling you."

"You think I can't figure it out?"

"If you can, why'd you ask?"

She couldn't quite make out the details of his face, but he seemed to be glowering. "You don't want me against you, little missy."

"I don't want you at all."

"I'll remember you said that." And he faded into the shadows around him just as Shad and Canton entered the room. They stopped dead when they saw Nigel's body.

"Well?" Bo-Kate said harshly. "You ain't never seen a dead nigger before? Get him out of here."

34

The Tuesday night of the full moon arrived bleak and cold. The temperature dropped into the single digits, which froze the snow in its clouds, allowing only the occasional flurry to escape. Ordinarily this would have kept most people at home, but the Pair-A-Dice parking lot was full, and cars parked along the road wherever the old, dirty banks of snow allowed them. It turned a mile-long stretch of highway into a one-lane road, but since no one was likely to drive by unless they were headed to the roadhouse, it wasn't a problem.

Inside it felt like a combination of the excitement before the Beatles appeared on Ed Sullivan, and the gallery at the Scopes Monkey Trial. Every Tufa capable of movement had arrived, drawn to this event as much as, if not more than, they'd been to Rockhouse's funeral. Everyone had shed their coats and hats, and the heater had long since been turned off as unnecessary. The kitchen was closed, and Arshile the cook now worked beside bartender Rachel to keep up with demand for cold beer and Cokes. There was an unspoken demilitarized zone that ran down the middle of the room. The two groups kept to themselves, and the conversations were low and slightly menacing. Everyone present knew this night would change everything for Needsville, Cloud County, and all the Tufa.

On the little stage, a single microphone stood, connected to a PA. Both the contenders would have their say. The decision, though, would be up to the crowd.

Bo-Kate and Byron waited in the darkened kitchen. She peeked out through the serving window at the simmering crowd with a mixture of apprehension and smug glee.

Byron, antsy and claustrophobic, clutched his guitar and said, "Can we get this over with?"

"Not yet," Bo-Kate said without looking at him.

"Waiting for that old boyfriend of yours?"

"No, I shoved him off a cliff."

He waited, but there was no punch line. "Man, when you people break up with each other, you do it for real."

She turned to him. His sour attitude, even when they were having sex, had just about killed off her teenage crush. She saw him now as merely a bitter punk, useful at the moment but of no lasting value. She no longer had any second thoughts about the fate she had lined up for him. "What are you complaining about?"

"Nothing," he muttered. "Nothing at all."

"Good. This is your revenge, too, you know. You're helping destroy the very soul of the Tufa. Isn't that better than killing them one at a time?"

When he said nothing, she resumed looking out the window. Byron went to the back door and peered through the little square of glass at the cars in the parking lot. He'd show them, all right. And he'd show her, too.

"I don't think you should go," Bliss said to Mandalay in her bedroom as the girl decided what to wear. Bronwyn waited in the living room with Leshell and Darnell. "We can't protect you there."

"I appreciate that," Mandalay said. "But everyone else is there, so I have to be."

"What's the worst thing that could happen if you don't go?"

Mandalay turned and looked at her. "Bo-Kate walks away with everything. Needsville becomes Scarborough. And we are all lost to the night winds."

"That would never happen."

"You don't think so? Rockhouse isn't around anymore to uphold the status quo. Marshall can't even step in as the civic authority. It's entirely my job now, and if I don't show up, then it's the same as saying I'm too afraid to face her."

"But you must know she intends to—"

Mandalay smiled. "Bliss, I appreciate what you're trying to do, really. But I'm going, and that's it."

"Mandalay—"

"I'm *going*!" Mandalay said. Her voice, normally soft and deferential, blasted forth like a physical slap. Bliss gasped, not just at the sound but at the fury in the girl's face as well. Bliss had never seen that before.

"Don't ask me what I'm going to do, because I don't know," Mandalay continued. "I only know I have to be there tonight. Are we clear?"

"Yes."

"Good." She decided on an outfit and began to change clothes. "Warm up your truck. It's late, and we need to go."

If Junior Damo knew how to do one thing, it was stir the pot.

He moved from table to table, group to group, speaking in whispers and being careful not to draw attention. He stood only when at least three other people were on their feet, so no one would notice his movements, and always slid into conversations by agreeing with whoever was speaking. It didn't take much—a slight comment about Bo-Kate, a supposed story about Rockhouse, a lewd joke about what Mandalay would be like in a few years—and the tension grew. That was what he wanted, because if they were tense, and a little angry, they'd be more inclined to listen to him when he really lit the fuse. And then, after the explosion, he could honestly claim he'd known it would happen all along.

He eased in between an immensely fat man who smelled of bacon grease and a broad-shouldered, glowering young man who idly tapped a quarter on the table. A middle-aged woman finished a story with, "And I swanny, he acted like it was no big thing, like a man diddles a goat every day."

"They do," the fat man said, "down in Mississippi."

They laughed. Junior waited patiently, and when the laughter had almost died, he interjected, "So what do you think Bo-Kate is going to do? Think she's gonna kill Mandalay Harris right here in front of us?"

"Wouldn't mind that a bit," the quarter-tapper said.

"She's just a kid," Junior said, mock-offended.

"She's trying to get us all thrown off our land," the fat man said.

"Who is?" the woman asked.

"Bo-Kate," Junior said, going with the flow. "That's her plan. She wants to buy up all the land and turn it into a damn shopping mall. Wasn't any of you here the other day when she came in?"

"That don't make no sense," quarter-tapper said.

"It'll be one of them outlet malls," the fat man said. "They like to put them off the main path, so's you feel like you're being sneaky when you go there, like that one they used to have down in Boaz, Alabama. That's a fact."

Two men from other tables stood and made their way toward the bar, and Junior stood to join them, content that he'd done his job with this group.

Jeff came down the stairs and entered the Catamount Corner lobby. Peggy Goins sat behind the counter, staring into space, a cigarette in her fingers. She didn't look up until he said, "Hey, Peggy."

"Hello, Mr. Powell. What can I do for you?"

"Nothing, really. I'm on my way out of town, I need to settle up my bill."

She waved a hand dismissively. "Doesn't matter. Consider it a freebie. It won't be my problem soon."

He picked up a postcard that advertised the Smoky Mountains, and gazed at the wisps of cloud that clung to the treetops. "So, are you going down to the Pair-A-Dice tonight?"

"Me? Good Lord, no. I wouldn't trust myself in the same room with that cancerous bitch."

"I know the feeling," he muttered.

Peggy spoke with the flat voice of someone wearied by tragedy. "When she changes the name of the town, I'll have to sell out to her. She already told me she wants the place, and with Marshall gone, there's nothing keeping me here. I suppose I could go over to the Pacific Northwest. I visited that once as a young woman, it's always been in my mind to go back."

"Maybe the people here won't want her. Lot of 'em got long memories, you know."

Peggy took a drag on her cigarette and smiled coldly as the smoke came out. "There's no one else. Junior Damo? Please. And Mandalay's a child. I hate to say it, because I love her to death, but when it counts, she's just a child. She can't stand up to a full-grown woman with as much hatred and spite in her heart as Bo-Kate has."

Jeff nodded. He agreed with that, even though he didn't want to. The memory of that little girl, with the strand of hair in her face, came back to him, and he had to force it down.

"Well," he said at last, "if I don't ever see you again, Miss Peggy . . . you take care."

"You, too, Jefferson. Travel safe, and tell New York I said hello."

"I'll do it." And with that, he left.

Byron peered over Bo-Kate out at the crowd. "Any sign of her?"

"Not yet."

"I'm getting antsy."

"Just drink your beer and calm down."

"You calm down. You don't have to go up there in front of them."

She turned and looked at him. "Stage fright, Byron? You?"

"Elvis gets stage fright, too, you know."

"Elvis died when he was forty-two, sitting on the commode."

She resumed looking out at the crowd, and so didn't see the look on Byron's face as he took in this information. He knew from his brief experiences with the Internet that, of his peers, only Jerry Lee Lewis was left alive; but he hadn't really dug into the circumstances of their various deaths. Somehow he assumed they'd all died old and rich. But if Elvis—the one they all wanted to be, the one who set the template—could die such an undignified death, then what did that say? Was rock-and-roll music, which had once seemed like it could change the world, really just a waste of time like all the preachers, teachers, and parents said? And did that make him even more useless and pitiful for outliving his time so egregiously?

The Pair-A-Dice door opened, and Mandalay entered, followed by Bliss and, lumbering uncomfortably, Bronwyn. Bliss and Bronwyn looked around nervously as they took off their coats, but Mandalay had the serene expression of a girl going to church . . . or an execution.

Three men stood and offered their chairs, which the women took. They were near the front, close to the stage, and the expectation in the room grew exponentially until the air vibrated with it. Mandalay sat with her hands demurely in her lap, holding her purse, like a girl at church. With her presence, it was now all over but the singing.

"And there she is," Bo-Kate said. She looked back at Byron. "Are you ready?"

"Sure. You still want me to play 'Rough and Ready'?"

"That's your signature tune, isn't it? People who don't even know who you are know that one, don't they?"

"I don't know," he muttered. "I been out of circulation for a while."

She patted his arm. "And here—I want you to use this." She held up the pick he'd given her at the fire in the woods.

"Why?" Byron asked.

"It's absorbed sixty years' worth of magic, that's why."

He took the pick and twirled it slowly in his fingers. It felt no different from any other guitar pick. "So it's magic now, huh?"

She patted his chest. "Just like you, baby."

35

There was no announcement or obvious signal, but almost as soon as Mandalay sat down, silence spread through the crowd. Beer bottles settled onto tables, chairs stopped scraping across the concrete floor, and eventually all eyes turned to the back of the room.

Byron and Bo-Kate emerged from the kitchen. He held his guitar at his side like a gun, had his leather jacket zipped halfway up, and his hair was perfectly styled into a ducktail, gleaming with the vintage Brylcreem he always carried. He met the gaze of every Tufa he could, drilling into them with the contained fury he felt for every last one of the smug sons of bitches.

Bo-Kate gently touched his back. "Wait here," she said softly. "I'll call you up in a minute."

She walked to the stage and stepped up to the microphone. As if she did this every day, she said casually, "How's everyone doing out there? Don't forget to tip Rachel and Arshile, it's all that keeps a roof over their heads."

No one laughed.

She wasn't fazed. "I guess, given how many people

are here, everyone knows how important this is. That's good; y'all ain't as dumb as I remember."

Again there was no response.

"So, here we are. Y'all know what I want: your agreement that I'm in charge. That we change the name of this place from Needsville to Scarborough. That Mandalay give up her position, either willingly"—she smiled and winked at Mandalay—"or not."

Mandalay said nothing, and her expression remained neutral.

"Now, I know one big thing many of you are worried about is that, with me being gone for so long, I might not know enough about you people to lead you. Well, I know more than you think. For example, I know that Big Sam Washburn over there lost all his money at that Cherokee casino over in North Carolina and had to beg his mama for money so Little Sam and his brothers and sisters could eat."

Everyone turned to look at a disheveled, corpulent man. "That ain't—," he started, then stopped.

"And Ellie Shannon, what were you doing parked at Curtis Stock's house in the middle of the night when his wife was off seeing about her mother?"

An attractive woman in her thirties just stared, her mouth open. A man with a thick mustache got to his feet and whipped out a big Case knife. He glared at his wife. "Is that true, Ellie? Is it?"

Two of his friends grabbed him by the arms and pulled him away before the woman, red-faced with shame, could reply. Another man, the aforementioned Curtis, slid down in his chair.

"And how many of y'all know that Carney Tesla is cooking meth up in that old farmhouse out back of his property?"

"That's a damn lie!" a man shouted, but he lacked conviction. It was a minor taunt, anyway; whatever the law might say, the production of meth was considered, like moonshine, no one's business except the seller's and the buyer's. Still, the Tesla

family was noted for its public propriety, and this airing of their
dirty secret would have repercussions in their immediate circle.

"And there's more," Bo-Kate assured them; Carolanne Pollard, seated with her parents, sank in her chair, aware far too
late why Bo-Kate wanted her aid. "Lots more. I'd love to spend
the next hour regaling you with it, but I reckon I've proved my
point. But I'll leave you with just one more thing."

She looked straight at Bronwyn Chess and said in a mock-
concerned voice, "Bronwyn, honey, does that preacher husband
of yours know who the father of that baby *really* is?"

Bronwyn's face turned white with rage. She grabbed the edge
of the table, intending to launch herself at Bo-Kate, but Bliss
held her arm, and Mandalay turned to look a warning at her.

Bo-Kate said. "And now, I'd like you to meet my special guest."
She stepped aside and gestured for Byron to come up.

He worked his way to the stage. With each step, his leg iron
squeaked and the heel brace struck the concrete floor with a solid
thunk. He stood beside Bo-Kate and glared out at the Tufa.

"This," Bo-Kate said, "is Byron Harley. You heard me right:
the Byron Harley, one of the guys who created rock and roll, who
supposedly died in this very county sixty years ago up on a lonely
mountainside. And he's standing here right now because the
night winds blew him right to me."

Faint murmurs of disbelief went through the crowd.

Bo-Kate looked at Mandalay. "Have they ever done anything
like that for you, Little Britches?"

Mandalay said nothing. She couldn't claim she knew Byron
Harley was stuck in slow time, because until the other night,
she hadn't. She clenched her hands into fists of frustration, but
kept her face neutral.

"I didn't think so," Bo-Kate said. "That must mean they approve of me, and what I want to do. They must want me to be
in charge, because they gave me proof of their goodwill."

"How do we know he's not just some look-alike you brought

from Nashville?" Bronwyn demanded. "Or does he only talk when you stick your hand up his ass and move his lips?"

"I talk," Byron rumbled.

"See?" Bo-Kate said. "He talks, and he also sings. And what better proof than that, right?" She stepped aside and gestured to him.

He shifted until his feet were spread enough to bring him down to the microphone's level. He looked out at the expectant crowd, and despite his anger, his sense of abandonment and dislocation, he felt the old rush of excitement that hit at the beginning of every show. He said softly, "One, two, three, four . . ."

Then he fiercely strummed with the pick Bo-Kate gave him.

My baby fights like a junkyard dog with a bone
My baby hits like a bullet from Al Capone
My baby screams like Fay Wray in a monkey's paw
But when the lights go down, none of that matters at all.

Some girls like it soft and sweet
And some like it hot and heavy
But my girl likes it the way I do
Like Teddy Roosevelt, rough and ready.

He glanced to one side and saw the delight on Bo-Kate's face. At the front of the crowd, the little girl, the one who scared Bo-Kate so much, kept her expression blank, but her two minders were clearly concerned.

Byron laughed contemptuously and snarled into the next verse.

My baby likes me when I make her scream real loud
And kiss her the way a thunderbolt kisses a cloud
She says she's mine forever, and nothing'll tear us apart
And I know she holds the key that starts the engine of
*   my heart.*

Then he roared then, a cry of such rage and anger that he worried he might pop a vocal cord. But all the emotions he'd kept tamped down, waiting for this chance, came out in a rush. He wanted to swing his guitar into the first row of black-haired, white-teethed faces, then wade into the crowd with the mike stand like a club. He didn't care if he died—he would take as many of them with him as he could.

Snowy and Tain sat together, she with her chair leaned back against him, and he draped an arm over her shoulder. They held hands, and if anyone looked too closely, they'd see that both their knuckles were white with the intensity of their grip. Tain's lip was still swollen, and the skin around one eye was bruised.

She glanced occasionally at Byron, but mostly watched Bo-Kate. She was now terrified of her cousin, not because Bo-Kate had beaten her up, but because she had killed Nigel—a sweetheart, and the closest thing Bo-Kate had to a conscience. Canton and Snad came to the diner and told her, after they'd hidden the body in a cave to await the ground's thaw. They were unsure how to feel about it themselves: family was always primary, but sometimes that loyalty left a rotten taste behind it.

Without Nigel's influence, there would be nothing stopping Bo-Kate, and the cold, calculated amusement Tain saw in her eyes reinforced that. Bo-Kate would be happy if the whole crowd burst into a riot and left her the only one still standing.

She looked at Byron onstage. She wondered what sex with him would've been like: he was so huge, and the weight of his body pressing down would've been overpowering in the best way. He could've turned her anyway he wanted, easily pushed her into any position, and would've been impossible to resist. Ordinarily such thoughts would send her into a tailspin of lust, but this time, it was no more than a wistful longing that faded almost at once as her body registered Snowy's presence anew.

She squeezed Snowy's hand even harder and wished they were back home in bed. For all her protests about wanting to be free to have other men, she found herself wanting only him. His total acceptance of her was something she'd never experienced before, and it was like a cool shower on a hot day.

"Can we leave?" she asked softly.

"Not right now," he said, and kissed her cheek. "But soon, I promise."

Byron finished with a flourish, the kind of wild-eyed spin the girls loved, using his leg iron for momentum and stopping with his weight on his good leg, his bad one out straight behind him. And even though these were rednecks from the future, the crowd went as wild as any other he remembered. Good music was, evidently, timeless.

He smiled, tossed his hair back from his face, and looked over at Bo-Kate. She did not look happy, or angry. She mainly looked a little puzzled.

36

As the applause died down, the muttering began. The consensus was clear: Bo-Kate had done a pretty fucking good job making her case. If she wanted to lead, then maybe they should let her. She couldn't be worse than Rockhouse, and Mandalay had made no effort to stand up to her. When the vote came, it would be a landslide.

Bronwyn and Bliss exchanged a look. Both thought the same thing: that their faith in Mandalay, as strong as it was, might have been misplaced.

Mandalay sensed all this around her. She had anticipated it, and had a plan. She opened her purse and closed her small hand around the small semiautomatic pistol she'd stolen from her father's pickup.

Before she could withdraw it, though, Bronwyn firmly grabbed her wrist, and the older woman spoke softly and urgently in her ear.

"No, Mandalay. If it needs to be done, I'll do it. It's my job. I already have blood on my hands."

"Let go," Mandalay said, equally firm. "This is between Bo-Kate and me."

"It's between Bo-Kate and all of us."

"No!" Mandalay snarled, and wrenched free. She stood and aimed the gun straight at Bo-Kate twenty feet away.

Everyone saw this and stepped quickly back, clearing the space between the two women. Bo-Kate's puzzlement vanished, replaced by a smile. She put her hands on her hips and stepped away from Byron, presenting herself as a clear target.

The room grew hushed.

"Well?" Bo-Kate said at last. "Are you going to do it?"

Mandalay did not answer, and the gun did not waver in her hand. Brownyn and Bliss stood beside her, unsure what to do, knowing only that this was their place, whatever happened. Junior Damo stood close, but not quite in the line of fire.

"I took a shot at you, you know," Bo-Kate said to Mandalay. "And I meant it. It was only your dumb luck that I missed. Is that thing even loaded?"

Mandalay pointed the gun at the ceiling and pulled the trigger. In the silence, in this room perfectly arranged for acoustics, the sound was unbearably loud, and each person watching flinched. Dust trickled down from the hole in the plaster.

Mandalay took three steps closer to Bo-Kate. Then she said, "You just want to lead the Tufa so you can destroy them, Bo-Kate. You have no love for them, for the music, or for the night winds. You won't be happy until the Tufa lose everything that makes them special, and fade into memories and songs. Then you'll have your revenge, won't you?"

"Hey, I'm not making anyone do anything they don't want to do. If you people don't want me, I'll leave."

"This isn't about what they want," Mandalay said. "It's about you, and me. Who we are, what we want, and what we're willing to do to get it. You were willing to kill me."

"I still am," Bo-Kate hissed.

Mandalay took another three steps and put the end of the barrel against Bo-Kate's sternum. Someone in the crowd gasped. Mandalay looked into the older woman's eyes.

"I can kill you," Mandalay said.

"Then do it."

Mandalay grinned, cold and malicious and harder than any child's face should be able to convey. She stepped back and lowered the gun. "But I'm not like you, Bo-Kate Wisby. So I won't."

Then she extended the gun, grip first, to Bo-Kate. "Now it's your move."

The two women looked at each other. Then, with a raw scream, Bo-Kate grabbed the gun, aimed it at the girl, and squeezed the trigger.

At the last second, though, someone knocked her arm up. The bullet struck the ceiling.

Jefferson Powell didn't say a word. He wrenched the gun from her hand and tossed it to Junior. Then he pushed Bo-Kate backwards ahead of him into the empty kitchen.

He slammed her against the wall beside the pantry. She started to speak, but he grabbed her by the throat. She'd forgotten how physically strong he was. She tried to pull his arm away, then to kick at him. He squeezed until she couldn't breathe. But there was no hatred in his eyes, only anguish and, behind that, the kind of love that nothing, no horrendous behavior or blatant betrayal, could ever change.

"This is over," he said. "We don't belong here anymore."

Fury at his words replaced her fear, and she clawed at his face. How dare he say they didn't belong? They belonged more than anyone!

He punched her in the stomach, then pushed her toward the door. She gave no resistance as he shoved her outside.

Bliss and Bronwyn said almost in unison, "Are you all right?"

"I'm fine," Mandalay said. She turned to Junior, and he quickly offered her the gun. She took it and passed it to Bronwyn, then grasped his right hand in both of her own.

"Junior," Mandalay said.

"Y-yes, ma'am?" he stammered.

She looked up into his face, his eyes, his soul. She saw the small, trembling center of him hidden behind his paper-thin bluster, and within that, the core of manipulative power that flickered like a pilot light awaiting a surge of natural gas. She also understood that at this moment, with a word, she could either stoke it, or put it out forever.

You have until the full moon to find your opposite number, the night winds had said, *or take the crown yourself.* "You want to take Rockhouse's place and help me lead the Tufa, Junior?"

"I . . ."

"Shit or get off the pot, Junior. Right now."

She'd never seen anyone look so frightened, but he managed a nod.

"You'll have to listen to me, you know. You're not Rockhouse. I will always be stronger than you. Are we clear on this?"

Again he nodded.

"Good. We'll talk more later."

She released his hand. She wondered if she'd just made the expedient decision of a leader, or the cowardly choice of a child afraid of taking on adult responsibility. There was no way to tell until the damage was already done.

She turned to the rest of the Tufa. "Is that all right with everyone? Things go on like they were. Only difference is Junior instead of Rockhouse. What do you say?"

There were gradual murmurs of assent. If anyone disagreed, they were too frightened of the possible consequences to speak up. Still, the tension in the room remained cranked to the sticking place by the showdown between the two women. Folks glared at each other, and spoke in urgent, soft voices that were somehow worse than yelling. If everyone wasn't careful, the lid could still blow.

While Jeff took Bo-Kate away and Mandalay spoke to Junior, Byron was forgotten. He looked out across the crowd, everyone speaking at once, some people arguing and shoving each other. He realized that, whatever future he'd potentially had, it was gone now. Like Donna. Like Harmony.

It was time for him to go as well.

He lifted his guitar and dug in his pocket for the real pick he'd used at the campfire. That day she'd brought him out of the woods, he deliberately gave her the wrong one from the stash he always carried. It was an impulse born of his instinctive mistrust of strangers, particularly attractive women with their own agendas, but now he was glad he'd done it. If that pick had absorbed something from all that time, he suspected he knew what would happen when he played with it.

He played, and softly sang:

I went down to the depot
Lord, not many days ago
Got on my train
And the train went a-flyin'
I looked back behind
And my baby was a-cryin'
Said he's gone and left me all alone.

You can count the days I'm gone
On the train that I left on
You can hear the whistle blow a hundred miles
If that train runs right
I'll see home tomorrow night
Lord, I'm nine hundred miles from my home. . . .

With each chord, each note, Byron changed. He grew achy and stooped, and his hair thinned and turned gray, then white. His square-jawed face sagged and softened. All his borrowed time drained away, and he teared up as he contemplated seeing Harmony again. He hoped he'd recognize her on the other side, and that she'd understand why he'd failed her.

But because of the magic in the pick, most of the chattering Tufa didn't notice his rapid aging. When they looked at him, they saw the man they expected to see. When he finally fell to his knees and collapsed sideways, people gathered around to see an old man who was too sick to have any business coming out tonight, lying dead atop his guitar.

The few purebloods who were fully aware of what had really happened held their peace. The hand of the night wind was not something you idly discussed in crowds.

Outside, the wind picked up, whipping old snow from the ground and swirling it around the two former lovers. Jeff shoved Bo-Kate away from him, and she stood with her fists clenched.

"You hit me!" she yelled.

"You're lucky I didn't fucking shoot you with your own gun."

"That wasn't *my* gun, you moron. So now what? You going to beat me up? Did you suddenly regrow a pair? You got your own gun, maybe? How are you going to stop me, Jeff?"

He gazed at her with something she never expected to see on his face again: tenderness. For her.

"I don't plan to stop you, Bo-Kate. We've both just been marking time until this moment."

There was real pain in her voice when she exclaimed, "You had your chance up on the mountain, you gutless sack of shit!"

"Not that. *This* is the moment when we admit we haven't changed. We can't change. We don't *want* to change."

"I never did," she said proudly.

He looked at her with a sadness that carried the weight of all those years of exile. "Well, I did. And I tried. But some songs run too deep."

He took the class ring from his shirt and let it hang outside his coat. Then he stepped close and took her in his arms. She put a hand on his chest to push him away, but she gasped at the feeling of the ring against her palm. His embrace sheared away the years of isolation and bitterness, and she felt as she always did in his arms: safe, powerful, *loved*.

"Jesus, Jeff," she said over the wind. "I never thought I'd feel this again."

"Neither did I."

"Remember when Michael Finley tried to make out with me at the sock hop and you beat him up so bad, he got a concussion?"

"Yeah."

"And when we made love beside Jesse Spicer after you beat him to death for trying to see me naked?"

"Yeah, I remember that, too."

"Do you think we can ever feel that way again?"

"No, Bo-Kate. We never can. This is the last thing we'll ever feel."

And for the first time in forever, since that day on Emania Knob when the whole Tufa community gathered to banish them from Needsville, from Cloud County, from music and love and life, Bo-Kate Wisby and Jefferson Powell kissed.

And had anyone been there to witness it, they would've seen the two lovers rise slowly into the windswept sky, borne aloft on their love and their half-seen wings.

Less than a minute later, Mandalay, Bliss, and Bronwyn came outside. Bo-Kate and Jeff were gone.

"Where are they?" Bliss said.

Mandalay slowly looked up. "They're dancing," she said softly.

Bliss and Bronwyn followed her gaze into the sky, but it was too dark and cloudy to see anything. Then wet droplets splattered down on them. But it wasn't cold winter rain—these drops were warm, and in the glow of the security lights, red.

The three women quickly got out of the way. Bronwyn wiped her face with her sleeve and said, "What the hell was that?"

"The end," Mandalay said. "Of Bo-Kate and Jeff."

"What, did they *explode* or something?"

"They're gone," Mandalay said. "That's all that matters." But she kept looking up. "Go back inside. I need a moment alone here."

Bliss and Bronwyn exchanged a look. "Uhm," Bliss began.

"I'll be perfectly safe."

They couldn't really argue with her, or overrule her, so they did as she asked.

Mandalay stared up at the swirling sky. The silence was broken: once again the night winds spoke to her as they always did, plainly and clearly, conveying the truth about what had happened. She felt a sudden, unexpected jolt of sadness at the idea that these two lovers could neither live together or apart, and so chose not to live at all. Or at least, one of them made the choice for both.

And *that song* came back to her.

Shadows at midnight
Shadows at dawn
Why won't your shadows
Go and leave me alone
I hear footsteps on the stairs
Someone's sneaking out the back
It's two in the morning
And the moon has gone black. . . .

"I've made the choice," she said to the winds. She waited, but they said nothing back.

Then she heard a vehicle making its way down the road. A white Ford E350 church van pulled a single-axle trailer that looked as if it could fall apart at any moment. Behind it came another car packed with people.

The van slowed when the driver saw Mandalay. It stopped, and the driver rolled down the window. He had long black hair and a neat beard. "Excuse me," he said, "but we're trying to find the interstate. Are we anywhere near it?"

Mandalay looked at the trailer. "You're a band, aren't you?"

"Yes. We're out of Gatlinburg. And we're lost. Can you or someone else give us directions?"

"We need a band," Mandalay said. "Right now. There's a building full of people who need an excuse to dance and have fun."

The driver chuckled. The woman in the seat beside him, who had black curly hair, leaned over and said, "Well, honey, I'm sorry, but we've already got a gig for tonight. If we can find it."

Mandalay realized with a start that they saw, not a leader, but a twelve-year-old girl. It had been a long time since that had happened. And of course, it wasn't their fault.

Then Junior Damo appeared beside her. He smiled, all reasonableness and assurance. "She's right, fellas. We really need a good, kick-ass band tonight. We're a sad bunch, and we need a reason to not be. Like the song says, you can't dance and stay uptight."

Before the driver could reply, the van sputtered once and died. He tried to restart it, but nothing happened. He exchanged a look with the woman, who was trying to use her cell phone. "Still don't get a signal," she said.

"I bet it's that alternator." He sighed and said, "Well, looks like we're stuck here. The car can't carry all of us *and* pull the trailer."

The people in the car behind the van emerged, zipping up coats and pulling on mittens. They were all young, and beautiful, and Mandalay could see the music that danced around them, and through them. Whoever they were, they lived for the playing, and that was something any Tufa could understand.

She smiled. "So if you're stuck, you might as well play. Right, Junior?"

"Right," he agreed. "How long does it take you to set up?"

The driver looked from her to Junior, unsure whom to address. "Uh . . . half an hour, maybe."

"We'll pass the hat and pay you what we can," Junior said with a smile. "Whatever it comes out to, it'll still be more than you'd make sitting on the side of the road waiting for a tow truck all the way out here, ain't that right?"

"That's probably true," the driver agreed.

"What's your band's name?" Mandalay asked.

"Tuatha Dea."

Mandalay and Junior exchanged a look whose significance was totally lost on the band. As was the reason behind their wide, enigmatic Tufa smiles.

"I'm Junior. This here's Mandalay."

"I'm Danny, this is my wife Rebecca, and the rest of the band is all family, too."

"A tribe," Mandalay said.

"That's what we call ourselves," he agreed.

Rebecca said, "Can I ask y'all something?"

"Sure," Junior said.

"I know we crossed into Cloud County, because that was right before the Google Maps went out, so . . . are you folks Tufa?"

Junior looked at Mandalay. "We are," she said.

Now Danny grinned. "I've heard you folks are some kind of good players."

"We can be," Junior agreed.

"You think anybody'd want to sit in with us?"

"If you're up for it, I'm sure a bunch of us would be honored."

"Then let's get to it," Danny said. "We need to get the trailer off the road first."

Junior winked at Mandalay. She wanted to smack him, but couldn't deny that he'd made the situation go much smoother than it might have. She motioned him close and said softly, "Go get some help. We want to get this party started as soon as possible. And while you're at it, ask Canton and Snad Wisby what they did with the body of Bo-Kate's assistant."

"How do you know he's dead?"

"Because he's not here. And wherever he is, he deserves better. He tried to stop her."

Junior nodded and strode back through the cars toward the Pair-A-Dice. When Mandalay turned back, she let out a yelp. Luke Somerville stood right before her.

"Didn't mean to scare you," he said. He nodded at the van, where the members of Tuatha Dea were already pulling out instruments. "Who are they?"

"A gift from the night winds."

"Seriously?"

"You tell me. We have practically the entire Tufa population in there so wound up, they might all gut each other before morning if something doesn't happen to help 'em let off steam, and a band shows up out of nowhere. A band called Tuatha Dea."

His eyes opened wide. "No way."

"Yes way." She paused, then said, "Why are you here?"

"I snuck out."

"You mean now, or the other day?" she shot back.

"Yeah. I'm not too proud of that. I just got spooked."

The breeze tousled his unruly hair, and his shy smile melted her annoyance. She said, "You could've e-mailed, or texted, or even called."

"I was embarrassed. I didn't like to think of myself as a coward, or think . . . that you thought about me that way."

She was impressed with his honesty, but wasn't yet ready to let him off the hook. "So why are you here tonight, then?"

He looked down. "I was . . . well . . . kinda worried about you."

"Me? Why?"

He bit his lip, bashful and, to her, adorable. "Well . . . Bo-Kate and Jeff . . . they're like us. One from each side. It didn't go that well for them, and there's no . . ."

"No sign it'll go that well for us?"

He shrugged. "I've been asking around. Don't worry, I didn't mention your name or anything, just . . . well, anyway, it's never gone too well. When two sides go to war, like she said, you know? Love and war seem to be an awful lot alike."

The Pair-A-Dice door opened. Several young men emerged to help the band, followed by Snowy and Tain, who headed for their vehicle.

"It's going well for them," Mandalay said.

"Wonder what the secret is?"

"He didn't ask her to change for him."

"Is that important to girls?"

"It's important to anybody."

He looked down. "Well . . . I like you fine like you are."

"I don't scare you?"

"Sure you do. But so did my dirt bike at first, and I love it now." He blushed, although she wasn't sure if it was because he'd compared her to a motorcycle, or because he'd used the word "love."

"Well, I like you, too. But I don't know if we'll end up together or anything."

"Me, neither. I mean, we're twelve, right?" he added quickly. Then he grinned. "Want to dance when the band gets ready?"

"No. Follow me."

She took his hand and led him around the building.

Junior watched the others help the band unload, and held the door while they carried equipment and instruments inside. He saw Mandalay and the Somerville boy duck around the corner of the building, and filed that away for future reference. You could never tell what would be important someday.

A flash of reflected light caught his eye. On the ground, in the middle of the fresh blood splatter, something metallic gleamed. He picked it up, wincing as it cut his finger. It was a tiny axe.

At the corner of the building, a lone figure silhouetted by the security light watched him. With a jolt, he recognized it as Rockhouse Hicks, but not the way he'd been the last time Junior saw him. He was younger, with black hair again, and he smiled at Junior with a kind of knowing viciousness. He shook a finger in mocking disapproval, then faded into the darkness.

Goosebumps ran down Junior's spine.

The icy wind slapped both Luke's and Mandalay's bare faces, and tangled her hair. When they reached the edge of the woods and stopped, she said, "Now we can dance."

"There's no music."

She laughed. "Just listen."

He paused. And faintly, on the wind, he heard the sound of a distant fiddle. It took a moment for him to parse out the song, but then he recognized it from his grandfather's visits: "I'm Nine Hundred Miles from Home."

She put her arms around his neck. "Put your arms around me now," she said, and he did. "Do you trust me?"

"Yeah."

"Then hold on."

And again, if anyone had been there to watch, they would've seen two people rise into the cold, windy night, carried aloft by first love and half-seen wings.

Both Tuatha Dea and Fiddlin' John Carson are real.
You can find out more about Tuatha Dea at

http://www.tuathadea.net.

Their album *Tufa Tales: Appalachian Fae* is inspired by these novels.

The music of Fiddlin' John Carson (March 23, 1868–December 11, 1949) can be found in the excellent Complete Recorded Works in Chronological Order series from Document Records:

http://www.document-records.com.

SONGS WITH QUOTED LYRICS

Unless otherwise indicated below, all song lyrics are either public domain or original to this work.

EPIGRAPH
"Appalachia," written by Josiah Leming. Copyright © 2009 by Josiah Leming. Used by permission.

CHAPTER 1
"Lord Thomas and Fair Annet," found on pp 196–197 of *The English and Scottish Popular Ballads,* Vol. 3, by Francis James Child (Houghton Mifflin, 1882).

CHAPTER 2
"The Snows They Melt the Soonest," first published in *Blackwood's Magazine* (Edinburgh, 1821).

CHAPTER 3
"Paranoid," written by Alice Peacock. Copyright © 2014 by Alice Peacock Music/ASCAP. Used by permission. (The original video for Alice Peacock's song "Paranoid" can be found here: https://www.youtube.com/watch?v=R3ZQhVd0xFo)

CHAPTER 4
"The Unfortunate Rake," composer unknown, earliest date 1790.

CHAPTER 5

"I'm Nine Hundred Miles from My Home," traditional, composition date unknown. First recorded by Fiddlin' John Carson in 1924, http://www.secondhandsongs.com/work/29381.

"Babes in the Wood," composed by William Gardiner (1770–1853), composition date unknown.

"Across the Blue Mountains," traditional, http://www.fresnostate.edu/folklore/ballads/AF014.html.

CHAPTER 6

"Home, Sweet Home," lyrics by John Howard Payne, composed in 1823 for the opera *Clari: Or, The Maid of Milan.*

CHAPTER 7

"The Valiant and Fury Girls," written by Lou Buckingham. Copyright © 1994 by Lou Buckingham. Used by permission.

CHAPTER 8

"Engine 143," composer unknown, based on the true story of the wreck of the FFV (Fast Flying Virginian) near Hinton, West Virginia, on October 23, 1890.

"Johnny Faa," first documented in *The Tea-Table Miscellany,* 1740.

CHAPTER 9

"Poor Murdered Woman," first published by Lucy Broadwood in her collection *English Traditional Songs and Carols* (London: Boosey, 1908). Originally collected by Rev. Charles J. Shebbeare from a Mr. Forster of Milford, Surrey, in 1897. Slightly modified by Bledsoe for this book.

"The Curragh of Kildare," written by Robert Burns (1759–1796) in 1788, based on the stall-ballad "The Lovesick Maid."

CHAPTER 10
"Old Dan Tucker," composer unknown, first sheet music edition published in 1843.

CHAPTER 11
"Sugar Blues," lyrics by Lucy Fletcher, music by Clarence Williams (1893–1965), published in 1920.

CHAPTER 13
"Fire on the Mountain," traditional, earliest American publication date is 1814 or 1815 in *Riley's Flute Melodies* (where it appears as "Free on the Mountains"), and as "I Betty Martin" in *A. Shattuck's Book,* a fiddler's manuscript book dating from around 1801.
"The Parting Glass," traditional, earliest reference 1605.

CHAPTER 18
"Wayfaring Stranger," traditional. Earliest versions from the early nineteenth century.

CHAPTER 23
"The Dawning of the Day," published by Edward Walsh (1805–1850) in 1847 in *Irish Popular Songs.*

CHAPTER 24
"The Galway Shawl," traditional, first known version collected by Sam Henry from Bridget Kealey in Dungiven in 1936.

CHAPTER 25
"Marlborough Has Left for the War," traditional. First popular in 1780.